RESEARCH

RESEARCH
PHILIP KERR

Quercus

First published in Great Britain in 2014 by Quercus Editions Ltd

55 Baker Street
7th Floor, South Block
London W1U 8EW

A CIP catalogue record for this book is available
from the British Library

HB ISBN 978 1 78206 577 7
TPB ISBN 978 1 78206 578 4
EBOOK ISBN 978 1 78206 579 1

10 9 8 7 6 5 4 3 2 1

Printed and bound in Great Britain by Clays Ltd, St Ives plc

Typeset by Ellipsis Digital Limited, Glasgow

For Harry Armfield

'Write what you know.'
Mark Twain

DON IRVINE'S STORY

PART ONE

CHAPTER 1

It was the American novelist William Faulkner who once said that in writing you must kill all your darlings; it was Mike Munns – another writer but, like me, not half as good as Faulkner – who made a joke out of this quote when he telephoned my flat in Putney early that Tuesday morning.

'It's me, Mike. I've heard of kill your darlings but this is ridiculous.'

'Mike. What the hell? It's not even eight o'clock.'

'Don, listen, switch on Sky News and then call me at home. John's only gone and killed Orla. Not to mention both of her pet dogs.'

I don't watch much television any more than I read much Faulkner but I got out of bed and went into the kitchen, made a pot of tea, switched on the telly, and after a few seconds was reading a rolling strip of news across the bottom of the screen: BESTSELLING NOVELIST JOHN HOUSTON'S WIFE FOUND MURDERED AT THEIR LUXURY APARTMENT IN MONACO.

About ten minutes later the twinkly-eyed Irish news anchor was announcing the bare facts of the story before asking a local reporter positioned outside the distinctive glass fan entranceway to the Tour Odéon, 'What more can you tell us about this, Riva?'

Riva, a fit-looking blonde wearing a black pencil skirt and a beige pussy-cat-bow blouse, explained what was now known:

'The writer–millionaire John Houston is being sought by Monaco police in connection with the murder of his wife, Orla, whose body was found early this Tuesday morning at their luxury apartment in the exclusive principality of Monaco. It's believed that her murderer also killed Mrs Houston's pet dogs. The sixty-seven-year-old Houston, who hasn't been seen since Friday night, made his fortune as the author of more than a hundred books and is widely considered to be the bestselling novelist in the world, with sales of more than 350 million copies. He regularly tops the Forbes list of the world's highest-paid authors with earnings estimated at over one hundred million dollars a year. Mrs Houston was aged thirty-seven; as Orla Mac Curtain she was a former Miss Ireland and actor who won a Tony Award for Best Leading Actress in a Musical for her portrayal of Sophie Zawistowska in *Sophie's Choice: The Musical*. Orla Mac Curtain was generally acknowledged to be one of the world's most beautiful women and had recently written her first novel. The couple were married five years ago at Mr Houston's home on the Caribbean island of St Maarten. But other than the fact that they are treating her death as a murder the Monaco police have given us no information on the exact circumstances of Mrs Houston's death. Eamon.'

'Riva, Monaco isn't exactly a large place,' said the news anchor. 'Have the police any idea where John Houston might have gone?'

'Monaco's less than a square mile in area and bordered by France on three sides,' said Riva. 'It's only ten miles from Italy and I'm told you could even be on the North African coast in maybe ten or twelve hours. He owned a boat and he had a pilot's licence so it's generally held that he could be absolutely anywhere.'

'It's like a scene from one of his books. John Houston was on this programme just last year and I read one of them then and I thought it was very good – although I can't remember what it was called. He seemed like a very nice fellow. Have the police said how she died?'

'Not yet, Eamon—'

I turned off the TV, refilled my mug with tea and was scrolling through the numbers in the contact list on my cellphone to find Mike's telephone number when the landline rang. It was Mike Munns again.

'Are you watching this, Don?' he asked.

'Yes,' I lied. 'But I think you're jumping to conclusions here, Mike. Just because the Monty cops are looking for John doesn't mean John actually did murder her. We've both written enough of his books to know that's not how a plot works. The husband's always the first and most obvious suspect in a case like this. It's almost a given that he should be the early favourite. Any husband can be made to look as if he might have had a motive to kill his wife. Guilty until proven innocent, that's how it always works. Mark my words, it will be someone else who turns out to be the murderer. An intruder. Orla's lover, perhaps. Assuming she had one.'

'*Nil nisi bonum*,' said Munns. 'But Orla was a gold-plated bitch and I certainly can't imagine anyone loving her. If John did bump her off then I can hardly say I blame the poor bastard. I'm sure I'd have killed Orla if I'd had to live with her. Jesus, that woman would have tried the patience of Saint Monica. Do you remember the way she used to ignore Starri at the Christmas party?'

A dull and monosyllabic Finn from Helsinki, Starri was

Mike's wife, but I could hardly have faulted Orla for ignoring her at the Christmas party. I was none too fond of Mike's wife myself. I could easily have ignored her presence in a mug of tea.

I smiled. 'Say nothing of the dead unless it's good,' I said. 'That's what *nil nisi bonum* is supposed to mean, Mike.'

'I know what it fucking means, Don,' said Munns. 'I'm just saying that maybe Orla had it coming. Her and those bloody mutts. And I'm surprised to hear you of all people defending her. She didn't like you at all. You do know that, don't you?'

'Of course I know it but, strictly speaking, I don't think I was defending *her*,' I said. 'It was John I was defending. Look, our former friend and employer is a lot of things, and many of them have four asterisks on the printed page if it appears in a newspaper, but he's not a murderer. I'm sure of it.'

'I'm not so sure. John has one hell of a temper. Come on, Don, you've seen him when he gets into one of his rages. He was Captain bloody Hurricane. Strong, too. Those hands of his are as big as car doors. When he makes a fist it's like a wrecking ball. I wouldn't like to tangle with him.'

'You did tangle with him, Mike. As I recall you hit him and for some reason that is still beyond me he didn't hit you back, which I must say showed a remarkable amount of control on his part. I don't think I could have been as restrained as he was.'

This was truer than Munns probably realized; I'd always wanted to punch him on the nose – perhaps now more than ever.

'Yes,' admitted Munns, 'but that was only because he was feeling ashamed of the way he'd behaved already. For bawling me out so violently.'

'In fairness he might also have sacked you for hitting him, Mike,' I added. 'And he didn't do that either.'

'Only because he needed me to finish a book.'

'Maybe so, but I think you're being a little quick to judge him here.'

'Why shouldn't I judge him? No one knew John Houston better than us. Look, I don't owe him a thing. And in the long run, he sacked us all, didn't he? His friends and colleagues.'

'Not without compensation.'

'That was pizza money for a bloke as rich as him.'

'Come on, Mike, you could buy a whole pizza restaurant for what he gave the four of us.'

'All right, a watch then. He spent more on wristwatches than he did on our compensation. You can't deny that.'

I heard Mike's cellphone ringing – 'Paperback Writer' by the Beatles – on the other end and waited a moment while he answered it.

'Peter,' I heard Munns say. 'Yes, I have. He does, I'm on the line to him now. I'd better call you back. No, wait, I've a better idea. Why don't the three of us meet for lunch? Today. You can? Good. Hang on a mo, I'll ask Don.'

Munns came back to me on the landline. 'It's Stakenborg,' he said. 'Look here, why don't we all have lunch at Chez Bruce to talk about it.'

Chez Bruce is a restaurant in south-west London that was conveniently close to where both Mike Munns and Peter Stakenborg lived, in Wandsworth and Clapham.

'What's there to talk about?' I said. 'She's dead. John's missing. Maybe he's dead, too, only we just don't know it yet.'

'Come on, Don, don't be such a miserable cunt. Besides, it's been months since the three of us sat down and talked.

It'd be good to catch up. Look, I'll pay for it, if that's what's bothering you.'

It wasn't. 'Lunch gets in the way of my writing, that's all. I won't be good for anything after I've drunk a bottle of wine with you bastards.'

'You're working on something?'

'Yes.'

'In that case I insist,' said Munns. 'I'll do anything to interfere with a fellow writer's work. Come on. Say yes.'

'All right,' I said. 'Yes.'

'Great. The set lunch is a bargain. Pete? You still there? We're on. Don? Pete? Chez Bruce. See you there at one.'

In the culinary wasteland that is south-west London Chez Bruce is, quite justifiably, up itself; but while the kitchen is undeniably excellent it isn't a smart kind of place. The clientele is mostly pairs of bored housewives spending their city husbands' modest bonuses, final salary pensioners blowing their ill-gotten gains and middle-aged couples celebrating – if that's the right word – Pyrrhic wedding anniversaries.

Outside, on the narrow main road, was a long line of near-stationary traffic and beyond this lay the large expanse of unfeasibly green and pleasant parkland that is Wandsworth Common. Only the week before summer had finally arrived, but already it was looking like it had jumped on the first plane and was now headed somewhere warmer. They certainly hadn't seen much of the sun the previous weekend in Fowey, which was where I had a holiday home in Cornwall called Manderley after the house in *Rebecca*, by Daphne du Maurier. I think all holiday homes in Cornwall are probably called Manderley.

Naturally I was the first to arrive at Chez Bruce, as I had

travelled the furthest distance. I took a look at the wine list and ordered a bottle of Rully: at sixty quid it was hardly the most expensive wine on the list but it would certainly spoil us for anything cheaper and could hardly fail to deter Mike Munns from ordering too many more. I was determined to leave the lunch sober – more or less – especially since I had come by car.

Peter Stakenborg was the next to arrive, a tall, slightly anxious-looking man wearing a badger's coat on his head, a blue velvet jacket, a white shirt and brown corduroy trousers.

'Christ, what a morning,' he said. 'I've been fielding telephone calls from Hereward Jones, Bat Anderton and the *Evening* fucking *Standard*. You?'

Hereward Jones was Houston's literary agent; and B. A. T. 'Bat' Anderton was his publisher. I shook my head.

'Didn't answer the phone. I figured it was probably just people wanting to feed me gossip and speculation about John.' I shrugged. 'Besides, I never answer the phone when I'm trying to work.'

'Yes, I heard you were working on something.'

'I'm trying. Put it that way. I was in Fowey for the weekend but it wasn't working there either so I came back. I kept looking out the window and marvelling that it could rain anywhere quite as much as Cornwall.'

'A novel?'

I nodded and poured Stakenborg a glass of the Rully.

'What's it about?'

'I've already forgotten. When I'm away from my desk it really doesn't exist at all. That way I can't talk the book away. I think all writing should be conducted like a kind of exorcism.'

'Who said that?'

'I did, Peter.'

'You mean you've actually got a plot – an outline and every-thing?'

'Not exactly. I'm just writing, seeing where that takes me.'

'I tried that once.'

'And what happened?'

'To be honest with you, Don, very little.' Stakenborg made a face. 'Without one of John's leather-bound outlines to work from it was just typing really. And it didn't seem to go any-where at all. Like trying to drive to the Hay Festival without a satnav. I got lost before I had even started. The man has an extraordinary capacity for creating stories out of thin air. His plots are like Rolex fucking watches. I bet you could lock him in a room with a sheet of paper and a pencil and an instruc-tion to give you a five-hundred-word plot about – about this wine, and he could probably do it. Not only that but he'd actually start to believe it was a good plot, too. I've seen that happen. A germ of an idea that becomes a fully-fledged plot in the space of one lunch. I don't know how he does it.'

I nodded, recognizing this description of our erstwhile employer. 'That's true, although I've seen him get carried away with an idea, too. So much so that he starts to believe an idea might actually be true.'

'So, what's your take on today's sensational news?'

'Until today becomes tomorrow I think it's far too early to say.'

'Come on, Don. You know him better than anyone. From the beginning, as it were. You must have an opinion about what happened. I'm afraid that Twitter has already got John bang to rights.'

'That's it then. You might as well fetch the black cap and hand it to the judge. He must be guilty if a few tweets have said so.'

'It's more than a few,' said Stakenborg. 'God, the people of this country are without mercy. Especially the writing sisterhood. You'd think Orla had got them the vote the way they're writing about her now. But really. What do you think?'

'Yes, Don. Do tell.' Mike Munns sat down opposite me, poured himself a glass and then measured the Burgundy's golden colour against the white of the tablecloth. He was short, with floppy hair, large heavy-framed lightly tinted glasses and a checked suit that belonged in the window of a charity shop; but Munns had a personality that seemed the very opposite of charitable. 'The least you can do is give us your honest opinion. Guilty or not guilty?'

'For fuck's sake. With friends like you, what chance does the poor bugger have of clearing his name?'

'Friend? Who said I was his friend? I thought I already made it quite clear that John Houston was no friend of mine.'

I let that one go. Lunch was effectively over if I didn't. I shook my head. 'Beyond the few facts that were reported on Sky News at eight o'clock this morning there isn't much to go on, yet; surely we can all agree on that.'

'It so happens that's why I'm a little late,' announced Munns. 'Some cop from the *Sûreté Publique* just made a statement on TV outside John's building in Monty. Orla and the dogs were shot with a nine-millimetre handgun; and one of John's cars – the Range Rover it looks like – is missing from the garage. The cops have named Houston as a prime suspect and issued an international warrant for his arrest.'

'I always liked that car,' said Stakenborg. 'That's the one I'd have taken from the garage if I had to lit out of somewhere in a hurry.'

'Lit?' Munns frowned. 'I'm not sure I recognize that verb.'

'Huckleberry Finn,' explained Stakenborg.

'That explains it. Twain's always been a bit of a grey area for me.'

'I guess that means you haven't read him,' I said cruelly.

'John's Lamborghini is too flashy and too blue,' continued Stakenborg. 'And the Bentley is just too big to do anything but stay in the garage. With the top down he might have been recognized, and in Monaco, with the top up anyone would look conspicuous. No, the Range Rover is what I'd have selected. It's also grey – a useful colour for going anywhere unnoticed in Monaco.'

'That would have been my choice, too,' I said, deciding to play the car game – at least for a short while; if you can't beat them join them. 'The Range Rover is always the Goldilocks choice for a getaway: just right. Especially the particular model that John owned: it's the top-of-the-line Autobiography. A hundred thousand quid. There's not much that John had I envied except that particular car.'

'Will you forget about the cars for a moment?' insisted Munns. 'The point is that officially John is now a wanted man. Which probably means the Monty cops know a lot more about what happened in John's apartment than they're telling. John always did have a thing for guns.'

'Since when did the Monty cops ever know a lot more about anything very much except how to indulge and humour people with pots of money?' asked Stakenborg. 'They may have the largest police force in the world—'

'Do they really?' said Munns.

'Per capita. There are five hundred cops for thirty-five thousand people. But what I'm saying is while the crime rate is low, there's a hell of a lot that just gets swept under the silk Tabriz in the *Salon Privé*.'

'A sunny place for shady people,' I said, quoting Somerset Maugham.

'Exactly,' said Stakenborg. 'And what was that scandal back in 1999? When they fucked up the case of that billionaire banker guy who died in a house fire?'

'Edmond Safra,' I said. 'Dominick Dunne wrote a pretty good piece about how the cops buried that case, in *Vanity Fair*.'

'The Monty cops may have a bigger budget than Scotland Yard,' continued Stakenborg, 'but that doesn't mean they have the brains to go with all that loot. I mean nearly everyone who's anyone in that pimple of a country comes from Monaco itself, and that's not much of a gene pool to draw on when it comes to producing cops who can do more than write out a few parking tickets. I mean, look at the Grimaldis for Christ's sake.'

'For John's sake,' I said, 'I hope you're wrong.'

'That all depends on whether you think he killed her or not,' said Munns.

'Obviously I don't think he killed her. Which is why I hope the cops are equal to the task of catching the real culprit.'

'In spite of them naming John as their prime suspect? Jesus, Don, what makes you so loyal to that madman?'

'Loyal? I'm not loyal. Although next to you, Mike, it must seem as if I am. It's just that I refuse to see him hanged until I've heard his side of the story.'

We ordered lunch and I had what I always have when I go to Chez Bruce: the foie gras parfait and then the roast cod with olive mash. This is standard practice for me – ordering the same things wherever I go – and I dare say it's one reason my wife couldn't stand to live with me; but as my favourite

Genesis song goes – which is another reason my wife left me, I think – I know what I like, and I like what I know.

'His side of the story stopped counting for very much when he ran away,' said Mike Munns.

'Flight is only circumstantial evidence of guilt,' I said. 'Think about it. Maybe John argued with Orla and someone overheard that. And if the murderer used one of John's many guns to shoot her then there's your case, right there. Two plus two equals fifteen to twenty years in a Monty jail. Under those circumstances I might have lit out of there myself. Jesus, you don't need to be Johnnie Cochran to see how to defend your client against running away from shit like that.'

'Monty jail isn't probably that bad,' murmured Stakenborg. 'As jails go. I imagine the cells are quite cushy, with a sea view in the better ones. Just like the Hôtel Hermitage. I wonder if they forbid card games for the inmates like they do for the locals in the casino.'

'Who the fuck is Johnnie Cochran?' asked Munns.

'I think it's no accident that the novels Mike used to write for John were so often the biggest sellers,' Stakenborg said to me. 'John always valued that. He used to talk about Mike being the lowest common denominator of a set of very vulgar fractions.'

'Very funny,' said Munns.

'Cochran was O. J. Simpson's lawyer,' I said.

'That explains it,' said Munns. 'Jesus, that was twenty years ago. Sometimes I forget that you two are so much older than me. At least I do until I see your grey hair.'

'So much older and so very much wiser,' said Stakenborg.

'As it happens I think I wrote John's biggest-selling book of all,' I said. '*Ten Soldiers Wisely Led*. Which was the last one. Not that it matters very much now.'

'Not as long as you got your bonus.'

'Three bonuses as I recall. One for each million sales.'

'That was the one about the private detective, wasn't it?' said Stakenborg.

'No, *Ten Soldiers* is the one about the Pakistani arms dealer. *Fools of Fortune* was the one about the private detective. Peter Coffin. Who reappeared in *The Manxman*.'

'And then again in *The Riddle Index*. Which is the worst of the lot, frankly.'

'John's characters,' Munns sneered. 'I mean who could believe in a hero called Peter fucking Coffin?'

'As a matter of fact,' I said, 'Peter Coffin is a character in another novel you might not have read either. *Moby-Dick* by Herman Melville. For a man whose books the *Guardian* newspaper described as "Vogon novels" John is remarkably well-read.'

'The Vogons,' said Munns. 'From Douglas Adams's *A Hitchhiker's Guide to the Galaxy*, right?'

'At last,' said Stakenborg. 'A book Munns has read.'

'Vogon novels being like Vogon poetry, I suppose,' continued Munns. 'The third-worst poetry in the Universe.'

'And clearly one book he's read all the way to the last page,' added Stakenborg. Laughing, he ordered another bottle of wine.

'Fuck off,' said Munns, but he was laughing, at least until he checked the wine list and saw the price of the Rully.

The starters arrived; and the second bottle of Rully which Munns changed for something cheaper.

'You know, it's a pity Philip French isn't here,' said Munns. 'To make up the Houston quartet.'

'I suppose he's at his place in the South of France,' I said. 'The lucky bugger.'

'You make it sound like it's something special,' said Munns.

'I think it is, to Philip,' I said. 'It cost him all he had.'

'It certainly wouldn't have been my choice,' said Munns. 'It's a modest little house. There's an olive grove but there's no air conditioning.'

'It sounds quite idyllic,' insisted Stakenborg.

'Tourrettes-sur-Loup is hardly that. It's more of a syndrome, really.'

'Coming from you, Mike, that's almost witty.'

'Hey, I wonder if they'll make Philip a suspect,' said Munns.

'Why would they do that?' I asked.

'Because Tourrettes is just an hour's drive from Monaco,' said Munns.

'And?'

'And because Philip hated John Houston even more than I do. Am I right, or am I right?'

'You're never right, Mike,' I said. 'Even when you're not wrong.'

'You just think you hate him,' Stakenborg told Mike. 'Which is something altogether different from the way poor old Phil feels. Besides, Phil doesn't really hate John. It's just that he'd gone out on a limb to buy that house in Tourrettes; he assumed that his income from ghosting Houston's books was going to stay at a steady hundred grand per annum plus bestseller bonuses for the next ten years.'

'It's always a mistake to assume anything when you're a freelance hack,' I said. 'Which is what we all were.'

'So when John pulled the plug on our little *atelier*—'

I felt myself wince: I'd always been a little embarrassed by Houston's name for our writing quartet: the *atelier*. It made us sound as if we had all been employed in the workshop of a real artist, instead of someone whose only talent was for making tons of money.

'Philip felt especially aggrieved.'

'. . . And blamed Orla,' added Munns. 'For putting him up to it. That's what he told me at any rate.'

'Best keep that to yourself,' I said.

'What do you mean?'

'If the Monty cops turn up here asking questions it might be best if you didn't repeat that,' I said. 'For Philip's sake. There's no point in dropping him in it, too. And before you ask, no, I don't believe Philip killed Orla any more than I think it was John who did it. Or you, or Peter.'

'Do you think they will?' Munns asked. 'The cops. Turn up here, I mean?'

'Peter's right,' I said. 'The Monty cops have got plenty of money and not much else to do. Which means some cops are bound to show up here before very long. London is the most logical place to start an inquiry like this. Let's face it, his publisher lives in London. His agent lives in London. We all live in London. His two ex-wives and his kids live in London. His old mother lives in London.'

'And they all hate him, too,' said Munns. 'Yes, you're right. You just named the whole pack of Cluedo cards for those who might have had a bit of malice aforethought where John is concerned.'

'Never let the facts get in the way of a good story,' said Stakenborg. 'It's easy to see why John thought you had a talent for fiction, Mike.'

'Actually it was Don here who brought me into the *atelier*,' said Munns. 'Not John.'

'Mike used to bring those same rigorous talents to his journalism when he was a hack on the *Daily Mail*,' I said. 'Didn't you, Mike? But for that, who knows where you'd be now, post-Leveson? In prison for phone hacking, probably.'

Munns grinned. 'Maybe. I pulled a few strokes in my time, sure. But look here, you can't argue with the fact that when Houston switched off the *atelier*'s router he let everyone down. Not just the monkeys like us who wrote John's books to order, but a virtual industry that was dedicated to one man: the publisher, the agent, the whole fucking shooting match. He had his own bloody West Wing dedicated to his publishing brand at Veni, Vidi, Legi. How many was it? Ten, fifteen people? Not to mention those three girls in the Houston office. All of whom lost their nice jobs when John decided he wanted to go back to basics and write something on his own. To say nothing of the effect on VVL's share price, reduced lawyers' fees, accountants' fees, and Christ only knows what else. I reckon you've got more motives there than at the Lee Strasberg Theatre and Film Institute.'

'For murder?' I laughed.

'Certainly for murder. Why not? But you're right, Peter. That wasn't the reason why the ex-wives and the kids and his old mother hated him. They hated him already.'

'Need I remind you that it's poor Orla who's dead,' I said. 'Not John.'

'Listen to him. Poor Orla. Poor Orla, my arse. Poor Orla had it coming. Even so I reckon John must have used a silver bullet from a melted-down crucifix for her. He'd certainly have needed one.'

'Unless he's dead, too,' added Stakenborg. 'And we just don't know it yet. Russian mafia, a disgruntled hooker – Christ, there must be plenty of those, I never knew a man who liked having rentals more than John. A jealous husband or two – John never could keep his hands off another chap's girl. A dope dealer, perhaps – yes, he liked a bit of blow now and then, especially when he was partying with the ladies. Or, maybe you're right after all, Mike, his literary agent; Hereward's income must have fallen off a cliff since John got to fancying he could win the Booker Prize. And if it hasn't yet, it soon will. Agents are an egotistical lot. Always think they made their client's money for them. Or none at all, as in my case. Actually I'm sure my agent wishes I was dead. He could probably sell my novel – yes, *my* novel – if I could only do something that might make me a bit more of a marketable commodity, such as die in some trendy way. Like Keith Haring. You know, a dead John Houston might actually sell a shedload of his next book. The one Mike wrote.' Stakenborg snapped his fingers as he tried to remember the title.

'*The Merchant of Death*,' said Munns.

'So, who knows, maybe he's cooked up this whole thing to sell even more. No one knows more about how to sell a book than John Houston. I mean look how many records Michael Jackson sold after he checked out of Neverland. Or wherever it was. In the twelve months following his death the King of Crap sold thirty-five million albums.'

'I never thought of that,' said Munns. 'Not a bad idea at all. This celebrity slaying is bound to get more column inches than Jordan's tits.'

'Now who's writing fiction?' I said.

'But either way, however you look at it,' added Munns, 'you have to admit that John himself is totally fucked.'

It was past six o'clock when I got back to my flat in Putney. This was on the top of one of those gloomy but large redbrick buildings near the bridge and overlooking the river – what the Americans would have called a wraparound apartment, with a little corner turret and a round window; handy for the shops, some quite decent pubs, and the number 14 bus to Piccadilly. The writer J. R. Ackerley – the one who was overly fond of his Alsatian dog – had once lived opposite; and, in one of the other mansion blocks nearer the bridge, so had the poet Gavin Ewart and the novelist William Cooper, both of whom I had sort of known. Putney's a bit like that, with lots of writers you haven't quite heard of, which is why they live in Putney and not Monaco, I suppose. As I stared out of my turret window at the small boats that passed up and down the dirty brown river Thames I often told myself that the view from University Mansions was infinitely preferable to the one John had enjoyed of the Ligurian Sea from the double-height windows of his apartment in the Tour Odéon; but this was just another fiction in my life – like the one that I was happier living alone, or the one that I didn't need John Houston to get a novel published. The fact of the matter was that I hated London. The place was full of miserable people who were always moaning about the weather, or the bankers, or Europe, or this government or the last government; Cornwall wasn't any better; that was just moaning with a fucking fleece on. John was fond of describing Monte Carlo as a slum full of billionaires, but that sounded just fine to me. Billionaires have higher standards than yokels who buy all their clothes at Primark.

I was pissed of course. In spite of my best intentions we had drunk at least a bottle apiece, followed by vintage brandies off the trolley, which is when the Chez Bruce bargain set lunch stops being such a bargain. I'd paid for all six of those, which ended up costing more than the food. That's what they mean by vintage brandy: filling the tank of an old Rolls-Royce would have been so much cheaper.

There was no chance of me being able to write anything other than my name and form number at the top of the paper, so I switched on the telly and sat on the sofa in the hope of having a nap. It wasn't long before ITV News got round to the murder of Orla Houston in the running order of 'stories'. That's one of the reasons I never watch television news; because 'stories' used to be 'reports' (I have enough of stories during my working day); possibly this might be because there's nothing in the news that sounds very much like news – it's all speculation and opinion and stream of consciousness, or just plain bullshit. Facts are rare. Virginia Woolf could write the script for the six o'clock news. And so it was with the Houston 'story': John was still missing and the prime suspect – anyone who knew of his whereabouts was encouraged to call the Monty police; Orla's body had been removed from the apartment and taken to a local mortuary; and her family had been informed and some of them were travelling from Dublin, presumably to identify the body and arrange a funeral. Cruelly I wondered if there might be a colour party. Orla's cousin, Tadhg McGahern, was a Sinn Féin MEP and had already arrived in Monaco from Brussels. The last time I'd seen him he'd been at Orla's wedding, when he'd been wearing an expression that was not unlike the one his half-brick of a face was wearing now – the bastard.

The Mac Curtain family were a rough lot. One of her brothers, Colm, was a Fianna Fáil member of the Dáil Éirann, which is the principal chamber of the Irish parliament; of course there's nothing wrong with that, but at his sister's wedding in St Maarten, Colm and I had almost come to blows when someone – most likely it was Orla herself – told him that before working for the London advertising agency where I'd met John, I'd been a junior officer in the British army.

Colm had received this news with something less than the good humour that ought to have been required at his sister's wedding. As I recalled it now, sprawled on the sofa with eyes half closed against the undulating room, the conversation had gone something like this:

'So you're Donald Irvine.'

'That's right,' I said, extending my hand to shake his. 'And you must be Orla's brother, Colm. I'm pleased to meet you.'

Colm had stared at my hand as if it had been covered in the blood of Bobby Sands; but I still left it out in front of me, if only for the sake of Anglo-Irish relations. Not that I'm English, but you know what I mean.

'I can't shake your hand, Don,' he said. 'Not until I've found out if it's true.'

'If what's true, Colm?'

'If it's true that you were a British soldier in Northern Ireland?'

I smiled a conciliatory smile and dropped my hand.

'It was twenty-five years ago, Colm. It would be a real shame if the British Prime Minister and Gerry Adams can manage a handshake in Downing Street and we can't do the same at your own sister's wedding.'

'Tony Blair didn't murder any of my friends,' said Colm. 'And you still didn't answer my question.'

'It's not a proper question for a day like this. We're supposed to be celebrating, not opening old wounds. But for the record, I've never murdered anyone.'

'If you say so. But it certainly doesn't sound like you're denying that you were a Brit soldier in Ireland.'

'I'm not denying anything.'

'Then it is true. That you were part of an occupying force in my country.'

'Please, Colm,' I said. 'Let's not fall out over this. If you want to pick a fight with me then do it later, preferably outside, and I'll gladly accommodate you, all right? But not now, old son.'

'No one is falling out over anything. I asked you a civil question, Mr Irvine. The least you can do is to give me a civil answer.'

'You were hardly being civil when you refused to shake my hand, Colm.' I held it out once more. 'Look. There it is again. So, what do you say? Shall we let bygones be bygones, for John and Orla's sake? After all this day is not about the past, it's about the future.'

'Bullshit.'

Colm looked at my hand for a moment and then smacked it away, which transformed my hand into a fist; the next second he had caught me neatly by the wrist and held the fist in front of his face, as if it had been a crucial and damning piece of evidence in a court of law.

'Go ahead,' he said, coolly. 'Punch me. It's what you want to do, isn't it, soldier?'

'I think it's what you'd like me to do,' I said pulling my wrist from his wiry fingers. 'To prove a point to yourself, or perhaps to some of these other people. But you're not going to do that, Colm. I won't let you.'

By now several other guests had seen something of this incident and moved to separate us; but for some reason – I'm not sure how – Tadhg McGahern got it into his head that I had threatened his cousin, and it wasn't long before I was being painted by the wedding's Irish contingent as the old colonial villain of the piece. Later on, I tried to explain what had happened to Orla, but she wasn't having any of it; naturally she sided with her chimp of a brother. Blood is thicker than water, although in Northern Ireland it's more often just thick.

Now, as I watched the television footage of Orla's body being lifted into a panelled forensic van I heard the reporter's voice utter some nonsense about how following her tragic murder 'tributes' had been paid to 'the beautiful actress' by some of the people who worked with her. Then the doors of the van closed on Orla and she was driven swiftly away to her autopsy, which hardly bore thinking of with a woman as stunningly beautiful as she had been. That much was true at any rate. You could hardly blame John for marrying a woman like Orla – especially at his age; at the wedding John had been sixty-two and Orla just thirty-one. There were trophy wives and then there was Orla Mac Curtain, who had been nothing less than the FA Cup.

CHAPTER 2

The next morning I awoke feeling better than perhaps I deserved. I showered, put on a tracksuit, went for a run along the towpath, ate breakfast and tried to work up some enthusiasm for working on my novel. The day was cool and overcast, perfect conditions for standing at my desk; like Erasmus, Thomas Jefferson and Winston Churchill I prefer to stand while I'm writing; the human body is not best served by sitting on your arse all day. But whatever feelings of optimism I possessed about the day ahead lasted only until the moment when Peter Stakenborg telephoned.

'The bastard's only gone and written an article about John and us in today's *Daily Mail*,' he said.

'Who has?' I asked dimly.

'Mike fucking Munns, that's who. Two whole pages of crap that includes several less than choice remarks I made over lunch yesterday that I assumed were made in confidence. About Orla. About John. About his books.'

'I should have realized he'd do something like this,' I said. 'Once a reptile always a reptile. You know, I wondered why he went to the lavatory so often. He must have been taking notes.'

'Cunt. What amazes me is that he was sober enough to write a piece like that when he got home. Me, I was wasted.

I spent the whole evening in front of the telly sleeping it off. Where does he get his stamina?'

'That's part of the old Fleet Street training. Even the worst of them can knock out three hundred words on almost any subject when they're pissed. Some of those hacks write better drunk than when they're sober.'

'This is considerably more than three hundred words,' said Peter. 'More like nine hundred.'

'Look, I'll call you back when I've read it.'

'Do it on my mobile, will you? I've got a caller display on that; there are several people I'm going to try to avoid for the rest of the day. Hereward for one. My describing a list of people who might have a reason to murder John himself isn't likely to make me popular with him or John's publisher. I was rather hoping VVL might read my own book with some favour. But there's fat chance of that now, I should say.'

'Maybe it's not as bad as you think it is, Peter.'

'Oh, it bloody is, Don. They've even printed pictures of us all at the *atelier*. I'll kill that bastard the next time I see him. Read it and weep. All right. Catch you later.'

I put on some clothes and walked around the corner to a newsagent just off the High Street. Putney was a bottleneck of traffic, as always; and yet the river – wider than a ten-lane freeway and running from one end of the city to the other – was almost empty. To that extent London was like a body in which the veins and arteries were hopelessly clogged except for the aorta. I bought all of the newspapers and some cigarettes, which made nonsense of the run earlier on but there we are, I need the occasional ciggie when I'm working on a book. Orla's murder and John's disappearance was on the front pages of nearly all of them except the *Financial Times* and the *Guardian*. The *Sun*'s headline brought a half-smile to my lips: HOUSTON, WE HAVE A PROBLEM. It's not the half-naked girl on Page Three that sells that paper – not for many years; it's the anonymous guys who write the headlines. As an anonymous writer myself I always had a soft spot for those guys.

I bought a coffee from a Starbucks and carried it and the papers back to my flat where, after glancing quickly over the other articles, I finally read Mike Munns's story. The purpose of lunch the previous day was now plain to me: Munns had needed some quotes to spice up his piece, which was every bit as hurtful as Peter Stakenborg had said it was – worse, if you were John Houston, Stakenborg or Philip French. I came out of it marginally better than they did. Oddly the thing that irritated me most was that Munns had attributed Somerset Maugham's famous quote about Monte Carlo to me; it looked as if I'd tried to pass it off as my own, and since the subtext of the article was that I was the 'Machiavellian' mastermind behind a kind of grubby fraud in which a sweatshop of poorly paid, ruthlessly exploited authors wrote all of Houston's books in order that he might pass them off as his own work, I saw myself portrayed as a sort of literary forger, like Thomas Chatterton or, more recently, Clifford Irving. It mattered not a bit to Munns or to the *Mail* that over the years, in the many interviews he conducted with the press – including the *Daily Mail* – John had always been perfectly open about his modus operandi. And after all, what was so wrong with the idea of a writing factory? Hadn't painters like Van Dyck and Rubens kept *ateliers* where other artists skilled in painting landscapes or children or animals were employed to fill in the blank spaces on some of those enormous canvases? And like Andy Warhol, didn't Jeff Koons and Damien Hirst do something very similar to what Van Dyck and Rubens had

done? Why in the minds of critics – and the critics had been
very critical of John Houston, the author – was it all right for
a painter to rely on assistants but not all right for an author
to do the same? Would *War and Peace* have been any less of
a great novel if today it were to be revealed that Tolstoy had
employed another writer to pen that account of the Battle
of Borodino in exactly the same way that Eugène Delacroix
employed Gustave Lassalle-Bordes to help him paint some of
his larger murals? I doubted it very much.

But then I would say that, wouldn't I?

I called Peter Stakenborg back and tried to reassure him
the article wasn't nearly as bad as he had imagined it was;
he wasn't convinced; so I called Mike Munns and left a one-
word message on his cellphone that Samuel Beckett informs
us was the trump card of young wives. Then I stood in front
of my standing desk, switched on my computer and tried to
forget the whole wretched affair.

The thing is I feel more alert while I'm standing; when I'm
sitting behind my other desk I am too easily distracted by
the internet – the PC on the standing desk isn't connected,
so there's no temptation to send an email, to pay a visit to
YouTube or Twitter, or make a bet on the William Hill website. Writing is all about the elimination of distractions. I'm
always amazed how some writers have music playing in the
background. Like anything else, a standing desk takes a little
bit of getting used to; you have to learn not to lock out your
knees and to spread the weight between both legs; but there's
no doubt that I feel much more alert while I'm standing.
Above my desk there's a picture of Ernest Hemingway typing
something while he's standing up: the typewriter is balanced
on top of a music case which is on top of a set of shelves, and
so strictly speaking there's no desk involved, but it always

reminds me that a good writer ought to be able to write any-where. A standing desk hasn't made me the writer Papa was, but then again it hasn't done me any harm either: I couldn't fall asleep at my desk when I was standing up or browse any online porn. Being on your feet all day – like a beat copper – burns calories, too, and there are already enough lard-arse writers around as it is.

At lunchtime I wandered out onto the High Street and picked up a sandwich from Marks & Spencer; after eating it I had a short nap in my Eames chair, and then continued work until around 4.30. The phone did not ring again until almost six o'clock, which was a bit of a surprise; it was much more of a surprise to discover that it was the cops who were calling me.

'Monsieur Irvine?'

'Speaking.'

'My name is Vincent Amalric and I am a chief inspector of police with the *Sûreté Publique* in Monaco. My Commissioner, Paul de Beauvoir, has ordered me to investigate the murder of Madame Orla Houston. I believe you knew her quite well, yes?'

It was a masculine-sounding voice, masculine and very French; every few seconds there was a short pause and a quiet inhalation of breath, and I guessed he was smoking a cigarette. Cops should always smoke when they're working on a case; not because it makes them look cool or anything but because a cigarette is the perfect baton for conducting an interrogation; it gives the smoker pause for thought and a pregnant pause for disbelief, and if all else fails you can always blow smoke in someone's face or press it into your suspect's eye.

'I knew her.'

'Tell me, monsieur – and forgive me for asking this so soon

in our conversation – but has John Houston spoken to you recently?'

'No, not for several weeks.'

'An email, perhaps? A text?'

'Nothing. I'm sorry.'

'So. I am arriving in London on Saturday. My sergeant and I will be staying at Claridge's.'

'Very nice for you both. I can see that life as a policeman in Monaco has its rewards.'

'Claridge's is a nice hotel? Is this what you mean, monsieur?'

'It's probably the best hotel in London, Chief Inspector. Not quite as opulent as the Hermitage, perhaps, or the Hôtel de Paris, but probably as good as it gets in London.'

'*Bon.* In which case I feel there could be no problem in me inviting you there for dinner next Monday evening. I was hoping that you might help me with my inquiries.'

I could have pointed out that this was once a euphemism in English crime reporting – a phrase that implied a degree of guilt – but I felt this was hardly the time to help Chief Inspector Amalric with the subtleties of his English, which anyway was better than my French. Besides, the phrase seemed almost to have disappeared; these days the Metropolitan Police just arrested you and then tipped off the newspapers.

'Certainly, Chief Inspector. At what time?'

'Shall we say eight o'clock?'

'Fine. I'll be there. By the way, how did you get my telephone number?'

'Your colleague Mike Munns gave us your contact details. We saw the article in today's newspaper and spoke to him only a short while ago. He was most helpful. He said that if we spoke to anyone in London we should make sure that we spoke to you, since you have known Monsieur Houston the longest?'

'Longer than Mike Munns, yes.'

'And longer than his late wife, too?'

'Oh yes. I've known John for more than twenty years. Since before he became a published author.'

'Then I have just one more question for the present, sir. Is it possible you have some idea where Monsieur Houston might have gone?'

'I've been thinking about that. I know he'd been working on a book in Switzerland but he didn't think to tell me where and I didn't ask. He had a largish boat, as I'm sure you know. The *Lady Schadenfreude*. And a plane at Mandelieu. A twin-engined King Air 350. With a plane like that he could have gone anywhere in Europe in a matter of hours. In fact I know he used to fly it quite regularly here to London.'

'The boat is still in its berth in the Monte Carlo harbour. And the plane is still at the airfield. No, we believe Monsieur Houston must have left Monaco by road. A car has been taken from his garage.'

'Which one?'

'The Range Rover.'

I smiled. Got that one right. 'Okay. I'll see you on Monday. Goodbye.'

'Goodbye, monsieur.'

Goodbye. Easy. I never quite bought that last line in Chandler's *The Long Goodbye*: 'I never saw any of them again – except the cops. No way has yet been invented to say goodbye to them.' What does that mean? People give the cops the brush-off all the time; and if anyone was equal to the task of doing it for real it was surely John Houston; the man was very resourceful. Still, Chandler's is a great title. One of the best I'd say. That and *The Big Sleep*. Sometimes a good title helps you to write the novel. I wasn't at all happy with the title of my own novel. I wasn't happy with the beginning. And I certainly wasn't happy with the hero – he was too much like me: dull and pompous with a strong streak of pedantry. John was always picking me up for that when, earlier in our working relationship, he read a draft I'd written for one of his own books:

'As usual you've made the hero much too professorial, Don. He's a bit cold. Not likeable at all. You need to go back and make us like him more.'

'I don't know how to do that.'

'Sure you do, old sport. Give him a pet dog. Better still let him find an abandoned kitten. Or have him call his mother up. That always works. Or maybe there's a kid he knows who he gives a few bucks to now and then. People like that. Shows he's got a heart.'

'It's a bit obvious isn't it?'

'This isn't Nicholson Baker, Don. We don't sweat the small stuff. We tell it how it is in broad strokes, and people can take it or leave it. I'm not much interested in the finer aspects of characterization any more than I am in winning the Man Booker Prize. We're not writing for Howard Jacobson or Martin Amis.'

'But he's supposed to be a ruthless killer, John.'

'That's right.'

I shrugged. 'Which would imply a degree of unlikeability. Did people like the Jackal in Forsyth's novel?'

'I did,' said John. 'The Englishman, as Freddie more often calls him, is bold and audacious. Yes, he is cool and self-contained and a cold-blooded killer. But he also has style and considerable charm. Remember that French bird he shags when he's on the run. When he's with her he's a bit like James Bond. Smooth and full of smiles. Charm will take a character a long way. Even when he's also a bastard. Until I fix them your characters tend to lack charm, Don. A bit like you.'

He chuckled at his little joke.

'It's there – the old army officer charm – but you keep it hidden, old sport. It's buried deep along with a lot of other shit. Look, Don, if we're going to spend three hundred pages with this guy we have to like him a bit. If you write a biography of Himmler you at least have to find him interesting, right? So, it's the same with this guy in the novel. He has to be someone you might want to have a beer with. That's the key to any successful character in fiction, Don. No matter who he is, no matter what he's done, he has to be someone you might want to sit with in a bar. If it comes to that it's also how you get elected to be the President of the United States, or the Prime Minister of Great Britain. For that to happen you have to look like someone to have a drink with.'

'Right.'

'Remember what we did with Jack Boardman?'

Then there were only two, but Jack Boardman became the hero of six novels, of which the most recent was *The Second Archangel: A Jack Boardman Story.*

'Yes, I think so.'

'We based him on your best friend at Sandhurst. What was his name? Piers something or other? The one who was a lieutenant in the Parachute Regiment.'

'Piers Perceval.'

'That's right. I asked you what it was you liked about Piers and we drew up a list of all the things that made him seem like such a good bloke. And then I suggested you stick to that when you were writing about Jack Boardman. I told you to always be asking yourself, what would Piers have done in a situation like this? If Piers slept with this woman what would he say to her afterward? If Piers was going to tell a joke what kind of joke would it be? That kind of thing. It's how we put Jack Boardman together.'

'Yes, I'd forgotten that.'

'So. Think of another friend. And base this new character on him. Steal him, if you like. Steal him like a body snatcher. Simple.'

The trouble was that after writing almost forty books for John, I'd used up all of my own friends – and quite a few of my ex-wife's – so that there was no one left I could use now for my own novel. I could hardly use Piers Perceval again. After six Jack Boardman books I never wanted to think about or see Piers again. So it was probably just as well that he had been dead for more than thirty years.

I badly missed John's suggestions on how to improve what I'd written – he was brilliant at doing that. This is different from mere editing; in my experience most editors can tell you what is wrong with a page of writing but have little or no clue how to fix it. That's why they're editors and not writers, I suppose. Constructive criticism is the most difficult thing to give any writer. But mostly I missed John's carefully researched story outlines. These were 75-page out-lines of as yet unwritten books, with research appendices, maps and photographs – story epitomes in which all of the questions had been asked and answered – bound in red leather with purple silk bookmarks and their titles lettered in gold. Which seemed only appropriate: each of John's outlines was worth about four million dollars. Unlike my own novel; the way things were going I would be lucky to sell it at all.

CHAPTER 3

On the face of it the restaurant at Claridge's did not augur well; there was something about the art deco room with its purple chairs, high marble ceilings, telescopic peach lampshades and modern carpet that made me feel slightly nauseous. Maybe it was the prospect of dining with two French policemen, but the restaurant looked like the dining room on a passenger-liner that was about to sink.

The maître d' led me to a table where two men got to their feet and shook me by the hand. Amalric was a weary-looking man with grey hair, a neat, grey moustache and beard, and a good navy-blue suit with a custom lining, pocket silk handkerchief and Hermès tie that made him seem more like a banker. His sergeant, Didier Savigny, was about twenty years younger, with a shaven head and altogether more muscular; his suit was less expensive than his superior's but rather more fashionable, which is to say the jacket was cut a little too short for my taste and made his arms stick out like a chimp's. Each of them handed me a nicely printed business card with the embossed gold seal of the principality and which I read politely.

'Rue Notari,' I said. 'Why does that seem familiar to me?'

'It's close to the main harbour of Monaco,' explained Amalric. 'Your boss's boat, the *Lady Schadenfreude*, is moored less than fifty metres from police headquarters, on the other side of the Stade Nautique swimming pool. You can actually see the bridge of the boat from my office window.'

'That's handy,' I said. I collected the menu off the table and ordered a glass of champagne from the waiter. It's not often you get taken out for an expensive dinner by the police.

'You know Monaco?' asked Savigny. He reminded me a little of Zinedine Zidane. Tanned, muscular, not very patient. From the look of him I imagined his shaven head would feel every bit as hard butting against my sternum as the Marseille-born footballer's.

'Enough to know that Monaco is the name of the country; that Monte Carlo is just one neighbourhood; and that the capital is the neighbourhood known as Monaco-Ville, which according to your card is where your office appears to be located. I've been going there for quite a few years. Ever since John Houston relocated there for tax reasons.'

'Which is why you know the Hermitage, perhaps?'

'Not to stay there. Whenever I've been in Monaco I've stayed in Beausoleil. At the Hôtel Capitole on Boulevard General Leclerc. At a hundred euros a night that's more in my price range, I'm afraid. And by the way, John Houston was never really my boss. I'm a freelance writer. Self-employed.'

I neglected to add that on one occasion when I'd been staying in Beausoleil I had stood on my tiny balcony and urinated into Monaco which, at the time, gave me an absurd amount of schoolboy pleasure.

'You never stayed with him?' Savigny sounded a little surprised. 'In your friend's apartment?'

'No. I was never asked. Oh, I went to the apartment in the Odéon Tower several times to deliver or to collect something.

But ours was more of a business arrangement. It's been a long time since we were something so innocent as friends.'

The waiter came back with my champagne and I toasted the two policemen politely. They were drinking gin and tonic. The sergeant put down his glass and placed a little Marantz dictation machine upright on the table in front of me.

'Do you mind this?' he asked. 'It is difficult for us to eat and take notes at the same time.'

I shrugged. 'No, I don't mind. But look, what are you expecting me to say? I should tell you right now that I don't think John Houston murdered his wife. I've known the man for twenty-five years and he doesn't strike me as a killer. And believe me I know what I'm talking about. If he's done a runner it's probably because he's scared, not because he's guilty.'

'Let's order first,' said Amalric, 'and then you can tell us some more about why he's innocent.'

I ordered a beetroot tartare and a seared loin of venison; Amalric ordered his own food and a hundred-and-twenty-quid bottle of Vosne-Romanée.

'Your expense account must make entertaining reading,' I said. 'For a policeman.'

'The Interior Minister of Monaco, Dominique de Polignac, takes all crime in the principality very seriously,' said Amalric. 'His specific orders to me before we came to London were that no expense is to be spared in catching Mrs Houston's killer, and as you can see I am not a man who is inclined to disobey his superiors.'

'Under the present circumstances, I'm very glad to hear it.'

'Not that he reads much, you understand. The Minister is more interested in football. AS Monaco is his great passion. Did you know that Arsène Wenger used to manage the team?'

'Yes, I did. And you, Chief Inspector? Do you have much time for reading?'

'My wife died a few years ago and since then I have developed quite a habit for reading. Mostly I like to read history. Simon Sebag Montefiore. Max Hastings. But I confess I have never read a book by John Houston. Until his wife died I had never even heard of him. But Sergeant Savigny has read a lot of his books. Haven't you, Sergeant?'

Savigny nodded. 'I don't know the English titles, only the French. But the Jack Boardman books. I have read all of them.'

'Did you like them?'

'Yes. I buy one at the airport every time I go on holiday. What I like is that you always know exactly what you're going to get.'

The sergeant made it sound like a Big Mac. For some writers this would have been an insulting remark, but for Houston this was what his books were all about; a successful brand was based on a consistent product. *Give them what they want and then teach them that they can have it again. And again.* John had been a great believer in creating his own writing style, or more accurately his lack of one. He'd paid particular attention to the number of words in a sentence and the number of sentences in a paragraph. Verbiage, as he called the excessive use of words, was the great enemy of writers: *Words only appear to be your friends; but you should think of them as the speed bumps on your page; they can slow the story down as much as they can keep it bowling along.*

He had even created a writing lexicon of words that writers from the *atelier* were forbidden to use; words like 'corollary', 'detumescent', 'uxorious', 'polyglot', and 'felicitous'.

As a rough rule of thumb, don't use a word that isn't in the

Microsoft Word dictionary, unless it's a proper noun, of course. Equally, don't ever be afraid of using clichés. Not in my books. If you want your novel to be a page-turner then make clichés your friends. Clichés – the kind of writing that Martin Amis makes war on – are the verbal particle accelerators to finishing books. Original writing just slows a reader down and makes him feel inadequate. Like he's thick. Which of course he is, but there's no sense in rubbing that in. My readers actively approve of clichés. And forget about similes and metaphors; if you want to use similes and metaphors then go and write fucking poetry, not one of my books. People don't like it. That's why poetry doesn't sell.

About the use of swear words in his books Houston was equally circumspect:

No more than one per chapter. And only in situations of extreme stress. A lot of people in Middle America don't much care for profanity, so within reason, it's best avoided.

Sergeant Savigny was still explaining why he admired the Houston canon. Harold Bloom it wasn't, but listening to the Frenchman I had an idea that John would have been delighted with his deconstruction of John's work:

'The great thing about Jack Boardman is the way that you don't get too much useless description; the woman wore a white dress and that's it. Job done. I don't need to know if the dress came from Chloé and if her shoes matched her handbag and her panties. If I want that kind of shit I'll read *Vogue*. Also, I like the fact that you can just put the books down and then pick them up again without losing the plot.'

'As a matter of fact I wrote all of the Jack Boardman books.'

'You don't say.'

Amalric frowned. 'This is not something we understand. Houston puts his name to a book that you write, Monsieur

Irvine, and he gets the big money while you are paid – forgive me – like a hired hand. How is this possible?'

'He comes up with the story,' I said. 'The stories are pretty
good. As Sergeant Savigny has explained, the stories are
why people buy Houston's books, not because of any fancy
writing. We didn't go in for much in the way of metaphors
and similes. Just straight descriptions. You're not supposed
to notice the writing very much – just the story. He came up
with the plots and I – or someone like me – wrote them. The
actual writing was something that bored him greatly. Really
it's a bit like what Bismarck is supposed to have said about
laws being like sausages. You should never watch either one
being made. It's best just to read the final product and not
to pay any attention to the creative process. But that's only
my opinion. John himself loved to talk about the whole
business of writing and exactly how he produced his books.
He was really very open about it. Much more open than
I'd ever have been. Especially when you're talking to these
bastards on the *Guardian* who are just looking to trip you
up and tell the world what a fraud you are. The *Guardian*
is a left-leaning newspaper in this country. They don't like
anyone with a bit of money. A bit like *Libération* in France,
I think, but with less style. Anyway the lefties loved to hate
John. What was it they called him? The Mies van der Rohe
of the modern novel; because form follows function and
ornament is a crime. The novelist of the machine age; that
was another thing they called him. John loved that. He
thought that was a compliment. I told him it wasn't but he
insisted it was, even though they meant it to be insulting.
He had that page framed and hung on his office wall. And
as a quote on some of his publicity. He was very good at
creating publicity.'

'In the last forty-eight hours he's had more of that than perhaps even he could have bargained for,' said Amalric. 'With his face on the front of so many newspapers it won't be long before we find him. So it would be better for Monsieur Houston if he were to turn himself in. I'm only saying this in case he does decide to get in touch with you.'

'He won't. I'm almost certain of that. If he has decided to disappear he certainly wouldn't need my help. The man can manage on his own.'

I sipped my champagne and surveyed the starters as they arrived at the table.

'You see, John's a clever man, Chief Inspector. Very well read. Independently minded. Highly resourceful. He was always good at accumulating esoteric, sometimes forbidden wisdom. He prided himself on getting the facts right so that the books could seem more plausible. He said he didn't care if anyone faulted his style just as long as they weren't able to fault his facts. Facts were what he wanted. Painstaking, solid research was the part of the writing process that John really enjoyed. He knew everything from how to manufacture ricin, to the best place to buy an illegal assault rifle. That's Poland, in case you're interested. In Gdansk you can put in an order for a new Vepr and within the hour have one delivered to your hotel. That's why so many people read his books, Chief Inspector. Not because they seem authentic but because they are authentic. Isn't that right, Sergeant?'

Savigny nodded. 'That's right, sir.'

'John used to offer ten thousand bucks to anyone who could fault his research. To this date that money is unclaimed. Oh, he had the odd letter from some nutter claiming the money, but John was always able to write back and point out just where his correspondent was incorrect. No, he's quite a character, is John. If he doesn't want to be found you might have a hard job finding him.'

I winced a little as I heard myself saying this; it sounded very like some bullshit I'd read on the overheated blurb of the last Jack Boardman: *You won't find him unless he wants you to find him.*

Amalric nodded. 'Perhaps,' he said. '*Mais il faut cultiver notre jardin.*'

I nodded, recognizing this, the last line from Voltaire's *Candide.* 'Yes, of course. You are only doing your job. I understand that.'

'You know, so far you are the only one who talks about Monsieur Houston as if he might be innocent. We have spoken to his agent, Hereward Jones, his publisher, Monsieur Anderton, Monsieur Munns of course, and his first wife, Madame Sheldrake.'

'You've been busy.'

'And you are the only one who gives him the benefit of the doubt.'

'Maybe they know more about what happened than I do.' I shrugged. 'Which is only what was on television.'

'Then let me tell you what we do know. I'd show you some photographs only it might put you off your food.'

I shook my head. 'I was a soldier in Northern Ireland. Blood doesn't bother me. At least not any more. Believe me, there's nothing you could show me that could ever put me off a free dinner at Claridge's.'

Amalric nodded at Savigny, who reached down to his case and took out an iPad. A few seconds later I was looking at a digital slideshow of the Odéon crime scene: two dead dogs, and a woman – Orla – who might almost have been asleep but for the black and ragged hole in the centre of her Botoxed forehead.

Meanwhile Amalric explained exactly what was known; or at least exactly what was known that he wanted me to know.

'A week last Friday night, Mr and Mrs Houston had dinner at Joël Robuchon, where they were regulars.'

'Somewhere else I can't afford.'

Amalric nodded. 'While they were there they argued. It was a violent argument. Blows were exchanged. The maître d' at the restaurant says that Mr Houston twisted his wife's ear. The doorman says that Mrs Houston hit him with her bag. Soon after this they left, with Mrs Houston in tears. He drove them back to the Tour Odéon in her cream Ferrari. At around 10.30 Mrs Houston took a sleeping pill and they went to bed. Then, sometime between midnight and six o'clock that morning, she was shot at point-blank range in the forehead while she lay in bed. We think he probably got out of bed, fetched a gun and shot her while she was asleep. There's a burn mark on the skin of her forehead.'

'There's no exit wound,' I remarked. 'On the news they said it was a nine-millimetre. Only that can't be right. But for the fact that I know this woman I might say it almost looks like a neat job. There's hardly a hair out of place on this body. A nine-mill bullet would certainly have blown off the back of her skull, not to mention the fact that the pillow would have been covered in blood.' I shrugged. 'By the way, that's the writer in me talking, not the murder suspect. Just so you know.'

'You're right,' said Amalric. 'It wasn't a nine-millimetre pistol that killed her.'

Amalric glanced over the top of the iPad and, with a neatly manicured finger, moved the picture on to a shot of a smallish pistol. 'That's a Walther 22-calibre automatic,' he said. 'The same kind of gun that probably shot Mrs Houston. Mr Houston bought just such a gun in Monaco six months ago. We think it was probably bought for and owned by her. It's now the only gun missing from what was, after all, a substantial gun cabinet.'

I glanced again at the dead dogs, where considerably more blood was in evidence. It looked like a photograph from a press ad for the RSPCA.

'The Walther has a ten-shot magazine,' said Amalric. 'He used four more shots on the dogs, possibly to silence them, I don't know.'

'Four shots? Then I'd say whoever shot the dogs enjoyed it.'

'Why do you say so, monsieur?'

'They were small dogs. Two shots for each one. That's a little excessive. Like he was making sure they were dead. But to be quite frank with you, I think he might have enjoyed it, because I know that I would have enjoyed it. Those two dogs were a bloody nuisance. Not just the noise they made. But the hair they left on your clothes. Nor were they properly house-trained. John was always stepping on the crap they left around the house. It used to drive him mad that they weren't properly house-trained and so he did his best to have nothing to do with them.'

'I thought all English people love dogs,' said Amalric.

'Whatever gave you that idea? Anyway, I'm Scottish. And I thought they were a bloody nuisance.'

'Then perhaps the real motive behind her murder was to kill the dogs,' said Savigny. 'The husband shoots the wife because he really wants to shoot the dogs.'

Amalric shot him an impatient sort of look.

'Stranger things have happened,' said the younger policeman.

Amalric shrugged. 'At about 8.30 on Saturday morning the concierge knocked on Houston's door and gave him the English newspapers. According to him Houston seemed quite normal. Neither Mr nor Mrs Houston was seen all day, but that wasn't unusual. At around 5.30 in the evening Houston left the building on foot. He was out until about 7.30. He remained in the Tower until about midnight, when he went away in his Range Rover. He hasn't been seen since. Meanwhile the body of Mrs Houston was found on Tuesday morning by the maid.'

'Why not suicide?' I asked.

'The dogs, monsieur. Why would she kill her own pet dogs?'

'If she was going to kill herself she might have reasoned that John wasn't likely to care for them himself. I've already told you about those dogs; he was none too fond.'

'And the sleeping pill? How do you explain that?'

'She takes a pill out of habit *before* she decided to do it. And maybe she shoots herself in bed in order to embarrass her husband. To put him in a tight spot, if you like.'

'For what reason?'

'John would have given her plenty of reasons. Other women, perhaps. He was always a bit of a pussy-hound.'

Savigny frowned and spoke in French to Amalric, who provided what I presumed was the translation; my French isn't bad but the Chief Inspector was too quick for me.

Savigny smiled. 'It's an interesting theory but for one thing: the gun is missing.'

'I see. But that still doesn't rule out suicide. Not entirely. How about this, for example? John takes the gun when he finds out that Orla has killed herself. He takes it because it's his gun. Or at least one he'd purchased. I'm not sure if he owned a Walther 22, but I wouldn't be at all surprised. He owned quite a few weapons.'

Amalric nodded. 'Yes, he owned a Walther 22.'

'Anyway, he leaves Monaco because he recognizes that he's in a tight spot and takes the gun with him so that there's less evidence against him other than the mere fact of his flight.' I shrugged. 'Tosses it into the sea from the car window as he drives along the Croisette.'

'I can see how it is that you are a writer, Monsieur Irvine,' said Amalric.

'I have my moments. But to be honest plotting is not my strong suit. That was John's particular forte.' I finished my champagne and sat back on my chair. 'Or how about this? Someone else killed her while John was asleep. They didn't always share the same bed. Sometimes he slept alone. So maybe John wakes up after hearing the shots – although the shots from a 22 aren't so very loud. And it's a big apartment. He gets up. Finds her dead. Reasons that he's the most obvious suspect, panics and decides to take off. Can't say I blame him. Because in spite of all I'm saying I admit the case against him is strong.' I shrugged. 'But you know, from what he had told me they'd had some problems with the CCTV in that building, so it's going to be hard to prove he didn't go straight out again after they came home from Joël Robuchon.'

'Not problems. Issues. The residents of the Tour Odéon objected to their being filmed. They felt that the use of CCTV in that building invaded their privacy and so the system was switched off a while ago everywhere but the garage. Many of the other residents had bodyguards, of course, some of whom also lived in the tower. Others like Monsieur Houston made do with the security on the front desk.'

'Isn't that convenient for whoever shot Orla Houston? Doubtless her murderer was aware of this, too.'

'This is typical of people who live in Monaco, of course. They are very private people.'

'Those are the ones who usually have something to hide,' I said.

'Yes. You're right. And without them I would be out of a job.'

I shrugged. 'And that's it? This is all you have?'

Amalric smiled sheepishly. 'There were other forensics, which I can't go into right now. But it's already quite a lot, don't you think? A murdered wife. A missing husband. It's only in books that one can afford to ignore the convenience of such an obvious suspect as Monsieur Houston. And until we find him we have to go about building a picture of their marriage and what might have made him kill her. That's fair, surely?'

'Which is why we're here in London,' said Savigny, tucking into his scallop starter.

'*Who's Afraid of Virginia Woolf*, with better cars,' I said. 'That's a picture of their marriage.' I shrugged. 'At least it's the only one I ever saw. I don't know what else I can tell you about their marriage.'

'Perhaps nothing, but according to Monsieur Munns, you know all there is to know about Houston himself,' said Amalric. 'So why don't you tell us the whole story? From the very beginning. How you two met. The way things worked and then the way things changed. Recently, wasn't it? When he made the decision to wind up the *atelier*?'

'*Il était une fois*, as it were,' I said.

'Exactly. This is your métier, after all. And there's nothing policemen like more than to listen to a story. It strikes me

that this might be quite a good one, too. One minute Houston
is the most successful writer in the world, making millions
of dollars every year, and the next he decides to throw it all
up. Why?' Amalric sniffed the wine as it was poured by the
waiter and nodded his approval. 'I have the strong feeling
that this is the key to everything. Yes, indeed, I have the dis-
tinct sense that once one understands this then much else
will become clear. And perhaps we will have a good idea of
where to find the elusive Monsieur Houston.'

CHAPTER 4

My father died while I was still studying law at Cambridge. He left my mother very little and joining the army on an undergraduate bursary was the only way of finishing my degree; for this I had to give the army three years, but I ended up giving them six. I went to Sandhurst in September 1976, and stayed in the army until 1982 when I met a rather marvellous man called Perry Slater, who had known my father during national service in the Royal Scots Greys. Perry was the kind of chap who knew everyone and who everyone seemed to like. He'd been a keen motorcyclist, as was I – we'd both ridden bikes at the Isle of Man TT – and was famously a sports commentator for the BBC; he was also an advertising executive with an agency called D'Arcy MacManus Masius and he kindly managed to find me a job as an account executive in the summer of 1982.

In the late Seventies and early Eighties British advertising was undergoing something of a revolution; thanks to entrepreneurs like the Saatchi Brothers and commercials directors like Alan Parker and Ridley Scott, London's agencies were making much more creative work than their Madison Avenue counterparts and suddenly it was cool to be an advertising man.

At least it was unless you worked for Masius, which was

known in the business as the civil service of advertising agencies; Masius looked after clients such as Pedigree Petfoods, Peugeot, Mars, Beechams, Kimberly-Clark and Allied Breweries whose brands were long-established and distinguished by their dullness and conservatism. It might have been the after-effects of my military service – back then we hadn't a clue about PTSD – but the tedium and monotony of my new career left me rather depressed and, after a year as an account executive, I persuaded someone to let me become a copywriter. That was how I first met John Houston. He was my creative director, which is to say he was the person to whom I reported and to whom I was supposed to present the press advertisements, TV and radio commercials that I had written for various clients. I liked working for John, but only in so far as he let me do what I liked, and I quickly learned that John himself was interested in advertising in so far as it enabled him to pay his bills; his real interest was writing not advertising copy but a novel to which he had devoted every weekend and evening for almost two years. I'd been writing something myself, and jealously I was spurred to greater effort by the thought that John might beat me into print. From time to time after that we would each politely enquire how the other's novel was coming along; but John always played his cards close to his chest and I had no idea that his book was as advanced as it turned out to be. Because one day, to everyone's surprise but mine, he announced that this novel – *The Tyranny of Heaven* – was going to be published and simultaneously handed in his notice. It was, as John himself describes, his *Keep the Aspidistra Flying* moment, which is a novel by George Orwell wherein the hero, Gordon Comstock, quits an advertising agency and takes a low-paid job so that he can write poetry instead. Of course the major difference between John Houston and Gordon Comstock was that there was nothing low-paid about John's future prospects; he had obtained a lucrative three-book deal with a leading British publisher and very soon he landed similarly generous deals with American, Japanese, German and French publishers which seemed likely to make my former boss a millionaire before the first book was even published. But still he was not satisfied; he quickly discovered that publishers possessed none of the marketing and advertising skills that John himself had; in those days publishing was full of gentlemen with bow-ties and cigarette-holders who had an eye for good books but no idea how to sell them. And it was typical of the man that instead of spending his advance money on a house or a car John used it all to advertise *The Tyranny of Heaven* on television and radio, with the result that it was soon a number one bestseller. After that the people at John's publishers were not inclined to disagree with him about anything very much.

It was about this time that John called me up and invited me out to lunch. He told me he wanted to pick my brains about my army service in Northern Ireland for his follow-up novel and I pretended I was happy to let them be picked, although in truth I rather envied his success and hardly wanted to see him for fear that this might show. On the principle that lightning never strikes in the same place twice I'd let myself imagine that John's being published made it much less likely that the same good fortune would happen to me. But I put a smile on my face and went along to a restaurant near Masius in St James's Square called Ormond's Yard, bit my tongue and congratulated him effusively and thanked him for the signed copy of his novel which, of course, I'd not dared read in case it was actually any good. I'm afraid this is a very typical reaction among writers. No one reads anyone else's stuff if they can possibly avoid it: we're an insecure, spiteful, jealous lot. Nothing confounds like a good friend's success; and as Gore Vidal once said, 'Whenever a friend succeeds, a little something in me dies.'

'*The Tyranny of Heaven*? What's that?' I asked John. 'Shakespeare?'

He shook his head. 'John Milton. If you're looking for a good title you'll find there are lots of good titles in Milton, old sport. Shakespeare, no. Don't waste your time looking for a title in fucking Shakespeare. He's been raped more than a Berlin housewife. But Milton's great. Nobody reads Milton these days.'

'Congratulations,' I said, inspecting the signature and the dedication in his novel. 'I understand it's already a bestseller.'

'True. But it's America where I want to make it big, not here. In publishing terms this country is a sideshow with goldfish.'

'Easier said than done.'

'Not really. Whatever it is you're writing my advice is to make the thing American-centric, if you'll pardon that word. Get yourself an American hero and you're halfway to the big money, old sport.'

Old sport. He used to say that a lot; and since John's favourite book is *The Great Gatsby* and 'old sport' seems to be Jay Gatsby's favourite phrase, I sometimes wonder how much of Gatsby there is in John. He is as he would tell you himself, entirely self-invented: describing his own humble Yorkshire origins he used to say, 'It doesn't matter where the fuck you come from; what matters is where you're going.' And that is John's whole philosophy, in a nutshell.

'I just happen to be English, old sport. But that's not who I am or who I want to be. Yorkshire is a dump. I hate the place.

Never want to see it again. Cold. Miserable. Men in flat caps with pigeons and racing dogs and ill-fitting false teeth and homespun philosophy that all sounds like a Hovis commercial. The only people who care about it are the poor bastards who have to live there. Not me. I can't wait to live somewhere else. Tuscany. Provence. The Bahamas. To live somewhere else and be someone else. That's the great thing about being a writer, Don. You have a perfect excuse not just to make up the story that's in the fucking novel but your own story, too. You can invent yourself at the same time as you create the novel. It's wonderfully liberating to become someone else. You haven't asked my advice but I'm going to give it to you anyway. Make yourself more American, yes, even to the extent of using American spelling. After all, it's America where a publishing fortune is still to be made. Which is why I've already mortgaged my house to pay for the advertising campaign that will accompany the book's publication in the US.'

'Jesus, John, is that wise?'

'Probably not. But I don't think that making big money has very much to do with wisdom, do you? It's about having the balls to take a risk. History shows that all great fortunes are based on taking risk. What is it that T. S. Eliot says? Only those who will risk going too far can possibly find out how far one can go. I truly believe that, Don. The greatest danger would be not to take a risk at all. Of course, the ad spend would be doubly effective if I had a paperback and a hardback out at the same time. I mean you can always sell the paperback on the tail of the hardback. So it's a bit unfortunate that the money I'm spending will be only half as effective as it might have been. That's my one regret about all this: that I didn't have two products ready when I made the publishing deals.'

John sighed and lit a cigarette and stared across the yard because it was a nice day and we were sitting at the three or four tables that were grouped outside Ormond's' front door. His use of the word 'products' was telling. John has never quite lost the adman's phraseology; even today when you meet him – twenty years after he left Masius – it's more like talking to David Ogilvy than David Cornwell. Some writers talk about metafiction and genre and romans à clef and unreliable narrators, but John talks about the USP and the brand and focus groups and distribution and point-of-sale.

'So what is it that you want, John? You've dug your tunnel out of the advertising *Stalag*. You're out and you're as free as Steve McQueen on a motorcycle and yet you don't really seem like you're happy although there is any number of copywriters who would love to change places with you. Even the ones who are gods at trendier ad agencies like GGT and AMV. To me who's going back to write a couple of shitty radio commercials this afternoon for Ribena it seems like you have it all, pal: a three-book deal, plenty of money, some social significance, no boss, no nine-to-five, no Monday morning client meetings at fucking Perivale.'

Perivale in West London was where another dull-as-ditchwater Masius client was to be found: Hoover.

'I could go on with that list but I would only depress myself so much that I'd feel obliged to fall on my Mont Blanc.'

John shrugged. 'I want what anyone in this business wants, old sport: success, money, and then lashings more of both. I want the same thing that Ken Follett, Jeffrey Archer, Stephen King want when they sit down in front of the word-processor: one international bestseller followed quickly by another. My only regret right now is that I can't write these books any faster. I mean, I've got this three-book deal that's worth a million bucks if you add together the Yanks and the Brits and the Japs and the Krauts. But at the rate it takes to write a book I'm going to need at least another eighteen months to write the next two because quite frankly the actual writing part leaves me cold. I'm someone who needs a damn sight more than a room with a fucking view to make me write five hundred words a day. I mean I'm only human, right? Of course, I figure there will be some royalties by then; even so, the big money – the fuck-off money, which is a really substantial advance against future royalties – is still a way off. Meanwhile I've got all these ideas for half a dozen other books down the road. No, really, I've got files full of ideas. Sometimes it seems there are just not enough days in the week.' He grinned. 'Sorry, old sport. I know that's not what you want to hear when you're trying to finish and publish your own book. But that's just the way it is right now. I'm older than you by a decade, which means that I'm a man in a hurry. I want a taste of that outrageous Stephen Sheppard type money while I'm still young enough to enjoy it.'

Stephen Sheppard was a British novelist who wrote a novel called *The Four Hundred* that, back in 1976, Ed Victor, the literary agent, had famously – every newspaper in Britain had covered the story – sold for one million pounds.

I thought for a minute. 'There is a solution, perhaps.' I said. 'Albeit an unorthodox one in the ascetic, left-liberal world of publishing.'

'Oh? I'd like to hear it.'

'At the English bar there exists a practice called devilling, when a junior barrister undertakes paid written work on behalf of a more senior barrister. The instructing solicitor is not informed of the arrangement and the junior barrister is paid by the senior barrister out of his own fee, as a private arrangement between the two. It's a way older barristers have of making themselves even richer than ought to be possible. So, why not something similar for you? In other words you could pay me a fee to write one of your books. You give me the plot in as much detail as you can manage and then I do the hard slog of knocking out one hundred thousand words; I give it back to you six months later and you edit the manuscript I've provided to your own satisfaction – putting in a few stylistic flourishes to make it truly yours. Or taking a few out, as the case may be. It'd be like what Adam Smith says regarding the division of labour in the manufacture of pins. It strikes me that you've always been the one with a powerful – not to say overactive – imagination and that you're better at creating stories than you are at writing them. Which is where I might come in. In a sense you would just carry on being the creative director, so to speak, and no one need ever know. I can even sign some sort of non-disclosure agreement. Meanwhile, you write the other book; then you hand both books to your publisher in quick succession and claim the balance of the advance.'

'Go on.'

I didn't know that I could say very much more about this, but now that I'd mentioned it I rather liked the idea of quitting my job and using John's publishing windfall – what was left of it – to stay at home and subsidize my own writing; so I was selling it now and selling it with more than a hint of flattery.

'After all, you wouldn't be the first to pull a stroke like this. Shakespeare may have had a similar arrangement with Thomas Nashe when he wrote *Henry VI, Part One*. Or with George Wilkins when he wrote *Pericles*. And with Thomas Middleton when he wrote – something else.' I shrugged.

'Don't ask me what. But I rather think Elizabethan theatre was a bit like the modern film industry. With one writer replaced by another at a moment's notice. Or writers step-ping into the breach to help someone out with a first act, or a quick polish. That kind of thing.'

'You know, that's not a bad idea, old sport.' John deliber-ated for a moment. 'That's not a bad idea at all. A bit like Andy Warhol's factory, in New York.'

'Precisely. I suppose you might even argue that the Apple Macintosh is the modern equivalent of the silkscreen printing process. A technology that makes for the rapid reproduction and alteration of the basic creative idea.'

Back in the 1980s – and following the famous Ridley Scott *1984* television commercial – every writer coveted a Macintosh computer. John actually owned one; whereas I was making do with a cheaper and certainly inferior Amstrad; but even that seemed a vast improvement on the IBM Selectric typewriter which is what they gave us to use at work.

'How much would you want? To do what you've just described.'

'Let's see now.' I shook my head. 'Naturally, I'd have to give up work. I mean, to write a whole book in six months – I couldn't do that and continue to be a copywriter. I mean, we're talking nine to five here to produce that many words in that amount of time. So it would have to be enough money to allow that to happen.'

'You were on twenty grand a year when I left.'

'Twenty-five, now. They gave me an extra five to make up your workload after you left. I'd be taking a risk, of course. Giving up work like that. To do something as chancy as this. If it doesn't work out then I'm out of a job without the means to pay the mortgage.'

'You'd really give it up? Come on, Don. You love it. All those nice dolly birds to shag. I sometimes think that's why you came into advertising, old sport. For the birds.'

I shook my head. 'That's bollocks and you know it. I'm fed up with it. Just like you were, John. If I have to write another telly commercial for Brooke Bond Red Mountain coffee I think I will scream. Besides I've already shagged all the birds I'm ever going to shag at Masius. They're wise to my act. I need to move on. But no one at another agency is ever going to take on a copywriter from Masius. We're like lepers. So, this might just be my ticket out of St James's Square. I can subsidize my own novel with what I make from writing yours.'

'I'd have to see a few specimen chapters.'

'You mean my novel?'

'I don't mean your advertising copy. I know how crap you are writing that. David Abbott you're not, old sport.'

I shrugged. 'As if I ever gave a damn about writing copy. Look, you don't need to see my novel. You know I can fucking write. I had that story in *Granta*, remember?'

'Oh, yes. I'd forgotten about that.'

'Unless that is you're not serious. Because I am.'

'Of course I'm serious. Writing all day and every day like Henry fucking James is a royal pain in the ass, Don. No wonder authors all look like swots. Did you see that picture of those Best of Young British Novelists? Christ, if that's what the young ones look like . . . No, it's putting the plot together that I enjoy, not typing all day and night like some tragic bespectacled cunt.'

'I really don't mind it at all,' I confessed. 'I feel like my life has some meaning when I'm in front of the keyboard.'

'I don't know how you have the patience.'

'That's what Northern Ireland teaches you, John: patience and an appreciation for the quiet life. Whenever I sit down at the typewriter I tell myself, "Count yourself lucky; it's not the Falls Road."'

'So, how much?' he repeated. 'That's the sixty-four-thousand-dollar question. Or not, since I'm not about to pay you anything like that.'

'Twenty-five grand.'

'Fuck off. Ten.'

'I can't do it for ten. I can't take the risk. Twenty.'

'Twelve and a half.'

I shook my head. 'Fifteen. And with a bonus if the book is a bestseller.'

I could see John doing the maths in his head. 'Agreed.'

We shook on it and then continued with the minutiae of further negotiations for a while – delivery dates, penalties for failing to meet John's deadline, bonus payments; then John said, 'You know if I can make this arrangement with you, Don, there's no reason I couldn't make it with someone else.'

'I'm sure you could find someone cheaper than me, John. Perhaps if you were to put a small ad in the back of *Books and Bookmen*. Or *The Literary Review*. Writer in a Hurry Seeks Amanuensis. Must be able to spell "amanuensis" and write bestselling novel to order. Thomas Pynchon need not apply.'

'No, I didn't mean that. What I mean is that if I can make this deal with one writer then why not with two? That way I could have two novels being written while I research another story. That's what I'm good at.'

I shrugged. 'Why not? Like you said, it's what Warhol does. I could be your Gerard Malanga.'

'The question is, who? Who else is there who can write that's as desperate as you, old sport?'

'You mean at Masius?'

'Why not? Everyone who's any good wants out of St James's Square one way or the other.'

'What about Sally?'

'One of the many pleasures I have enjoyed in leaving Masius is that I will never again have to see or hear Sally van Leeuwenhoek. Or try to spell her fucking name.'

'Might be useful to have a woman on your team.'

'No, I disagree. You see, I know my market, old sport, because I've researched it very carefully. And before you ask, yes, I paid for a proper research company to carry out some market research and make a report. I'm writing for men; men who want to read books about solidly heterosexual men who think the female eunuch is a fucking mare with a horn on its forehead; who think a problem shared is a fist-fight in a bar. Blokes who grew up thinking that Ian Fleming is a better writer than Christopher Isherwood. Anyway, I never met a woman yet who could write like a man. Did you read *The Sea, The Sea* by Iris Murdoch? The narrator of that novel is supposed to be a man, but he's a man who's interested in curtain fabrics and hence not a real man at all but some daft old bat's idea of what a man sounds like. Hence he sounds like a complete fucking poof. No, this is a good idea we've had here today but no fish, old sport. Besides, I have an idea that we'll have a lot more fun if we keep this a purely stag do.'

'All right. How about Paul Cliveden?'

John thought for a moment and then shook his head. 'He's

queer and therefore similarly disqualified from writing about heterosexual men.'

'Yes, I'd forgotten about that.'

'You worry me, sometimes, old sport. How anyone could forget that Paul Cliveden is queer, I have no idea. He makes Quentin Crisp look like Burt Reynolds.'

I thought for another moment. 'How about Peter Stakenborg?'

'He failed the copy test, didn't he?'

'Yes, although I think it's to his credit that you thought he wasn't suitable copywriter material. As I recall it was you who told him there was no shame in not being able to think at the elevated intellectual level required to write a Ribena commercial featuring a talking blackcurrant bubble.'

'True.'

'Besides, he got a degree in English at Oxford. Not only that but I happen to know he's just started to write his second novel.'

'The first one having been rejected all round. Yes, that's right. It was about advertising, wasn't it? I remember him boring me about it during the D and AD dinner last year. I don't know why people should think a story about the sad hucksters who work in advertising should be interesting to anyone. The adman as a sort of modern class warrior was already dead and buried when Michael Winner made that crappy film about the business back in the Sixties. What was it called?'

'*I'll Never Forget What's'isname.*'

'So what's the new one about?'

'He said that it was a comic novel about what it was like growing up in Malawi. It sounds like another *Good Man in Africa*, I think.'

'Jesus. I bet Jonathan Cape is just gagging for that. Still, Stakenborg has been absolutely everywhere. Mostly to the sort of fly-blown countries I wouldn't ever want to go myself. Kashmir, Afghanistan. It might be handy to have someone who knows what some of these ghastly places are actually like. It would save me from having to go. And you're right. He can write. He wrote those press ads for American Express when Vic Cassel was too pissed to write them himself.'

'They won an award, didn't they?'

'That's what encouraged him to think he could become a copywriter in the first place.' John nodded. 'Okay, okay. Talk to him. See if he's interested in my idea.'

I smiled and did not try to correct him, which I ought to have done, but back then it didn't really seem to matter whose idea it was, as neither of us had any idea that a convenient working arrangement between two advertising copywriters for one or two books would result in more than thirty *New York Times* bestsellers and sales of more than 175 million books. Only James Patterson and J. K. Rowling sell more. These days, whenever the subject of his squad of co-writers comes up in an interview, John always claims that the idea of employing a back-room of ghost-writers was his and his alone; perhaps it's what C. P. Snow describes in his novel *The Sleep of Reason* as 'the hallucinations of fact'. More likely it's just John being his usual selfish self.

The following week I gave in my notice at Masius, and four weeks later I started work on the storyline provided by John for a novel that was published the following year as *The Golden Key is Death* – the first of five novels featuring Dougal Haddon, an ex-SAS officer turned trouble-shooter and mercenary. For a long time I couldn't believe my own good luck: to get paid to stay at home all morning and write a book, and still have time and energy enough to spend the afternoon writing my own. Pigs in shit do not feel as good about themselves as I did.

Even before it was published it was clear that John's new book was destined to be a bestseller – as things turned out it was his first *New York Times* number one – and almost immediately it was finished I started work on the next plot-driven title. I was already making more money than I would have done if I'd been a going-nowhere copywriter at an agency that was held to be the civil service of advertising. For the first time in a long time I was smiling when I got up in the morning.

Meanwhile, Peter Stakenborg joined John's new team of writers, followed by a third writer – another ex-copywriter from Ogilvy & Mather called Brian Callaghan – and then a fourth named Philip French, a freelance journalist. Within three years of that lunch at Ormond's Yard, John Houston employed a team of five writers and was worth more than twenty million pounds. After that John moved first to Jersey for tax reasons – where he met and divorced his second wife, Susan – and then, briefly, to Switzerland, where I believe he still has a house.

In truth, more or less anyone could write the books, so long as they understood a little about pace and structure, and how to write reasonable dialogue; but only John could edit them so they all read the same, uncomplicated way. It's not what's written that makes the difference in John's books, it's what doesn't get written. I quickly learned that the writing is just the connective tissue for John's stories. He's very well-read and extremely literate and he can write beautifully constructed prose when he wants to, but there's a simplicity about his books that reminds me of Picasso; you see, before Picasso, artists painted exactly what they saw, but it was Picasso's genius to know exactly what you could leave out of a picture; it's the same with John. Knowing what you can leave out of a book is one reason why he's so successful and why I have such admiration for what he does.

While I think I'm a much better writer than John I have never been particularly good at devising a good story, and in the current publishing market it's story not fine writing that sells. This is the other reason John is so successful at what he does: he's the most story-led person I've ever met. John once told me that he never goes looking for new plots because they always seem to find him; to that extent they're like orphans, he says, looking for a good home, or perhaps electrons looking to attach themselves to a vulnerable nucleus. For this reason he never goes anywhere without one of his little Smythson notebooks in which he is forever jotting ideas down – the notebooks even have the word GENIUS printed on the covers in gold letters, and he's got a whole boxful of them; sometimes he just jots down some things a character might say, or plot-points, but just as often a plot will come to him wholly formed, as if a stork had delivered them to his desk like Dumbo the elephant. John is the kind of person who could find you a good plot from the in-flight magazine on the plane and famously did with one of his earlier novels, *The Liberty to Know*; incidentally, the film rights on that one were bought by Jerry Bruckheimer for two million dollars.

When she divorced him, John's second wife alleged that his constant note-taking was a kind of obsessive compulsive disorder; she even alleged that he had stolen some of her own ideas and passed these off as his own intellectual property; but that's another story.

Somewhere along the line I published my own first novel
– *Dreams of Heaven on the Falls Road* – which limped into print
and was quickly remaindered, then forgotten. Which is the
fate of most novels, of course, and the normal condition
for any writer is to be rejected or to be out of print; this is
what I tell myself – that being a published writer is a bit like
what Schopenhauer says about life itself: non-existence is our
natural condition. Unless, of course, you're John Houston.
Because make no mistake about it, what John Houston does
is very rare indeed; to make money by your writing is incred-
ibly difficult. To that extent John Houston is truly one of
the greats and the living embodiment of what Andy Warhol
meant when he said that good business is the best art.

When John read my novel and noted my disappointment
at its cool reception he gave me his own critical reaction,
which was a little less F. R. Leavis and a bit more Jack Regan:

'Forget about it, old sport – that's my advice. Forget about
this and write another; that's what separates the men from
the boys; any dumb fuck can start writing a novel – and
they frequently do – but very few can finish writing one; and
there are even fewer who can put that novel behind them
and start another. The important thing is to learn from your
mistakes. My opinion is that your novel is beautifully written
and very atmospheric but too often you seem like you're
peeking across your shoulder to see if any of those bloody
clever writers you say you admire are paying attention to
your nice, pretty sentences. The Martins and the Julians and
the Salmans. The trouble is your story doesn't stay afloat.
About halfway through it's as if you forgot where you put
it. It's almost like you were shagging some bird and even
while you were doing it you decided you didn't want to shag
her any more. With your next one you've got to work out

the story and everything about the story and nothing but the fucking story before you start writing a goddamn word, after which everything becomes subordinate to that. More importantly you have got to learn to tell Martin and Julian and Salman to go and fuck themselves.'

Someone's mobile was ringing out a tune – a piece of tinny piano music I vaguely recognized. Sergeant Savigny got up from the table and left the half-empty restaurant to answer his *portable*. I tasted the wine and then frowned, trying to place the clunking melody.

'You don't like the wine?'

'The wine is excellent. No, it's the ringtone that's perplexing me.'

'Irritating, isn't it?' said Amalric. 'It's the theme from *Betty Blue*. The sergeant has a thing for Béatrice Dalle.'

I shrugged. 'That's easy to understand. She was very beautiful. Whatever happened to her, anyway?'

'Like all beautiful women, monsieur, she got older. Savigny keeps a copy of the DVD in his suitcase. Always.'

'That and a novel by John Houston. But then with 140 million books sold, I guess that's a little less unusual. Statistically speaking. It's said that one in every thirty books being bought in the world right now is likely to be written by John Houston. Did you know that? And your sergeant certainly fits the standard profile of a John Houston reader.'

'Is there such a thing?'

'Oh yes. Every so often Houston commissions a piece of market research into who is reading his books. Impact – that's the name of the research company that John used – they carry out focus groups and sometimes John insists that the writing team come along and watch what the groups are saying, through a two-way mirror. Which is the way these things are done in an advertising agency. He'll end up with a report that describes socio-economic profiles of readership, buying habits, income – in the exactly same way that Heinz will try to find out who is buying what soup and why. John has never quite stopped being a successful advertising man. Having read several of those research reports I can probably tell you quite a lot about your sergeant. What is he – thirty-five?'

Amalric nodded. 'This is fascinating. Please go on.'

'All right. He buys no more than two or three books a year and rarely ever reads a newspaper, unless it's free. The chances are that in all the years you've known him you've never seen him read anything you'd like to read yourself. The one time you looked at the book he was reading you were a bit shocked at how simplistic it was, how short the chapters seemed to be, how small the sentences were. Mostly the sergeant doesn't have time to read because he thinks of himself as a busy sort of guy – if that's even possible in a place like Monaco. One time he bought the same book he bought the last time and read half of it before he realized he'd read it already.'

Amalric tried to conceal a smile, which only encouraged me to show off a little.

'Voltaire and Molière, he couldn't get on with them at school, and as for history, he probably thinks Philippe Pétain was a male prostitute, or even something you say when you get cross. He's easily amused with quite a short attention span so he reads in short intense bursts – maybe ten or fifteen minutes at a time, with a very furrowed brow, as if he's actually doing something quite difficult, almost like he's trying to solve a puzzle. He doesn't read in the bath because he prefers a shower. He always rolls a book like a magazine, which probably irritates you; no one who loves books could ever treat a book the way he treats them. But then you probably don't know that for this same reason all of Houston's books are printed in a B or C format, with stitched binding which is more durable than just glue, so they don't fall apart when you treat them like a football programme. He watches a lot of television – football, mostly – and he has an Xbox or a PlayStation at home, and there are certainly more than a few games he keeps on that iPhone of his: *Temple Run*, *Extreme Road Trip* – something like that. He lives out of the microwave and his favourite actors are Tom Cruise, Matt Damon and Brad Pitt. He prefers beach holidays to doing anything cultural. He never goes to art galleries or museums. He likes fast cars, big yachts, sleazy-looking women, but these are more of an aspiration than a reflection of his own life. He has a tattoo, smokes too much but still keeps himself fit. He doesn't drink much and he's certainly not interested in fine wine like you. His spelling and grammar leave a little to be desired. He never questions your orders or comes up with suggestions of his own, but he's a useful man to have along in the same way that another policeman might bring a dog; after all, someone has to do the paperwork.'

'Not bad. Not bad at all. But I doubt you got all of that from Houston's research.'

'Not all of it, perhaps; but most of it.'

'He's a good man. Policemen are like engineers, monsieur; sometimes you need a very small screwdriver and sometimes you need a wrench. Savigny is very good at applying torque to a problem.'

'I don't doubt it.'

'It's true, he did once buy the same book he read last

year. And it was by John Houston. But instead of learning something from this experience, he continues to be one of Houston's loyal readers. Which I have to say, strikes me as absurd. I confess I don't understand why it is that Houston sells so many. The plots are all over the place and have no real point to them. The characters are one-dimensional and the dialogue absurd. To me they seem like books for people who have never read a book before.'

'That's right. That's exactly what they are. It's like what H. L. Mencken said: No one ever went broke underestimating the intelligence of the American public.'

Amalric nodded wearily. 'I fear you're right. But it's the same with the French-speaking public. People seem more stupid than I remember.' He shrugged. 'In twenty years you wrote how many of his books?'

'Almost thirty. One every nine months. Like giving birth you might say.' I shrugged. 'That's what writing a book is like. A child to which you give birth. And like a child, some of them are more popular than others. I know I have a few favourites. The first one, most of all, I suppose.'

'Didn't it ever bother you?' asked Savigny. 'That Houston got the fame, the money and the kudos? By comparison with him you're a failure, aren't you?'

'"What I aspired to be, And was not, comforts me: A brute I might have been, but would not sink i' the scale."' I shrugged. 'Robert Browning.'

'But what about the money? The jet-set life in Monaco?'

'Perhaps not all the money. I've been very well paid. In twenty years I've made almost two million pounds, before tax. True that's not a fortune. In fact it's chump change by Houston's own elevated standard. But then again it's more than I would ever have made as a copywriter. Plus, toward the end of my relationship with John I was also receiving a credit – an acknowledgement of my assistance, albeit in very small letters somewhere near the name of the cover designer and the name of the printer. And along the way I published a few more of my own novels. One or two of them were actually quite well reviewed. Working for John, I thought of it as a bit like an Arts Council grant; but for what he paid me I would have been obliged to go back to advertising and do a proper job writing commercials for toilet paper and lager. If you can call that a proper job. Oh, there are worse jobs than being an advertising copywriter, Chief Inspector; but I much prefer working from home. The commute is so much easier. And at least I had the illusion of being my own boss.'

Savigny returned to the table and for a moment he and Amalric spoke in French. It seemed that there were still no clues as to Houston's whereabouts. The sergeant's accent was warmer and friendlier than Amalric's and I guessed he was from Marseille and that Amalric might originally hail from Paris.

I shrugged. 'Like I said. If he doesn't want to be found.'

'You speak French?' For a moment Amalric looked positively vulpine.

'Yes.'

'You didn't say.'

'You never asked. Besides, I think your English is better than my French.'

'Thank you. I spent six months working with the FBI in Washington.'

'How did that work out?'

'Fascinating. I liked Washington. I like Americans. It's the food I had a problem with. There's so much of it. And so very little that's any good. I must be one of the few people ever to live in the United States who ended up losing weight.'

I smiled. 'They do like their chow.'

'Your arrangement with Houston? How did that work?'

'You might say that I was John's maître d'. The head writer. I helped to manage the *atelier*. That's what John called us – the people who worked in his ship's boiler room – although I usually thought of it as a bit like the *Pequod*, because we were such a pagan bunch of misfits. At its peak we were producing four or five new books a year. And John was making between eighty and a hundred million dollars per annum.'

'That much?' Savigny whistled quietly. 'Just from writing books?'

I nodded.

'Incredible; perhaps I should write a novel about the *Sûreté Publique*,' said Savigny. 'In Monaco.'

'I think an Italian author already did,' I said. 'Not that something like that should ever stop you, Sergeant. Lots of cops become writers: Joseph Wambaugh for one. And some of the most successful writers steal their best ideas from other writers. The book world calls that kind of thing an *hommage*. But mostly it's downright theft. It happens every day and no one ever goes to prison for it.'

'*Je prends mon propre partout où je trouve*,' said Amalric.

'I believe you've already met John's agent, Hereward Jones. A year or so ago he negotiated a fifteen-book, world English rights deal with VVL – that's John's US publishers, Veni, Vidi, Legi – which the *Wall Street Journal* reported was worth $170 million. It's a little hard to connect this with how things were in publishing twenty years ago. When John told his then UK publishers what he was planning to do – write and publish more than one new book a year – they were appalled.

It's said they actually thought of ending his contract there and then. At least they did until they saw the sales of his first book. Before that moment they had been living in a little Bloomsbury bubble with writers who were rather unworldly Angus Wilson types who smoked pipes, and wore tweedy jackets with leather elbows. They turned out a book every couple of years and generally did what they were told. Yes, there were a few writers like Jeffrey Archer and Dick Francis who were a bit more commercially minded than the rest of the field, but John Houston was really the first writer to come along and tell them that he was first and foremost a businessman whose business was writing and selling books.

'He came up with the stories, and we, his collaborators, wrote the books. He preferred having English writers. For one thing he said we were cheaper than Americans. And for another he said he didn't have to explain his jokes to us. For all of John's love affair with America he thought the English easier to edit and more in awe of his power and wealth, he'd say, in a way that Americans never are. Over the years the ghost-writers came and went, with some working out more successfully than the others. One or two went on to be quite successful in their own right: C. Boxer Revell, for one and Thomas Chenevix for another – although Chenevix himself denies he was ever contracted to write one of Houston's books and is inclined to sue anyone who says he did. They hate each other and famously came to blows in a London club called The Groucho with John punching Tom Chenevix down a flight of stairs; the police were called and both men were cautioned.'

'What was the fight about? And when?'

'Four years ago? Five? John rejected Chenevix's manuscript. You see the way John usually works is that he sees material every four weeks. Like maybe ten or fifteen chapters. Chenevix had missed one of those meetings and had eight weeks' worth of work that John rejected out of hand, which Chenevix – who has a very high opinion of his writing – took very personally. He called John all sorts of names and took a swing at him. More than one if the reports are correct. Pissed probably – Chenevix, I mean. John never drank very much. I've never seen him drunk, at any rate.'

'This man, Chenevix. I should like to speak to him.'

'I believe he lives in France. Somewhere in Provence. But I couldn't tell you where. You could ask his publishers – HarperCollins. They'd probably know.' I shrugged. 'That was probably the last time John came to London to meet someone from the team. Soon after that he moved to Monaco and opened the Houston office in Paris. That's what he called it. In fact, it wasn't an office but a rented house in the western suburbs of Neuilly-sur-Seine – a pretty fabulous sort of place. Exquisitely furnished. Beautiful pictures.' I frowned. 'With one insightful exception.'

'Yes?'

'In the conference room where we had our meetings there was a large framed photograph of lots of chimpanzees in a library; all of the chimps were seated at desktop computers, as if they were writing something. John had seen the original – which was by a photographer called Louis Psihoyos – in *National Geographic* magazine, as the illustration for a feature about the information revolution. One or two of us thought it was insulting but John thought it was very funny. I think he meant that it should remind those of us who were part of the *atelier* of our true status in the Houston publishing empire. And it did. Certainly he used to think of us like his children and, in the case of some of his writers, that wasn't so very wide of the mark. Some of these characters need careful handling. But John was good at that. It was only Chenevix who fell out with him badly. And perhaps Mike Munns, who also hit him.'

'This was at the Houston office?'

'Yes. Me, I'd have fired him. But Houston showed great restraint and kept him on. He said that writers are passionate and that sometimes you have to respect that.'

I paused and drank some more of the excellent Burgundy. The bottle was empty and Amalric was already beckoning another from the sommelier. I had to hand it to Amalric, he was very different from the kind of policemen we were used to in London. It's not many cops who have a taste for Vosne-Romanée and Hermès ties, and who can quote Molière and Voltaire.

'Tell me more about the Houston office,' he said.

'You mean before he closed it down?'

Amalric nodded; Savigny checked the Marantz recorder and then replaced it on the table.

'At the Houston office he employed a couple of secretaries – both English and rather fetching – and a couple of webmasters, who were Dutch. They did all the things that VVL didn't do for John; which isn't much. But he liked to keep a close eye on his public image. Whenever John wanted a meeting with one of the writers, which was probably once a fortnight, we would get the Eurostar to Paris – standard-class, John could be a tightwad with the expenses like that – and meet him there; he would drive up from Monaco, or from some location where he'd been doing research for a book, in his latest supercar. A Lamborghini. A Ferrari. An Aston Martin. You name it, John drove it. Usually he drove back to Monaco in a different car from the one he'd arrived in. That was part of the fun. John liked to have fun. And he loved that drive. He used to see how fast he could do it, of course, and try to beat his previous record. I think eight hours was about the record. I did that drive with him a couple of times and it scared the shit out of me. He tended to use the plane only to fly straight to London, or to Corfu where he had a place. Anyway, we would meet him – sometimes there were two or three of us there at the one time. He would read through what we'd written, making notes, and we'd wait for his comments, a little anxiously. It was like being back at Cambridge, for your supervisor's assessment of an essay you'd written. If he was pleased with your progress he would take you out to lunch or dinner. Somewhere expensive. La Grande Cascade, Lapérouse, Alain Ducasse, La Tour d'Argent. John liked his food almost as much as he liked his fast cars. You could always tell just how much he liked what you'd written by the price of the wine he ordered.

'At other times, when he was too busy to come to Paris, or had used up his tax-free visits – John was very scrupulous like that – I, or one of the others, would fly to Nice, hire a car and drive to Monaco for a meeting there.'

'Which is why you had to stay in Beausoleil.'

I nodded. 'Sometimes he went to London from Paris, on the Eurostar. To see his children. He was close to them. Tried his very best for them. But quite frankly, they're a shiftless, idle lot. Sometimes I look at them and think how lucky I am that I don't have any kids myself. John's children have always got their hands out for something. The ex-wives aren't much better. I once heard John lament that he had brought up the largest family with the smallest disposition for doing anything for themselves. In that respect at least he's rather like Charles Dickens, whose sons all inherited their grandfather's

Micawberish trouble in handling their finances. But John has always tried his best for them. They all had trusts and flats and cars, and a few had expensive drug habits, too. For example, his eldest son, Travis, got a place to study history at Queens' College, Cambridge; but after a failed career as a rock star he's now in rehab at some place on the island of Antigua founded by Eric Clapton that costs $24,000 a month. He's been there for a while now. All paid for by his pa.'

'So, what went wrong?' asked Savigny. 'Why did he decide to stop writing books?'

'He didn't,' I said. 'He just decided to stop producing as many. To change his whole modus operandi.'

'All right,' said Savigny. 'Why did he do that? Give up on the big money. His agent said Houston just walked away from being the richest writer in the world. He said he thought that Monsieur Houston had suffered a midlife crisis, perhaps.'

I laughed. 'I'm afraid John was a little too old for one of those. If it comes to that, so am I.'

'Or a nervous breakdown,' suggested the sergeant.

I shook my head. 'That's another cute explanation. People like the easy explanations that you can fit into a magazine headline. It restores a sense of order in the universe to think that things can be so easily explained philosophically, I tend to adhere to the A. A. Milne explanation of the universe which goes something like this: "Rabbit's clever," said Pooh thoughtfully. "Yes," said Piglet, "Rabbit's clever." "And he has a brain." "Yes," said Piglet. "Rabbit has a brain." There was a long silence. "I suppose," said Pooh, "that that's why he never understands anything."'

Savigny was looking blank but Amalric was smiling. 'That's wonderful,' he said.

'With all due respect to Hereward Jones, it's more

complicated than a midlife crisis or a nervous breakdown.'
I shrugged. 'John is a complicated man. And you might say
that it was an existential choice, although I hesitate to argue
such a thing before two Frenchmen.'

'What do you mean by that?' asked Savigny.

'I have to go to the bathroom, first.'

On my way to the men's room in Claridge's I checked my
phone for text messages and thought a little about what I had
just said and tried to remember exactly what John had told
me before telling everyone else that he was closing the *atelier*.
I wanted to get it right for the cops; as Raymond Chandler might have said in *The Long Goodbye* – more realistically,
perhaps – it's advisable not to invent too much when you are
talking to them.

I drank some water from the tap – quite a lot – to help
keep my head clear; I wouldn't have put it past the wily Chief
Inspector to try to loosen my tongue with fine wine. A mix-
ture of Louis Roederer and Vosne-Romanée was an excellent
way of doing it, too; what writer could ever have resisted
something as subtle as that? And looking like a fox as much
as he did, I didn't doubt that Chief Inspector Amalric could
probably smell a lie with almost as much certainty as he
would recognize the bouquet of a good red. Two bottles of
hundred-quid Burgundy were probably a much more cost-
effective means of conducting an interview than paying
someone to operate a polygraph machine.

I drank some more water and then washed my face.

It wasn't that I was lying – not exactly – but then I'd hardly
been honest either because, in spite of what I had told the
Chief Inspector, there wasn't a doubt in my mind that before
very long John Houston would telephone me; nor did I have

any doubt that I would never have betrayed him to the Monty cops.

I went back to the table, where I found Savigny had gone and my glass had been refilled with wine. For a moment I left it alone and waited to resume my story.

'Where's the sergeant?'

'He's gone outside for a cigarette.'

'Shall I wait for him?'

'No. Besides, it will be his job to transcribe what's on the tape. I mean the digital recorder. He will hear everything you say again soon enough. That's another reason I brought him to London. Savigny's English is almost as good as mine. His mother is Canadian. From Quebec City.'

'I thought they spoke French in Quebec.'

'Oh, they do. But Didier's mother was raised to be bilingual. And so was he. So, I think you were about to tell us about John Houston's existential choice.'

'I was only going to say that money gave John an enormous amount of freedom. He was free to behave like a fool. Free to marry, several times. Free to have many homes, and fast cars, and even faster mistresses. He was free to be his own boss, to say yes, to say no – free to be and to do whatever he liked. And yet, in the end he wasn't free at all. I think it was the fifteen-book contract with VVL that did it. One morning John woke up with the idea that he was a prisoner not just of that but everything else too. It was the responsibility of his position as an employer and the sense that so much was riding on him that began to weigh on him.'

'*Noblesse oblige*,' said Amalric.

'Perhaps. At least that's what he told me. As a matter of fact I think it was me he told before anyone else.'

'Told you when? How?'

'We were on the autoroute, driving to Paris from Monaco early one morning about three months ago in an Aston Martin Vantage, ostensibly to discuss a book I was writing for him called *Dead Red*. But he'd been quiet and I could sense that something was bothering him, not least because he was driving below the speed limit. I thought it might have something to do with what I'd written and asked him about that, but he said it wasn't, and finally he told me what was on his mind:

'It seems only fitting that you should be the first to know, old sport.'

'First to know what, John? Are you ill?'

'No, but thanks for asking, Don. You were always the one who I could talk to like a friend. It's just that I've had enough of all this – I've had enough of producing six books a year. I've had enough of overseeing websites, supervising blogs about my wonderful life and my books, employing all these fucking people, the marketing meetings in London and New York with VVL. I've had enough of agents, fucking agents. Did you know that Hereward drives a fucking Rolls-Royce? The other day I read an interview with him in *The Times*, and there he was pictured sitting astride the bonnet like he was Tom fucking Jones. The self-importance of the man staggered me; he talked like everything he'd achieved was by his own hard work; and like somehow I owe everything to him. He went on and on about his legendary New Year's Eve parties at his legendary Windsor house with his smart lefty fucking friends. I thought, "What a cunt", and "That cunt is your agent"; and then I thought, "Let's see what happens to your legendary Windsor house and your smart Rolls-Royce and your legendary party when I'm not around to generate the ten per cent that pays for it, you cunt." Did you know he didn't invite me to his last party?'

'He probably thought that living in Monaco, you wouldn't come.'

'Bollocks. It's because he and his lefty friends all read the *Guardian* and the book world still regards me as a kind of literary pariah. That's why he didn't invite me. I vote Conservative. I don't pay UK taxes. I'm his guilty little secret.'

'Perhaps the invitation got lost in the Christmas post. I'm sure he didn't mean to upset you.' I shrugged. 'But he didn't invite me either, if that's any consolation.'

'So, I've had enough of all that,' said John, ignoring me. 'And I've certainly had enough of living in Monaco. It's a dump. A housing estate for billionaires. A traffic jam. I've had enough of the travel. The tax-exile thing. The IRS and the Inland Revenue. The meetings with financial advisers. The accountants. The lawyers. The hedgies selling their funds. The boats. The plane. The cars. Do you know I rent a garage in Monaco with my own personal mechanic just to look after all the cars? It's ridiculous. Who needs all these fucking cars, anyway? I mean some of them are just more trouble than they are worth. The Ferraris especially. The other day I spent a thousand euros just to have the wheels aligned on the F12. A thousand euros. I told them – I'm not Fernando Alonso, you thieving bastards. And as for the houses. Jesus, the fucking houses with their caretakers and *gardiens*. Whenever we go to our house in Courchevel we spend a whole morning listening to the *gardien*'s problems: the roof has a leak, his child was sick, the gardener is unreliable, the sauna still isn't fixed; could I have a cheque for this, and one for that? It's the same everywhere else. Bastards moaning that you don't pay them enough or stealing from you when you do. I think I know how God feels on a Sunday. All of these fucking people complaining about this and that must drive him mad; no wonder he sent a flood to destroy the world and drown everyone. I'd have done the same, just to get some peace and quiet. Several times over, probably. No, I've had enough of it, old sport.

'Lately it's all begun to weigh on me rather. When I was taken ill a few years ago, remember? And I was only able to produce three books in one year instead of five? I never told you this, but VVL's share price actually fell by five per cent when that happened and so VVL's publishing director – Bat Anderton – had to go to Wall Street to explain why VVL's profits were going to be down on the previous year. And while he was there I had to do a conference call from my sickbed to reassure a load of wankers I'd never seen that my output would soon be back to normal. Then there's the fact that VVL have employed a whole department of copy-editors and publicity people to look after my output.'

'They are trying to keep you happy, that's all.'

'Oh, I understand why they're doing it, old sport. I get it, all right. But it's started to annoy me that I am personally responsible not just for the shares in some tosspot institutional investor's pension fund but also the livelihoods of as many as forty people. And for what? So that my wife can blow it on fucking handbags and hats. Orla's got more hats than Ascot races.'

'Handbags and hats don't sound so bad, John, in the scheme of things. It could be cocaine. Or American miniature horses, like your last missus.'

'True. True. And as for my kids. They're useless, one and all. Stephen has given up his legal studies at Bristol and decided he wants to go to film school, in L.A. While Heddy wants to open a shop in Chelsea selling her ghastly fucking jewellery. You know, the rough diamond stuff she designs herself that was inspired by her gap year in Thailand?'

I smiled; Heddy Houston's jewellery designs – 'every bracelet tells a story' – were beloved of magazine editors and fashion mavens everywhere, but to me they looked childlike and naïve, and I guessed that like me John was a man who liked a diamond ring to look like a diamond ring and not a half-eaten boiled sweet.

But my smile lasted only as long as it took for it to dawn on me that I was probably out of work.

'Let me get this straight,' I said. 'You're saying that you want to wind the whole thing up. The *atelier* – everything?'

'That's right, old sport. The whole shooting match. Everything. I've bought a house in Chelsea – in St Leonard's Terrace. As soon as the builders have finished with it I'm going to sell the penthouse in Monaco and move back to London. And to hell with the income tax. I want to go to the Garrick Club on a Friday, walk down the King's Road on a Saturday, and see Chelsea play football on a Sunday. I want to watch the BBC and ITV and eat fish and chips in the Ivy and have Christmas with all the trimmings. And I'm going to spend the rest of the week writing a book – I mean not just the plot, but the whole thing, the way I did when I first started writing. I've got an idea that I might have one good book in me – the sort of book that might last a bit longer than the glue on the spine, if you know what I mean. I think perhaps that if I go back to basics, so to speak, I might even win one of those smaller awards – a dagger, or an Edgar. Maybe something better. Fuck knows.'

'But what about your fifteen-book contract with VVL?'

'To hell with it. And to hell with them, too. I'll just have to pay them back the twenty million dollars advance.'

'Just like that?'

'Just like that.' John grinned. 'Yes.'

'But what about *Dead Red*?'

'Don't worry, you can finish *Dead Red* and get paid just like we agreed, old sport; for that matter all of you guys can finish whatever it is you're writing now. That should also help to soften the blow for VVL. Naturally I'll try to cushion the blow for you and everyone else in the *atelier* with some sort of severance package. Which, of course, will be rather more generous in your own case, Don, since you've been with me the longest. Fifty thousand quid. How does that sound?'

'Very generous,' I said, although I could have pointed out that in any normal year this was only half of what I made from writing John Houston books.

'And I certainly haven't forgotten my promise – to try to find you a decent outline for a bestseller of your own, old sport.'

I felt my heart skip a beat; this was something much more worrying than a catastrophic reduction in my earnings.

'Holy shit, John. You goddamned asshole.'

'What?'

'What do you mean "try"? You already said you were going to give me the outline of *The Geneva Convention*.'

As a reward for twenty years of loyal service, John had previously promised to 'donate' me the very much-needed plot for a book I was going to write myself, just as soon as I'd finished writing *Dead Red*. This was to be a stand-alone thriller about a Geneva-based hedge fund called *The Geneva Convention* and John had said it was one of the best outlines he'd written in a long time; when I read it I knew he wasn't wrong, and I had no doubt that provided I observed all of the lessons I had learned while writing thrillers for John then *The Geneva Convention* might actually make me a small fortune. Perhaps even a large one. My own agent, Craig Conrad, had listened to my description of John's outline and assured me he could probably sell it to someone at Random House for at least fifty grand; all that I had to do was write the damn thing.

'I think I said that it was probably the best outline I *could* give you. Which, to be fair, is not quite the same thing as actually agreeing to give it to you, old sport. Or even saying that I was *going* to give it to you. I hate to split grammatical hairs here, but I really don't think what you're saying truly reflects our conversations about this idea.'

'Come on, John. You certainly led me to believe that this was the outline you were going to give me.'

'No, you led yourself to believe it, Don. I think that's more accurate. And it's not like I gave you the finished article, is it? Bound in leather, with gold letters on the cover, like we normally do? With a contract? No. Look, don't worry about it. I told you, I'll try to give you something else. Something just as good, I promise. But it so happens that *The Geneva Convention* is the book I'm going to write myself. The whole damn thing. After all, it is my story to do with as I like. I don't know why I feel I have to justify this to you. It's not as if you've ever had anything to do with writing the outlines, old sport. Besides, this book needs to be a little different from what we've been writing up until now. This book is going to need more atmosphere. More detail. Closer observation. Which is precisely why I want to write it myself.'

'Sure, John, sure. It's your damned outline to do whatever you like with.'

We were both silent for about thirty or forty miles of autoroute. I stared out of the Aston's passenger window as we hurtled through the French countryside. Outside, the car's V12 engine sounded like some wild beast in distress; but cocooned inside, the quiet was a little unnerving and the silence nothing short of awkward. John felt it, too; and after a while he said, 'Tell you what, old sport. I've had a great idea. You can write the next Jack Boardman book.'

'What do you mean, the next? I already wrote the last six, remember?'

'What I mean is, why don't you take him over? With your name on the jacket, and only your name. I'll give him to you. The character. Yours to do with as you like. Book six sold a million and a half copies, right?'

'Yes, but book five sold twice as many, which is why you decided not to pursue book seven, remember?'

'Maybe so. But it's still a valuable franchise, Don. And I do have a finished outline for book seven which I will gladly give you as my parting gift. There's absolutely no reason why you shouldn't squeeze another three books out of that character. Maybe five, which could be worth millions; I bet VVL would go for it, too. Especially now that they know I won't be writing any more of those books myself. There are plenty of precedents for doing that sort of thing: Kingsley Amis, John Gardner and Sebastian Faulks with James Bond. The Faulks book *Devil May Care* was actually very successful. Good title, too. I had plans to use that title myself. And of course you wouldn't have to cut me in for a percentage the way Faulks was obliged to do with Ian Fleming's estate. Whatever money the book made would be yours and yours alone.'

I bit my lip and grunted as if I was thinking about it. I hadn't in the least enjoyed writing the sixth Jack Boardman book; after six I was heartily sick of him – as sick of him as Ian Fleming had been of James Bond, perhaps – and I'd hoped never to write another one again, but, all the same, I didn't want to say no; an outline for another of Boardman's adventures was still a valuable property, John was right about that much.

'At least say you'll think about it, old sport. Look, I'll even mention it to Anderton when I see him to tell him I'm through with all this.'

'All right. I'll think about it.' I thought for a moment. 'Are you planning to tell the rest of the guys when we get to the *atelier* in Paris?'

'That's right, I am. And then I'm going to catch the Eurostar to London and tell Anderton and everyone at VVL and then Hereward. I can't wait to see his fucking beard turn fifty shades of grey.'

'You're enjoying this, aren't you?'

John grinned and pressed his foot down on the accelerator as if he was anxious to get to Paris so that he could action his new plan as soon as possible.

'I have to confess I am a little. You know, part of being a winner, old sport, is knowing when enough is enough. When it's time to give up the fight and walk away and find something new. Like J. K. Rowling. I mean, good for her, I thought. Knowing when to quit is the essence of real creativity, wouldn't you say?'

'I don't know. I'm just glad I chose not to buy any of VVL's shares when they came on the market. You do know that Bat Anderton is going to have a heart attack.'

John laughed. 'He'll survive. And so will VVL. Bloomsbury survived after Harry Potter, didn't they?'

'Yes, but their shares halved after the series came to an end. They had to invest heavily in the German publishing market. They bought Berlin Verlag.'

'Then VVL will have to do something similar, won't they? Besides, it's not like they won't get *Dead Red* and the three books that Munns and Stakenborg and Philip French are writing right now. And *The Geneva Convention*.'

I shrugged and drank some wine. 'When we got to Paris, Houston told everyone he was ending our arrangement, like he said he would, and then he went on to London where he did the same. We've spoken on the telephone since then but I think that might have been the last time I saw him, Chief Inspector.'

'How did they take it? Your fellow writers?'

'Not well. Philip French had just bought a house in the south of France – in Tourrettes-sur-Loup – and I think he'd been counting on continuing his working association with John in order to pay for it. Things have been difficult for him ever since. Peter Stakenborg was predictably underwhelmed by the news. Nothing ever surprises Peter. I think he even said he'd seen it coming. Mike Munns probably received the news with the least amount of good grace – which is because he hadn't much grace to start with. Myself – I was a bit shocked at first. But it wasn't like John just cast us all adrift. He did pay us off very handsomely. As he promised he would.'

'And did he give you the outline for a seventh Jack Boardman book? Like he said?'

'Yes. He did. Although as yet I've not been able to work up any great enthusiasm to write it. To be quite frank I was burned out on that series long before book six. John knew that, which is another reason why we didn't write any more. That's how it goes, you see. After a while a series character becomes the creature to the writer's Victor Frankenstein; he's a hideous monster that you're obliged to spend time with but who you would happily see destroyed. Right now I could no more sit down and write another Jack

PHILIP KERR | 89

Boardman book than I could go back in the army. He was a two-dimensional character, Chief Inspector, and without depth to a character about whom you're writing, it's just typing. I mean check out the reviews for those books on Amazon and you'll see what I'm talking about. It is soon plain that the people who enjoy these books and give them five stars aren't what you and I would call readers. A typical Amazon review for a Jack Boardman book reads something like "Houston's books are easy to read and the ideal choice if you are unable to read for very long at a time". The true readers, the real readers – readers like you and me, Chief Inspector – these are the people who give those books one-star reviews.'

I smiled and shook my head.

'What?' asked Amalric.

'It's just that John – always sales-led – was never ever bothered by those one-star reviews. Most writers – me included – get very hung up by what's written in the Amazon reviews. But John said that if you actually read the one-star reviews they're almost always better written than the five-star reviews, and that these always reveal readers who were never the true target market for John's books in the first place. He used to call this kind of reader a "mal-purchase". His real market he insisted was the authors of the illiterate, badly spelt five-star reviews, which is of course a much larger number of people than the authors of the better-written ones.'

'Interesting,' said Amalric.

'Perhaps. Anyway, I can't quite bring myself to get down to that sort of level again – the reader as lowest common denominator. I expect I will do, eventually, when I need the money. But right now I'm just ploughing my own little furrow and telling myself that a book which makes nothing but money is a poor book.'

This was another lie, of course; but writers lie for a living; at least, that's a truth I've always believed.

'How did Anderton take the news? And Hereward Jones?'

'Badly. VVL's shares nosedived on the news, as I expect you know. Lots of editors and marketing people lost their jobs. There was talk of a lawsuit against VVL and their bank by shareholders who felt that VVL had misled investors about John Houston's future sales. There are still three more Houston books for them to publish, so I expect this year's sales figures will hold up. But they can forget next year being any good. Especially now that John won't be delivering *The Geneva Convention*. Or at least I assume he won't be delivering it now that he's suspected of murdering his wife. When I checked Bloomberg this afternoon I noticed that VVL shares had been marked down again.

'As for Hereward, I imagine his situation is even bleaker. As someone who was earning between eight and ten million dollars a year in commission, he'll be lucky if he makes a tenth of that now. I believe he's had to sell his beautiful house in Ascot. Not to mention his famous Rolls-Royce.'

'When Mr Houston told you that he was terminating the *atelier* and moving back to London, did he lead you to suppose he'd discussed it with his wife?'

'It was all "I am going to do this" and "I am going to do that". I don't recall him mentioning Orla at all, except to make a disparaging remark about her hat-buying habit.'

'You're sure about that?'

'Oh yes. He said, "I've bought a house in St Leonard's Terrace", not "We've bought one", which would have been rather more uxorious.'

Uxorious: a word forbidden in John's lexicon of banned words.

'"We" is what a good husband would have said. On the other hand John always bought just what he wanted. He was quite impulsive when it came to spending. Recently he paid a million dollars for a watch. You probably read that in yesterday's *Daily Mail*.'

'Yes, an Hublot Black Caviar Bang, wasn't it?' said Amalric.

'A million dollars for a watch,' breathed Savigny.

'Ridiculous, isn't it?' I said, but I could see Savigny didn't agree and I knew I was looking at another man who would love to have owned a million-dollar watch. 'He bought it with the film rights money for *The Prisoner of Kandahar*. At least that's what he told the *Wall Street Journal* when they interviewed him.'

'This was the novel which caused all the WikiLeaks fuss, wasn't it?' said Savigny. 'With the coalition forces in Afghanistan.'

I nodded. 'According to WikiLeaks the CIA used John's book as the model for a Taliban prisoner swap in 2013. In John's plot, the CIA is looking for a way to close Guantánamo without losing face; so they persuade an American sergeant to let himself be captured in Afghanistan in order that they can swap him for several top Taliban prisoners in Gitmo. Your guess is as good as mine just how much truth there was in that rumour. But he himself never commented on it. Like I say, he could be quite secretive about some things. Except with his accountants, of course. You might ask them some questions. Citroen Wells, in Devonshire Street, London. I believe they handle a lot of top writers.'

'Do you think he might have been planning to return to London alone?'

'That's hard to say. I can't imagine for a moment that Orla would have wanted to go along to Stamford Bridge with John – to see Chelsea Football Club. She hated football. Or to Lord's to see the cricket. Not her scene at all. It was all too English for her. Even so, he never mentioned that he was unhappy with her. And she was a very beautiful woman after all.'

'What about other women?'

'Now you're asking. John was always a busy man in the ladies' department. He told me a joke once which I didn't think was particularly funny since I was happily married at the time. If you're married it's a very subversive sort of joke. He said, "What do you call a man who is always faithful to his wife? Gay." John thought that was very funny. But I think he really believes that. I'm certain he has girlfriends in places other than Monaco. There was a girl in New York I think he used to see when he was there; but I couldn't give you a name, or an address. Probably one in Paris, too, but again I have no firm information about who she was or where she lived. I think I saw him with another woman in London, once. But he denied it afterward. John is highly compartmentalized. Which is entirely typical of the writer of course. I've yet to hear a better description of what it means to be a writer than the lyric from the song in the Bond movie of the same name: "You only live twice; once in your dreams and once in real life". Works rather better than Bond's failed attempt at a Basho-like haiku that's in Fleming's book, I think. And it's a more or less perfect description of John Houston: a man who wrote one life and lived another – perhaps several others. I guess you'll find out how many when you catch up with him. If you catch up with him.'

'What about her?' he asked. 'Do you think she might have played around like he did?'

PHILIP KERR | 93
'I really couldn't say. She always struck me as a bit of an ice-maiden. You know, cold. I couldn't ever imagine her flirting with anyone. But even if I could it's my impression that the smallest country in the world would be a poor place to conduct a secret affair.'

'Not the smallest,' said Amalric, correcting me. 'The Vatican City is smaller. And I don't think that size ever stopped scandal there. Do you?'

I chuckled. 'Maybe not.'

Sergeant Savigny came back to the table and sat down, smelling strongly of French cigarettes, which only made me want one; but I have a rule about smoking: unless in a situation of stress I only smoke when I am writing and only then when I am stuck. I don't like my habits to become too much like a habit.

Amalric sat back in his chair and tugged at the end of his little beard.

'It's said that God never takes away something,' he said after a moment or two, 'without giving something better in its place. But not in this case. When Houston put an end to the *atelier* it seems everyone was a loser by his decision. Even him, perhaps, since he was obliged to hand back a cheque for twenty million. You, your fellow writers, the people at Veni, Vidi, Legi, the Houston office staff, shareholders, the publisher Mr Anderton, Mr Houston's literary agent Hereward Jones. Some of these people lost only their jobs; but some lost a great deal of money – or at least they didn't make the money that they were quite sure they were going to make until Houston's bombshell announcement. Which is almost the same thing. Of course, no one lost their life, unlike Mrs Houston; but I can't help but feel her murder is connected with everything you have told me, Monsieur

Irvine. As a policeman I've come to the conclusion that the Bible is wrong; it's the lack of money that's the root of all evil.' He shrugged. 'Perhaps Mrs Houston didn't want to accompany her husband back to London. Perhaps she liked living in Monaco.'

'Anything is possible, I suppose.'

'Perhaps that's why he killed her,' said Savigny.

'Maybe.'

'Was he a jealous man?' Savigny was warming to his line of questioning.

'John? No. Not at all. I have the impression that if he'd found out she was fucking someone else, he'd have been pleased.'

'Pleased?' Savigny was frowning. 'How?'

'It would have let him off the hook, that's how. And of course he'd have forgiven her because, in his own way, he loved her. Love will hide a multitude of sins.'

'Talking of which,' said Amalric, 'would it surprise you to know that the contact list on Orla Houston's iPhone included a number of sinners in the persons of several prominent Irish republicans? Two of whom – according to an officer we spoke to today at Scotland Yard – served long sentences at Portlaoise Prison for arms smuggling?'

'Does that surprise me? No. As a matter of fact I believe those two guys you mentioned helped John with the research for one of his books. *Ten Soldiers Wisely Led*. That was the last book I wrote for John. Before *Dead Red*, I mean.'

Savigny nodded thoughtfully. '*Dix Soldats Sagement Conduits*. That's the follow-up book to *Le Prisonnier de Kandahar*, isn't it? One of my favourite books, sir.'

'Is it?' said Amalric.

'There's this guy who wears diamond-encrusted shoes. An arms dealer. Fantastic.'

'The title comes from Euripides,' I added helpfully. 'Ten soldiers wisely led will beat a hundred without a head. I always thought it was Orla's brother who put John in contact with those two characters. But it could just as easily have been her. John always suspected she was giving money to Sinn Féin. His money. I know they argued about it. John did not approve.'

I don't know why, but I mentioned the incident at Orla's wedding to John when Colm Mac Curtain had tried to pick a fight with me.

'They sound like quite a family,' observed Amalric.

'They are.'

'Is it possible that perhaps she might have offended someone in those circles?' asked Savigny. 'According to Scotland Yard, some of these people are still active and violent.'

'You mean Irish nationalist paramilitaries?' I smiled. 'I'm a writer, Sergeant. It's my job to make you believe that anything is possible.' I shrugged. 'With a sound-suppressor on a gun, it just might be, I suppose. John slips out of the Odéon Tower – for whatever reason – and comes back to find that his wife has been murdered by the Real IRA. I like that story better than him shooting his own wife in cold blood. But frankly I think I've got too much imagination to be a cop, don't you?'

I tried and failed to suppress a yawn, and then glanced at my watch, which wasn't an Hublot but a hundred-and-fifty-pound Bulova that was a poor imitation of the rather more expensive Rolex Sea Dweller. 'But even my imagination is a getting a little dull. And my throat a little dry. I'm not used to talking as much as this. So perhaps you'll excuse me.' I took out my wallet.

'No, no, monsieur,' said Amalric. 'You were our guest.'

'Thank you, very much.'

'No, thank you, monsieur.'

I allowed him to carry on thinking that I might actually have offered to pay my share while, from my wallet, I took out the two business cards I'd been reaching for all along. I handed one to Amalric and the other to Sergeant Savigny, who was standing up to say goodbye.

'I enjoyed it very much,' I said. 'Especially the wine.'

Amalric was nodding circumspectly, which excited my curiosity. 'What did you think of the restaurant?' I asked him.

'It's trying hard to be something it's not,' he said. 'But then again, isn't everyone?'

'Don't hesitate to call or email if you have any more questions,' I said. Then we all shook hands and I left.

It was a warm, clear Monday evening in London. From Claridge's I walked up to Oxford Circus where I caught a Central Line train west to Notting Hill Gate, and then the District Line south to Putney. I walked onto the bridge and about halfway across stopped and stared across the river, hoping that the air would help to clear my head. Putney looked better at night when it was almost as glamorous-looking as Monaco; almost, but not quite. Saint Mary the Virgin Church, immediately to the east of the bridge, was bathed in sharp white light like a ghost ship. Next to the church, the blue lights from Putney Wharf Tower – a rather smarter, more expensive apartment building than my own – reflected on the metallic surface of the water in a way that made the river seem almost benign when it was anything but that. Strong currents and whirlpools made the Thames much too dangerous for swimming while the tide – which was now at its highest – was playing its usual game of trying to catch out the motorists who had unwisely parked along the Embankment to the west of Putney Bridge. It was not uncommon to return from dinner at one of Putney's many inexpensive restaurants to find your car filled up to the roof with Thames water. This was certainly an entertaining spectacle to watch from the safety of an upper window in a pub, and the customers drinking at The Star and Garter often did just that.

There's nothing that seems to give people more pleasure in Britain than watching a disaster happening to someone else in slow motion. Except perhaps what George Orwell would have called 'a perfect murder', which is to say a murder involving money and celebrities, of the kind that encourages not just extensive write-ups in the Sunday newspapers but also lots of books and melodramas – in short, the kind of murder that had befallen Edmond Safra and now Orla Mac Curtain. Her death really did seem to have all of the qualities that Orwell required to make a murder memorable. If Dominick Dunne had been alive he'd certainly have been on the next available plane to the Côte d'Azur. But if the Monty cops working the Edmond Safra case had screwed up – as the Vanity Fair journalist had implied – they didn't look like they were about to make any of the same mistakes again. I might not have learned anything from Chief Inspector Amalric and Sergeant Savigny that made me change my mind about what had happened in Monaco, but I had certainly revised my opinion concerning the efficiency of the Monty cops. Amalric had been especially impressive and served to remind me that a well-read cop is like a supermarket steak: not as thick as you might hope.

Back in the flat I took off my one good suit and wearing just my underpants and a T-shirt I checked my emails and decided to finally open the one headed 'News about your ticket' from the National Lottery; I'd been delaying this in order that I might enjoy the property pornographic fantasy of just what I'd do if I won a rollover jackpot of eight million pounds and I felt absurdly deflated – as if I really could have bought that seven-bedroom manor house in Bouches du Rhône – when I discovered I'd won only ten quid.

I was about to log off for the day when the Skype ringtone came through the desktop speakers with a sound effect that was like a robot farting in a paddling pool. I almost fell off my Herman Miller with surprise. John Houston was the only person who ever called me on Skype and thus my only Skype contact; his Skype Name was *Colonneh*. This wasn't because John cared about the cost of international telephone calls but because he had a thing about privacy and security and, while researching one of his meticulous outlines, he'd learned from the FBI that because Skype was what they call 'peer to peer' there was no way that anyone – the Feds included – could eavesdrop on your conversation. I suppose this was something else I had neglected to mention to Chief Inspector Amalric.

I clicked the mouse to answer the call and a second later I was staring at a very different-looking John from the man I had last seen in a car on the French autoroute. For one thing he was now wearing a short grey beard and had lost a little weight, which rather suited him. What with the salt-and-pepper beard and the way his head was leaning on his hand he reminded me more than a little of Thomas Carlyle or perhaps John Fowles. But I could see nothing particularly desperate about the figure on the screen. His shirt collar was clean and the million-dollar Hublot watch was clearly visible on his thick, tanned wrist. The room behind him had lots of bookshelves and a high ceiling. He might have been about to give an online interview to a creative-writing class.

'John. How the hell are you?'

He gave a wry sort of smile.

'Aside from being a fugitive from justice and wanted for my wife's murder, I'm fine, old sport.'

'As a matter of fact I just had dinner with the Monty cops.'

'They're in London already? Jesus.'

'Two of them are.'

'Where'd they take you?'

I smiled. It was a question that only John would have asked in these circumstances.

'Claridge's. That's where they're staying.'

'Fucking hell. They must really like me for this one. Claridge's.'

'You're the obvious suspect, all things considered.'

'And that's precisely why I left. Because I looked so bang to rights for it. I figured my best chance was to get out of Dodge and try to clear myself from outside the principality. Unpleasant things in Monty have a habit of getting tidied away rather too quickly.'

'That comes of there not being much room for anything – the place being smaller than a pimple on France's arse.'

'Maybe. Or just lazy cops.'

'I don't know, John, the two detectives I met tonight seemed quite equal to the task of tracking you down.'

'What did you tell them?'

'The truth. What else could I tell them? John, I don't know anything. I told them about the last time I spoke to you. I told them what we talked about. But if you're asking me if I told them I thought you were guilty, no, I didn't tell him that, because I don't.'

'Thanks, old sport. I appreciate it. And for what it's worth, I really didn't kill her. What does everyone else think?'

'Peter and Mike think you're probably guilty as charged. I don't know about Bat and Hereward. I'm seeing them tomorrow, at their offices in Eastbourne Terrace. They asked me to come in and see them.'

'I see.'

'So what did happen?'

'I've been framed, that's what happened.'

'Then why don't you tell that to the cops? On Skype, I mean. I could set it up. You could talk to them like you're doing with me now. Put your end of the story to them from wherever it is you are and you'd still be safe. Without having you in their custody they'd have no option but to check out your side of the story.'

'I already considered that, and the answer is no.'

'Why not?'

'Look, Don, I don't want to go into any details right now. What I want to say is this: I know you might think I let you down and maybe I did and I'm sorry about it. But you're the only one who can help me. You're the only person I can trust, old sport. I need a favour. A big favour. And it's the kind of favour you simply won't be able to do if you set up a Skype call between me and those two Monty cops, because if that happens then it stands to reason the British police will start watching you in the hope you'll lead them to me.'

'I get it. I'm to come and see you, is that it? Sure. Just tell me where you are and I'm there.'

'Look, I know this is asking a lot. You'll be aiding and abetting a serious crime and subject to prosecution. If you were found guilty you could go to prison, Don.'

'What am I, Forrest Gump? John, I trained to be a lawyer, remember? Say what you want me to do and then you can read me the Miranda.'

'There's a sort of box containing some stuff which I'd like you to pick up and bring to me here.'

'You mean like a safety deposit box?'

John laughed. 'Jesus, Don, that stuff is strictly for the Ludlum movies. Nobody bothers with safety deposit boxes these days. At least no one who wants to keep things secret. For one thing you can't trust any of the fucking banks to keep their mouths shut – least of all the Swiss ones. And for another I happen to know of at least two Liechtenstein banks that are under constant surveillance by the CIA – I mean you walk out of some of these places it's like the red fucking carpet. You might as well pause and smile and tell the folks watching back home that Domenico Vacca made your fucking tuxedo. No, if you really want to keep your stuff safe and secret you use a self-storage facility. And it's a hell of a lot cheaper than a fucking bank, too. UK has eight hundred self-storage facilities – more than the rest of Europe put together. It's a 350 million pound a year industry in Great Britain alone and there's no way that any law enforcement agencies can keep eyes on them. Al-Qaeda probably has shares in these companies.'

I laughed. The way John talked sometimes, it was like reading one of his novels.

'So, here's what you do,' he said. 'You drive to Big Yellow Self Storage on Townmead Road in Fulham. Next to the Harbour Club where I used to be a member.'

'I know it.'

'I rent twenty-five square feet of storage space on the first floor. Number F14. And that's where you'll find this box. The pin number to get in the place is 1746, Battle of Culloden, so a Jock like you shouldn't have any trouble remembering it. And there's free parking so it won't cost you a penny either. There's a combination padlock on the door. It's another Scottish defeat. Flodden Field, 1513. Anyone asks you – not that they will – then the space is rented to a Mr Hanway. You'll see that your name is also on the system. A little precaution I took at the time. In the storage space you'll find a box. Really, it's more of a foot locker. Or a small trunk. The combination on that lock is Bannockburn. 1314.'

'So what's in the box?'

'You could call it research, I suppose. You know how I always tried to get things right – how far I would go. Yes, of course you do. Sometimes a little too far, right? I got myself a fake British passport and driver's licence, sourced an illegal handgun, and bought some of the last US Treasury bearer bonds. I broke a few laws in the cause of checking out what was actually possible, sure. But that's what made the books work; because the stories were watertight. I always figured that if I got caught doing any of that shit I'd deploy the Forsyth defence. I'd get my lawyer to say that I was merely practising the same research techniques used in undercover journalism – in the same way that Freddie did when he wrote *The Day of the Jackal*. Of course, I never did get caught; and I held on to the stuff for what you might call romantic reasons. I mean I suppose I always rather fancied myself as Jason Bourne. Anyway, that's what's in the box, old sport. A thriller writer's career contraband. Look, bring the cash and the documents – in fact bring everything except the gun and the bonds. Yes, you'd best toss the gun in the river. But inside a Mont Blanc Meisterstück pen you'll find there are some conflict diamonds, so for Christ's sake don't try to use it to sign anything.'

'How much cash?'

'There's about a hundred grand in euros.'

'Suppose they see it on the X-ray?'

'They won't. It's all new 500-euro notes. So, you buy a copy of a nice big history book. Something thick and very worthy-looking by Max Hastings or Antony Beevor. One banknote between two pages. Simple as that. Besides, the law says that you can actually move as much cash as you like around the EU. You only need a cash declaration form if you're leaving or entering the EU and it's more than ten thousand euros. But even so, you wouldn't want to have to explain it to them because then the Revenue would want to know where you got a hundred K. So best use the book.'

'Okay, I get your box. Then what do I do?'

'Wait for the Monty cops to fly home, just in case they have any more questions for you; and then come and see me here. Use some of the cash to pay your expenses. Air fare. Car hire at the airport. Just make sure you're not followed.'

'Where?'

'Geneva.'

'Hang on, that isn't actually in the EU.'

'Depends what exit you choose at Geneva airport, doesn't it? There's a Swiss side and there's a French side. Look, the worst that can happen is that they'll confiscate the money. Which isn't yours anyway. So don't worry about it.'

'All right.'

John gave me the address and phone number. 'I've been staying here on and off since I closed the *atelier*. To write my book. The place belongs to a hedgie I know. I keep a few million in his fund so he's cool about me being here. He's in the Antarctic, right now. On some charity expedition to drive across the continent. At one stage I was going to go with him. I wish to Christ I had. Anyway, he won't be back for months.'

'I should have guessed you were there.'

'Look, call me when you get to Geneva. It's about a thirty-minute drive to the house from the airport.'

'Okay.'

John nodded silently. For a moment he looked overcome; then he said, 'Don. Thanks, old sport. I really appreciate this.'

'I doubt that. I really do, John. But you can rely on me. I'll be there.'

I clicked the mouse and ended the Skype call while he was still staring sincerely into the camera on his laptop and trying to look properly grateful but not bringing it off.

CHAPTER 5

A few days later I took the 14.00 British Airways flight to Geneva. For a change I flew Business Class. I figured John could afford it. As well as five stones in his Mont Blanc that were each about a carat in size and probably worth at least thirty thousand pounds, the box at the lock-up in Townmead Road had contained 100,000 euros in cash. At Cointrin Airport I breathed a sigh of relief that I had arrived 'without let or hindrance' as a British passport has it. I called John on a payphone to let him know I'd landed and then went to the Avis desk to rent a car. I had to use my own credit card for that, so I chose something small – a VW Golf – just in case I ended up doing more driving than I anticipated. But in the car I helped myself to a generous amount of John's folding to cover a week's car hire and petrol and then keyed the address he'd given me on the phone into the satnav. The highlighted route away from the airport took me east onto Lake Geneva and then north along the Quai de Coligny.

I've never liked Geneva that much. Before going up to Cambridge I went to summer school at the University of Geneva for six weeks to improve my French, fell in love with a peach of a girl from Italy called Ernestina who wasn't in love with me, and had a thoroughly miserable time. And when I was still in advertising I went to the Geneva Motor Show with some suits from the agency to view a range of shitty French cars before we pitched for the manufacturer's account; we didn't get it. These days I associate Geneva with EasyJet flight delays at the end of ski holidays that had already proved disappointing, or ludicrously expensive, or both. It's hard to feel enthusiastic about a city that was once home to a bigot like John Calvin and which in *le jet d'eau* has a landmark that resembles nothing so much as a giant stream of piss.

Twenty-eight minutes from the airport (Rolex time), the village of Collonge-Bellerive is one of the most exclusive places to live in the world, not just Geneva. Houses on the lakeshore cost anything up to sixty million euros. I knew that because I'd been on a website called *The Leading Properties of the World* and I'd also explored the area a bit on Google Maps. From the air the house where John was holed up, on Chemin Armand Dufaux, was surrounded with trees and looked like a small hunting lodge, but only if you were the Crown Prince of Austria. With its own jetty and boat house, a box-hedge maze, and a drive longer than the Hadron Collider, the red-roofed manor house was as cosy and private as a ruby ring in a green velvet box; Martin Bormann could have been living there and no one would have known, or cared. The Swiss are like that. It doesn't matter who you are or what you did somewhere else just as long as you wipe your shoes and wash your hands before you walk off the plane.

I pulled up in front of an impressive-looking gate, leaned out of the car window, tapped the number John had given me into the security keypad and waited to be admitted. A camera moved, the lens twisting as it focused on my face.

'It's me,' I said. 'Don Irvine.'

Minutes later I was approaching the house.

'Jesus,' I exclaimed as the real scale of the place became more apparent to me. 'What is this place? East Egg?'

In front of the house was a courtyard that lacked only Captain Dreyfus and a full court martial while the enormous, dihedral roof properly belonged on the massif of a small Alpine range. As I stepped out of the car the front door opened to reveal not a count or a baron, nor for that matter a cadaverous butler, but John Houston wearing a tweed suit and a big smile, and looking more than a little like Toad of Toad Hall. He tap-danced his way down the stone steps to the door of my car and shook me firmly by the hand.

'Don,' he said, fondly. 'I appreciate you coming all this way to help me try to unfuck my life.'

'That's okay, Mr Hanway,' I said, pointedly. 'And it makes a pleasant change for me to try and *unfuck* someone's life.'

'You brought my passport and driving licence?'

'Of course. I was wondering why you picked that name.'

'Charles Hanway?' He shrugged. 'I didn't pick it. Not exactly. That's not how it works, old sport. You have to find some poor bastard about the same age who died young. And apply for a new birth certificate in his name. So you can then apply for the passport. The police do it themselves when they want to go and work undercover. At least, that's what *The Guardian* says.'

'Only you picked someone who was a bit younger, I see.'

'Why not? Applying for a false passport is an excellent way of knocking a few years off your mug. Cheaper than surgery. You know, there's a small part of me that's going to enjoy being someone else for a while. Come in and have a drink and I'll show you around Xanadu.'

'Who owns this place?'

'A fellow named Bob Mechanic. He runs a hedge fund in

Geneva called The Mechanism. It's one of those funds run by a series of algorithms that no one understands which adds up to a licence to print money. Last time I looked in Forbes he was worth about two billion dollars.'

'Two billion's a figure I can understand. He's the guy driving across Antarctica, right?'

'Yeah.'

'Sounds like a useful friend to have.'

John led me into a large hallway which was dominated by the sculpture – if that's the right word – of a seated golden nude woman with several hundred surgical syringes instead of hair.

'That's quite a conversation piece,' I said.

'It's by Mauro Perucchetti,' said John. 'Bob is quite a collector. This house is full of modern art. Some of it is worth a small fortune.'

'This one looks like a bad trip to the hairdressers.'

John laughed and pointed at the large stairway on the opposite side of the hall. 'She gave me quite a start the other night when I came down here in the dark. Her body is made of Swarovski crystal which was catching the moonlight through the window and makes her look rather ghostly. For a moment I thought it was Orla. I nearly had a heart attack.'

'Sounds like a guilty conscience. You sure you didn't shoot her?'

'Funny, but not funny.'

He led me into a kitchen which could have served a good restaurant and poured me a glass of cold wine from a bottle of Corton-Charlemagne that was cooling in a refrigerator as big as a bank vault. The kitchen was immaculately clean and it was hard to imagine that anyone was actually living here. Even the stainless steel sink was gleaming like a suit of armour at Windsor Castle.

'Cheers.' He raised his glass and I caught sight of the massive Hublot on his wrist; it looked like a Range Rover parked on a beach towel.

I drank some of the wine and nodded appreciatively.

'It's the '85,' he said.

'I think that being a fugitive has some very obvious advantages if this is what you're drinking.'

'There are worse places to go into hiding,' he admitted. 'Bob keeps a superb cellar here. I'll say that for him.'

He was leaning nonchalantly against a white marble worktop except that the nonchalance never lasted for longer than a few seconds. He was too restless to quite pull that off. There was always an oven clock to adjust, a glass to top up, a mark on the marble to wipe, a shirt cuff to correct, and once a handful of vitamins to swallow.

'I'm taking these because I need to stay sharp,' he explained. 'Three times a day. The stress I've been under, I haven't been eating very much.'

'That would explain why the kitchen is so neat,' I said. 'I thought you'd lost a few pounds. It suits you. Unlike that suit.'

'What's wrong with it?'

'Nothing. I'm sure they wear that kind of thing at Balmoral all the time.'

'I had to leave Monaco in a bit of a hurry. I was stuck with the winter wardrobe I'd already brought here on a previous trip.'

'That's what it looks like.'

He was looking at my cabin luggage.

'It's all in there? In that toilet bag you call a suitcase?'

'Everything except the gun. I chucked that off Putney Bridge. Not that it would have worked anyway.'

'What do you mean?'

'Your nice Brocock Magnum with the inox finish. It had been deactivated.'

'What? I paid two grand for that off some natty dredd on the Barking Road.'

'You were done. He saw you coming. He sold you a weapon that was perfectly legal. You'd have needed someone with a lathe and the curiosity of a dead cat to make that thing fire again.'

I laughed and so did John.

'You're right. I was so fucking nervous when I bought it that I didn't think to actually test-fire the thing.'

'That's not so easy to do, even in Newham.'

'So why did you chuck it if it didn't work?'

'Because these days the Met is very trigger-happy. They shoot you dead when you're only carrying a table leg. It's best not to have anything that even looks like a gun. They shot a blind man the other day because he was carrying a white stick.'

'Buying a gun is so much easier in Monaco.'

'Evidently. Or we wouldn't be talking like this now.'

'Point taken.'

I put my hand in my jacket and brought out my passport-wallet, from which I withdrew John's passport and then his driving licence. He frowned.

'You brought it through customs like that?'

I shrugged. 'Of course. Best place for a passport, wouldn't you say? A passport-holder.'

'But where's your own passport?'

'In my other pocket. They make you take it out of the

holder when they look at it anyway. So what the fuck? I figured no one is going to look in the passport-holder if they're already holding your passport.' I shrugged. 'That's just the Father Brown principle of concealment. G. K. Chesterton? *The Innocence of Father Brown?*'

John started to nod. 'Where does a wise man hide a leaf? Sure. I remember.'

He looked at the picture in his false passport and nodded. 'It's lucky I wore my glasses and grew a beard for my passport picture.'

'Yes, it is.'

'Not that I've ever dared use this, you know. I mean, I stuck to the Jackal's recipe, for how to get one. PO Box and everything. I mean it ought to be kosher enough. But I really don't know for sure.'

'You could try to assassinate the President of France. That's one way of finding out if it works like a passport should.'

'The way things are going there right now, they'd probably give me the *Légion d'honneur*.'

'Or you could go back to the UK, like any other British passport holder. That's probably the best road test you could give it. On the other hand if you want to use it without anyone actually looking at it, then Corfu is your best bet. No one ever looks at your passport when you fly there. The Greeks are glad to see anyone who's going to spend some money. Robert Mugabe could fly into Corfu without a problem.'

John didn't answer and I wondered where he was thinking of going. South Africa? Colombia? New Zealand? What was the destination of choice these days for people who wanted to do a Lord Lucan?

I put the Mont Blanc on the worktop and lifted my case

onto the kitchen table. I unzipped the case and placed Charles Moore's biography of Margaret Thatcher in his hands.

'What's this? A joke? You know I couldn't stand that woman.'

'Oh, I think you'll like this book, John. In fact, I wouldn't be at all surprised if that's the most absorbing biography you'll read all year. Especially chapters ten to thirty.'

'Ah.' He flicked open the book and tugged out one new 500-euro bill. 'Yes, I see what you mean. God bless Mrs T. Thanks, Don. Without a credit card I've been paying for nearly everything with Bitcoin until now.'

'Where do you get a hundred thousand euros in new bills anyway?'

'You remember that trip I made to the Lahore Literary Festival? The French DGSE got me to do a job for them while I was there.' He shrugged. 'Can't say any more than that.' John grinned. His grin got even wider when he unscrewed the pen and emptied the five stones onto the marble worktop. 'Thanks again, old sport.'

'And the diamonds?'

'I bought them in Amsterdam. I was going to have them set in a necklace for someone.'

'For Orla?'

'No,' he said, quietly.

'So,' I said. 'What happened to her? And don't tell me you were cleaning the gun and it went off. Cleaning the kitchen I might believe, but not a 22 automatic. According to the cops she got it right between the eyes and probably while she was asleep. I've seen the pictures.'

'Look, I'll tell you the truth. About everything, Don, I promise. And then I'm going to ask you another big favour. But why don't I show you around first? Take you to your room and let you unpack. You can see some of Bob Mechanic's art collection. Then we'll order in some sushi from Uchitomi. It's Geneva's number one Japanese takeout. And the best part is, it's on Bob's account. Now that you're here at last I'm starting to feel hungry again.'

'All right.'

I shrugged. I've never cared very much for modern art, by which I mean the sort of crap that wins the Turner Prize. The last twentieth-century artist I had any time for was David Hockney.

John walked me through some other rooms with modern art installations and pictures until we came into an otherwise empty conservatory that was dominated by a female version of Michelangelo's greatest sculpture, *David*.

'Who's this? Davina, I suppose.'

'This is another Perucchetti,' explained John. 'It's half size and made of the same Carrera marble as the original.'

'I always wondered who buys this kind of shit,' I said. 'I guess now I know.'

'You don't like it?'

'On the whole I prefer something with a little less novelty and a bit more original thought. You know – stuff that doesn't need a whole catalogue and Waldemar Januszczak to explain it.'

'Hmm. You could be right.'

The drawing room was dominated by a huge blue chandelier that looked like a sort of amoebic creature from a *Men in Black* movie. I had to admit that this was impressive, but couldn't help but add that I wouldn't care to try and dust it.

'You know, I'd forgotten what a fucking philistine you are, old sport,' said John.

'That's what I am, I guess. But then again, isn't that why you used to pay me to write your books?'

'Oh, I see.' John grinned, patiently. 'Now that I'm a wanted man you figure you can insult me with impunity, is that it?'

'You've been doing it to me for years. And you're going to have to get used to me telling you what a cunt you are, John. At the very least you'll have to put up with it until you've explained what the fuck happened in Monaco. So why don't you skip the Jay Jopling, White Cube tour of this absurdly impressive house and try to take this situation a bit more seriously? Out of respect for the person who just brought thirty grand's worth of diamonds through customs for you. I've been very patient, John. But as you yourself pointed out on Skype I'm running quite a risk in helping you here. And I certainly didn't come all this way to Geneva just to see Michelangelo's *David* missing a dick and wearing a nice pair of tits. So let's hear it: the undisputed truth or I swear I am leaving on a jetplane.'

'You're right, Don, I'm sorry. I'm afraid I just don't know how to behave in this situation. I suppose I was trying to put on a brave face; to play the good host and make you feel welcome after coming all this way. Especially after the way things ended between us. Really, I'm so grateful you came. But I don't know how to be myself. I've got quite a lot on my mind, old sport. It's not easy to talk about any of this. Not easy at all. You hear me chattering away about fucking art but inside I'm mute with horror at what's happened.' He tapped his diaphragm and swallowed uncomfortably. 'I have this persistent feeling of indigestion. Look, sit down. I'll fetch another bottle and we'll talk. I'll talk. The fact is I haven't talked to anyone since it happened. Since I arrived here in Geneva.' He shook his head. 'I've just sat around in silence and stared at the walls, wondering what the fuck to do. I'm like a monk in this place.'

I sat down on a large cream sofa and raised my glass. 'At least it's a nice monastery.'

John went away to fetch a second bottle and I stood up and walked around the room. Photographs of Bob Mechanic and his family were arranged along the broad white piste that was the mantelpiece; in pride of place was what looked like a Grayson Perry vase featuring a series of obscene cuddly toys that resembled the children in the photographs. Grey-coloured faux fur throws were arranged neatly on a crescent of cream sofas, only they weren't faux, they were real; the silver foxes who had worked closely with the interior decorator were doubtless glad to have given their lives to keep such a nice family warm on colder Geneva nights. In the centre of the crescent was a coffee table on which you could have dried a year's entire crop of arabica beans.

How the other half live or, to be more accurate, the other 0.001 per cent. Were the rest of the Mechanic family crossing the Antarctic continent, too? If so it probably made a stimulating change from a summer in the Hamptons. It certainly made a change from Switzerland. Outside the window a lawn as big as a polo field led down to the lakeside and a stone quay. An American flag hung limply on a tall pole and a couple of swans were dozing in the sun. There wasn't much happening on the shores of Lake Geneva, either. Then again that was why you lived on the shores of Lake Geneva. That was probably why they had built *le jet d'eau*; so something harmless could happen in Geneva, even if it was just a few people enduring the momentary discomfort of getting hit with the spray.

John came back in the room bearing another bottle of liquid gold.

'"Things fall apart,"' I said. '"The centre cannot hold; Mere anarchy is loosed upon the world, the blood-dimmed tide is loosed, and everywhere The ceremony of innocence is drowned; The best lack all conviction, while the worst Are full of passionate intensity."' I smiled and came back to the coffee table. 'Although not in Switzerland.'

'What's that?'

'With apologies to William Butler Yeats.'

'I think I'd forgotten what a fucking lefty you are. Cheers.'

'I'm only a lefty by your rough, bestial standards, John.'

He arranged fresh glasses on the table and poured the wine.

'Old sport, I have the strangest feeling that any minute now, you're going to give me a lecture about brotherly love and the cuckoo clock. Are you?'

'I'm not the one the police are looking for, Mr Lime. Cheers.'

'Is that really how you see me?'

'Why not? You've always reminded me a little of Orson Welles.'

'Don't be so melodramatic. We're friends, you and I. We've always done everything together. And when all this is over, when I've cleared my name, it will be just like it was before. Maybe not exactly like it was before. Orla won't be there of course, and that's a tragedy. She had her whole life before her, poor girl. Oh, I know you and she didn't get on and I always regretted that. But she was a great woman and a wonderful wife and I really did love her, Don. In my own way. You mentioned Yeats and I suppose you could say she was my Maud Gonne. It's true, I have a bad conscience about some things that happened between us – times when I didn't behave as I ought to have done, that's the real pain;

then again, my conscience is not so bad, in the great scheme of things. I remember the first time I saw her. She was the centrefold in a magazine. I can't remember the one but it might have been *Playboy*. As soon as I saw her picture I promised myself that I was going to marry her and I did.'

He paused for a moment as something welled up from deep inside him and then two tears that were full of white wine and self-pity trickled down the sides of his broad nose, and his big shoulders started to shake as if there was something almost seismic about what was happening to him; it was nothing less than a tsunami of grief.

For a moment he wept without a sound, his face a grey, Guernican rictus of agony and bereavement which reminded me of Michael Corleone's silent scream of agony at the end of *Godfather 3* when he has seen his beloved daughter Mary murdered on the steps of the Palermo Opera House. It was painful to watch, much more painful than I might have expected.

There's something about another man's tears that's more awful than a woman's. In Northern Ireland there had been several occasions when I'd seen the boys from my platoon crying – I wept myself after the Warrenpoint ambush. Nothing wrong with that. No one is unmanned by tears. Mostly you just sat it out in the Bulldog, waited for them to finish – if there was time – and then never mentioned it again. Not ever. That was it, done, and it was all right. This was all right, too – it was all right because as I watched John weep his heart out in front of me I knew he couldn't have murdered his wife. Not him. Not in a thousand years.

JOHN HOUSTON'S STORY

PART ONE

CHAPTER 1

After publishing more than one hundred books you might be forgiven for thinking I'd know how to begin a story, but with this one I'm not at all sure how or where. I've always believed that a bad beginning makes a bad ending. You know me, Don: I like to start with a title and a great first line – something that really arrests you. I think my favourite first line in all literature must be 'The past is a foreign country; they do things differently there.' Christ, I wish I could write something as simple but as good as that.

I suppose I could start from the moment you and I last saw each other, old sport, in the Aston on the French autoroute, when I told you that I was shutting down the *atelier*; but I could as easily start a few weeks after that, from the moment when I arrived in Geneva for the first time, to begin writing *The Geneva Convention* – which was before Orla's murder – because it seems to me now that a number of strange things happened to me here in Switzerland that could be easily connected with her death. Then again if this was film noir I'd probably begin the story in medias res, as Horace has it – with the night of her death. You know? The poor husband comes back home in the wee small hours to find his wife dead. Now that's what I call a cold opening. Except that I didn't find her dead when I came home. Not exactly. When

I came home I thought Orla was asleep. She was in bed and it was dark after all; and I had good reason not to want to wake her. The plain fact of the matter is that when I got back into bed beside her she was more than likely already shot. And if I hardly thought it unusual she didn't stir when I climbed into bed beside her that's because she never did, on account of the fact that she took sleeping pills: Halcion. When Orla took Halcion there was very little that could wake her for several hours. Only who would believe that? Certainly not the police. That's what happened, however, and frankly if I'd been going to kill my wife I'd hardly have done it in a way that left me looking as guilty as Crippen – I'd have pushed her out of a high window, or something; I mean, I'm a thriller writer so it's second nature to me to analyse the circumstances of the crime and offer a critique of her homicide, right? But you can't tell the cops that. Suggesting an alternative and better way of killing your own wife – moreover one you stood a better chance of getting away with – doesn't exactly encourage them to think you're innocent. Cops are the purest form of the bourgeoisie, for whom fiction is the frivolous privilege of aristocracy, or people who play at being aristocrats, like writers. In their eyes an allegiance to hard facts is what distinguishes honest, ordinary folk.

I don't know what the Monty cops have told you about what happened in the hours leading up to Orla's murder. On a Friday night we often went to Joël Robuchon at the Hôtel Métropole on Avenue de la Madone. I don't know why we went there so often. Robuchon is ridiculously expensive but the reason I hated going there with Orla was not because of the food – which is excellent – but because there is something slightly corrupt about the atmosphere. It always made me feel like one of the old roués who go there with their very much younger mistresses and rentals like characters from the pages of *Nana*; I felt like some old fool in love – Comte Muffat or La Faloise. Also, they give you a delicious lemon cake when you leave, which Orla always insisted on taking although it was never her who ate it, but me, who could least afford to consume the extra calories. But Orla truly loved the place. She enjoyed dressing up and people-watching, which is a serious sport at Joël Robuchon. And since she seldom drank anything it was also an excuse for Orla to get behind the wheel of her Ferrari. Frankly we could have walked there in about the same time it took to drive there. People watch the Monaco Grand Prix and imagine the place is some kind of motoring Valhalla; but driving in Monaco is a bit like shifting your car around one enormous parking lot.

On the telly I saw that Orla's local fans have been leaving flowers and photographs to her memory in front of the entrance to the Odéon Tower, Diana-style. I don't know why I'm surprised about that. Orla was one of the few people I ever met who actually liked living in Monaco. After we moved there she developed a thing for Grace Kelly. Orla always believed she bore a strong resemblance to her. She was just as bad a driver. And of course she was in that disastrous remake of *Rear Window*, which only contributed to her stupid little conceit. There were certainly other people in Monaco who commented on the resemblance and perhaps that's why she took the place to heart. On the walls of her dressing-room at the Tour Odéon she had hung some framed movie posters of Grace Kelly in *High Society* and *To Catch a Thief*, although, in retrospect, *Dial M for Murder* might have been more appropriate. And I suppose that in the eyes of the public I'm just as much of a cad now as Ray Milland was in that movie. More so, if the truth was known.

Anyway, she really didn't like the idea of us moving back to London – not one bit – and when we were in the restaurant we argued about it. Orla was dead against the idea. As you know she had no great love for the English and was even less enthusiastic about the weather, not to mention the tax situation. People seem to have forgotten that Orla was quite a wealthy woman in her own right. She made a ton of money from that stage musical about WikiLeaks that she invested in: *WikiBeats*.

Anyway, the argument became quite loud and at one point I grabbed her by the ear and twisted it, which she didn't take kindly to and kicked me hard on the shin. I let out quite a yelp because Orla could always give as good as anything she got. She called me an arrogant cunt and I called her a fucking cow and then the maître d' came and asked us to keep our voices down. No doubt the cops have already told you about that. There's nothing like a lover's tiff in public to provide a convenient background for a murder. It's pure Agatha Christie. You have an argument, perhaps a face is slapped, some harsh things get said, very probably you meant some of them and therefore you must have killed her. The way the cops are you'd think a bit of a barney between husband and wife was one of Aristotle's four fucking causes.

Actually, it was a fairly wide-ranging sort of argument, and not just about the move back to Blighty. I'd found out that Orla was giving money to all sorts of people and institutions I didn't much care for. UNESCO was something we were both passionate about and we were actively involved in events like World Book Day and International Literacy Day. But I'm rather less keen on the RSPCA, the Labour Party, Julian Assange and Sinn Féin. Probably it was just her way of making me pay more attention to her, which I admit sometimes I didn't do enough of; quite the opposite. But I'm not telling you this to excuse what I'm going to tell you, old sport, merely to illustrate that my relationship with Orla was occasionally tempestuous. I was capable of driving her mad; she was capable of irritating the hell out of me, but not enough to kill her. Jesus, no. As George Clooney says in *From Dusk to Dawn*, 'I may be a bastard but I'm not a fucking bastard.'

As we were leaving the restaurant I made some tasteless remark about Irish republicans which she greeted with silence. That wouldn't have been so bad, but Orla can make a silence as cold and loud as a blast of air conditioning. Then, outside the hotel entrance, as we were waiting for the valet to bring us the car, Orla hit me with the Robuchon carrier bag containing the lemon cake. Hard enough to knock me off balance. I expect the doorman saw this and then me trying to laugh it off. Now a Ferrari is not a good car to drive when you're angry – especially when it's almost new – so I thought it best to apologize and, to my surprise, she started to cry, accepted my apology, told me she was sorry for hitting me with the cake, and then handed me the car keys. I don't expect anyone saw us make up in the car.

When we were back home I apologized again, for good measure, and I really thought everything between us was all right and that everything had blown over. We even had a good laugh about the incident and reflected it was fortunate that the *Daily Mail* weren't there to see what happened. I made a joke about it being lucky it was a Robuchon lemon cake and not one cooked by her mother – who's the world's worst baker – which Orla thought was very funny. Then we kissed and made up again – I swear that's exactly what happened, although in view of what now took place you could be forgiven for thinking our making up was hardly sincere on my part.

I went into my study and checked my emails and read a bit while Orla had a bath. Then she took the sleeping pill so I knew she would be soundly asleep for several hours. Which left me with ample opportunity to do what I often did when she took Halcion, which was to go out again; at least out of our apartment – which, as you may remember, is the sky duplex on the forty-third floor of the Tour Odéon – and down to an apartment on the twenty-ninth which is occupied – for the time being – by a friend of mine, a girl called Colette Laurent.

At least it was; Colette Laurent seems to have disappeared.

Until the night of Orla's death I'd been seeing her for a while. Colette was originally set up in the Tour Odéon by a Russian oligarch called Lev who abandoned her, although it's hard to imagine why, because girls don't come looking any more spectacular than Colette Laurent. I used to see her in the Odéon's gymnasium and it was lust at first sight on my part. One day we got talking. She's a French-Algerian who looks a bit like Isabelle Adjani. Tall, shapely – I mean she had tits to die for, real ones – and as fit as a butcher's dog. After we got to know each other a little better I agreed to offer her some help with her English and at first that's all that happened. Everything was above board between us for almost a month – I mean it was like the matchmaker was keeping her beady eye on us; but I'm only human and one thing led to another and before very long we were sleeping together at least once or twice a week. At first it was only on the boat, but one day Orla showed up and almost caught us at it; after that I only saw Colette at her Russian's apartment in the Tour or occasionally in Paris: she'd fly up for the weekend to the house in Neuilly-sur-Seine, when there was no one working there. It was an arrangement that suited us both because her job left her with little opportunity or energy for a social life. Colette was a yoga teacher and a masseuse and in Monaco that can keep you very busy; it's possible to make at least a thousand euros a day. But I'd also give her a bit of money now and then, just to tide her over when the poor thing had to miss a client to see me.

On what turned out to be my last night in Monaco there was nothing that seemed at all unusual. At about 11.30 when I was satisfied Orla was genuinely asleep – she snored – I swallowed a tablet of Cialis and armed with nothing more than a cold bottle of Dom I took the stairs down to the twenty-ninth floor, which is what I always did – to avoid nosy-parker neighbours and the CCTV. No one ever takes the stairs in our building. Most of the other residents would need a defibrillator if they climbed into their beds a bit too quickly. But not as quickly as I did when I saw Colette. She was wearing a baby-doll nightdress that was as light as a summer morning mist and I spent a very happy thirty minutes mapping every inch of her fabulous body. And before you say anything, old sport, yes, I know, it was a dreadfully deceitful and underhand thing to do, like something from the pages of the *Decameron*. Peronella, is it, who tells her husband how to clean a large wine jar that he's inside while she's being fucked from behind by her lover? That's what it was like. I really do feel ashamed of myself; and yet I know I'd probably do it again if I ever got the chance. That's the funny thing about being a bloke; to some extent we're ruled by our pricks. I've tried to understand it but I'm afraid I still haven't found a better description of male-pattern sexuality than what John Lewis says in *That Uncertain Feeling* by

Kingsley Amis when he asks himself why he likes women's breasts. 'I was clear on why I liked them, thanks, but why did I like them so much?' That's it, in a nutshell. We know we shouldn't fuck around but we do and then end up rather pathetically feeling ashamed of what we've done and hoping for the best. You might just as well call the male libido Russia and say that it's a riddle, wrapped in a mystery, inside an enigma.

At about two o'clock I went back upstairs to my own apartment. Again, nothing seemed unusual. No, that's not quite true. I stepped in some dog shit; the dogs – who slept in Orla's dressing room – were always crapping in the apartment and I spent the next ten minutes tracking it down and cleaning it off the fucking carpet before I went back into the bedroom. As usual our bedroom was like a fridge so I put on a T-shirt and some pyjama bottoms, slipped into bed and went straight to sleep. I awoke at about 7.30, got up, made myself a cup of tea and cleaned some more dog shit off the carpet. I bet the cops loved that. Traces of fucking bleach all over the place as if I'd tried to clean away something incriminating. Anyway, at that stage, as far as I was aware, Orla was still asleep. Again, there was nothing unusual about that. After she'd taken a sleeping pill it would have been quite usual for her to have slept through until about eleven. I had a shower and went into my study to work, like I always did. I emerged at around two and was a little surprised to find Orla wasn't around. It simply didn't occur to me that she was lying dead in our bed. I assumed she must have gone out somewhere. And besides, I couldn't hear the dogs. If that sounds at all unlikely you have to remember that this is an apartment that's twelve hundred square metres, which is about five tennis courts.

I made a bite of lunch, watched a bit of TV and then went back into my study for a couple of hours. At around five I came out again and still finding no sign of Orla I called her mobile to find out where she was, and when I heard it ringing in her dressing room I realized something was very wrong, especially when I came across the bodies of her pet dogs. It was only now that I went into the bedroom and found her lying just as I had left her earlier that day, facing the curtains and away from my side of the bed. I drew the curtains and saw that she'd been shot at close range, as if she'd been executed. My own gun – a twenty-two calibre Walther – was lying on the floor. Orla's skin was cold to the touch and it was clear she'd been dead for several hours.

For a while I just sat there on the floor beside her body and wept like a baby. I was horrified. It's a sight that will stay with me for as long as I live. Every time I close my eyes I can see her beautiful face and the bullet hole in the centre of her forehead, like a dreadful caste mark. I hope to God it never happens to you that you see something like that. The only consolation I have is that I'm certain Orla was asleep when it happened and that she could have experienced neither fear nor pain. After a while I took off my shirt and covered her beautiful face with it, almost as if I wanted to preserve her dignity and give Orla some privacy from those who were going to come into our home now and look at her. Crazy I know. After all the crime scenes I've described in my books you'd think I'd know exactly what to do. But in truth I wasn't thinking straight at all. The cliché 'I was beside myself' describes me very well; it was like I was hardly functioning in my own skin. My hands and my feet hardly seemed to belong to me at all. I remember pouring myself a stiff drink and going out onto the balcony to get some fresh air before I called the police. For a while I watched the swallows dive-bombing the air for insects near the top of the tower; out in the sea a pod of dolphins was clearly visible in the water; and I wondered how it could be such a beautiful evening when one of the most beautiful women in the world had just died so horribly.

I picked up the phone and was about to call the police and then it dawned on me that Orla must already have been dead when I returned from Colette's apartment. Clearly I must have got into bed with a corpse. It was obvious that the only time Orla could have been murdered was when I was downstairs with Colette, but I didn't think the cops were going to buy that. The more I thought about it the more I realized that I was about to become their number one suspect: my wife, my bedroom, my gun, my opportunity and, I dare say, with a little help from the staff and customers at Joël Robuchon, my motive, too.

I considered calling Ince & Co, who are my lawyers in Paris and Monaco, and asking their advice about what to do next; but then I decided to go down to Colette's apartment and discuss what to do with her. She was my alibi for the time that Orla had been murdered after all, although the precise time of death was going to be difficult to prove. Of course, my alibi in such an alluring shape as Colette was equally problematic; there's nothing cops like more than a lover's triangle.

I had a key to Colette's apartment but she wasn't at home. That wasn't unusual, she often worked on a Saturday. I was going to call her on my mobile and then changed my mind on the assumption that, if I was arrested by the police, my call would probably incriminate her. I tried to use Colette's landline but for some reason it wasn't working, so at around 5.30 I walked out onto the Boulevard d'Italie and called Colette's mobile from a payphone next to the BNP Paribas bank. Again, I wasn't alarmed that she didn't answer. I assumed she had a client and that she would be free to talk on the hour. I walked a bit further down the boulevard to an Italian restaurant called Il Giardino, had a coffee and then called her again at exactly six o'clock. Several times, without reply. I called her again at seven and when she still didn't answer I went back to the Odéon where I checked her car-parking space and saw her car wasn't there. I went back to Colette's apartment and it was now, as I searched the place for some clue as to where she might have gone, that I made a very unwelcome discovery: an empty bottle of Russian *Shampanskoye* in the very same ice-bucket I'd used to chill the Dom. You know? That awful sweet fizz that Russians call champagne and that frankly only they find palatable. When I first saw it I thought it was the Dom. But as soon as I realized what it was it was clear that someone else had visited Colette after I had left her and that more than likely this someone was Russian.

You might wonder why a man whose wife had just been murdered would devote any thought to something as trivial as a bottle of Russian champagne.

I can assure you it wasn't out of jealousy. After seeing the bottle of Russian champagne I decided to take a good look around the apartment and see what else I could find. In the wastepaper bin I came across an empty packet of Russian fags. And some other stuff, too. A book. A newspaper. *The Moscow Times.* And it was now that I began to consider the frightening possibility that Colette's former boyfriend, Lev Semyonovich Kaganovich was now back from Russia and had returned to his apartment. Thinking I'd better make myself scarce, I went back up to my apartment, made myself a drink and considered my options.

Was it possible that Lev's arrival back in Monaco was connected with Orla's death? Was it possible that Lev had intended to frame me for my wife's murder? Not for a moment did I think that Colette had killed Orla by herself. The only time I'd been out of my apartment was when I was with her. I was her alibi, as much as she was mine. But I could hardly ignore the idea that Lev had turned up while I was fucking his girlfriend and perhaps killed Orla in revenge. According to her he was like all Russians – a very violent man with connections in the world of organized crime; I'd only ever started seeing Colette on the understanding that Lev was completely off the scene. But it was now perfectly obvious to me that he wasn't and before very long I was absolutely shitting myself.

To be honest I'd never been completely satisfied at Colette's explanation concerning Lev's protracted absence. According to her, Lev was the kind of man who had a girl in every port and she was required to look after the apartment and him whenever he was in Monaco. But the telephone number she had for Lev in Moscow had been disconnected and the email address he had given her no longer functioned either. The service charge on the apartment in the Odéon was paid up until the end of the year, at which point it looked probable that she would have to leave Monaco and return to her family home in Marseille. I didn't mind that Colette was obviously looking for someone to replace Lev and that I might be it. I'd already considered the possibility of renting her a small place in Beausoleil. What I did mind hugely was the idea that a Russian gangster might now have me in his sights.

For several minutes I wandered through my apartment in a cold sweat and trying to figure out what to do. I don't mind telling you, I was sick with fear, old sport. I mean I actually vomited with fear. Since there was no sign of a break-in at my own apartment, it was clear that whoever had killed Orla must have had a key and that more than likely this was the key I had left on the hall table while I was fucking Colette.

Until now I don't suppose I had even considered robbery as a motive, so I went to the safe and found everything there that should have been there: a couple of thousand euros, some chequebooks, and a few smaller pieces of Orla's jewellery – all of the decent stuff was in a security box at Jacob Safra's Bank. None of the pictures were missing. What kind of burglar was it who ignored a decent-sized Picasso on our living-room wall and yet was compelled to shoot a sleeping woman? There were no answers that came my way. Just more questions, and one thing was soon obvious: the only way I had a chance of answering any of them and clearing my name was not to contact the police. Whichever way I looked at it I was squarely in the frame for my wife's murder, which bore all the hallmarks of a professional hit. For this reason it seemed to me that there was also a very real possibility that I was in danger myself. All of this meant I had to get out of Monaco, and fast.

I packed a bag, returned to Colette's apartment and waited around in the hope she might come back; I even took a gun with me in case Lev showed up. But by midnight I was convinced that something must have happened to her, too, and the possibility that I might find myself incriminated in two murders seemed all too possible. Perhaps her body was already lying in a cabin in my boat and I'd be kneeling there on the floor holding her body in one hand and a knife in the other like Roger Thornhill in *North by Northwest* when the cops showed up.

So I went down to the garage, where I got into my car and drove straight here.

Not exactly straight, no; the obvious route from Monaco to Geneva would have been on the A10, via Italy. Instead, I took a much longer route along the coast road west – there are lots of traffic cameras on the A8 out of Monaco – and then north, through the Écrins National Park, to avoid any toll roads. That's another way they have of tracking you. I mean things have changed a bit since Tom Ripley went on the lam. Not that anyone was looking for me when I got here – and I figured I had seventy-two hours before the maid found Orla's body – but Interpol can be quite tenacious when it sets its mind to catching someone. There was always a slim chance that the Monty cops would pay the French some serious cash to spend thousands of man-hours combing through CCTV footage of the roads in and out of the principality. Stranger things have happened. I recently read a couple of excellent thrillers by a fellow named Mark Russinovich – *Zero Day* and *Trojan Horse* – that really made me think about digital forensics, old sport. Russinovich is a PhD computer scientist and Microsoft Technical Fellow and really knows his stuff. There's not much the geeks can't find out with their drones and their satellites and their 'digital bloodhounds'. You should check him out before you write the next Jack Boardman. Some of that high-tech stuff

I put in the outline already looks like an old version of Windows.

Anyway, by the time poor Orla's body was found in the Tour Odéon I was safely hidden here in Collonge-Bellerive, which really is one of the most private places in the world; forget South America – you could hide the whole of the ODESSA here, in Jerry uniform, too, and no one would be any the wiser. Bob Mechanic – the guy who owns this place – has lived in this house for five years and he's never even seen his fucking neighbours. For all he knows he could be living next door to Joseph Kony and he wouldn't have a clue. And he's so bloody paranoid about being spied on he has his own pet geeks at the hedge fund's office in Geneva block Google Earth street views; the image that's on the site right now is at least a year or two old.

When the cleaner turns up I lurk down in Mechanic's study where she's forbidden to go in case she ever tries to dust his PC, which is on twenty-four hours a day, and Mechanic loses some important data. I think he must log into it remotely from an internet café on the Ross Ice Shelf to check his trades. Anyway, she's also the one who fills the fridge, not me. Mechanic had a butler for a while. So, as you can see, this is an ideal place to hide when you're a wanted man. It was an ideal place to write, too, which is why I came here in the first place. I just wish I'd stayed on to work through the summer instead of going back to Monty that weekend. I wouldn't have gone at all, but it was our wedding anniversary – something the cops don't seem to have noticed. I mean why would I have murdered Orla on her wedding anniversary? If I stayed on here in Switzerland then perhaps none of this would have happened. I wrote at least thirty thousand words of *The Geneva Convention* before Orla was murdered. Frankly, it's the best work I've done in a long time.

Seriously, old sport, if you want to drive life and all its attendant cares into a remote corner, forget Walden Pond, this is it. This is what I call a writer's retreat. You can really think in a place like this, which is all I've been doing, of course, since I left Monaco.

I paused and waited for Don to say something. His habitual demeanour is always pretty calm and unflappable, as befits a former army officer with two tours of Northern Ireland under his belt. Don's more of a Guy Crouchback than a Christopher Tietjens, but he was looking even more composed and unemotional than was normal even for him. His fingers were laced and his thick forefingers were touching the end of his square jaw, like a man contemplating a chess move. To my surprise he was still wearing his wedding ring, although Jenny, his wife, gave him the heave-ho more than eighteen months ago. Found herself someone else, apparently – and of all people he was a High Court judge, with a title, so the former Mrs Irvine is now Lady Somebody with a nice house in Kensington and a holiday home in Fiesole. Frankly I think she did him a favour; Jenny was always a bit too fast for old Don. On one occasion she even made a pass at me.

'I can imagine,' was all he said.

I rather doubted that. Don was never all that imaginative. I sometimes think he and the others would never have managed to become writers at all if not for me. And too late I'd realized that was the real thing I'd taken away from them when I closed the *atelier*; it wasn't the money they missed most, it was the delusion that any of them could hack it as proper writers. It's one thing to take away a man's livelihood; but it's something else – something terrible – to take away his dreams.

'At least say that you believe me, old sport.'

His cornflower-blue eyes narrowed; he tried a smile, then thought better of it, as if remembering that my wife was dead after all.

'It's not me you have to convince, John. It's the police. Frankly, I really don't give a damn if you killed her or not. I mean, it hardly matters between you and me. But if you're suggesting that this Lev character killed your wife and framed you in revenge for shagging his girlfriend, I just don't buy it. And for fuck's sake, when will you learn not to shit on your own doorstep? Why fuck a girl who lives in your own building? It's bloody madness. What on earth possessed you to do something so utterly crazy? Didn't I always say that something like this would happen? That you would always be getting into scrapes so long as you believed that you did things to girls instead of with them? You were crazy to get involved with this woman.'

'You have to be a bit crazy to fall in love with anyone, don't you think?'

But Don wasn't really listening. 'No, the idea that Lev killed Orla simply because you were shagging some bimbo he doesn't sound as though he cared two kopecks for makes no sense to me at all. It's a serious crime for a pretty trivial motive, if you don't mind me saying so. Not all Ivans are as crazy or as lethal as the ones Jack Boardman meets in your novels.'

Don shook his head and drank some wine. He was wearing his usual uniform: beige chinos, a plain white shirt, and a blue blazer. His brown brogue shoes were beginning to seem rather more venerable than sensible and the watch on his wrist looked like a knock-off. But he looked pretty fit, as always; every year he did a triathlon in the Cornish town where he had a small holiday home; I looked it up online one year after he'd told me he'd finished near the back of the field and was surprised to discover he'd actually come third. That said something important about old Don. There was more to him than met the eye. It was easy to underestimate him.

'Mind if I smoke?' he said.

'Go ahead.'

Don took out a silver cigarette case – he was the only person I knew who used one; he said it meant he could ration his day's smoking – and lit one with a silver Dunhill I'd given him for his fortieth birthday; I was touched to see he was still using it. He puffed, licked his lips and continued speaking:

'And forgive me, John, but it's really not like he could have killed Orla without Colette's help, is it? Think about it for a moment. Lev would have to have pinched your key while you were shagging her, nipped upstairs, shot Orla and the dogs, come back downstairs, returned your key without you noticing, and hidden somewhere until you'd gone home. And she helps him to do all this because what – she's afraid of him? If any of that was true she could have told you and then dialled 112. It's John Houston's basic rule to writing a thriller, number one; the whole house of cards falls down if you can't answer a simple question: why didn't X or Y call the police? And here's another thing: are you seriously suggesting that the first thing Lev does after killing Orla is open a bottle of Russian champagne? That doesn't strike me as very likely either. It doesn't matter who you kill, champagne – cheap or otherwise – is not and never has been a post-homicidal drink. You drink a scotch or a brandy, or maybe even vodka to calm your nerves but you don't crack open a bottle of bubbles.'

I nodded. 'Yes, you're right, Don. None of it makes any sense when you think about it.'

'Oh, I didn't say it didn't make any sense. I just don't think it makes the sort of sense you think it does. I believe it's quite possible that the champagne bottle was a message, for you. That maybe Colette meant you to see the bottle and to put two and two together and make *pyat*. A Russian code. A message from Otto Leipzig. Tell Max that our Russian friend is back in town.'

'You mean, she meant me to think that Lev had returned to Monaco and was now on the scene with malice aforethought.'

'Exactly. She would have known the effect that seeing something Russian like that bottle would have on you. Because it was her who gave you the legend about Lev in the first place – his connections to the mafia, the fact that he was a violent man, an oligarch with an attitude. And just to underline that she leaves an empty packet of Russian cigarettes in the wastepaper bin and a recent copy of *The Moscow Times*.'

'But Colette couldn't have killed Orla. Could she?'

Don shrugged and hurried some tobacco smoke down into his lungs. He wasn't a heavy smoker so much as an enthusiastic one. He enjoyed smoking in the same way that I enjoy a plate of perfectly *baveuse* scrambled eggs.

'I don't know. You're assuming Orla and the dogs were shot while you were shagging Colette. But she knew your habits and Orla's too. Isn't it possible that she might have carried out the shooting while you were working in your study? You said yourself that it's a large apartment. My own recollection of being in the Tour Odéon is that the walls and doors are rather thick. I also seem to recall the research you carried out for one of your early books – *The Lethal Companion*, was it? An experiment with a Walther nine-mill. You fired a whole clip of blanks from the Walther in the study of your old house in London while your ex-wife was serving Sunday lunch in the dining room upstairs; nobody heard a thing because nobody ever really expects to hear gunshots. And remember what happened in Truman Capote's *In Cold Blood*. The hired hand didn't hear the twelve-gauge that killed the Clutter family even though he lived fairly close by.'

'Yes, that's true,' I said. 'I remember that. There are lots of things you can mistake a gunshot for. A car backfiring; a balloon bursting; a door being slammed. And now I come to think of it, I always had a mid-morning nap on the day after I'd shagged Colette. Forty winks at eleven.'

'Would she have known that, do you think?'

I nodded. 'For sure. She used to make a joke about it. Jesus. She made a lot of jokes about my nap. At the time I thought they were affectionate but now I'm not so sure.'

'You're right not to be sure. Even if Colette didn't pull the trigger it's entirely conceivable she's in this up to the neck of her womb. She could have had an accomplice who carried out the murder while you and she were on the job. It doesn't have to be Lev who murdered Orla. In fact, I'm sure it wasn't. She could have had a younger boyfriend who put her up to it.'

'But why?'

'She needed money, of course. You said yourself she was little better than a squatter in that apartment. What was going to happen to her when the service charge wasn't paid at the end of the year? The building management would have kicked her out on her shell-like. And then what would have happened to her? No, wait, you were going to buy her an apartment in Beausoleil. Jesus that's generous of you, John. *Not.* From Monaco to Beausoleil – that's a hell of a change in lifestyles. An eighteen-million-euro apartment swapped for something costing less than a tenth of that, I'll bet. Fuck off. She knew you were loaded. I'll bet she wanted a lot more than you were planning to give her.'

'And she was going to get it by killing my wife? That makes no sense at all.'

'Sure it does, if you're stuck in the frame for it. Think about it, John. This could be blackmail. After all, she's your alibi. It could be that she's planning to contact you and tell the Monty cops you spent the night with her just as soon as she's negotiated a pay-off. In fact she might already have tried to do so. But perhaps she didn't anticipate that you would have turned off your phone to stop the cops from tracking you. No, that would seriously interfere with her plans.'

Don stubbed out his cigarette in a big glass ashtray and leaned forward on the sofa, as if warming to his theme. Most of the time he was a strait-laced, poker-up-the-arse sort of bugger, but I had the strong impression from his rather animated demeanour that he was taking some pleasure in pointing out my naïveté. Like I really was the complete cunt he'd called me earlier on. Naturally I'd considered Colette's involvement – indeed, I'd been planning to suggest that he helped me track down her family in Marseille – but I felt rather chastened by Don's persuasive analysis and all right, yes, *a bit of* a cunt for not seeing what now seemed obvious. Plots were supposed to be my department, not his.

'But look here, if I turn the fucking phone on to find out if she's called or sent a text then the cops will get a fix on my electronic exhaust and I'll be arrested, won't I?'

'Have you tried calling her again?'

'Of course. Several times. But on Mechanic's landline. There's no chance of anyone ever tracing that. He has a scrambler on all his telephone lines – here, and at the office in Geneva.'

'Did you leave her a message?'

'No, I didn't like to. Just in case I dropped her in the oomska.'

'In which case she could be hiding out somewhere, until she's negotiated a deal with you for her cooperation. Maybe in Marseille like you said.' He shrugged. 'It's a nice scheme, if it's true. After all, just how much money would you be prepared to pay to have her stand up in a Monaco courtroom and tell the jury that she spent the night with you? Not just a couple of hours but the whole shagging night. A million euros? Five? I mean what's money versus the next twenty years in your very own *salon privé*?'

'Jesus Christ, the little bitch. After all I've fucking given her – cash, a nice watch, a new laptop, some expensive ear-rings from Pomellato – and this is how she repays me.'

'But to be quite frank with you, the shooting of the dogs is what puzzles me the most,' said Don. 'In a Silver Blaze sort of way.'

'Silver Blaze? I don't think I understand.'

'Sherlock Holmes? The curious incident of the dog in the night time?'

'Oh, yes,' I said, although I still didn't know what Don was driving at.

'Think about it, John. What was the possible motive for shooting the dogs? If the shooting occurred while you were shagging Colette then her accomplice – supposing that she had one – would surely have known that Orla had taken a sleeping pill, in which case he would hardly have shot the dogs because he was worried the sound of their barking would awaken *her*.'

'Good point.'

'But if the shooting occurred at around eleven in the morning, while you were taking a nap in your study, is it likely that the murderer would have risked waking *you* by firing four shots instead of one? Shooting the dogs makes a lot more sense if you were in bed with Orla at the time – between the hours of 2 and 7.30 a.m. – in which case it seems more than probable that the murderer must have used a sound suppressor. I assume you don't own one for any of your weapons.'

'No, of course not. And the weapon I found on the floor wasn't fitted with a sound suppressor.'

'Did you check to see if it had been fired?'

'What, you mean did I sniff the barrel? Come on, Don, that stuff is for amateurs. There was a spent cartridge on the floor of the bedroom and four more on the floor of Orla's dressing room. The brass certainly looked like it had come from the Walther. I mean it was the right size. Besides, I checked the Walther's magazine. There were five bullets missing.'

'Perhaps. But the murderer would hardly have risked bringing along a sound suppressor in the hope that it might fit one of your guns. Ergo if a suppressor was used then almost certainly the gun used to kill Orla was not your own. So, perhaps the murderer merely wanted you to think your gun was the murder weapon. Now you see why I was thinking about the curious incident of the dogs in the night time. I think if we could figure out why they were killed then we'd be a lot closer to working out exactly what happened.'

'I'm glad you think so, old sport. Jesus Christ, Don. You're doing my fucking head in.'

'I'm not trying to confuse you, John. I'm just trying to think through all of the possible permutations. That's fair, isn't it? After all, before advertising, before the army, I did train to be a lawyer.'

Don took off his blazer and tossed it down on the sofa. It was a blazer I recognized. The label said Huntsman of Savile Row but I was certain Don had been wearing that jacket for at least twenty years. The buttons were brass, regimental ones. He had been out of the army for even longer but he always managed to make his clothes look like military attire. He smoothed his hair; once a very English shade of blonde, it was now streaked with grey, but there was something – a firm set to his jaw, a clipped way of speaking, his wiry frame, a lean ascetic way about him – that made me think he could easily have taken command of a brigade of guardsmen. Don refilled his glass from the bottle, sniffed the bouquet for a moment and then swallowed a generous mouthful.

'Sorry, Don. I know you're only trying to help.'

'Look, I'm not saying that this is what happened, John. I'm just saying that it could have. Painting a picture for you. But it might not be like that at all. For all I know the girl is completely innocent and worships the fucking ground you walk on. And perhaps there's a simple explanation for Colette's protracted absence. Then again she might be dead after all. Although now we can at least be sure that her body is not on your boat – the police have already searched that.'

I got up and went to the window again, trying to get my head around the idea of Colette's duplicity. I was also obliged to concede Don's argument: the idea that Lev might have killed Orla was ridiculous. It was a rare occasion in which

I'd been the victim rather than the beneficiary of my own imagination. Perhaps I'd been too hasty in fleeing from Monaco after all.

'I was going to ask you to help me try to find Colette,' I said. 'But maybe I should just hand myself in after all and take my chances with a trial. Hire that French lawyer, Olivier Metzner – the one who defended Dominique de Villepin when he was accused of a conspiracy to defame Nicolas Sarkozy. He's supposed to be the best defence attorney in France.'

'I think that would be a mistake,' said Don. 'I really can't see that handing yourself in now is going to be any better for you than in a few days' time. Besides, I happen to know that Metzner won't take your case.'

'Oh? Why's that?'

'Because he was found dead in the waters around his private island in Brittany, just a year or two ago.' Don shrugged. 'No, if you decide to hand yourself in, John, you'll have to think of someone else. The best firm in France is probably Baker and McKenzie. And a female attorney would play better with a jury than a man. Like the one Phil Spector had when he was tried for the murder of Lana Clarkson. What was her name? Linda Kenney Baden.'

'Sure. I'll find a fright wig-maker now, shall I? Besides, she can't have been that good. The guy's in jail, isn't he?'

'Yes, however *the first time* he went to trial she got him off. Which has to count as some kind of fucking miracle, right? I mean he was much guiltier-looking than you are. Spector's chauffeur saw him with the murder weapon *in his hand*. Anyway, all that's beside the point. Until you've told me about some of the other strange things you mentioned that have happened to you here in Switzerland, I'm not sure I can properly judge your best course of action.'

'What's that?'

'When you were starting your story earlier on you said that some strange things had happened to you here in Switzerland that you thought might be connected with Orla's death.' Don shrugged. 'Look, if this was a military operation we'd certainly want to gather all the intelligence before we sent a patrol into the Bogside to snatch a couple of Paddies, so to speak.'

'There were a couple of things that seemed unusual, yes.'

I pressed my head against the windowpane. To my surprise the glass wasn't cold and didn't shift under the weight of my skull; it was clearly thicker than I had expected. Might it also have been bulletproof? I tapped it with my finger experimentally. The glass sounded reassuringly dull and solid; and bulletproof. I don't know why I was at all surprised. I certainly wouldn't have put having bullet-proof glass windows beyond someone as security-conscious as Bob Mechanic. When I'd first arrived at the house in Collonge-Bellerive I'd had a good nose about the place. As well as a rather ornate safe in Mechanic's study that was formerly the property of the Emperor Louis Napoleon the Third but was just for show, there was also a more substantial Stockinger in the wine cellar that would have been the envy of many a small bank. The house itself had more security cameras than the London Underground. But most impressive of all was a panic room with a tunnel that led to a secret boat house – you probably wouldn't have found it from the garden – where a high-performance RIB with a powerful Yamaha 350 outboard could have provided an immediate getaway onto Lake Geneva, although from what I wasn't quite sure. Whoever or whatever it was that Bob had prepared for – the Swiss financial authorities, Interpol, the mob – it was clear he wasn't about to risk being arrested or worse for lack of careful preparations for a swift exit, and I almost wished that I'd been able to ask for his advice instead of Don's.

'Such as?' said Don. 'Give me an example.'

'Such as . . .' I sighed wearily. 'I can't think. I thought things would seem a little clearer when you got here, Don. But they're not. Not so far. Look, I need to take a break. And I need some fresh air. You go and change and in a short while I'll order in. And we can resume this conversation after dinner. Okay?'

'Sure, John. Whatever you say.'

CHAPTER 3

I went for a walk across the sloping lawn, past the sleeping swans and down to the neat shores of the shimmering blue lake where there was a short dog-leg of a stone jetty built at right angles to the house so that Mechanic's moneyed, pampered visitors might arrive by boat even more discreetly than via the lightly travelled road. A soft, Alpine breath of cool wind stirred the tops of the recently pruned trees and somewhere in the distance I could hear the clamour of some local children playing. As if inspired by that very un-Swiss, carefree sound I walked to the end of the jetty and down the polished stone steps to the water's edge, where I took off my shoes and socks and paddled in the lake, and sat there in a solitary vigil, brooding on the charmed life I had once known and might never know again. I was bound to be convicted, I could see that. How could I hope to escape? And I wanted the whole thing to come to an end. What was the point of going on? I knew how this story was going to finish, so why see it through to the credits?

To give up and to disappear for ever, was that so bad? I had escaped from Monaco and the Monty police. Could I also now escape from myself?

It was odd how my feet had almost vanished in the seductive water, as if, with a little more effort, the rest of me might also disappear underneath the icy surface. The water – from the Rhône glacier, and a thousand feet deep at the lake's deepest point – was remarkably cold for a summer's day and seemed to slowly anaesthetize my feet, so much so that I wondered how painless and easy it would be just to step off the jetty and into the lake, to swim away from the house and then perhaps, when I could swim no more, to let myself sink into the black depths to meet a quiet, cold and very private death. Something had broken in my soul – assuming I had a soul – and I wanted to fall asleep for a very long time. To escape from everything. To avoid that final, judicial moment when all that I had was taken away from me. The relentless, inductive truths offered by Don Irvine in the brisk, no-nonsense manner of a serving army officer were more than I could stand. Talking to him I felt like I was back before the headmaster at school. It was only too easy to see that this was how it was going to be from now on: cunts who were friends offering me advice, cunts who were policemen asking me questions, cunts who were lawyers and journalists and God knows who else commenting on my inadequacies as a husband, as a man, as a human being, and as a writer. It really didn't bear thinking of.

Then, a neighbour's peacock called for help and it was as if my own soul had cried out in agony – or so I thought, but for only a moment; the next second I began to laugh at my own stupid conceit and loathsome self-pity; for wasn't this the very kind of hackneyed, pathetic-fallacy bullshit scene I had banned from ever being written in my own novels?

'You're not Gerald Crich,' I murmured. 'Nor are you Oliver fucking Reed. And this is not *Women in Love*.'

I collected my shoes and socks, stood up, and walked back to the house to order sushi and tell Don the next chapter of my story.

CHAPTER 4

After dinner from Uchitomi, and another bottle of Mechanic's best white Burgundy, I ushered Don into the living room and hauled a fur throw over myself.

'This place is never as warm as it ought to be,' I said. 'Even in summer. And smoke if you want. Bob likes a good cigar so I doubt he'll object to you having another fag. Matter of fact I think I'll have one myself. I really think a smoke might help.'

'Sure,' said Don, and offered me one from his cigarette case.

I lit us both with a silver table lighter the size of Aladdin's magic lamp and puffed happily for several seconds.

'Orla would kill me if she saw me now,' I said. 'Smoking, I mean. She was a real fascist where smoking was concerned.'

'Don't I know it,' said Don. 'But that was probably just one of many reasons why she didn't like me.'

I didn't contradict him. Don Irvine's army service in Northern Ireland during the Troubles had made him *persona non grata* as far as Orla and her family were concerned; my old advertising colleague had done his best to avoid confrontation – he was the least confrontational person I'd ever met – but that was never easy with Irish nationalists, especially when they'd had a drop of the hard stuff. Frankly there wasn't one of Orla's murderous clan I wouldn't cheerfully have punched on the nose.

We smoked in silence for another moment before Don glanced around and shivered. 'Christ, I don't know how you can stand it here. On your own. Rattling around in a house as big as this. And I thought Cornwall was fucking quiet.'

'You've still got your place down in Fowey? Mandalay, isn't it?'

'Manderley. The same as in *Rebecca*. And actually it's in Polruan, which is on the other side of the estuary from Fowey.'

I nodded, but really not giving a shit about the difference. Cornwall was just Cornwall to me: a care-in-the-community, backward, *Go-Between* sort of place – all right, that was Norfolk, but you get the picture – full of red-faced, cider-drinking, deliberate people. With my parents, I'd often visited Cornwall on holiday as a boy but I had no interest in ever visiting the county again. It wasn't just the past that was a foreign country, it was Cornwall, too, where they were so independently-minded and did things so differently from anywhere else in England that it might as well have been fucking Hungary. Don being Don was suited to living there, I thought. Me, I'd have hated it.

'It was a couple of weeks after terminating the *atelier* that I fetched up here,' I said, beginning the next chapter of my story 'You can imagine how that went. Telling Hereward and Bat that I was calling time on our heroic little enterprise. They were fit to be tied. Bat told me I'd ruined his life and destroyed the company. Which was nonsense, of course. People wind up successful rock bands all the time. The Beatles. Pink Floyd. Guns N' Roses. The Smiths. Bowie pulled the rug on the Spiders while they were on tour, at the peak of their success. This wasn't any different from that.

'Anyway, I came back to Monaco, collected some clothes and some papers, and my laptop, of course, and drove up here the very next day to start work writing the book. By myself. Not that Orla wanted to come. She's always hated Switzerland and the Swiss. Which is why we had a ski chalet in Courchevel 1850 instead of Gstaad or St Moritz. Colette Laurent did want to come with me, however. But if she had I'd never have got any writing done. Plus she'd have been bored. That's the thing about writing people just don't understand. It's about making yourself so bored that there's nothing else to do *except* to write. You can't do it when there are any distractions. At least that's how it is for me. Colette would have been itching to go shopping in Geneva every day and that would have been distracting. So, I was determined to come and do it by myself – write, I mean – in the way I'd done when I first got started. On retreat. Like a monk. Without so much as a choirboy's arse to divert my mind. Actually, I was really looking forward to it. I had a hollow craving for loneliness and self-sufficiency. I'd been here before of course, when I was writing the plot of *The Geneva Convention*. Mechanic had listened and he made a few suggestions and he was full of admiration for what I'd come up with. He made a few suggestions but he left me with the clear impression that he thought that the new kind of hedge fund I described to him might actually have worked. I mean he got the idea right away. Bob is nothing if not quick. In fact he's quite devious and a natural plotter. Anyway, it's a stand-alone thriller and you know the story. Of course you do. At one stage you thought you were going to write this book yourself.'

'Actually,' said Don, 'it's been a while since I read the seventy-page outline, John.'

'Ninety-five,' I said. 'That outline was ninety-five. I expanded it quite a lot after you read it. I was going to make this one a bit more of a doorstop than some of the others. You know: airport-sized. Like Wilbur Smith when Wilbur Smith used to write the books himself.'

'In which case perhaps it would be useful if you refreshed my memory. About the plot. It might be relevant. I do remember that it's rather complicated. And a bit technical. But skip the algebra if you would. There's no need to include the algorithm. I only just passed O-level maths.'

'Oh, the algorithm is gone, old sport. No, I decided that was just too much for my readers to cope with. An equation in a thriller is about as welcome as a skid mark on a wedding dress. I learned that with *Ten Soldiers Wisely Led* when I put in all that stuff about how modern cryptographic software – and in particular the Hermetic Algorithm – is now regarded as a munition by the US government and subject to arms-trafficking export controls. You look on the Amazon reviews and that's the bit they always complain about: not knowing what the fuck an algorithm is.'

'I'm not sure I know myself.'

'Doesn't matter.' I took another of Don's cigarettes and lit it. 'So, to come back to the story of *The Geneva Convention*, Charles Colson is a hedgie who lives and works here in Geneva. He's an alpha type: an orphan, and near-genius – mildly Asperger's, probably. His fund is called the Geneva Convention and it's one of the most successful in the world, with forty billion dollars' worth of assets under management. In spite of the name there's nothing particularly benign or humanitarian about Colson's Geneva Convention. It's simply a large group of very wealthy people who share a common interest, which is to become even wealthier. Don't they always?

'Now, as you might expect, Charles is a ruthless investor

and a bastard with several Geneva Convention subsidiary companies that lend money to some of the worst people in the world: dictators to start up joint-venture oil and mining companies, that kind of thing. He does business in North Korea, Equatorial Guinea, Zimbabwe, Paraguay, El Salvador and nearly all of the Stan countries. If you were looking for a model of the detestable capitalist you couldn't do better than Charles Colson, which is why in the book the *Guardian* newspaper names him on their own version of the ST Rich List as the one of the top ten hate figures of the liberal left.

'But Colson's Geneva Convention is about to get even richer, after Colson acquires a company called Galatea Genomics run by two geneticists – Daniel Weinreich and William Williams. Weinreich, who deeply disapproves of Colson, disagrees with the board of Galatea and leaves the company. Then, with Williams's help Colson constructs an innovative and highly confidential computer program that's soon the basis of what the two men believe is nothing less than a new social science they now dub *Phenomics*.

'Now, the big drawback of conventional economics of course is that it doesn't act like a science at all, because human activity makes economic agents much too unpredictable. Put another way, Adam Smith was simply wrong because he believed that it was possible to make laws and rules for economies of the kind that Sir Isaac Newton had established for the universe. It just isn't. Economies don't behave like that with physical laws – with forces that act in a mechanistic and predictable way. If you've ever talked to three economists you'll know what I'm talking about; they'll all hold very different opinions about everything from unemployment to the price of eggs, which proves that economics really isn't a science at all but a form of clairvoyance.

'In my story Colson and Williams believe Phenomics remedies the defects of economics because the essence of the analysis is not the observation of rational laws that make economies easy to predict, but of the kind of human irrationality that makes economies impossible to predict – at least by the application of conventional economic principles. Crudely speaking, Phenomics purports to provide its inventors with a data-based method of making economics work as a true science. Without wanting to get too technical the Phenomics program is able to analyse companies as organisms with genetic codes that can be mapped, just like the DNA of a sheep or a human being. It's Phenomics that provides Colson with an ensemble of observable characteristics displayed by a company; the program looks for company phenotypes, which is to say it attempts to identify the composite of a company's observable characteristics and traits such as its morphology, heredity, development, business cycles, investment behaviour, products and personnel. Using an enormous amount of accumulated data the Phenomics program looks to predict those company phenotypes and the effect the company will have on the outside world – and, by extension, its chances of becoming a successful corporate organism.

'Of course, this is fiction, and the beauty of this fiction is that since there are very few people who understand how hedge funds and their products actually work, this is the kind of story where the reader really does have to suspend disbelief. Especially my fucking readers. But after all that is the novelist's job. Making people believe the unbelievable is no trick, it's work. Damn right. So that when the Phenomics program makes the Geneva Convention the most successful hedge fund in the world, it doesn't strain credibility too much.

'Colson and Williams create a special tracking fund of 100 million dollars using Phenomics as the basis of its investment philosophy, and within just six months this shows a forty per cent return. Colson and Williams now proceed to sell Phenomics as the basis of modern investment to GC's investors. And all goes smooth. Until it doesn't. And of course this is where one says bollocks to Christopher Booker's idea that there are seven basic plots. Frankly that just looked like rehashed Quiller-Couch, anyway. There is only one fucking plot in the whole of literature: in fiction nothing is what it ever seems to be. I mean everything comes down to that, right?

'And this is where everything in the story gets turned upside down. In the book we've always known that Charles Colson has a skeleton in his closet; but now we discover that this is almost literally true. Charles once had an identical twin brother called James. As boys James and Charles had concluded that they could never live normal lives just as long as they were both alive. They did too many weird things to make people feel comfortable around them and decided that one of them should disappear. So they tossed for it and James lost; soon after that he vanished. Charles was even suspected of killing his twin. But a body was never found.

'Now, using international criminal DNA databases, one of the people who worked for Galatea Genomics – Daniel Weinreich – has found out about the twin and traced him to Casuarina Prison in Western Australia, where he's serving a sentence for a bank robbery he didn't commit; he was framed by his brother Charles, to make sure he kept out of the way for ever. Weinreich and a bunch of people get together and spring James Colson, to take his brother's place. They also kidnap Charles, take him to a motel in the outback, and then inform the police, who naturally assume they've caught his brother, James, who returns to Geneva with his liberators, where he assumes the place of his brother Charles; he starts to use the Geneva Convention money for good. Charles, locked up in Casuarina – which is the hardest prison in Oz – protests that he's someone else; but of course, the prison officers assume he's gone nuts and ignore him.

'Of course, it's the same story as *The Man in the Iron Mask*, in which the King's musketeer, Aramis, substitutes the twin brother of Louis XIV, Philippe, for the king. This was always one of my favourite stories when I was a boy. And it's long seemed to me that the founders and owners of modern hedge funds are the modern equivalent of the aristocracy and royalty that once ruled Europe.'

Don nodded. 'It's a good story. Your novel, I mean. I always liked it.'

'I wish to God I'd let you write it, Don, like you wanted to. Seems like everything's gone wrong since I started this fucking project. The minute I got here, shit started to happen.'

'Such as.'

'The very first night in Geneva. It had turned a little chilly and so I borrowed Mechanic's coat to walk into the village and have dinner at the Café des Marronniers. Just before I went out I caught sight of myself in the mirror in the hall and thought how like Bob Mechanic I looked wearing his overcoat. And that might have been funny except that between here and there someone fucking mugged me. They didn't get much. Just a couple of hundred euros. Fortunately, I wasn't wearing this watch.'

I lifted my wrist to show Don the Hublot Caviar watch I was wearing. With a case made entirely of black diamonds which glistened in the light it did indeed look like a little pot of Beluga caviar.

'Did you report it to the police?' asked Don.

'No. It was my own fault. It's dark and very quiet around here at night and everyone in Geneva knows that people in Collonge-Bellerive have more money than sense. At the time I thought nothing about it. But then I got a call from Mechanic on his satellite phone warning me to be careful; he'd received an email from Keith Levin, the head of security at the Mechanism – that's the name of Bob's fund – advising him of the existence of a boiler-room company called Mechanism New Investment Capital that was offering discounted securities to UK investors. In other words these were scammers who were pretending to work for Bob Mechanic's hedge fund. The head of security at the Mechanism thought it possible that the scammers were taking advantage of Bob being in the Antarctic to operate the boiler-room scam. When Bob told me this I rang Keith and told him about the mugging and Keith said it was quite possible that these two events were connected; and that I shouldn't go anywhere on foot while I remained in Geneva. After that I didn't go out for several days. I had my head down and wrote the best part of ten thousand words. Good stuff, too. Not just dialogue – which is easier to write, of course – but narrative. It was the best writing I'd done since I first started. After a while I felt I'd earned myself a break. I'd thought about taking a trip down to Lyon to see Philip French. He was always inviting me to his house in Tourrettes-sur-Loup. Anyway I didn't go. Besides, it was my wedding anniversary and I had to go back to Monaco.'

'It's probably good you didn't go and see Phil,' said Don. 'The last time we spoke he was very bitter about what had happened. He told me he would never have bought that house in Tourrettes if he'd had any idea that you were going to close the *atelier*. I think you'd have got a poor reception.'

'Yes, I know. That's what Munns said in the *Daily Mail*. How much did it cost, anyway?'

'The house? About a million euros. Which was pretty much all he had saved. I haven't seen the place myself. But I understand he's had to take a local job, as a waiter, to help with the maintenance.'

'That's too bad. But what about the redundo money I gave him?'

'Most of that went to pay the builders for the swimming pool he'd had built.'

'That's too bad,' I said. 'I'm sorry.'

Don shrugged. 'It's not your fault, John. No one asked him to buy that house. Or install a pool. Frankly, a freelance writer should know better than to buy anything like that. What did Robert Benchley say? The freelance writer is a man who is paid per piece or per word or perhaps.' He shrugged. 'Is that it, then? The sum total of the strange things that have happened to you while you were in Geneva?'

'You think I'm paranoid, don't you?'

'I can see why you think there might be a connection. If someone was trying to scam the Mechanism fund then it might be useful to have Bob Mechanic – or even someone who looked like Bob Mechanic – out of the way. One way or the other.'

'But actually that's just the half of it,' I said.

Don smiled. 'I don't suppose there's a shaggy dog around here, is there?'

'Not so much as a bloody campfire,' I admitted. 'This is all on the level, unfortunately.'

'And what you're going to tell me now – this also happened in Geneva? Is that right?'

I nodded. 'There's a club in the Calvin district of Geneva called the Baroque, popular with Middle Eastern types. I don't know why I went there. Yes, I do: Mechanic said that there were always plenty of beautiful girls in the Baroque. They have these girls called ambassadors, although for what, I'm not quite sure, since they never seem to want to negotiate anything, if you know what I mean. There was one girl called Dominique who worked there who had a body from your best wet dream: not so much an hourglass figure as a twenty-four-hourglass figure. Anyway, it must have been about two or three in the morning and there was a guy on the next table who seemed to have gathered quite a crowd of girls around him, which was hardly surprising given the size of the bottle of champagne on his table. He seemed to be Indian or Pakistani – I wasn't quite sure, at the time – and he was accompanied by a couple of bodyguards. Anyway, he was having a good time – a better time than me – and I was just about to call it a night when he put his feet up on the table and I noticed his shoes. The heels of his white loafers were encrusted with diamonds, Don. And if that wasn't bad enough he seemed to be looking not at the girls, who were all very pretty, but straight at me.'

I paused, assuming that Don would realize why this was significant. He didn't.

'Don't you remember? The character of the arms dealer, Dr Shakil Malik Sharif, in *Ten Soldiers Wisely Led*? He had diamond-encrusted crocodile leather shoes, too. They were especially made for him by Amedeo Testoni at three million dollars a pair.'

Don shrugged. 'So?'

'Maybe I never told you, old sport, but Dr Shakil Malik Sharif was based on a real guy – someone who people told me about when I was doing my research in Islamabad. You know how it is with me and research. I like to make things as accurate as possible. I become my characters. If my characters are involved in a dodgy arms deal then you can bet your bottom dollar that I was involved in one myself. And I was. With this guy's representative in Islamabad. Now this was a man I never met myself but whose reputation went before him like a troop of Janissaries. His name was Dr Haji Ahmad Wali Khan, and he's a major player in international arms trading. The South Asian press call him King Khan while the Western media refer to him rather less affectionately as Doctor Death. He owns a company called gunCO which deals in everything from gold-plated handguns to ballistic missiles. I remember when the book was published my Pakistani source – a useful fellow named Shehzad who works at the Serena Hotel in Islamabad – rang me up and said that Khan had recognized the portrait of himself in my book and was none too pleased by it. Or by me. And there he was now, sitting at the next fucking table, and giving me the bad eye.'

'How do you know it was the same guy? Perhaps Aldo were having a sale of diamond-encrusted shoes that week.'

'I asked Mehdi, the club manager, and he confirmed that it was Dr Khan and that he was celebrating a major deal with the new government of a flea-bitten, fucked-up somewhere. Not that Khan only deals with governments. It's said he deals with everyone from Somali pirates to Al-Qaeda Al-Shabaab. That man would sell a gun to Anders Breivik.'

'Please tell me you got up and left,' said Don.

'Of course I did. The only thing is that to book a table at the Baroque you have to give your name and address and mobile number, right? So it's quite possible that if Khan did recognize me, he could easily have persuaded the club to give him my address here in Collonge-Bellerive.' I shrugged. 'Which must have been what happened, because a couple of days later I went out to the wheely bin on the other side of the front gate here to put a bag of trash in it and inside, lying on top of the other trash bags, was a copy of my book.'

'You mean, *Ten Soldiers Wisely Led*?'

'Yes.'

'Ah. A critic.'

'Critics I can handle. Even that cunt of a woman who used to work for VVL who described me in *The Times* as a cancer on the face of publishing. What was her name?'

'Helen Channing-Smith.'

'Exactly. No, people like that I can take. That's the game we're in, after all. Someone doesn't like your stuff, that's fine. You read critics, it can make you strong. And my book in the garbage, I can deal with that shit, too. Only someone had given my book the Richard Ford treatment. There was a bullet through it.'

'I remember,' said Don. 'That was Alice Hoffman's book, wasn't it? After she gave him a lousy review for *The Sportswriter* in the *New York Times*, he shot her book with a 38 and sent it to her in the mail.'

'It doesn't matter whose fucking book it was,' I said. 'It's the bullet hole that matters. And by the way this was bigger than a 38. This was a rifle bullet. Maybe even a Barratt 50-calibre. It went straight through the first letter "O" in my fucking surname. Like a scene from *Winchester '73*.'

'And you think that might have been this arms dealer fellow with the diamond-encrusted loafers – Dr Haji Khan?'

'Don't you?'

Don shrugged. 'Maybe. Yes, probably I do. Then again, shooting a book – your book – it's not like he shot you, is it? It seems to me that if he wanted you dead, he'd have had some hit man shoot you when you went to the gate to put out the trash. Instead of which he told you – rather stylishly, it seems to me – exactly what he thought of you and your book. I mean, hasn't every writer wanted to do something like that to a critic? I know I have. I always rather admired Richard Ford for doing that.'

'I thought maybe you'd be a little more sympathetic. You did write *Ten Soldiers Wisely Led*, in case you'd forgotten.'

'Yes, but your name is on the cover.'

'Thanks, old sport.'

'You know, it has to be said, John, yours is an interesting life. In a Chinese curse sort of way. Much more interesting than mine. If it wasn't for you the most interesting thing in my life would be my daily newspaper.'

'To that extent, you're a typical writer, Don. Being boring is an essential prerequisite to getting any writing done. Whenever I meet creative writing classes I always tell them the same thing: don't think that to be a writer you have to be like Ernest Hemingway. If you want to write a book don't do anything, don't go anywhere, don't talk to anyone, don't tell anyone you're writing a book, just stay home with a pencil and paper. Thanks to my interesting life I may never write again.'

'I can't see that happening.'

'I'm glad you think so.'

'At the very least you should get a fascinating memoir out of this story. Like Jeffrey Archer. He managed to publish three volumes of his prison diaries. They were the funniest books I've read in a long time. Made me laugh, anyway.'

'Oh, I see.'

'My God, John, you've given me a lot to think about. Russian gangsters. Pakistani arms dealers. Boiler-room scammers. Wannabe *femmes fatales*. Friends in the French DGSE. To say nothing about all of the people Mike Munns identified as your enemies when he wrote that piece of poison for the *Daily Mail*. Disgruntled publishers and agents and ghost-writers. Irish republicans.' He frowned. 'Do tell me if there's anyone I've left out, John.'

'Yes, I see what you mean, old sport.'

'I need to think about everything you've told me, John. I can't imagine more plot for plot's sake outside of a novel by Agatha Christie. You've got a whole Orient Express of likely suspects there. I'll have to spend some time with my own little grey cells before I can suggest your best course of action. Until then I'd like a cognac. Ever since I sat down I've been wondering what some of that bottle of old Hine on the drinks tray tastes like.'

I got up and fetched a bottle of cognac and a couple of brandy glasses off the silver tray by the mantelpiece.

'You've a good eye, Don. This is a 1928. And I'm going to have to leave Mechanic several hundred euros when I leave because I've already had a couple of glasses of it myself.'

'From what you've told me it sounds like you needed it. So. Let's talk about this again over a decent breakfast. And I don't mean a bowl of fucking Alpen.'

We both laughed; for a while we'd both worked on the Weetabix advertising account writing commercials for muesli.

'It's not the tastiest hamster food for nothing,' I said, bowdlerizing the slogan we'd helped to devise.

Don laughed some more. 'That's the thing I never get

about *Mad Men*,' he said. 'They take all that shit so seriously. We never did. Did we?'

'Never.' Still shaking my head, I handed Don a glass of Mechanic's best cognac and then toasted him. 'Thanks, Don. You know, I really appreciate you coming here. I don't know what I'd have done without you.'

'You already thanked me.'

'So, I'm thanking you again. If I ever manage to clear my name you won't find me ungrateful.'

'All right, but promise me one thing: if you do decide to write a prison diary, don't for Christ's sake say that I used to work on the Weetabix account. Come to think of it, don't mention any of the advertising accounts I used to work on. That kind of shit can follow you around. Remember Salman Rushdie and his naughty but nice cream cakes and his fucking Aero chocolate bars? Of course you do. Everyone does. The poor bastard. Forget the Ayatollah Khomeini and his bloody fatwa, *that*'s the sort of stuff that can really harm us. Crummy advertising slogans stay with a writer like a dose of herpes.'

CHAPTER 5

In the morning I worked hard in the gym as though trying to punish myself for my earlier crimes and misdemeanours; after all, there were so many; Colette, me going on the lam, me going to the Baroque – what was I thinking of, looking for girls at my age? – me alienating the very people who ought to have been most on my side: Hereward, Bat, Munns, Stakenborg, French – I was spoiled for choice; and severe punishment was what I most deserved. A heart attack after forty minutes on the running machine might have solved all of my problems. And, after I'd checked into a posh Swiss hospital and kept the police and an extradition to Monaco nicely at bay for several more weeks without compromising my own legal defence, I could have engaged a team of private detectives to find Colette Laurent, not to mention some forensic evidence that might even clear me.

Heart attacks were on my mind again when I surveyed the breakfast that Don had cooked in Mechanic's dauntingly minimalist kitchen: eggs, bacon, sausage, mushrooms, tomatoes, fried bread, buttered toast and plenty of hot coffee.

'Jesus, Don, you weren't kidding about breakfast, were you? I haven't seen so much cholesterol since I left fucking Yorkshire. Do you eat like this in Putney?'

'Sometimes. At weekends. When I'm on my own. Which

is pretty much all the time, these days. Women don't go in much for the full English any more. Not the ones I know. Not that I know very many. Since Jenny walked out that whole area of my life seems to have been closed down pretty comprehensively.'

'Perhaps I should have married you instead of Orla. She couldn't abide the smell of fried food, even when it was what I most wanted in the world. You'd think – her being a Mick – that she'd have liked the smell of a good fry-up.'

'That and the stink of a fucking petrol bomb,' observed Don.

'You old racist, you.' I grinned. 'But entirely bloody accurate, of course. She used to cheer when she saw nationalists on the telly throwing Molotov cocktails at the security forces. Can you believe it?'

'Yes,' said Don. 'I can.'

I sat down in front of a generously heaped plate and inhaled happily.

'Jenny was just the same – about a fry-up,' said Don. 'She said the smell of frying bacon and eggs stuck to her hair and to her clothes.' He shrugged. 'Not that she had many good clothes. But that's one of the reasons she left me, I think. To get herself a better wardrobe.' He sat down and started to eat his own breakfast. 'Anyway, we ought to have a good meal inside us, when we get on the road.'

'Are we going somewhere? Geneva's not exactly a tourist city, old sport. The Ron Jeremy memorial fountain just shoots its load all day and the Rolex factory isn't much fun unless you're going to buy a watch. I'd buy you one myself – as a thank you – but I figure the money you brought from London is going to have to last me an unfeasibly long time.'

'Yes. We are going somewhere.'

'Where? Do tell? But it will have to be somewhere better than this. I'm feeling just a bit like *Le Grand Meaulnes* now that the prospect of leaving this particular lost domain has been mooted.'

'When we first talked, John, you mentioned trying to find Colette Laurent.'

'Yes. I did.'

'I think that's a good idea. I think it's best to be pro-active in this situation. Everything else I can think of involves doing nothing very much except sit here on our arses. You said this girl had family in Marseille, so that's where I think we should go and search for her.'

'Okay, Popeye, but the trouble is Marseille is a city of one and a half million frogs and I don't have an address.'

'That's a pity.'

'But I do know where I could find one. In her apartment.'

'At the Tour Odéon? In Monaco?'

'Of course, she might actually be there. Just not answering her phone. Wouldn't that be interesting? But her iPad was lying on the kitchen worktop when I left. That's got her diary on it. And an address book. We might also look for her Apple Mac. The one I bought her. If it's not there we'll know for sure she's not dead.'

'How's that?'

'She took it everywhere. It had her whole life on it.'

Don was nodding, thoughtfully. 'It's risky.'

I shrugged. 'Yes, but it's almost the last place the Monty cops will expect to find me. And after all I still have a key for her apartment. Not to mention a pass for the Odéon's underground garage. If we wait until this afternoon before we leave, we can arrive in Monaco when it's dark. There's less chance of me being recognized then.'

Don shook his head. 'There's no question of you going in the building. That would be crazy. You can wait in that wop restaurant around the corner you mentioned before.'

'Il Giardino.'

'I'll go in your building, fetch her iPad from the apartment, and her laptop if it's there. Then we can get the hell out of Monaco. Spend the night in a hotel in Beausoleil, finding an address on Colette's iPad. And head to Marseille in the morning.'

'Using what? Your hired car?'

'Of course. Why not?'

'We can do better than that, I think. And as a matter of fact, I rather think we should.'

After breakfast I led Don to Mechanic's garage, opened the side door, and switched on the light to reveal a whole series of *Top Gear*: Ferraris, Astons, Lamborghinis, Bentleys, there was even a Bugatti Veyron. 'Bob Mechanic's an even bigger petrol-head than I am.'

'Magnificent,' said Don. 'It's like Jay Leno's garage. Christ, there must be at least a million quid's worth of cars in here.'

'Two million. You're forgetting the Veyron.'

'He won't mind if you borrow one of these?'

'Mechanic is worth at least a couple of billion dollars. He once left a new Porsche Turbo in the car park at Nice airport and forgot all about it. By the time he remembered he'd run up a bill for almost seven thousand quid. So, no, he won't mind at all. Anyway, I have the best part of two million quid invested in his Mechanism fund. If we wreck his fucking car he can deduct the cost from my year-end dividend. Besides, if we're going to drive into the Tour Odéon, we'd better do it in a car that looks like it belongs there. And that also means we'd better stay somewhere other than

Beausoleil. Èze, probably. I hear Le Château Chèvre d'Or is pretty good. I should think they're used to smart cars there. And in Marseille, we'd better stay at Villa Massalia; they have an excellent business centre. It actually works, unlike most business centres in France. It's just the spot to do a bit of research, if necessary.'

'Makes sense.'

'We'll drop your car off at the airport and take the A1 out of Geneva.' I watched as Don ran his hand along the wing of the Bugatti, open-mouthed with envy. 'But not this one, obviously. Even in Monaco this will attract a lot of attention. I think we'd better borrow the Bentley. They're ten a penny on the Côte d'Azur. And unlike the Ferrari the boot offers room for more than just a tart's clean panties.'

'One thing before we go, John.'

Don was looking grave again. Resentful, even. To be honest, it was his natural default expression, but on this occasion he had also deployed an accusatory forefinger, like I was a soldier in his platoon who was now on report.

'What's that, old sport?'

'I want your word of honour. Yesterday, when I said that I didn't care if you killed your wife or not, it didn't, but I think it matters now, if I'm going to help you like this, don't you? I think it matters a lot. So I want your word that you didn't murder Orla. If it doesn't sound too much like a cliché I want to be sure that I'm not helping a murderer to escape justice instead of enabling an innocent man to find it. That you're not making a complete fucking chump out of me, *old sport*.'

In my head I tapped a little tuning fork, stood it on the rough surface of my conscience and listened to the clear, true sound of the times when I had been less than honest with poor Don Irvine. He was quite right of course – what he'd said about me the previous day. On occasion I *had* behaved badly toward him just the way Harry Lime had behaved to Holly Martins in *The Third Man*: not like a real friend at all; there had been several times when I had treated Don like a chump. He'd chosen exactly the right word. Times when I'd regarded him as someone to use and exploit and ultimately betray. I don't know how else you can describe paying him so very, very little to do something for which I was being paid so much. I felt bad about that now – especially now that I desperately needed him to help me. For a moment I considered a confession and an apology for all those years when I'd taken ruthless advantage of him, but the words melted in my mouth, and when I swallowed, they were gone, like a single Malteser. Of course, he was right, it did sound exactly like a cliché, but I could see that he really did need to know I was innocent and so I did my best to look honest, and steadfast. This is certainly not *my* natural default expression. I'm much too much of a cynic to look anything but world-weary and contemptuous – even Orla had accused me of smirking at her in front of the altar on our wedding day, as if I'd been amused at her dress; she was wrong, of course; she'd looked wonderful; all the same I'd had the devil of a job to assure her that this was just the way my face was – but for a brief moment I think I did manage to appear to be as honourable and trustworthy as Don seemed to require me to be. I thought that was best.

'Of course,' I said. 'I understand perfectly. And I certainly don't blame you for asking, old sport. I rather think I would, if I was in your shoes. So, to answer your question: no, I did not murder Orla. On my honour, Don. On a stack of bibles, Don. I'm innocent. I'm guilty of a lot of things – you know that more than anyone. But a murderer I'm not.'

'All right.' He smiled. 'That's all I need to know.'

And then we shook hands on it, just to make sure the bond of trust was firmly there between us.

DON IRVINE'S STORY

PART TWO

CHAPTER 1

It was almost three o'clock on Saturday afternoon when after returning the hire car at Cointrin Airport, we got into the leather-lined passenger cabin of the blue Bentley and, with me at the wheel, started for Monaco. We were soon driving in France. John talked incessantly, excited and happy to be doing something, but his voice was full of anxiety about exactly what we would find in Colette's apartment and whether or not we could pull off our plan without being arrested and put in prison. With the hood down and wearing Mechanic's expensive sunglasses – there were several pairs of Persols in the glovebox – we must have looked the very picture of two rich, carefree Swiss friends driving down to the Côte d'Azur or perhaps the Italian Riviera, for the weekend. This was an image we were content to hide behind. A clear and innocent conscience fears nothing, and that's usually the best way to behave when you have committed or are committing a serious crime. And I know what I'm talking about. After all, I'd been feigning innocence for weeks.

Ever since I murdered Orla.

You might have thought that play-acting has its limits – that it's only too easy to become weary of constant dissimulation and to get caught out in a lie; but this simply isn't true. Once you commit to an egregious deception – really commit to it – there's very little that can break your resolve. The fact is that it's exactly as Joseph Goebbels said: if you tell a big enough lie and keep repeating it people will eventually come to believe it. The evidence of this was right beside me, in the passenger seat, in the person of John Houston, who was much too naïve ever to have asked me the same question I had asked him. He really did believe I was his protector – the solid, dependable type with a stiff upper lip you see in so many old British films, when in truth I was more of the James Steerforth sort who turns out to have run off with Little Emily. Or put a bullet in her head. And it struck me as ironic, but the man with all the imagination didn't seem to have considered the possibility that the true author of his misfortunes was not some Pakistani arms dealer, some local hedge-fund scammer, or even a Russian mafioso; it was me, his oldest friend. But there's a coda to what Goebbels said: the fact is if you tell a big enough lie and keep repeating it, after a while you start to believe that lie yourself. In fact that's almost necessary if you stand any chance of getting away with it. Honestly, there were plenty of times since my arrival in Geneva when I'd managed to convince myself of the possibility that John might actually have murdered his wife just so that I could look him straight in the eye and treat him exactly like the prime suspect the Monty police thought he was. But if you're going to kill your friend's wife and make out that he did it, you have to become a good dissembler: the need to smile and smile and be a villain is found on page one of the Sparknotes on how to play the scoundrel.

'The quickest route back to Monaco,' explained John, 'is via Italy and the A10. We go right through the Alps. Should take us about five hours. It's one of my favourite drives in the world. Especially in summer. It's interesting how most of

these ski resorts – Chamonix, Courmayeur, Aosta – look completely different at this time of year. And there's a very good
hotel-restaurant in Vercelli we should stop at – the Cinzia –
where they serve twenty different kinds of risotto. You'll love
it, Don. Years ago, I had this thing with an Italian publisher
who worked for Mondadori – the publishing house in Milan
– and that's where we used to meet. Lovely she was; I think
her name was Domitilla.'

'Not exactly the sort of name you forget,' I said.

'Monaco is only sixteen kilometres from Italy and there
have been a lot of Italians in my life, one way or another.
Sometimes I wonder how I didn't marry one. I used to go
there on the *Lady Schadenfreude* a lot. To Portofino, Santa
Margherita.'

'You've led a charmed life,' I said. 'And no mistake.'

'Until now. If I go down for this it will be my only compensation, old sport. That at least I'll have lived life to the full,
you know?'

'Anyone can say that, surely.'

'Yes, but I can say it and mean it. Like Roy Batty in *Blade
Runner*. "I've seen things you people wouldn't believe."'

'"Attack ships on fire off the shoulder of Orion".' I laughed.
'But if I'm "you people" that must make you a replicant. One
thing's for sure: you're just as fucking ruthless as Roy Batty.'

'Me? Ruthless? That's not how I see myself at all.'

'John, the last time the two of us were in a car on a French
autoroute like this you told me you were closing down the
atelier for no other reason than you wanted to leave Monaco
and watch bloody Chelsea play football. You knew the
damage and disarray that this would cause to those around
you: all the people who would lose their jobs because of your
decision, the effect it would have on VVL's share-price, the

friendships it was probably going to cost you; but you still went ahead and did it. I seem to recall you even rather relished the damage it might do to poor old Hereward. To say nothing of the damage you must have known it was going to do to me. Now that's what I call fucking ruthless.'

'But I compensated everyone, didn't I? In what way was I ruthless?'

I paused for a moment as I steered the big Bentley into a slower lane. A big truck crept along the near side and the driver's mate stared down at me. From the look on his dark, unshaven face I was just some rich bastard in a Bentley with no idea of what it was like to really work for a living. His arm was hanging out of the open window and I was close enough to see the pink, bubble-gum patch of eczema on his elbow and the cigarette in his thick, yellowish fingers, but he might as well have been on another planet; there was nothing about what I had to say to John that would have made sense to him and I knew instinctively that he dearly wanted to treat the Bentley like a large, expensive ashtray and tip his fag ash onto our heads. In his position it's what I would have done. It's what anyone would do.

'The trouble with you, John, is that you think that the answer to every problem is to throw money at it.'

'That's bollocks.'

'Really? Has it occurred to you that your relationship with Travis might have been better if you'd just spent more time with the boy and less money trying to please him?'

'Let's leave my son out of this, okay, old sport? This has got nothing to do with Travis. And exactly what damage did my closing down the *atelier* do to you? You had the best compensation package of anyone, Don.'

'John. You weren't listening. For me and the people like

me – Peter Stakenborg and Philip French – the money was irrelevant. Surely it must have occurred to you that none of us has ever been able to make a decent living from his writing on our own? When you closed the *atelier* you extinguished the flame that we called an artistic life. You took away all our dreams that we could be something other than nine-to-five men who were part of the awful rat-race called full-time employment – that we too were writers and part of the exclusive club that's London literary society. It's one thing to take away a man's livelihood, John; it's something else to shatter his dreams. And there's no amount of money can compensate for something as terrible as that.'

'You're exaggerating, surely.'

'Am I? You turned my life upside down, like a bloody egg-timer. One minute I'm going one way and then the next minute I'm going the other. It's been months now but I still don't know where I really am. I've been trying to write a novel of my own but I've got a dreadful feeling I've become hopelessly addicted to John Houston's crack-pipe. That I can't do it without the stuff you supply. I might end up having to look for a job myself – like Philip French. I might even have to go back to advertising. At my age. Can you imagine how awful that would be? Me writing copy at sixty. Christ, I'd probably have to work on retail, or below the line.'

'So what do you want me to do about it now? Jesus, Don, you know how to pick your fucking moments.'

'I want what any friend would want in a situation like this. Some recognition on your part that you behaved like an arsehole. And an apology. After twenty years of loyal service I think I'm entitled to one.'

Of course this wasn't what I wanted – not in the least – but, before I put into motion the real point of our journey, it was fun making him jump through yet another hoop like this. Pure sadism on my part.

'Okay,' he said impatiently. 'Yes, you're right. I was wrong. I behaved badly. And I apologize.' He paused for a moment. 'All right?'

I shrugged. 'It might be, but only if you said it like you mean it.'

Out of the corner of my eye I saw John shrink into the diamond-quilted leather seat and let out a sigh. Then he said:

'For fuck's sake, Don, you've no idea of the pressure I was under. The pressure to deliver the goods. Again and again. I needed to get out from underneath it all. You remember that scene in *A Clockwork Orange* when Alex and his droogs tip the bookcase on top of poor old Patrick Magee? That's what it felt like. A man buried under a whole library of fucking books. But, you're right. I didn't ever take into account your feelings, Don; and the feelings of everyone else. And I'm truly sorry about that. It was thoughtless and inconsiderate of me. And I should like to offer you my sincere apology. Okay?'

I nodded. 'Thank you. Your apology is accepted.'

'Twenty years,' he said. 'I'd forgotten it was that long.'

We both lapsed into silence after that – or as much silence as can be encountered in an open-top sports car travelling at a hundred miles an hour on a French autoroute – and I let my mind drift for a while. You would be forgiven for imagining that I was racked with guilt about Orla's murder; but I wasn't. Not for a second. I had no regrets on that score. She'd had it coming for a long time and while it's true, I'd enjoyed killing her – rather more than I had expected to enjoy it – in truth Orla's death was only the means to an end. In my defence I should add that it has been a long time since I was obliged to pull the trigger on someone in cold blood – the last time was in Northern Ireland. That was on another Mick, of course, while I was on active service, and not exactly to the sound of trumpets, as what happened with the Int and Squint boys in County Fermanagh was murder pure and simple. I'm not ashamed of what happened there. But all the same if things work out the way I've planned then it's to be hoped I won't ever have to kill anyone again.

Several minutes passed before John glanced over at the Bentley's speedometer and said, 'Better keep to the speed limit, old sport. In case the local filth pull us over. I wouldn't like to answer a lot of awkward questions about who this car belongs to.'

'No, you wouldn't want that, would you?' I said, and lifting my foot off the gas pedal a little, I let our speed drop back to a more respectable eighty-five miles per hour.

'Thanks,' he said. 'That's always how wanted felons get nicked, you know. Committing some ordinary misdemeanour like that.'

I nodded.

'I mean, it's John Houston that Bob Mechanic thinks he's lent his cars to, not Charles Hanway. Not that Bob's around to answer any nosy-parker cop questions. But all the same. Best keep our noses clean, eh?'

'Sure, John, I can do that. As a matter of fact, I've been keeping my nose clean for years.'

CHAPTER 2

We stopped for an early dinner at the Hotel Cinzia, which was a nondescript modern building of red and yellow concrete set back from a deserted crossroads in Vercelli, and not at all what I'd been expecting; it looked about as charming as my local launderette. But after a delicate lemon and asparagus risotto every bit as good as John Houston had said it would be, we drove on, with him at the wheel, which allowed me a chance to doze for a while.

When I opened my eyes again, about an hour later, we were already on the Italian coast and driving west, away from Genoa toward Ventimiglia and France. The Bentley ate up the road with a voracious appetite that showed no sign of abating.

'Wish I could sleep like that,' said Don. 'In the car, I mean. I can manage it at home, in a chair, but never in a car. Especially with the hood down.' He shrugged. 'Not that anyone could sleep when Orla was driving. She was a terrible driver.'

'Me, I can sleep anywhere,' I said.

'You must have a clear conscience, old sport.'

I pretended to think about that for a moment. 'I suppose I have.'

'It was a joke,' said John.

'All the same, there's nothing much that I do feel bad about. Except perhaps Jenny. Yes, there is Jenny. Perhaps, if

I'd fought a little harder to keep her, I might still have her.'
I shrugged. 'But I don't blame her for leaving me. Not in the
least. No, I expect she needed a bit more excitement than I
was able to give her.'

'With a High Court judge?' John shook his head. 'Surely
not. He's seventy-something isn't he? Lord Cocklecarrot or
whatever his name is?'

'Yes. Seventy-three.'

'He doesn't sound very exciting. How old is Jenny? Fifty?'

'Fifty-one.'

'So what kind of excitement was it that you were thinking
of? I can see what's in it for him. She's a very good-looking
woman. But I can't see what's in it for her. Apart from the
thrill of being Lady Cocklecarrot.'

'I expect they talk. I was never one for talking very much.'

John laughed. 'So I'd noticed.'

'And I think they go to Fiesole a lot. Apparently Harold
Acton used to be a neighbour, when his lordship's parents
owned the place. I'm told it has a rather fine garden. Not to
mention a fantastic, E. M. Forster view of Florence. I think I
might easily have left someone like me for something like
that. Unlike the Reverend Eager, I've always rather liked that
particular view of Florence. Of course, I'd have Jenny back in
a heartbeat, you know. If that's what she wanted.'

'Have you even had another woman since she cleared off?'

'No.'

'Christ. What, not even a rental?'

'I'm not like you, John. I'm not led by my cock.'

'Oh, I'm not led by my cock. But I do think it's there to be
used, at least while I can. It's a short time we have on earth,
I think, and perhaps it's just as well that I've got a very big
cock.'

'Not that I think Jenny's coming back any time soon.'

I might have added that the real reason she wasn't coming back was that I scared her. I'd never told my wife exactly what I did when I was in the army but she knew that there was something I wasn't telling her. Something importantly horrible. Of course she did; wives always know when they're being lied to and sometimes they can even see the killer in your eyes. I'm certain mine could.

In July 1977, after Sandhurst, I'd joined the Queen's Own Highlanders, and I went with them to Belize and then on their second tour of Northern Ireland. We were there until 1980. 1979 was the worst year for British security personnel killed in the province. My own regimental CO, Lieutenant-Colonel David Blair, was one of them. On 27 August 1979 – the same day that the Duke of Edinburgh's uncle, Lord Louis Mountbatten, was assassinated by the Provos, along with the boatman and three members of his family, in County Sligo – Blair was killed in the Warrenpoint ambush. A British army convoy drove past a 500-pound bomb hidden by the road, killing six members of 2nd Battalion, the Parachute Regiment. Thirty minutes later, the Provos detonated a second bomb, at a nearby command point, killing twelve more soldiers – including my CO, Blair – who'd gone to assist the dead and injured. I was at the scene soon after the second explosion and it was a butcher's shop, with body parts all over the road, in the River Clanrye, and hanging from the trees. Only one of Colonel Blair's epaulettes remained to identify him, as his body had almost completely disappeared in the blast. I gave the epaulette to a brigadier from the 3rd Infantry, David Thorne, who took it with him when he briefed Prime Minister Margaret Thatcher, who apparently wept when she saw it.

I must say that Warrenpoint affected me very deeply, too. This was what motivated me to volunteer for military intelligence duties in NI when the QOH tour ended; being a Scot I was very good at doing an Irish accent. After an eight-week course with the SAS I returned to the province as part of the 14th Intelligence Company, who used to conduct undercover ops alongside loyalist paramilitaries. Which is an army way of saying we helped the UVF to murder members of the Provisional IRA. I did this until 1982, when I left the army and went into advertising, although at the time I'd wished I'd stayed on, as my regiment went to the Falklands soon after that; I remember them reaching the South Atlantic in July 1982 on the same day that John Houston and I had a meeting on the agency's toilet paper account – although by then hostilities were over, of course.

'You're well out of it,' said John. 'You did your best with Jenny, I'm sure. But sometimes women are just like the clients we used to meet when we were in advertising. They really don't know what the fuck they want. All they know is that it's not you.' He laughed. 'Hey, do you remember the time we did all those commercials for Brooke Bond Red Mountain coffee?'

'How could I forget? *Coffeez never been so full of beanz.*'

'That was a really crappy coffee. How many fucking scripts did you write for it?'

'Twenty-two. And they still wouldn't buy one.'

'I remember you brought a bloody starting pistol to the client meeting and you laid it on the boardroom table and told them that before the meeting was over they were going to buy your commercial. That was very funny.'

I smiled, remembering the incident, but I neglected to add that it hadn't been a starter's pistol at all but a real Smith &

Wesson 38 – the same weapon I'd used for my wet work in Northern Ireland. I doubt that everyone would have thought this quite so funny if they'd known the gun was loaded with live ammunition and had been used to off more than one Fenian bastard.

'But still, I learned something important from that whole process,' I said.

Taking the gun with me had been a test of whether or not I could live again in the normal world. Could I take criticism without using a gun? Fortunately for the Brooke Bond execs, it turned out that I could.

'Oh? What was that?'

'How not to take it personally when someone doesn't like your stuff. How to pick yourself up, dust yourself off, and start all over again.'

'I guess you must have done,' said John. 'I've never known anyone who is as even-tempered as you, old sport. The number of times you must have wanted to kill me.'

'It never entered my head to kill you,' I said. 'Lord, no. That would spoil everything. No, you're the goose that lays the golden eggs. And will do again, I'm sure of it.'

'Me, I'm hopeless at taking criticism,' admitted John. 'Christ, many's the time I've wanted to kill someone who criticized my work. Most writers do, I think. It's just that some of them are better than others at pretending they don't care about that sort of thing. You know, I sometimes think that writers are just people who might have become criminals except for the fact that they were lucky enough to learn how to read and write. Although in my case the *Guardian* thinks I am a criminal *because* I learned to read and write. My God, if my critics saw me raise fucking Lazarus from the dead they would say I'd only done it to help promote one of my books.'

'I think it's simpler than that. Being a writer is a kind of elegant sociopathy, that's all. I don't know how else you'd describe a person who doesn't care about other people very much, who thinks mainly of themselves, who has a complete disregard for rules, and who lies for a living. Some sociopaths become murderers, it's true; but probably just as many become writers.' I laughed. 'Hell, I know I did.'

After a few miles we changed seats again and we reached the tiny barnacle on the bottom of the hull of France that is Monaco. The sun was setting but John still wore his sunglasses and insisted on putting up the hood, since every single car entering Monaco – even a newish Bentley – is scanned by police CCTV to keep criminals out. High-summer tourists were in more obvious and plentiful supply. Most had come to rub their tattooed shoulders with big money, or so they fondly imagined, and the main square was full of people who were as pink as the Beaux Arts-style casino that occupied its pride of place, taking pictures of anyone loitering on the steps who looked remotely famous or of the several expensive cars that were busy arranging their own very shiny and exclusive Saturday night traffic jam. As always the lawn in front of the Café de Paris was so impeccably green and the fountain so perfectly wet and the surrounding palm trees so uniformly sized it looked as if the whole area had been sponsored by some Qatari irrigation company, or perhaps a Disney cartoon about a cute little talking oasis. It might have been, too, except that Santander and UBS had got there first, like Germans marking their territory on a beach with a strategically placed towel. The sea itself was only a few yards away but it might as well have been somewhere back in Switzerland. You couldn't see the water for white boats, and any sea breezes had been strictly forbidden by the principality out of deference to hairpieces and hemlines and the more-is-best flower-beds, while the only gull wings in evidence were the doors of outrageous candy-coloured Lamborghinis and top-end Mercedes-Benzes.

'The horror!' whispered John as we drove through the dusk. 'The horror!'

'Isn't it just awful?' I said, but in truth I only half agreed with him: parking my orange Lamborghini in Casino Square and taking some dolly bird shopping at Chopard while side-stepping the holidaying lumpenproletariat looked just fine to me. As Oscar once said: I'm a man of simple tastes; I usually find that the best is quite good enough.

We drove out of the square and past the Métropole Hotel where John had famously argued with Orla in Joël Robuchon's restaurant. He didn't mention it so neither did I.

'Christ, now that I'm back here I'm as nervous as a kitten,' said John. 'I couldn't feel more nervous if I'd actually murdered her.'

'You're doing fine.'

'Suppose someone recognizes me?'

'They won't. That beard really does make you look different. Like Orson Welles in *Macbeth*.'

'At least you didn't say *Chimes at Midnight*.'

'You'd best keep a hold of that sense of humour,' I told him. 'I've a feeling you're in for a nerve-racking wait while I'm in the tower.'

A little further on we drove slowly along the Boulevard d'Italie until we came to a mini-roundabout.

'You can let me out here and I'll walk,' said John. 'The Giardino is about a hundred metres ahead, just past the Lexus showroom. You can come and find me there when you're done. I'll be sitting outside awaiting your return. The Odéon is up the hill to the left.'

I steered the Bentley around the roundabout and pulled up in front of a Maserati showroom; outside the entrance to an apartment building immediately next door, a suntanned woman wearing a white dress and the gold reserves of a small country on her ears and not insubstantial chest was sitting on a bench and smoking a cigarette. A small white dog was sitting beside the six-inch heels of her scarlet-soled Louboutin shoes. She looked like a hooker; but then all of the women in Monte Carlo look like hookers, which is all right with me as that's the way I like my women to look. These days the only women in Monaco who don't look like hookers are the hookers.

John twisted around in his seat.

'Here.' He handed me his electronic parking fob that would open the door to the Odéon's garage, and another one for the door to Colette's apartment. 'You can take the lift straight up from the garage to the twenty-ninth floor. We need the iPad and, if you can find it, her Apple Mac. That should tell us everything we need to know. And don't forget the charger, in case the batteries have run down.'

He stepped out of the car and was about to close the door when he remembered something else.

'And give me a ring on Bob's mobile, if everything's all right.'

We'd found a number of old mobile telephones in Mechanic's desk drawer – so many they looked like burners – and had borrowed one for John to use on our journey.

'Define "all right",' I said.

'Ring me when you're in the flat, and again when you're on your way back.'

'Sure,' I said. 'If it will make you feel any better. But I can't see what the fuck could go wrong. After all, it's you the police are looking for, John, not me, and certainly not Colette. The cops don't even know she exists.'

I drove slowly up the hill in the direction of the tower and, in the rear-view mirror, watched John walk down the Boulevard d'Italie. At the top of the winding Avenue de L'Annonciade, surrounded with several high-rise apartment buildings, and in a small walled garden, was a tiny red stucco chapel. Whenever I saw this little chapel I wondered who went there and how it managed to survive in a country where worship was no longer a special act of acknowledgement of all that lies beyond us but the more everyday response its polyglot citizens made to the glorious reality of zero taxation.

On the opposite side of another mini-roundabout – home to a solitary tree – was the curving, grey glass entrance of the enormous Tour Odéon, a building so tall and featureless and ridiculously expensive it resembled nothing so much as the launching gantry for a Saturn V rocket. Floral tributes, photographs and soft toys for Orla Houston still lay on the ornamental shrubberies in front of the main door and even now were being inspected by her fans or those who were fascinated with premature death or just curious to see what all the fuss was about. I have to confess I was surprised by the reaction to Orla's death; surprised and more than a little horrified, too; that someone as ordinary as her could in death have generated such an outpouring of grief.

But I was more horrified to see the person of Chief Inspector Amalric coming out of the front door; he even glanced at the Bentley, and it was only the car's tinted windows that prevented him from having a clear sight of me. This was fortunate, as I would have found it hard to explain exactly what I was doing there. Were there other policemen still in the building – Sergeant Savigny, perhaps? Was it possible the police were still questioning the other occupants of the Odéon about what they had seen, or more likely – this was Monaco – not seen? Were there still scenes of crime officers searching John's apartment for minute and important clues as to who had killed her?

I almost kept on going round the mini-roundabout and back down the hill to the restaurant. Instead I held my nerve and drove into the Odéon's underground garage, where I parked the Bentley, closed my eyes and drew a deep breath before deciding what to do next. I tried to telephone John, to let him know what I was doing, but found that I couldn't get a signal. Not that this mattered much; it suited me nicely to keep him on edge. So I just sat there, listening to the hot, six-litre engine at rest; after almost 300 kilometres without a stop there were so many taps and ticks and knocks it sounded like a tiny silver mine.

Waiting awhile before venturing upstairs seemed the wisest course of action; I had no wish to meet Sergeant Savigny again, least of all in the Odéon lift. Of course, I could easily have driven away without doing anything because I knew exactly where Colette was at that particular moment – she was my accomplice, after all; but to have abandoned my mission to recover her iPad from the apartment would have left what happened next to chance, in which case John might easily have panicked and given himself up to the Monty police, and that was the last thing I wanted. So long as we seemed to have a definite plan about what to do next I had control of things, which, ultimately, was what this was all about.

To my surprise there was a copy of Merrychristmas Makeba's new novel, *Drowning in the Kalahari*, in the Bentley's glovebox underneath the car's manual. I started to read a chapter – either it was terrible stuff or I was too much on edge because it didn't make any sense. The Canongate blurb said it was African magic realism, but to me it was more mundane than realistic and had nothing up the sleeve, so that it was rather less magical than a three-card trick. I was puzzled as to why a man like Bob Mechanic should have had a Man Booker shortlisted novel by an African woman writer in his car until I saw that someone called Grace de Beer had written all of her contact details and some kisses, as well as an injunction that Bob should feel free to call her any time, in a neat copperplate hand on the flyleaf. In this, the age of the e-book, it's reassuring to know that the printed page still has its uses.

After about fifteen minutes I left the car and having checked the garage for police cars – there were none – I went to the lift and rode up to the twenty-ninth floor, where the lift chime quietly announced my arrival like a butler's cough into a corridor already hushed by an inch-thick Wilton and ostrich-leather walls. It's only on the streets of Monaco that money talks; in the principality's more expensive apartment buildings it always lowers its voice discreetly.

I walked to the door of Colette's apartment and pressed my ear to the kauri wood for a second before touching the keyless lock with the lacquered plastic fob, and then stepped inside with the speed of a tango-dancer. All was quiet as I stood in the tiny hallway and closed the door behind me. Apart from the sour smell of rotting garbage that lingered in the air, everything else was much as I remembered: the balcony sofa where we had sat and planned everything; the little dining room where she had cooked me more than one supper; the bed where I had fucked her several times. The fucking had helped to cement our pact, like Frank and Cora in *The Postman Always Rings Twice*, which is a pretty good book. Movie's pretty good, too; as a matter of fact, it's one of my favourites. When Frank fucks her it's like he's wrestling God's angel. '*I'm getting tired of what's right and wrong*,' says Cora. Amen to that, little sister.

I went into the kitchen and double-bagged the contents of the bin to drop into the chute when I left. I even cleaned up a bit and watered her pot plants, which was very considerate of me. At the same time I noted the iPad on the marble worktop where Colette had carelessly left it. But before collecting this and making my exit I opened the doors onto the balcony to let in some air; that was the good thing about the private apartments in Tour Odéon: it was so high above the streets of Monaco that cars and their exhaust fumes were hardly noticeable; even in summer the air was as cool and fresh as if you were standing at the top of a schooner's main mast listening to the whip and snap of a dozen sails. The air was the best thing about the Tour Odéon; that and the view, of course.

I glanced around the coastline amphitheatre of tall buildings that was Monaco and Beausoleil. It was hard to tell where the backdrop that was France ended and the tax-free principality began. The buildings of Beausoleil were no less ugly or featureless than those of Monaco, and the idea that property in one cost more than four times as much as in the other would have seemed laughable to anyone who had never heard of what the French called *l'impôt de solidarité sur la fortune.* Whenever I looked at this view – which some consider spectacular – I thought of my financial advisers back in London and the yearly reviews they used to produce with 3-D bar-graphs showing you how much your pension might be worth in fifteen years' time; or, in my case, how little. I wouldn't have been surprised to see nine- or ten-figure numbers hovering in the sky over the primary-coloured rectangular bar of each building, as if to indicate the collective net worth of its privileged, tax-free occupants.

Beyond the harbour and out to sea, things were rather more obviously picturesque; a slowly shifting constellation of brightly lit boats on the darkening blue surface of the sea looked like an inverse planetarium. Above these the moon was a red circle on the eastern horizon, although any iniquity or spilling of blood that this might have foretold was long past.

I glanced back through the window glass into the apartment and for a moment I caught sight of my reflected self, locked in animated conspiracy with Colette. A moment later we seemed possessed by each other and I drew her into my arms and kissed her before pushing my hand deep between her thighs. She dropped her head back on her shoulders and gave herself up to my impudent fingers before climbing on to my lap. I think at that point I might even have told her I loved her, the way you do sometimes when you're trying to persuade a nice girl to help you commit a murder.

CHAPTER 3

We met for the first time at the Columbus in Fontvieille Port, which is the best bar in Monaco. I'd flown in for a meeting with John, to discuss the first draft of *Dead Red* – after him closing the *atelier* it was to be our last meeting before Orla's murder – but as usual I was staying in Beausoleil, which meant opportunities for a drink or dinner were limited, and while the Columbus is expensive it's not as extortionate as a lot of other places in Monaco. Just as importantly, the Columbus serves the best fish and chips on the Côte d'Azur and is a welcome antidote to anything the Hôtel Capitole has to offer. In Beausoleil nightlife is a contradiction in terms, although sometimes there is a certain kind of entertainment to be had when the French police and tax authorities operate night-time spot checks on cars with Monaco licence plates passing through on their way to the clubs in Antibes and Cannes, looking for people who are cheating on their 182 days. You take your pleasures when and where you can.

It had been a long day and all I wanted was to eat a quiet meal and to read, but leaving the Capitole I'd mistakenly brought one of Houston's books instead of the one I'd been hoping to finish. Not one I'd written, but even so, I had no interest in reading it. So I found a copy of *Monaco-Matin* – the Monaco edition of the Nice morning newspaper – and settled down on the roof terrace, which enjoys a fine view of the Princess Grace Rose Garden, to try and improve my French, leaving Houston's latest book unread on the table, where it ended up catching Colette's eye. As did I.

There were one or two more women around the bar at the Columbus than was usual, but then it was early summer and the fishing fleet of hookers had arrived in port. Whatever naïve ideas John Houston may have entertained about Colette's profession it was obvious to me the first time I saw her that it could only have been the oldest one. Perhaps the Columbus was her first call on an evening that would have taken in Zelo's, Jimmy'z, the Buddha Bar, the Crystal Bar at the Hermitage, the Black Legend, the seventh-floor bar at the Fairmont Hotel, and, if things were desperate, the Novotel.

'Are you a fan of Houston's work?' she asked, speaking English.

'Yes, you could say that.' I stood up, politely.

'Which one is your favourite?'

'That's quite a hard question. You see, I help Houston write them. As a matter of fact I've been helping him to write them for twenty years. I'm a sort of ghost.'

'That's where I've seen you before,' she said. 'You were in the Odéon today, weren't you?'

'You're not supposed to see a ghost,' I said. 'That's rather the point. But yes, I was. Only I don't remember seeing you.'

'Colette Laurent.'

'Don Irvine. Pleased to meet you.'

She sat down and arranged her legs neatly under the table. They were certainly worth a little bit of care and attention; her short black business skirt revealed a pair of bare knees that were as shapely as they were tanned: with legs like that she could have modelled an elasticated bandage and made it look sexy.

'I got out of the elevator as you and John got in,' she said. 'Are you staying here?'

'No. Are you a neighbour of John's?'

'In a way, yes. For now. I'm just looking after the apartment for a friend, until I can find something of my own. I couldn't possibly afford something like that on my own.'

'Me neither. Like I said, I'm just the ghost. One of several. There's a whole haunted house of us.'

'Yes, he mentioned that. The studio. No, what is it he calls it?'

'The *atelier*.'

'Yes.'

'You're friends then, you and he?'

She shrugged. 'We see each other in the gymnasium almost every day. And now and again we have a drink afterward. Anywhere other than Monaco that would count as an acquaintance. But here, that's almost a close friend.'

She glanced over her shoulder as if mentioning a drink had prompted her to look for a waiter.

'I'm sorry,' I said. 'Would you like a drink?'

'Yes. Thank you. That's very kind of you. I would.'

I waved a waiter over and she ordered a Badoit, which impressed me, since Cristal seems to be the only drink that most women in Monaco have ever heard of.

'Your name is Don, you said?'

I nodded.

'How do you end up being a ghost?'

'First it's necessary that you should die,' I said. 'As a real writer, I mean.'

It was a joke that everyone in the *atelier* had made at one time or another, and while it contained an element of truth, I didn't really expect her to get it; her English was good but I didn't expect it was equal to my sarcasm. I certainly didn't expect her to smile and then to say what she said:

'Yes, that's what John says about all of you guys.'

'He does? Oh. I see.'

'No, I meant, how did you become a ghost for John?'

'Years ago, we both worked as copywriters for the same advertising agency. In London.' I shrugged. 'I've known John for a very long time indeed.'

'Since the very beginning, then.'

I nodded. 'Since the very beginning. As a matter of fact it was me who gave him the idea of setting up the *atelier*. For the mass production of bestselling novels.'

'Very successfully, too.'

'It was good while it lasted. At one stage we were producing five or six books a year. And selling millions. John is the Henry Ford of publishing.'

The waiter came back with our drinks, shot her and then me a look as if to say 'You lucky bastard', and then left us alone. He was right, of course. She was worth a look. Since Colette had sat down I hadn't once looked at the Princess Grace Rose Garden.

'It was an excellent arrangement, too. I was never much good at plots. And John never had much patience with nailing himself to a PC and knocking out 3,000 words a day. He always enjoyed the research much more than the writing.'

'Yes, but you speak about it as if this is over. Are you leaving John's *atelier*?'

'We all are. The *atelier* is over.'

'But why? Why, when you're doing so well?'

'He wants to go back to basics, apparently, and write something a bit more worthy. Something for posterity. Something
that will win him the Nobel Prize for Literature.'

'And do you think he could?'

'Win the Nobel Prize?' I laughed. 'No. I was joking.'

'You think he couldn't?'

'I know he couldn't. For one thing he's not Swedish. The
prize committee seems to award the Nobel to a dispropor-
tionate number of Swedes you've never heard of. And for
another – commercial literature makes money, not merit.
I've got more chance of winning the Euro Millions jackpot
than John Houston has of winning a Nobel Prize for Literature. Not that John is about to become poor any time soon.
Even if he does start paying lots of income tax.'

Colette shook her head. 'But I don't understand. There
isn't any income tax in Monaco.'

'No, but there is in England.'

'It can't be true.'

'I'm afraid it is. And I should know. I've been paying tax
there for more years than I care to remember.'

'No, I meant . . . are you saying that John's going back to
live in London?'

'Yes. At least, that's what he told me when he said he was
closing down the *atelier*. Misses the football apparently. And
the cricket. Not to mention the Garrick Club. He longs for
the greenness of his native land, he pines for the Gothic cot-
tages of Surrey; already in his imagination he catches trout
and enjoys all the activities of the English gentleman.'

By now I was quoting from the final scene of *Lawrence of
Arabia*; and doing rather a good job of it, too.

Colette smiled faintly. 'And he misses his children, I suppose.'

'Them rather less, I think. John has always had a difficult relationship with his kids.' I laughed. 'That's why he had a vasectomy. So he couldn't have any more. At least, that's what he told me.'

'You're not serious.'

'I've known John for more than twenty years. There's not much he doesn't tell me, eventually.'

'Oh,' said Colette, as if she'd felt a sharp pain or a heart palpitation. She closed her eyes and looked away for a moment. It was clear from her expression that John's plan to leave Monaco was a blow to her. Her Colgate smile had quite disappeared, her already noticeable chest had become quite agitated and her neck was turning as rosy as the blooms in the Princess Grace Garden. Without meaning to, I'd said too much. Without intending it, I'd also discovered that John and Colette Laurent had enjoyed or were still enjoying a relation-ship that went way beyond an innocent chat in the Odéon's gymnasium of a morning. Looking at her now, I couldn't find it in myself to blame him for this: the Archbishop of Canterbury would have jumped on the bones of a girl like that and people would have understood.

She stood up, abruptly, let out a deep breath and shook her head.

'*Alors*,' she said quietly.

'You're not leaving?' I said.

'Yes. I have to go. There's someone I have to meet.'

'Not John.'

'No, not John.'

I stood up and offered her my hand. 'It was nice to meet you.'

'Yes,' she said, distracted as she shook my hand. 'Yes, it was. Goodbye, Mr Irvine.'

She turned to walk away.

'Hey, don't forget your handbag.'

She came back and fetched it, nodding her thanks.

I sat down and watched her go. The waiter came back.

'That's a very nice-looking girl,' he observed with considerable understatement. 'A friend of yours?'

'No.'

'I've seen her here before.'

'She's gone now.'

'Better luck next time.'

'What do you think? Is she a working girl?'

He smiled. 'Monsieur, this is Monte Carlo. All of the girls who are here are working, one way or another. Even the ones who are married.' He paused. 'Perhaps the ones who are married, most of all.'

I picked up my so-called newspaper. I started reading an article about yet another lovely gala evening at the casino. It was for charity, of course, but as always the charity was a way of clearing the conscience, in order that the rich residents might be able to do what rich people like to do, which is to go somewhere smart and eye-wateringly expensive with lots of other rich people and still feel that by doing this they are also doing the world a favour. The celebrities attending the gala were the usual fashionable suspects, which is to say the here today, gone tomorrow crowd of pretty girls and even prettier boys. But after a moment I saw that Colette was back at my table. She was wearing a light pair of wire-framed glasses now and her eyes were red as if she'd been crying, but that didn't diminish her beauty – at least not in my eyes; indeed, the glasses and the tears made her seem like less of the pneumatic fantasy figure I'd imagined earlier – more real and therefore sexier.

'That was rude of me,' she said. 'Juvenile. You'd just ordered me a drink. And then I left.'

'Not at all. You were upset. About John going back to England. I could see it came as quite a shock to you.'

She took out her handkerchief, removed her glasses for a moment and dabbed her eyes.

'It wasn't only that,' she said, 'but yes, it was a little.' She sat down again. 'And now I think I should like a real drink. In fact I'm certain of it.'

We waved the waiter back and she ordered a large cognac.

'I'm sorry. I had no idea that you and he were such good friends.' I lifted my head to have another look at her. I suppose she was about thirty. Good-looking but perhaps not so very bright either. Her hair was gathered in a ponytail and shone like a newly groomed horse. She was tall and athletic and I wondered not what she was like in bed – I knew the answer to that just looking at her – but what I would be like in bed *with* her: restored, rejuvenated? There is no Viagra quite as powerful as a woman half your age. 'I spoke out of turn. Really, it's none of my business.'

The waiter returned with her cognac. She took it straight off his tray and drank half immediately before placing the glass on the table. Had she not been so unworthy of a famous writer like John I might almost have felt sorry for her.

'Oh, but it is, I think, Mr Irvine. Your business and mine. We've both been disappointed, haven't we? You as a writer; and me as a GFE.'

'A what?'

'Girlfriend experience. That's the abbreviation men use these days for someone like me who's effectively a girlfriend for money. In my defence I must say that I did think I was something more than that, but evidently I'm not.' She tried a

smile but it came out ill-shapen and bitter-looking. 'It seems
that I've been deluding myself and that after all I'm just a
talonneur, like all the rest.'

'You shouldn't talk about yourself like that.'

'I'm just being honest. I'm not an escort. No, I'm not that.
At the same time it would be dishonest of me to tell you that
I loved John for himself. But I do love him. It's true, the fact
that he is so very rich didn't discourage this feeling in me.
Indeed, it helped convince me that I have feelings for him.
Nevertheless I do have feelings for him. Even now that I find
he was planning to abandon me. I love him, yes. And that is
why this hurts so very, very much.'

'We don't know any of what I said for sure,' I said. 'For
all I know, what he told me was not the whole truth. In
fact I'm sure of it. The truth is never whole with John.
In fact I think he only gives you half or three-quarters of
the truth at any one time, depending who he's slicing
it for. But it's still the truth. Only not all of it, you see?
It's because he's a writer, I suppose. A lot of the time his
mind is dwelling in some fantasy place – he's thinking
about a book he's planning, not about anything real. Sometimes the two get blurred. John can tell more truth with a
lie than a lot of people can do by telling the truth. So, just
because he said that he wanted to move back to London
doesn't mean to say that he was actually going to do it – at
least, do it right away. He might just have told me that in
order to furnish me and the other guys with an excuse to
close down the *atelier*. To get rid of us with a minimum
of explanation. It might be several years before he moves
back to London.' I touched her knee and gave it what I
hoped would feel like an encouraging squeeze. In truth
I just wanted to feel what her skin was like: it was taut,

and slightly moist and when I brushed my nose with the same hand a second later, I could smell the scented body-butter on my fingers. Body butter: just the words made me want to spread her on a thick slice of bread and stuff it in my mouth. 'Honestly, you should ignore everything I said before. I have no idea what his plans in Monaco are.'

'You're very sweet.' She smiled. 'And I understand exactly what you say. John lives his life in compartments. You in one. His wife in another. Me in a third.' She shrugged. 'Although perhaps I flatter myself. I know there are others beside me, so perhaps I am in a lower number than three. Maybe six or seven, I don't know. But I haven't heard so much as a little slice of what you said before. Not even a sliver. The last conversation I had with him, on the subject of him and I, John told me that . . .' She stopped. 'Or perhaps you don't want to hear this. You are his friend, after all.'

I made a wry-looking face.

'I used to think that was true. But the truth is he's always regarded me not as a friend but as a long-term employee. As half of a professional relationship that has endured. Which isn't friendship at all – at least not for me – but a kind of indentured servitude. So I do want to hear it. Like you said before, perhaps we have more in common than we know.'

She looked around. 'Not here,' she said. 'I don't like this place.'

'No? I quite like it.'

'That's because you're a man. Everywhere seems different when you're a man. Monaco is a little like the Vatican in that it's set up for men, not women. But women go along with that. For all the obvious reasons.'

'All right.' I stood up and waved the waiter over. 'Where shall we go?'

'Your hotel?'

'The Capitole.'

She frowned. 'I don't know that one.'

I grinned. 'It's in Beausoleil.'

'But, I don't understand. You're working for John. Why doesn't he put you up somewhere nice? Somewhere in Monaco. Even this place would be better than Beausoleil.'

'I have to take care of my own expenses.'

'Let's go back to my apartment,' she said. 'In the Odéon.'

'Suppose we bump into John?'

'Do you really care if we do?' She shrugged. 'I know I certainly don't. Not any more. And if he's with her, what can he say?'

'Good point.'

I paid the waiter, who shot me the same 'lucky bastard' look he'd given me earlier, only this time it was alloyed with an element of amused respect, as if he'd underestimated me. And her perhaps: the glasses made her look much more formidable.

In the lift, Colette said, 'But why doesn't John let you stay in that enormous apartment? Or on his boat? Which is almost as big.'

'Like I said. It's a professional arrangement. Not a friendship. Besides his wife, Orla – we don't exactly get on, she and I. It's all she can do to say hello to me when I come through the door. Which isn't very often.'

'What do you think of her?'

'Beautiful. Irish. Bitch. To be fair, I only dislike her as much as she dislikes me. You see, I used to be a soldier. In Northern Ireland. And I think she holds me responsible for the death of every Irish man and woman since Oscar Wilde was sent to Reading Gaol.'

We left the hotel and walked east from Fontvieille Port to Larvotto and the Tour Odéon. Colette took my arm, not because she wanted to be close to me but because her high heels made it difficult to walk. It was a fine evening and we walked in companionable silence for a while, enjoying the Silvikrin sunset and the warm air. Out of the corner of my eye I took in the sexy toe-cleavage in her Louboutins, the Fabergé lacquer manicure, the sugar and gold Rolex, the tailoring details on her jacket sleeve; after more than a year of monastic celibacy it felt exciting to be out with a good-looking woman. As we made our way through the streets we got a few looks from other people who were out that evening, which is to say that Colette was the subject of more than a few appreciative glances. But with a much younger woman on my arm – even one wearing eyeglasses – I looked like any other old fool in Monaco: a slightly gnarled olive tree next to a rather luscious pink bougainvillea. If Toulouse-Lautrec had been alive today he might found much to inspire him in the principality.

We went into the Odéon and rode the lift up to Colette's floor without seeing either John or his wife.

Her apartment was small but nicely furnished, if you like that very French idea of modern living, with several armchairs that were more comfortable than they looked and, above a plain hardwood dining table, a sort of chandelier or light-fitting that resembled Jupiter and its four largest moons. On a coffee table in front of the window was a copy of a stick-thin Giacometti figure that had once inspired me – if that's the right word – to write a television commercial for a building society using a snatch of music from Lou Reed's *Transformer*: 'Take a walk on the safer side, with the Nationwide'. (I'm always haunted by some of the shit I wrote back then.) On another table – somewhat incongruously – there was small pot-plant holder, shaped like a baby donkey with a basket on its back. I guessed the Giacometti copy was the Russian's and the stupid donkey planter was hers.

Colette opened a bottle of white wine, which we didn't drink – at least not right away – because then she went into the bedroom and started to undress. I could hardly ignore that as it wasn't a big apartment and besides, she rather helpfully left the door open. Even I could recognize where this was going now and about that kind of thing I'm usually laughably slow; at least so I've been told – by John, of course. I joined her in the bedroom and swiftly removed her panties, just to be helpful. I stood back and looked at her for a moment, as if appraising a work of art, which wasn't so very far from the truth. She enjoyed being looked at, too, which hardly surprised me, all things considered. And I did consider them. Very carefully.

'There's probably a better way of getting even with Houston than this,' I said. 'Although right now I'm not at all inclined to try and think of one.'

'Shut up and fuck me,' was all she said.

John left for Geneva the next day; Orla went to visit her family of Fenian fuck-ups in Dublin. Neither of them knew that I had stayed on in Monaco, at the Odéon, fucking Colette and wondering how to broach with her a subject I'd been thinking about for a while – ever since that day on the autoroute when John had told me he was closing down the *atelier*. Exactly how *do* you suggest murder to someone? It certainly doesn't happen the way it does in Hitchcock – all that *Strangers on a Train* 'I can't believe you're really serious about this' crap. No, it was much more like *The Postman Always Rings Twice.*

As things turned out I hardly needed to bring up the subject of homicide at all. There were lots of small, bitter things that Colette said – 'I hope his brakes fail' and 'I wish she'd just go away and die', that kind of thing – which persuaded me she was on the same wicked wavelength as me.

And she was scared, of course; scared about what was going to happen to her if John went back to England.

'I'm thirty-four,' she said. 'Nearly thirty-five. That's old for a girl like me in Monte Carlo. That's right, I'm old. I used to look in the mirror and think it would last for ever. But it doesn't. It never does. At my age the choices are fewer for a girl than they are when you're ten years younger. No, really, Don, I'm not exaggerating. Why have a girl in her thirties when there are so many to be had in their twenties? Believe me, in Monaco, if you haven't met your *grand-père gâteau* who's prepared to take care of you by the time you hit thirty-five then you're probably lying about your age and spending a fortune in the beauty salon and doing escort work: fucking rich Arabs who use women like Kleenex down here. And sometimes worse than that. This is not going to happen to me. But I really thought I could rely on John. I trusted him, you know. He told me he loved me, and that he would look after me. I do not say that he promised to marry me, but he did say he would take care of me – to help me out with some of my expenses, to help me with my English and to find me an apartment of my own when I have to leave this place. If he leaves Monaco then I'll simply have to go back to Marseille and get a job somewhere. In a real estate office or a travel company. But shall I tell you what really upsets me?'

'Yes.'

'It was when you told me he'd had a vasectomy.'

'Oh, I see. You'd hoped that you and John might eventually have a child together.'

'No, not eventually,' said Colette. 'As soon as possible. I wanted to have a child and that he would help me to support it. That was the express condition of me becoming John's lover. At my age your biological clock starts ticking quite loudly. But the fact is I'd been on the pill so long I couldn't conceive. So I was having fertility treatment at a clinic here in Monaco. Paid for by John and from a doctor he knew personally. Of course that now looks like a complete waste of time, given that John is physically incapable of fathering any more children.'

Colette swallowed with difficulty and then started crying again. I let her weep for a while and then handed her my own handkerchief. She wiped her eyes while I fetched her a glass of water.

'I'm sorry,' I said.

'I said it looks like a complete waste of time,' she said. 'But it's more than that. What he's done to me is really criminal, I think.'

I nodded but I have to admit it sounded all too typical of John; and I certainly couldn't blame him for not wanting any more children at his age. I have to say I'd probably have done the same thing myself.

'Have you any idea of how painful IVF can be?' she asked. 'You have to inject hormones into the wall of your stomach. No doubt John had persuaded my doctor not to say anything about his own little problem. It was all a way of keeping me quiet. So now I feel destroyed. *Il m'a prise pour une belle connasse.*'

An hour or so later, when she was chopping cucumber for *salade niçoise*, I saw her holding the big Sabatier in a way which made me think that if John had been standing in front of her she would have pricked him with it, right through his cheating heart.

There's something about the whole idea of murder that just arrives in the atmosphere, unbidden, like a ghost, and starts to shadow everything you do. That's how it was with us. I knew what she was thinking because after a couple of years in County Fermanagh, when I was operating off-reservation with the Int and Squint boys, I'm a bit like a Geiger counter where that kind of thing is concerned. I only have to detect just a few homicidal particles in the air and I start to amplify that effect. Back then nobody ever said 'We're going to kill some left-footers tonight'; nobody had to; it happened as a sort of malign understanding between like-minded people, as if you were playing a rather lethal game of bridge. You might be in a pub talking about football with a few loyalist boys and then, an hour later, opening the boot of a taxi to reveal some trussed-up Mick you and them had snatched off the street; you would have questioned the bastard first, but no one there would have been in any doubt that someone – usually me, as it happened – was always going to trepan the fucker's head with a bullet. But there are ad campaigns I wrote that I regret more than any one of those killings. For a while, after Warrenpoint, I really learned how to hate.

But on my third morning with Colette we were eating breakfast on the balcony staring out to sea when she finally brought the subject a little more into the open.

'When you were in Ireland, Don, did you ever shoot anyone?'

I stood up silently and, leaning over the handrail, looked

up and then down to see if there was any chance we might be overheard.

Colette shook her head. 'I've never seen anyone on these balconies,' she said. 'Most of the people who live here don't actually live here, if you know what I mean.'

'Your Russian included.'

She shrugged. 'I don't know anything about what happened to him. I tried to ask around – you know, there are lots of Russian girls in Monaco. I even tried to watch the Russian news on TV. But I think he's dead. I really do. I was desperate. And then I met John. He seemed like the answer to my prayers.'

I sat down and lit a cigarette and waited for her to say something else, and when she didn't I started to steer the conversation back in the fatal direction I wanted.

'You were asking me if I'd ever shot someone. The answer is that I have.'

And then I told her the truth. In fact it all came out; oddly, she was the first person I'd ever spoken about it with. But unlike my wife Jenny, who'd certainly guessed about what I'd done, Colette didn't look shocked or revolted. In fact, she looked excited, even a little pleased, at what I'd told her.

'I thought as much,' she said. 'My grandfather was in the Foreign Legion. He was in Algiers, in the mid-1950s. And I think he did some bad things there, too. He had the same faraway look in his eyes that you do.'

'Of course,' I added, 'in Algeria and Ireland it was a damn sight easier to get away with that kind of thing. Back in the day, they were finding bodies all over the province. Not just the ones we did, but the ones they did, too. I lost several friends to IRA murder squads. It was like bloody Chicago. They'd hit one of ours and we'd hit one of theirs and so on.'

'And since then? Have you ever been tempted to kill anyone else?'

I smiled. 'When I worked at the ad agency there were several account executives I'd cheerfully have killed. One guy in particular. He hated my guts and enjoyed tearing a strip off me in front of everyone. More than once he tried to get me fired. He usually worked late, so one night I waited for him near his car in St James's Square, close by the office. I was going to kill him but, at the last minute, I changed my mind and gave him a good working over instead. Took his wallet to make it look like a mugging. He was lucky I only put him in hospital. It could so easily have been the morgue. I regretted that a little afterward. Not killing him, I mean.'

'So, you're not so squeamish about such things?'

'Me, squeamish? No. But don't get me wrong. I'm no psychopath. All of the people I've killed really needed killing.'

'Did you ever want to kill John?'

'Once or twice, maybe. But not seriously. To be sure, he can be an infuriating man. But now that you've suggested this—'

'You mistake me, Don. I haven't suggested anything of the kind.'

'Colette. Please. You've every right to feel upset. It's perfectly normal that you should want to hit back. If something like that happened to me I'd be as angry about it as you are. But I think we both know why you're asking these questions. And I understand that, too. What he did was quite unforgivable.'

She didn't contradict any of this. Instead she started to cry. So I put my arm around her and hugged her close, and kissed the back of her neck for a while until she stopped; and then I wiped her eyes with my handkerchief, and stroked her hair.

'You've been through a lot,' I said. 'I can tell. I've seen it before. And there's no need to feel ashamed about what's in your mind right now. Not a bit. However, I'm thinking that John's hardly the best person to kill in this particular situation. Not if it's your own future you're really concerned about.'

'He isn't?'

'No. It seems to me that John is our golden goose. And you don't kill your golden goose so long as he keeps on laying golden eggs. It's the giant you want to kill. The giant that owns the goose. The one who collects the eggs.'

Colette thought for a moment, but without any apparent result. It might have been the language barrier or maybe she was even less bright than I thought she was. She looked like I'd handed her a particular fiendish Sudoku puzzle.

'Who is it who benefits most from all those golden eggs that John lays, right now?' I asked her patiently.

'You mean Orla, don't you?'

We were on the same wavelength, at last.

'Precisely.'

'But she hasn't done anything, to either one of us.'

'You might think so. But now that I come to think about it, with Orla out of the way a lot of problems – yours and mine – are solved.'

'They are?'

'Oh yes. Besides, I'm quite sure it's her who's behind this move back to London. This would certainly explain why he hasn't told you about it. From one or two things he said to me at the time I think it was probably Orla's idea that they should move back to London, not his, and that he was simply too scared to tell you about it. In some ways she's a very intimidating woman. And John hates confrontation.'

I paused to allow that to sink in. You have to take a

conversation like ours very carefully. There's no sense in rushing things. It's like painting an enamel miniature. You need fine sable brushes and a very steady hand.

'Perhaps, if Orla was off the scene, things might be very different. In fact I'm quite sure of it. For one thing you might even marry John. And once you were married to him you could easily persuade him to restart the *atelier*. You could get your man and secure your own future and I could get my old job back. John could start earning the top money once more and you could avoid going back to work in a Marseille estate agent's.'

'You make it sound very simple. But I don't think it is that cut and dried, Don. He hasn't ever mentioned divorcing her to marry me. Not once. Unless he's mentioned something to you.'

I shook my head. 'Really, I had no idea about you and him until you mentioned it.'

'Then I don't know what we're talking about. And even if I did, I'm not sure I could marry anyone who has been as deceitful as John has been. I really do want children, you know. Like I told you already, I'm not getting any younger.'

'And you can have children. You see, I was rather hoping that if you married John then you and I might continue to see each other. That we could be lovers. You might have my child. In fact, you could even conceive right now. I certainly haven't had a vasectomy. And as far as I'm aware there's nothing wrong with my fertility either.'

I paused, waiting to see if she would actually be dumb enough to swallow that. Dumb or desperate. Either way, she was.

She brushed my cheek with her fingertips and smiled. 'I see.'

'It's perfectly understandable that you should want to have a future. To have a child. I understand all that. It's what any normal woman wants, isn't it? To be a mother?'

I looked at her as tenderly as I could manage whilst suppressing a flash of contempt for John who, when he could have had any woman, had chosen someone so unforgivably stupid.

After a while she said, 'I still don't quite see why you need to kill her.'

'Everything I described just now – about a new start for us both – that can quite easily happen, but only if we kill Orla in a way that makes you John's only alibi. If we kill her in a way that leaves him as the prime suspect and means you're his best chance – perhaps his only chance – of staying out of jail.'

By now Colette had told me all about John's habit of sneaking downstairs from his apartment several nights a week, to fuck her while Orla was asleep; and this had given me an idea which I now described to her in detail. She listened attentively and then nodded.

'That's so simple it really might work,' she said, nodding sagely. 'You're very clever, Don.'

I pretended to be flattered.

I nodded. 'From what you've told me, John won't even notice she's dead when he gets back into bed. He'll be so anxious not to wake her that he'll creep in – as you've described – and go straight to sleep. By the time he wakes up in the morning, you'll be miles away, with your family in Marseille, perhaps. Or better still in Paris. Yes, in Paris, I think. But wherever it is, you'll wait there for a while, until he's good and desperate of course, and ready to make a deal, and then you can call to offer him the lifeline. In fact you should offer to say that he was with you for almost the whole night when Orla died. It's important that you should lie on the record for him. That way he'll always be in your debt. You can leave it to me to suggest that you and he ought to get married in order to make sure that you never go back on what you tell the police. After all, a wife cannot be forced to give evidence against her own husband.'

Not that it really mattered but I had no idea if this was still true or not.

'That will make us both look guilty, won't it?'

'By then it will be too late. Look here, in the beginning the police will make it rough for you both, but as long as you both stick to your story – that he spent the whole night with you after giving his wife a sleeping pill – then you and he should be in the clear. After all, the autopsy will certainly support John's story. They'll find the drugs in her system. And who would give his wife a sleeping pill if he was also planning to shoot her? Why not just give her an overdose and tell the police she had talked of suicide? And who would get back into bed with the body of someone he had already murdered? It just doesn't make sense, does it?'

'No, I can see that.' She paused. 'How would you kill her?'

'Do you really want to know?'

She shook her head. 'No, perhaps not.'

Colette put her feet on the handrail and lit us both a cigarette; she hoovered it into her lungs and then blew the smoke at the sea, where it hung over a little flotilla of boats like a sudden fog.

'Suppose he doesn't give himself up to the police after he finds Orla's body? Suppose he makes a run for it? If he looks as guilty as you say he will, then he might panic and leave

Monaco. On his boat. Or in his plane. I think I would, if I was him. Wouldn't you?'

'Perhaps.'

'What then?'

'Then he'll still try to call you, Colette. My guess is that in those circumstances you'll continue to be the linch-pin – the *déclic*, if you prefer – for his whole future. In fact I should say he'll be even more desperate to find you than before.'

'But won't he suspect that I've had something to do with Orla's murder? Surely I'll be the obvious suspect in his eyes.'

'No, not if you think about it logically. Look, before he comes downstairs from his apartment Orla is very much alive, so you're in the clear then. You're certainly in the clear while he's in bed with you here in your apartment, of course. And afterward, when he's back in bed with her, you're in the clear then, too. You can hardly murder Orla while he's lying next to her. He's your alibi as much as you are his. Don't you see? That's what makes it so perfect.'

I paused to let that sink in a bit before adding, 'But look here, she's not without enemies. Her family are all Irish republicans. And they have enemies, too. Dangerous enemies in the Irish Protestant community, the UDA and UVF. These people are just as dangerous as the IRA. I should know. I worked with them. Orla has been giving Sinn Féin money for years. When it comes to court I'm sure that this is what John's defence will rest upon. Orla's connections in Irish nationalism.'

Colette nodded. 'Yes. John told me about her family. But won't it seem suspicious that I went away on the very night his wife was murdered?'

'Not if you send him a text first thing in the morning; you can tell him that something unexpected came up – your sister in hospital, something like that. That way your absence will be easily explained. He'll call you of course. But you won't answer. Not for a while.'

'And where will I be?'

'In Paris. The minute I come back downstairs from John's apartment we'll go straight to the airport. You'll catch the first plane and stay there until I can get to you. Meanwhile I'll go to London and wait for the police to get in contact with me and the other guys. Which they will, of course. So it's important I'm there when they make contact. If it comes to that I expect John will call me, too. If he's on the lam, that is. When he's needed some dirty work done before I've been virtually the first person he calls.'

I described three such occasions to Colette: once when he got done for drink-driving and needed someone to go and collect his car; a second time when he wanted me to hire a couple of students to become his personal sock-puppet, posting five-star reviews for John's books on Amazon – there's a lot of that goes on, these days; and a third time when he wanted me to sack one of the writers in the *atelier*. But there were many more I could have told her about.

'Wait, won't the police know you were in Monaco on the night of Orla's murder? Won't that make you a suspect?'

I shook my head.

'That might have been the case once. But the staff at British border control don't bother to record the names of people leaving the UK, so no one will know that I was out of the country. If the Monty cops ask I'll tell them I spent that weekend at my place in Cornwall. Besides, I'll be using a false passport. Both John and I managed to get one when we were researching one of his books. No one will ever know I was even here.'

'You seem to have thought of everything already.'

'Yes, I think you're right. And perhaps I have. It is curious that since you mentioned the idea this plan seems to have arrived in my head as one whole, like the plot for a novel.'

'It seems that you are much better at plots than you thought you were.'

'Isn't that interesting? On the other hand maybe it's not so surprising. After all, I'm beginning to realize that I would do anything for you, Colette. Even commit a murder.'

'But why do you say so?'

I stood up and surveyed the Legoland scene below. The summer sporting club, on the promontory of land that marked the eastern edge of Larvotto, was no bigger than a one-euro coin, while the old port – Port Hercule – to the west, was the size and shape of a bottle opener. It was not a view for the faint-hearted – anyone with vertigo or acrophobia could never have inhabited the Tour Odéon – but it was the very place a more modern-minded devil might have chosen if he had been looking for a high place to tempt someone with ownership of the whole world. And Monte Carlo is as near to being a holy city as there is for the world's wealthiest people. It was certainly worth a try. I turned to face her and leaned back confidently on the handrail of the glass balcony; only in a novel would the rail have given way, sending me to a probably well-deserved death a couple of hundred feet below for my Icarus-like hubris. A warm breeze stirred my hair and then hers, but it might as easily have been something altogether more sinister – a subtler, more ethereal ectoplasm that contained the essence of pure temptation.

'Honestly, Colette, it's no accident our coming together in the Columbus Bar the other night. No accident at all. The way it happened – John's book as the nexus of our meeting – that was fate pure and simple. I know it. You know it. I've thought a lot about it and I think it happened because, frankly, it's within my power to give you exactly what you want in life; to enable you to live the life of luxury you've probably always wanted: a beautiful apartment, a lovely town house in Paris, a home in the Caribbean, an expensive sports car, *a child* – all of these things I will give you, Colette, if you'll let me help you. And I tell you without fear of contradiction that after all that's happened to you, you deserve these things. You know it and I know it. But we needn't dwell on any of that because while material things are important they're not *that* important. Happiness, fulfilment in life, love – these are the things that really matter. So now I'm going to tell you exactly why I want to help you – why I'm your most devoted servant in this matter. Please don't be embarrassed if I tell you it's because I think I love you. What do the French call it? *Un coup de foudre?*'

'Really? After so short a time?'

'Is that not how lightning strikes, Colette? Suddenly? Like something which is beyond our control. Perhaps that's one of the few benefits of being older. You make up your mind about things like that so much more quickly than when you're a bit younger. *Carpe diem*, so to speak. Anyway, I'd hardly be contemplating such a drastic course of action if I didn't love you, I think. Do you? Only a truly devoted lover could be willing to do what I am willing to do for you, which is murder, my sweet.'

I was on the verge of mentioning *Thérèse Raquin* – Zola's marvellous book about a love triangle and a murder – until I remembered that it hadn't ended well for any of them. I pressed my belted waist hard against the brushed steel hand-rail, as if testing the absolute limits of the world I was in.

I remained exactly where I was, with my feet not exactly on the ground but still very firmly on the polished wooden decking of that little twenty-ninth-floor balcony.

'No, I suppose not.' She finished her cigarette and smiled. 'I'm very fond of you, Don. But please, give me a little more time. For my feelings to catch up with yours. Yes?'

'Of course. I understand.'

'And look, I think it's a good plan. But tell me please, is ours a perfect plan? After all, we don't want to get caught, do we? It's odd how getting caught never seems to be part of anyone's plan. I'm terrified of going to jail.'

I wondered if Colette had ever read Camus, like every French schoolchild. I certainly didn't want to end up in jail like Meursault, talking to a priest about the absurdity of the human condition. Because that's the part of the plan that *les hommes d'action* always fail to consider; and yet it's the one that needs debating most of all – the possibility of failure and of being caught. Looking at Colette though, I didn't think the existential niceties of crime were worth mentioning.

'The perfect plan?' I smiled and flicked my still smouldering cigarette in the general direction of Beausoleil, where I hoped it might ignite the lacquered hair of some elderly French matron. 'It's an oxymoron, a contradiction in terms. It doesn't exist. Order always tends toward disorder; this is called entropy. So there is only a good plan, and this is a very good plan. But a good plan is only a good plan if it's flexible enough to deal with something that goes wrong, even sometimes very wrong. In my experience something always goes wrong. That's why there's no such thing as a perfect plan. Or a perfect murder. Because something always goes wrong.'

She nodded. 'When are we going to do it?'

'When's he back from Geneva?' I said.

'In two weeks' time, they're both here for their wedding anniversary, I think.'

'Then that's when we'll do it.'

CHAPTER 4

I picked up the iPad and surveyed the apartment, satisfied that I had everything I had come for. But I didn't bother searching the place for Colette's laptop; I knew where it was: she had taken it with her when she had gone with me in the car to Nice Airport. Her leaving the iPad on the kitchen worktop had been a mistake; I simply hadn't noticed it and nor had she. It had been the kind of thing I'd been referring to when I'd talked to her about entropy and was just one of a couple of things that had gone wrong with the plan immediately after I'd murdered Mrs Orla Houston.

It still felt a little weird saying that. I didn't regret it for a moment, however. In truth I was having the most fun I'd had since leaving the army. Nothing – not the huckster/wanker world of advertising nor the solitary/autistic life of a writer – can compare with the exhilarating thrill of getting away with murder.

I used the Judas hole in Colette's door to check that the corridor was empty and thinking the coast on floor twenty-nine was clear I went out of the apartment and closed the door behind me.

'Hello at last,' said an American voice.

I turned to see a smallish man in a grey suit with a Van Dyck beard, a paunch and an unlit Cohiba shuffling toward me. He was perspiring heavily and in his other hand was a handkerchief as big as a flag of truce. He looked like a Confederate Army general.

'You must be my Russian neighbour – Mr Kaganovich, isn't it?'

I fixed a smile to my face and nodded, vaguely.

'Colette – Miss Laurent has told me so much about you, but I was beginning to think you didn't exist.' He smiled. 'Unless you're a ghost.'

I smiled, enjoying the irony and said, 'There are no ghosts in this building.'

'I wouldn't be too sure about that.'

He held out a hand that only just cleared the sleeve of his ill-fitting jacket. 'Michael Twentyman. Originally from New York but now of no fixed abode. Hey, but we all are if we're here in Monaco, right?'

'Lev,' I said, shaking Twentyman's hand. 'Originally from Smolensk, but now mostly travelling somewhere on business. Pleased to meet you.'

I'd always been quite good at imitating accents; back in my advertising days, I'd often voiced a radio commercial when the so-called acting talent couldn't quite manage it to my high standard. Most of the actors who do voice-overs are drunken has-beens you haven't seen for so long they look like Dorian Gray's picture. In truth I'd never done a Russian accent, professionally, but seeing *The Hunt for Red October* on television as many times as I had, I figured I only had to be as good as – or no better than – Sean Connery or Sam Neill to persuade the American that I was the gènuine article. With any accent, less is more.

I turned and walked toward the lift.

'Not as pleased as I am,' said Twentyman. 'I'm having a

few friends over for Sunday night cocktails in my apartment tomorrow. And then we're going to dinner at Joël Robuchon. My girlfriend is from Kharkov. So it'd be great if you could join us.'

It figured that someone like him would have had a Russian girlfriend and, for a brief second, I tried to picture her: blonde, blue-eyed, glass-cutting cheekbones, with hooks and gut-suckers like a liverfluke – which is a parasite in sheep almost impossible to be rid of. Russian girls in Monaco would have looked at Twentyman the way a wolf on the steppe might have seen a lost lamb.

'I'd love to,' I said. 'But I'm on my way somewhere.'

'Business or pleasure?'

'Is there a difference?'

Twentyman laughed. 'You're right. Not in Monaco.'

The lift arrived and we stepped inside. I pressed the button to take us down to the Odéon garage.

'I'm headed out myself.'

I nodded politely.

'I assume you heard about our news,' he said.

'What news might that be?'

'What news?' Twentyman laughed. 'My God, you have been away, haven't you? Why our murder, of course. Mrs Houston. The actress. In one of the sky duplexes nearly two weeks ago. That's why I mentioned ghosts.'

'I did hear about that, yes. Terrible. I hadn't met the poor lady myself. But it was my information that the husband did it. The writer. And that he's still at liberty.'

'He's the number one suspect, yes. But that's the French police for you. The husband is always the number one suspect, right? This is the home of *le crime passionnel*. But if you ask me, the culprit could be anyone in this building. The first twenty floors are affordable housing. For Monégasques. Which means this place is hardly as exclusive as I'd hoped it might be when I bought it. All right, maybe the locals have a different elevator, but you wouldn't ever get this kind of European social engineering in an apartment building on Park Avenue. It smacks of communism.'

'You think it is one of them, perhaps? The locals?'

'Why not?'

I shrugged. 'Then perhaps it's good that I have alibi. I was in Geneva when this happened. At least that's what my wife thinks.'

Twentyman laughed. 'Who knows? Maybe we'll all need an alibi before this is over. It's almost two weeks since it happened but the police are still here and no further forward with their inquiry. Asking questions and being a general pain in the ass. I mean you can't blame them, they're just doing their jobs. But I really hate cops. You don't want to hear about that right now. Suffice to say that I've been thinking of getting out of town for a while. Until today there were television cameras outside the front of our building. And I just hate that.'

'Me, too,' I said. 'If my wife saw me *here* she would also kill me.'

The lift door opened not in the garage but in the ground-floor lobby; with its geometric bronze wall patterns which might have signified some ancient hermetic meaning and enormous beige marble pillars, it resembled something from a big-budget sci-fi movie. Whenever I was in it I half expected to see Mr Spock standing on the polished floor; instead I caught sight of someone who was just as unwelcome as any extraterrestrial creature: it was Chief Inspector Amalric and he was talking to the concierge by the front desk.

'That's him there,' said Twentyman. 'The Chief Inspector of Police. His name is Amalric and he's a suspicious son of a bitch. Shit. He's seen me. Hell, now I really am going to be late.'

'Monsieur Twentyman, hello.'

Amalric's gravelly voice echoed through the lobby; he was wearing a little straw hat and holding a glass of water in his hand.

'Chief Inspector,' Twentyman said weakly. 'How are you?'

I pressed myself into the side of the lift, hiding behind the side wall and control panel as the Monaco detective set out across the enormous floor toward us. I was pretty sure he hadn't yet seen me but I figured it was only a matter of seconds before he did and Twentyman introduced me as his neighbour, Lev Kaganovich, which was going to be very hard to explain. I was surely the living proof of the old wives' tale that murderers always return to the scene of the crime.

'Good, thank you. Could I have a word with you, please?'

'It's a little inconvenient right now,' he said. 'I'm just on my way out somewhere.'

'It won't take a moment,' insisted Amalric, nearer now. 'I just have a few questions to ask you.'

I'd already pressed the close doors button, several times, and to my immense relief the doors started to slide shut.

'*Attendez un moment.*'

Twentyman pushed his face close to the narrowing gap between the doors and called out 'Perhaps later' and 'Sorry' before they closed completely and the lift continued smoothly down to the Odéon garage.

'That was fast work,' said Twentyman and chuckled. 'I can see you're a good man in a tight spot, Lev, my friend. But for your nifty work with those elevator buttons I'd have been stuck with that fucking nosy cop for twenty minutes.'

'Why does he want to speak to you anyway? The twenty-ninth floor is a long way from those sky duplexes.'

'Because I knew her. Mrs Houston was a fellow Tifosi – like me a keen supporter of the Scuderia Ferrari. We met in the Ferrari hospitality suite at the Hôtel de Paris during the last Grand Prix. I imagine the Chief Inspector thinks that I can shed some light on some of the people she knew here in Monte Carlo.' He chuckled. 'Even if I could, I'd rather not, if you know what I mean. One question leads to another and before you know it, you're in handcuffs. I had a similar experience on Wall Street a few years ago. I went from witness to wanted in twenty-four hours. So fuck that, right?'

'I just hope I haven't got you into trouble.'

'Hey, you're not the only guy who can produce an alibi,' said Twentyman as the car arrived in the garage. 'It so happens I was in the library with Colonel Mustard at the time.'

I frowned as though not understanding what he'd said. 'Please?'

'American humour,' said my putative neighbour. 'Come to think of it, Chief Inspector Amalric didn't see the joke either.'

'French, Russian – cops are the same all over. The only jokes they like are the ones they make up themselves. In Russia we sometimes call these jokes "evidence".'

Twentyman laughed again. 'That's very good. Are you sure you can't come along tomorrow night? My girlfriend, Anastasia, would love to meet you. More importantly so would her friends.'

'You're forgetting about my wife. One murder in the Odéon is quite enough, don't you think?'

Twentyman was still laughing as he walked toward a red Ferrari 599 GTO. 'Knock me up next time you're in town, as the actress said to the bishop.'

'I will,' I said.

'Promise?'

'Scout's honour.'

I followed Twentyman's Ferrari out of the garage and into the street, where it was as if his V12 engine was in competition with my W12 for the amount of high-performance noise they could both generate. The roundabout in front of the Odéon echoed with a din that was like a very small and exclusive Grand Prix.

I drove down Boulevard d'Italie in search of Il Giardino – the Italian restaurant where John was awaiting my return. I pulled up in front of a tall privet hedge that shielded the outside tables from the street and started to ring John's mobile number, but he was already opening the Bentley's door and dropping into the passenger seat. A strong smell of scotch came with him, not to mention an air of general grievance.

'Where the fuck have you been?' he said. 'It's nearly nine o'clock. I was beginning to think something had happened to you.'

'Sorry about that,' I said. 'There wasn't any mobile reception in the garage and then I'm afraid I just forgot about it.'

'You forgot? Thanks, Don, and fuck you. I've been having bloody kittens since you left.'

'I forgot because your building is still crawling with Monty cops,' I said. 'Oddly enough I was rather more concerned with avoiding arrest than with your fucking nerves.'

'It's me they want to fucking arrest, *old sport*,' protested John. 'In case you'd forgotten.'

'Perhaps. But they would certainly want to know what

the fuck I was doing in the Odéon, *old sport*. With your girlfriend's iPad tucked under my arm. You see, they're the same
cops I met in London. The ones who came to interview me.'

'How do you know?'

'Because I fucking saw them, you ungrateful cunt. In the
lobby. And outside the entrance. I just hope to Christ they
didn't see me.'

'Oh, Jesus, Don, I'm sorry. I thought they'd have cleared
off by now.'

'They haven't. Then I got caught by one of Colette's neighbours. Fellow named Michael Twentyman.'

'What did you tell him?'

'Don't worry, he's now under the impression that I'm her
missing Russian lover, Lev Kaganovich.'

'How does that happen?'

'I did my impersonation of Uncle Vanya. Even though I say
so myself it was worthy of an Emmy, or whatever it is they
give those tossers for a bit of dressing up and make-believe.'

'Yes. You always fancied yourself as a bit of an actor, didn't
you? When we were in advertising.'

'Actually, my best performances were done in the army,'
I said, momentarily affecting a Northern Irish accent. 'But
that's another story.'

John started to relax a little.

'Michael Twentyman. I recognize that name. I never met
him myself but I think Orla used to know him.'

'Come on. Let's get out of here before he sees us and invites
us to a party.'

As I put the Bentley in gear and accelerated slowly away
he found the other end of the Apple wire in Colette's iPad
that I'd positioned down the side of the passenger seat in its
faux snakeskin cover.

'Is this it? Is this her iPad?'

'Yes.'

'Thank God for that.'

He plugged it into a charging socket underneath the Bentley's armrest and pressed the iPad's home button to start it up, but for now there wasn't enough power in the thing.

'We can open that when we get to the hotel in Èze,' I said. 'It will give us something to talk about over dinner.'

'I fucking hope so.'

'What do you mean?'

'She had a passcode on her iPad.'

'Don't you know the number?'

'I thought I did. But now, I'm not so sure I haven't forgotten it.'

'This is a fine time to forget it given that I just risked my ass retrieving that piece of junk from under the noses of the Monty cops. Because that's what it is if you can't remember the goddamn number.'

'Keep your hair on. I'm sure I'll remember it.'

'Let's hope so. Otherwise this whole journey will have been a waste of time.'

John grunted. 'Don't I know it.'

We made our way up the hill into Beausoleil and out of Monaco.

I said, 'But even if you don't, it's only four numbers. How difficult can that be to break?'

John made an error noise.

'Clearly you know nothing about Apple. If you repeatedly enter the wrong passcode, it disables the iPad. The only way to unlock an iPad that has a passcode, other than by entering the correct passcode, is to restore it to the original factory settings. And that deletes all of the data – which is the very thing we're after.'

'Everything?'

'Everything.'

'I see.'

'Did you find her laptop?' he asked. 'It might be a different story if we had Colette's laptop. We could plug the iPad into the computer and that would restore the data.'

'No sign of that, I'm afraid. And believe me I looked every-where. She must have taken it with her when she left Dodge. You'd better start trying to think of the right number. Or we're fucked.'

'Yes, you've made that abundantly clear already, old sport.'

As I steered the Bentley west – toward the small medieval village of Èze – John fell into sombre silence and I guessed he was trying to remember the iPad passcode. I already knew Colette's passcode, but I was trying to work out how I was going to give him the correct four numbers without drawing suspicion on myself.

CHAPTER 5

'What are you doing?'

'Pulling my cock out. I don't want to come inside you.'

'Why the hell not?'

'Because when John fucks you he'll notice that someone has fucked you already.' I paused. Colette was keeping me inside her. 'Won't he?'

'Of course he won't. Not unless he goes down on me and he never does. With him it's always the same *cinq à sept, douche comprise*. It's become a sort of joke with us. Besides, I don't want to change these sheets before he comes down here. So, go ahead and come in me.'

I shifted a little, pushed my cock right up to the neck of her womb – thank God for Cialis – and almost immediately rediscovered some urgency in my pelvic movements; a couple of minutes later I was rolling off her and giving her a tissue and struggling back into my underpants – to protect her Frette bed linen.

'Anyway,' she added, 'I thought you'd like the idea of – what's that disgusting phrase you have in English? *Remuant sa soupe.*'

'Stirring someone else's porridge.' I laughed. 'You're right. Now I come to think of it, I do like that idea. Or else I am a Turk.'

'What does *that* mean?'

'Nothing.' I glanced at my watch. 'Now then. You're quite clear about what to do when he gets here?'

'Yes. Only I'm trying not to think about it. I feel terribly sick when I do.'

'So, forget about it. Pretend it isn't happening. That it's got nothing to do with you. If it makes you feel any better you can ask me not to go through with it.'

'Please,' she said. 'Let's not do this, Don. Really. I've got cold feet about the whole thing.'

'There you are,' I said. 'And now that you've asked, I bet you're feeling better already. Look, I'm happy to have this on my conscience.'

'I don't believe you have one.'

'Not since Warrenpoint, no.'

'Warrenpoint. That's the place in Ireland where your friend was killed, wasn't it?'

I nodded. For a moment I replayed some very vivid frames of that particular horror movie. A beautiful sunny day in August – the bank holiday; and me, an Armalite rifle over my shoulder, a cigarette between my trembling lips, picking through the still smoking, mangled wreckage of a four-ton lorry with a stick, looking for human body parts, finding a man's hand with a wedding ring on the finger and then vowing eternal, undying hatred for the Irish.

'Look, I'd better have a wash myself. He'll be here in less than an hour.'

I showered and dressed and checked over the automatic I'd sourced from a dealer in Genoa. It was a Walther 22, identical to one that John had bought for Orla but still only a back-up weapon in case her gun wasn't in the bedside drawer where, according to John, she usually kept it. Then I lay down on the bed in Colette's spare room and read a novel on my Kindle to help take my mind off what I was about to do. The novel was by Martin Amis and, in spite of what the critics had said, I was enjoying it rather a lot. No one writes a better sentence than Marty, even if it does take several attempts to scale the sheer cliff-face of his intellect and know exactly what the fuck it is he's driving at. Sometimes I wonder who the critics would beat up if they couldn't beat up Marty.

At about 11.30 I heard a knock on Colette's front door, and when she went to answer it she was wearing a rather fetching little baby-doll nightdress that had me smiling at the predictability of John's taste. He'd always had a thing for the kind of sleazy bedroom wear that was hardly worth wearing. She pulled a sheepish, embarrassed sort of face before pushing me back into the room and closing the door. I switched out the bedside light and tiptoed into the en-suite bathroom. Then I heard the low murmur of voices, some laughter, the pop of a champagne cork and then silence as they moved swiftly into the bedroom. Colette had not exaggerated about John getting straight down to business: if anything, *cinq à sept* was optimistic. A few seconds later I received a text on my phone; it was a prewritten *Vas y* message from Colette that John's tracksuit – she hated the fact that he always wore a tracksuit for his midnight visits to see her – containing his all-important door key, was now lying on the drawing-room floor.

I hurried through and searched John's pockets for his door key, but to my irritation and horror there was no sign of it, and several valuable minutes passed before I spied it lying beside his phone on a table in the hall beside the front door. Then I put on John's tracksuit, pulled up the hood, picked up my backpack, went out into the corridor and headed up the fire stairs to the forty-third floor. The tracksuit was an inspired, last-minute touch, just in case anyone saw me.

But no one did.

I opened one of the double doors, stepped into the sky duplex and closed the door behind me. None of the curtains or blinds was drawn and it was easy to find my way around the apartment, which was as big as the rooftop palace in a Sinbad movie. I went straight through to the master bedroom. Scenting a stranger in the apartment Orla's dogs had started to bark and I was half inclined to go back and shoot them in case they woke her up. But opening the bedroom door and illuminating the darker room with a small LED flashlight it was immediately plain that the figure in bed and facing away from the room toward the double-height window was soundly asleep and that the hounds of hell could not have awakened her, let alone a couple of irritating spaniels. They say people with dogs live longer; Orla was about to become the proof that this is not always the case.

It was a while since I had looked at Orla without seeing a scowl appear on her face the moment she saw me; she looked as peaceful as she was undoubtedly beautiful. Her long blonde hair – the roots seemed much darker – was strewn across the white pillow and she was wearing a night-dress made of peach-coloured, almost transparent silk. I was irresistibly reminded of a painting entitled *Flaming June* by Sir Frederic Leighton and which – thanks to the toxic ole-ander branch that also features in the picture – symbolizes the fragile link between sleep and death; this seemed only appropriate in the circumstances. I wasn't about to allow the recollection of a nice pre-Raphaelite painting to stop me, of course. I've never believed Ruskin's nonsense that art is morally improving. The hideous Ulster Museum – is there an uglier building in the whole United Kingdom? – has a rather fine painting of St Christopher carrying the Christ child that I was always rather fond of while I was serving in the province, but it certainly never deterred me from putting a bullet in anyone's head. Besides, I'd been dreaming of killing Orla for a long, long time; ever since the wedding.

I rolled on a surgical rubber glove, opened her bedside drawer and found the Walther exactly where John had said it was, not to mention a number of sex-toys that had my eyes out on stalks. I fetched the gun, screwed on the Gemtech sound suppressor I'd brought along – there was no point in making more noise than was needed – checked the breech and then racked the slide to put one in the chamber. I'm not a cruel man and I'd already rejected the idea of waking Orla up so that she could see it coming. If it was done it was best done quickly and without much drama, so I pointed the silencer at the centre of her Botoxed forehead, muttered a quiet 'Good night, you Fenian bitch' and then – holding a thick square of Kevlar behind her skull, to prevent the possible egress of the bullet – I squeezed the trigger. The gun shifted in my hand with a sharp click almost as if the pistol was empty; with the Gemtech a Walther P22 makes no more noise than a table lighter and certainly nothing like a silencer sounds in movies. Her head jerked a little on the pillow at the impact as though I'd struck her, but the rest of Orla's body hardly moved; then, slowly, her mouth sagged a little as if the life had indeed gone out of her and pressing a finger against her larynx I felt for a carotid pulse but did not find one.

To my relief her cranium had remained intact. I checked for any blood with my finger but there was none. This was important. Any of the 38s in John's gun cabinet would have blown the back of her head off, and this, of course, was exactly why I'd preferred to use the smaller, less powerful 22. Meanwhile a small snail trail of blood trickled down her forehead, along the line of her eyebrow and underneath her cheek. Just as crucially, her body remained in the same attitude as when she had been alive, so that it was now quite possible that in the absence of any blood on Orla's pillow John might climb into bed beside her later on without knowing that she was in fact dead.

'I'm sorry, Orla,' I said. 'It was you or me, I'm afraid.'

I placed the gun on the bed for a moment and, for the forensics, I dabbed a little blood on the right sleeve of John's tracksuit before hunting for the ejected brass cartridge on the floor; when I found it I used a Q-tip to extract a fine amount of cordite which I smeared on the same sleeve. These days, thanks to people like Patricia Cornwell and Kathy Reichs, everyone's a scenes-of-crime expert and you wonder how it is that anyone is dumb enough to get caught.

I picked up the Walther and was on the point of making it safe, but the constant barking of the dogs persuaded me I'd always hated her fucking dogs almost as much as I'd hated Orla and that I'd certainly relish killing them, too. So I went along to her dressing room and, carefully, so as not to let the dogs escape, opened the door and switched on the light.

My first thoughts were not of the dogs but of Orla's wardrobe, which revealed such a large number of dresses, coats and shoes that it looked like a designer sale – albeit a shop with two very irritating dogs. On the only area of the walls not given over to closets were several movie posters featuring Grace Kelly – including *Rear Window*.

'Hello, boys,' I said. 'I've just come to say hello.'

The 'boys' – which, nauseatingly, is what Orla used to call

them – were black-and-white cocker spaniels and yapped furiously at my ankles. Is there a more irritating breed of dog than a cocker spaniel? I don't think so.

I chuckled. 'And goodbye.'

The second dog uttered a rather pleasing yelp as I shot the first twice in the chest. Then I pumped two into the second mutt, and I must have hit the dog's aorta or something because in the seconds before the thing died it started haemorrhaging blood all over the place. I'd never shot an animal before; not even for sport. I never see the point of all that Glorious Twelfth stuff where you shoot as many grouse as you can. But it gave me enormous pleasure to silence these two dogs, for ever. This wasn't exactly akin to Atticus shooting the mad dog in *To Kill a Mockingbird* – besides, that dog is only really a metaphor for the lynch mob that features earlier on in the book – but both of 'the boys' badly needed killing; and suddenly the world felt like it was a less malodorous and canicular place without such loathsome creatures in it. Quieter, too.

I made the little Walther safe and, unscrewing the silencer – after just five shots it was surprisingly hot to the touch – I pocketed it, went back into the bedroom, and tossed the .22 onto the carpet on Orla's side of the bed, where it was not likely to be discovered immediately. Job done.

And yet you might say it was the dogs who had the last laugh, for as I made my way out of the door and hurried back along the corridor and downstairs I realized that I'd stood in some of their shit. This discovery caused me to slip and almost fall down a whole flight of steps, and I pulled a muscle in my shoulder as I held on to the handrail, narrowly arresting my fall. I turned around and saw a neat series of footprints ascending the stairs behind me like a trail of stinking breadcrumbs. I took off my shoes and for a moment I stood there debating with myself what to do next. This would have been funny if it hadn't been so forensically awkward. You didn't have to be working in CSI to see that.

'This never happens in Agatha Christie,' I said. 'Talk about the curious incident of the dog in the night.'

But there was little time for any postmodern analysis of my predicament. It seemed I had little option but to return to John's apartment, find some cleaning materials and try to erase my footprints. To do otherwise would have left the police in no doubt that Orla's murderer had left her apartment after killing her, which might easily have left John in the clear.

I left my shoes where they were and ran back upstairs in my socks; in John's apartment I switched on my flashlight and went into the kitchen where I found some rags and some bleach. By now I had decided that I hardly needed to clean the dog shit from the carpet in the apartment; that could have happened to anyone, including John himself; it was the shitty footprints between the front door and the door to the fire stairs that were the real problem, and inside the apartment I restricted myself to dabbing a bit of dog shit on one of his shoes. But in the corridor outside the apartment I spent the next ten minutes cleaning away my own footprints, and it was fortunate for me that the owners of the sky duplex next to John's were – according to Colette – away for the summer on a yacht in St Barts. Glancing at my watch, I saw that I'd been gone for just over thirty minutes.

I moved out onto the fire stairs and worked my way carefully down almost ten flights, checking each step with my flashlight for traces of shit; and only when I was satisfied that every trace of the stuff was gone did I pick up my shoes and open the fire door on 29.

Then, if all that wasn't enough, outside Colette's door I couldn't make her key work and another nervous minute passed before I discovered it was actually John's key I was using and not hers, since the two were more or less identical. These small errors can mean the difference between success and failure, of course; they're not exactly Freudian slips – I had no subconscious desire to get caught – more what you might call fate's attempts to trip you up. That's what makes life interesting; and of course murder creates its own unique gestalt. *The Gestalt of Murder*; it's probably the title of a crime novel by John Creasey; with more than six hundred novels to his name something usually is.

In Colette's apartment I placed John's key on the table by the door where I'd found it, jumped out of his tracksuit, tossed it back on the floor and, breathing a little heavily now, went back into the spare room, where I dressed in the dark and waited for him to finish what he was so vociferously doing in the bedroom. It didn't bother me that he was fucking Colette; on the contrary it meant that she was playing her part right and that he was quite unaware that his wife was dead.

Sitting in the dark I felt quite at home. Some people don't like the dark at all, but I have always loved it. I feel comfortable there. The thicker and more palpable the darkness around me, the better. As a boy I used to sit in the dark and without the distraction of light and colour I would make all sorts of plans for my life that seemed altogether more possible. It was a little like dreaming without being asleep. I still find a mental clarity in darkness that is hard to find anywhere else. Let's face it, after life is over the darkness is all there is, so you'd better get used to it. Jenny used to think it was creepy, my fondness for the dark. She would open a door and find me there in the dark and scream with fright, which is why she took to calling me 'the bat'. Another reason why she left me, probably. No one likes bats very much.

CHAPTER 6

The medieval village of Èze lies along the famous Moyenne Corniche and is the perfect antithesis of Monaco glitz. Friedrich Nietzsche was fond of Èze, and it's easy to see why. Perched on a rock fourteen hundred feet above sea-level, Èze is built around the ruins of a twelfth-century castle and commands perhaps the best view of anywhere on the Côte d'Azur, which probably went to Nietzsche's head; either way it's just the kind of high and magical place to write some unreadable German nonsense about God and the philosophical importance of having goblins around you. This and the lack of glamour, and two celebrated local perfumiers, make Èze popular with the older sort of tourist, which could explain the defibrillator you see on a wall as you begin to climb the steep, labyrinthine streets, although you would be forgiven for thinking that this might be more usefully located nearer the top of the hill.

Èze is also home to a famous hotel, the Château de la Chèvre d'Or. The Château is actually a haphazard series of jasmine-covered buildings, saucer-sized sun-terraces, fountains, waterfalls, private suites and precipitous Moroccan-style gardens that seem to be part of the village and yet somehow also manage to be very private. With its immaculate green lawns, giant-sized chess-set, croaking toads and crappy modern sculptures it all reminded me – a little – of Port-meirion in North Wales. It's the kind of place where you expect to see Number Six from *The Prisoner* striding around in a neat blue blazer and roll-neck sweater, although, according to the guidebooks, Robert De Niro and Leonardo DiCaprio are more likely to be seen there.

We checked in, sharing a room with twin beds to save money and because that's all they had; then we went to dinner in the hotel's terrace restaurant, Les Remparts, which enjoyed a spectacular view of St-Jean-Cap-Ferrat. Rather more than we enjoyed the food, thus confirming a prejudice I have long held that the quality of food declines in inverse proportion to the altitude at which it is served. I think the three worst dinners I ever had were up the Eiffel Tower, at the top of the Shard, and in the Piz Gloria revolving restaurant at the summit of the Schilthorn, in Murren.

Then again, our thoughts were not really on food at all but on the iPad we had brought with us to the table; and there was nothing wrong with the wine. We ordered a bottle of delicious Domaines Ott rosé, which is almost ubiquitous in that part of the world, and stared silently out to sea. *An Artist of the Floating World*. It's the title of a slight novel by Kazuo Ishiguro, and for a few moments it felt as if we two were at peace and had become so unmoored from the realities of everyday life that we were floating high above the rest of the world. Then again, that's how most writers feel, most of the time.

'I gave her this iPad, as a little present, on the twelfth of December,' said John. 'Her birthday. But I'm certain the passcode number isn't that, and I know it's not mine because I already tried those numbers.'

I lit a cigarette and nodded; knowing the number – as I

did – I now hoped to prod his memory with some helpful suggestions. But while it could easily have been a date, the actual number – 0507 – did not present any other obvious possibilities than a birthday or a significant date in July.

'I still can't figure her doing something like this to me,' he said. 'After all I gave her. I mean, there was a lot more than a fucking iPad, I can tell you. Money, trips, diamond earrings, clothes, an expensive watch. You name it.'

'The anniversary of when you met, perhaps,' I said, helpfully.

'March something or other.' John shook his head. 'Can't be that. We never really mentioned that kind of thing.'

'Her telephone number, perhaps.'

He thought about that for a moment, tapped the number into the iPad and then shook his head.

'How many tries did the internet say you got? Before the thing locks down?'

'Ten,' said John.

'So how many is that now?'

'Five.'

'I still can't figure why she wouldn't have got in touch with me, either,' he said. 'I mean, she knows my email addresses – even the secret one. The Hushmail address I have. Why hasn't she left a message on that?'

'What the fuck is Hushmail?'

'It's an HIPAA-compliant email service. HIPAA is the Health Insurance Portability and Accountability Act, which sets the standard for protecting sensitive patient data. Which makes it very fucking private for anyone else who uses it. Hushmail is the email equivalent of a burner phone. I was planning to use it in a novel and then decided not to just to help keep the existence of Hushmail a bit more hush-hush.' He shrugged.

'Anyway. I checked. There's no message from her on that account either.'

'My guess is that she probably wants to make you sweat a bit. To soften you up so you'll be more inclined to offer her a decent bit of wedge for an alibi.'

'She could be dead of course. This whole trip might be a wild goose chase.'

'Maybe. But we're doing this to be proactive, right? And because we can't think of anything else to do in the circumstances.'

John nodded. 'Think of a number.'

'*Le quatorze juillet.*'

John tapped the number into the iPad and shook his head.

'Six,' he said. 'Four strikes left.'

As John refilled our glasses with the excellent rosé my phone started to ring; to my horror this was a number I could easily identify. It was Chief Inspector Amalric. I felt my stomach empty. I excused myself and walked away from the table into a little private garden to take the call.

'Chief Inspector,' I said, pleasantly. 'What a pleasant surprise. How can I help you?'

'You're not in London?' he said.

For a moment I considered the possibility that he really had seen me in the lift, at the Odéon. But then I realized it was just as possible he had made this conclusion based on my ringtone. When you're in a foreign country the ringtone on an English mobile phone sounds different to the way it sounds when you're back in the UK.

'No, I'm in Switzerland. I'd been cooped up writing for too long. Cabin fever, I think. So I decided to get away from London for a couple of days. I needed to get some fresh air and to feel the sun on my face.'

'But the weather is nice in England right now.'

'Not in Cornwall it isn't. And besides, the food isn't nearly as good.'

'Oh, I don't know. That dinner we had at Claridge's was excellent. That's why I was calling actually. I'm coming back to London on Wednesday, and I hoped to have dinner with you again. I have some more questions for you. About Mr Houston.'

'I imagined you might, since you haven't yet caught him.'

'Now you sound like my boss, Paul de Beauvoir, the Commissioner. Every day he asks me the same question: where is Houston? I know that sooner or later I am going to answer "Texas" out of sheer frustration and I will be off the case. People are starting to avoid me. After almost two weeks they're as frustrated with my lack of progress as I am. Why just tonight, a man at the Tour Odéon – someone who knew Madame Houston – he virtually ran away when he saw me.'

When he said this it was as if I'd had a mild electric shock. Had he seen me, too? Or was he just fencing with me?

'I hope you don't think that I'm avoiding you, Chief Inspector.'

'You, monsieur? Why would I think such a thing? You are an English officer and a gentleman.'

'I was,' I said. 'I'm not so sure I'm either of these things now. They both sound like luxuries I can ill afford.'

'In fact, I would go so far as to say that no one has been as helpful as you have been.'

'I'm glad you think so.'

'Certainly not his ex-wives or his children. Nor his publisher. When are you going back to London?'

'I'm not sure. I'm staying with some friends. In Geneva.'

'Then perhaps I could meet you there. It's not so very far away from Monaco, you know. Five or six hours by car.'

'Yes, of course. But look, could I call you back about when and where? I'm a little tied up with something right now.'

'I hope she's nice.'

'I wish it was like that. But it isn't. I'm afraid I lead rather a dull life, Chief Inspector.'

'You? A writer? I don't believe it. All writers have a mistress, surely?'

'Not me.'

'Take it from a Frenchman. Perhaps it's time you got one.'

'Thanks for the advice. Look, I'll call you, okay? Tomorrow. But I really do have to go now.'

'Certainly. You have my number, of course.'

I ended the call; and then checked several times that the call was actually ended. Sometimes you think you've hung up and you haven't. All the same it had been careless of me to use my own phone in Monaco. It was probably too late but I switched it off anyway. That's how technology works against you. Did he suspect me? There was just enough in what he'd said to make me think he did but not enough to make me think he didn't. Surely it was just a coincidence that he had telephoned on the very night I had been in Monaco? I've never much liked that word, 'coincidence'; there's more comfort to be found in words like 'fluke', 'happenstance' and 'accident'; thanks to Jung no one believes in coincidence much any more. But Amalric had been helpful in one respect at least. I'd realized exactly what Colette's passcode number meant.

I dropped my phone into my jacket pocket and was walking toward the gate when it opened to reveal the one person next to Chief Inspector Amalric and Sergeant Savigny whom I least wanted to see on the whole of the Côte d'Azur.

'I don't believe it. Talk about coincidence, you coming here to the Chèvre d'Or. Gee, that's hilarious. Lev. I never ever see you before and then I see you twice in one evening.'

It was Michael Twentyman and he was accompanied by two permatan blondes wearing tiny skirts and heels as sharp as a leather worker's awl. They had all just started cigarettes.

'How the hell are you? Ladies, this is the man I was telling you about. This is Lev Kaganovich. My neighbour from across the hall. Lev? I'd like you to meet a couple of friends of mine. Anastasia and Katya. Say hello to my little friends, Lev. Ladies, Lev is from Smolensk.'

I bowed my head politely. '*Dobry vecher.*' That and '*Dobry den*' were two of only three things I knew how to say in Russian. I actually said it twice; perhaps I figured it would make me sound twice as Russian as saying it only once.

One of the women said something back in Russian which of course I didn't understand.

'Do you speak any Russian, Michael?' I asked him.

'Not a damn word,' he said.

'Then ladies, for Michael's sake, let us speak only in English. Or perhaps French. To do otherwise would be rude.'

'I don't speak any French either,' said Twentyman. 'No one speaks French in Monaco. And frankly these days, Lev, Russian will get you further than English. That and Arabic, of course. Hey, look, are you with someone? Why don't we all hook up? We're having dinner right now in the hotel's Michelin-starred restaurant and we just came out for a smoke.'

'Yes,' said Anastasia. 'That would be nice.'

'That's the great thing about France. No one minds if you smoke outside a restaurant.'

'I'd really love to, Michael.' I eyed Katya meaningfully as if nothing would have given me more pleasure than a couple of hours spent with her. 'But I have an important client waiting on the terrace restaurant downstairs and I'm on the verge of closing a very lucrative deal. So you'll really have to excuse me.'

I knew that wouldn't be enough for Twentyman so I took him by the elbow and led him out of the back of the garden to the door of the Michelin-starred restaurant.

'Give me your card,' I said. 'Perhaps, if I can finish my business in time I can join you somewhere afterward. I really like your two friends.'

'Stasia is my girlfriend,' explained Twentyman as he opened his wallet and thumbed out a business card that was as thick as an invitation to a royal garden party. 'But Katya is a great girl. Very warm. You and she would really hit it off.'

'I think so, too.'

Twentyman handed me his card. 'Do you have a card?'

'No,' I said. 'In my line of work, it's best to keep one's telephone numbers secret. But I will call you later, yes?'

'Great. Hey, maybe we can go to Studio 47 in Nice.'

'Sounds like a plan.'

'By the way, I meant to ask you earlier. Where's Colette? I haven't seen her in a while.'

'She's with her family, in Marseille.' I winced. 'She and I are no longer an item, as you Americans say. To be frank with you, it's been a little difficult with her.'

'Sure, I know what that's like.'

'See you later, I hope.'

I went back down to the table where I'd left John. He had one of his little Smythson notebooks open on the table in front of him and he was writing something in a small, neat hand.

'You're writing?'

'Keeping notes,' he said. 'For research purposes. You never know, some of these experiences might turn out to be useful. For a novel. Or perhaps my prison autobiography.'

'Or *The Geneva Convention*, perhaps. I'm sure you can work some of your recent experiences into a plot like that.'

John shook his head. 'I'm afraid *The Geneva Convention* is no more,' he said. 'It turns out that Robert Harris wrote a thriller called *The Fear Index* about a Geneva-based hedge fund.'

'But the plot you outlined to me is very different from his,' I said. 'Besides, you've always said that you should never be deterred by someone writing a book which is in the same ball-park. That sometimes the second book about something succeeds where the first one fails.'

'But his one didn't fail. That's rather the point, old sport. Anyway, what the fuck took you?' John drained his glass and poured another. 'I thought you'd run out on me. The food here's not that bad.'

'You know you're going to have to start trusting me, John.'

He nodded. 'Fair enough. I'm sorry.'

'I ran into Michael Twentyman. It seems he's having dinner with a couple of friends in the other restaurant.'

'What did you tell him? Suppose he recognizes me?'

'He doesn't know you.'

'No, but my picture has been on the front of *Nice-Matin*.'

I smiled, wryly. 'That picture doesn't do you justice.'

'I'm glad you think this is funny.'

'I also had Chief Inspector Amalric on the phone,' I said. 'It seems that he wants to question me again.'

'Jesus. About what?'

'I rather imagine he thinks I can tell him where you are hiding.'

John bit his lip and looked worried. He turned around in his chair as if expecting to see the Chèvre d'Or terrace surrounded by French gendarmes. 'Maybe they're undercover cops,' he said. 'These other diners.'

Several of the other tables were occupied by Chinese – imperceptibly different from the Japanese who'd once flocked to Europe. I shook my head.

'You don't suppose he's on to me? Your chief inspector.'

'No. But I'm not so sure that he wouldn't like to make me a suspect.'

'You? What the fuck for? You haven't killed anyone. At least no one I know about.'

'I had the sneaking suspicion he might have spotted me in your building. When I was in there fetching that iPad.'

'Christ, Don.'

John looked around again.

I shrugged. 'Look, I'm probably imagining it. He didn't get a good look at me. I'm certain of it.'

'I hope so.'

'He's under a lot of pressure to get a result. From the Police Commissioner. And the Minister of Interior. He probably called me because he can't think of anything else to do. That's what cops are like when they're not getting anywhere. They do everything they did before, again, in case they missed something. At least that's what the clever ones do, and like I said before, Amalric is nothing if not clever.'

'You're not just saying that, are you? To make me feel better. Because as it is I'm not going to sleep a fucking wink tonight. My heart feels like a bloody canary.'

'No,' I said. 'It was just a coincidence that he should have called me on the very night we went back to Monaco. Look, if they were really on to us, they'd have arrested us by now, don't you think? I mean what's to be gained by not picking us up now? He was on a fucking fishing trip, I'm sure of it. Because of the pressure from the top.'

I was trying to persuade myself of this as much as I was trying to reassure John that everything was all right. I was half inclined to climb in the Bentley and leave Èze as quickly as possible. Suddenly it seemed dangerously near Monaco. But I was dog-tired. Half a bottle of decent rosé will do that to you after a long drive. All I wanted now was to go to bed in a nice air-conditioned bedroom.

But I still had one thing to do.

'My heart bleeds for him,' said John.

I laughed. 'Typical bloody Frenchman though. Always thinking about their cocks. He more or less asked me if I had a mistress. And when I said I didn't, he suggested I should get one. He sounds like he's a shagger. A real DSK.'

John frowned. 'A DSK? What's that?'

'Dominique Strauss-Kahn. You know? He was MD of the IMF before he got caught with his trousers down and the French press turned him into *Monsieur Cinq-à-Sept*.'

'Oh him, yeah.' John smiled as light dawned on Marblehead. 'That's it, Don, old sport. You bloody genius. I remember now. 0-5-0-7. That's Colette's fucking passcode.'

'You're not serious.' I made an innocent face. 'Really?'

'That's what Colette used to call me. *Monsieur Cinq-à-Sept*. For obvious reasons.' John was already tapping the number into Colette's iPad. 'Brilliant,' he said. 'We're in.' His smile widened. 'And here it is. Her list of contacts.'

He scrolled down through the list.

'This must be it. Didier and Mala Laurent. Boulevard la Savine, in the fifteenth arrondissement. There's a telephone number.' John picked up his mobile – the one he'd borrowed from Bob Mechanic – and started to dial.

'No, wait,' he said, tossing the phone back onto the table. 'If she is there and she is involved in some sort of blackmail scam, then I'd just be putting her on alert, wouldn't I? Better to have this conversation if we're sitting outside the front door. Might be interesting to see what reaction it provokes.'

'The fifteenth. That's northern Marseille, isn't it?'

'I don't know.'

'There was an article about the Marseille *banlieues* in the *Guardian*. Pretty rough area to take a friend's Bentley.'

John shrugged. 'So maybe we won't wash it tomorrow.'

'But more importantly, have you given any thought to what you're going to say to Colette when we catch up with her? I mean apart from demanding to know where the hell she's been for the last two weeks?'

'No. I can't say that I have.'

'Let's suppose for a moment that she really did have nothing to do with Orla's murder. In which case she's probably scared witless that she's going to be a police suspect, too. It seems to me that she's not just your alibi, you're hers, too. In which case it might be better if you were both to say that you spent the whole evening together instead of your just having had a quick shag, like you say you had. In one sense that makes you more of a cunt – the fact that you were prepared to do something like that, under your wife's nose. But being a cunt doesn't make you a murderer.'

'Yes, I can see how that might play.'

'Then all you'll have to do is think of a way of making sure Colette stays onside.'

'How do you mean?'

'How long have you known her? Less than a year?'

'Six months.'

I shrugged. 'If it was me I would want to be sure that she knew that you were going to look after her after this is all over. For a start she'll need a good lawyer. And she'll need money. Probably quite a lot of money.' I laughed and then shook my head as if I'd thought better of saying something.

'What?'

'Nothing.'

'No, go on, say it.'

'Just that it might actually be cheaper if you married her. When this is all over.'

'What?'

'No, think about it. A wife can't give evidence against her own husband. So if she did ever retract her story, there would be no point.' I shrugged again. 'It might actually be a good move. After all, it's not like you have a wife, is it?'

'You're a devious fucker, Irvine. Do you know that?'

I smiled. 'It has been said.'

CHAPTER 7

'What's that book about a road trip?' asked John.

We were driving west, heading toward Marseille on the busy A8 which, according to the Bentley's satnav, was a journey of about two and a half hours. I was at the wheel and John had his notebook open on his thigh.

'There are several. *The Hobbit. Travels with Charley.*'

'It's not *The* fucking *Hobbit.*' John frowned. '*Travels with Charley.* Is that Graham Greene?'

'Steinbeck. You're thinking of *Travels with My Aunt.* Which isn't a book about a road trip at all.'

'Think of some others.'

I shrugged. '*The Alchemist*, Paulo Coelho.'

John looked nauseous. 'Ugh. No. I hate him. That's a real Richard and Judy book. Zero sugar philosophy for muppets.'

'*The Grapes of Wrath. On the Road.*'

'Kerouac. Yeah, that's a real life-changing book. After I read it I promised myself I would never waste my time finishing a book I wasn't enjoying ever again. It's the kind of road book that would give you road rage.'

I smiled. John's opinions of books were always amusing.

'Come to think of it, it's not a book at all, the story I'm thinking about. It's *Two-Lane Blacktop.* A Seventies movie with James Taylor and Dennis Wilson from The Beach Boys.'

'Haven't seen it.'

'Few have. But it's a cult classic.'

'What happens?'

'Not very much. They drive across Route 66 in a '55 Chevy. Don't say anything. Get in a couple of races with Warren Oates.'

'Sounds a bit existential. Not your kind of thing at all.'

'Nope. It isn't. But I was thinking. That's kind of like you and me, old sport. Taylor and Wilson. Except that we're twice as old as they were in that movie. And this is a much better car, of course. Plus, we've got a lot more money. And we don't have a girl in the back.'

'Not yet. Maybe we'll find one on the way.' I put my foot down. 'Hey, there's a green Porsche up ahead. We can race that if you like.'

'Just keep it to 130.'

We hadn't driven far past Nice when John noticed a French police car in our mirrors. He turned around in his seat and said, 'There's a cop on our tail.'

'I know.'

'How long's he been there?'

'Couple of miles,' I said.

'What's he doing?'

'Don't keep looking at them. It'll make us look suspicious. Just ignore them.'

'Easy for you to say.'

'Easy to say because I'm right.' I smiled. 'I know. Let's play the secret subtitle game. Like we used to do when we were on the road. To keep your mind off them.'

This is a simple game; you give me the title of some worthy book as if it's the beginning of a sentence which I complete with something funny; extra marks are awarded for vulgarity and political incorrectness. So, for example, if someone said *Farewell to Arms*, I might reply, 'Hello, Stoke Mandeville.'

'I'll go first,' I said. '*I Know Why the Caged Bird Sings.*'

John hesitated for only a moment. 'Because if it doesn't then we're going to feed it to the fucking cat.'

'Excellent,' I said. 'Your turn.'

'*And the Mountains Echoed.*'

'With the sound of an enormous fart.' I thought for a minute. 'Here's a hard one for you. *Disgrace.*'

John smiled. 'Dat's Glenda.' He chuckled. 'Here's an easy one. *A Million Little Pieces.*'

'Of shit, are what make Kilburn High Road so interesting to walk along. All right I have one for you, John. *The Elected Member.*'

'Made the Chinese woman's vagina wet just to look at it. *The Remains of the Day.*'

'Refused to flush away until they found a plumber. *How late it was, how late.*'

'Oops. It looked as if she was pregnant after all.' John smiled grimly. 'Here's one you won't get. *The Inheritance of Loss.*'

I was quiet for a moment; then I said, 'Was the leadership of a big band from his father Joe. *The Reluctant Fundamentalist.*'

'Was encouraged greatly by the regular application of electricity to his testicles.'

We carried on this childish vein for a while, but after another ten kilometres the police were still there and, despite our laughter, John was now a nervous wreck.

'What's *their* bloody game?' he said.

'That's all it is. A game. Just like ours. You must have encountered this sort of thing before.'

'No. What do you mean?'

'When you were making your road trips between Monaco and Paris in your Lamborghinis and Aston Martins. Look, they're just fucking with us. We've got an expensive supercar we can't drive like an expensive supercar because they're right behind us. That's the game. You'll see, in a few more miles they'll get bored and move on to someone else.'

'They're on to us, I'm sure of it. They'll probably try to arrest me at the next toll.'

'You're paranoid.'

'I don't think so. After what you told me last night, about that cop telephoning you, I think the game is up for me, Don. Really I do.'

'I don't blame you for being paranoid. But that's what you are. You've got to relax. Close your eyes. Zone out. Pretend they're not there. Just be calm and I'll tell you when they're gone. Look here's another one. *American Pastoral*.'

But John wasn't listening. He delved into the little black Tumi briefcase he'd brought from Geneva and, to my horror, produced an automatic pistol.

'What the fuck is that?' I demanded.

'What's it look like? It's Orla's Walther P22.'

'Are you crazy?'

'I'm damned if they're going to take me without a fight. I can't spend the next twenty years in jail like Phil fucking Spector.'

'Put that thing away. You'll get us both killed.'

'I fucking mean it, Don. I'm not going to jail. I'm sixty-seven years old. I'd rather go out in a hail of bullets than die in prison.'

I could see he was desperate – desperate enough to do something stupid, and he gave me little choice but to turn sharply off the A8 at the next junction. The cops however stayed on the A8, which left us heading north on the M336 toward St-Paul-de-Vence and me wondering what to do now. But first I needed to get the gun out of John's hand and him in a slightly calmer frame of mind.

I kept on driving north for about ten or fifteen kilometres. It was an uninspiring landscape typical of the crappy roadside hinterland of the Côte d'Azur: garden centres, Casino markets, builder's merchants, tyre centres, McDonald's, car showrooms, petrol stations and banks. The sort of road that makes the south of France look more like a ring road around Hemel Hempstead.

'They're gone,' I said after a while.

'I know.'

'The Monty cops said Orla was killed with a 22-calibre Walther,' I said. 'Is that the same gun?'

'Yes.'

'You brought the murder weapon with you? Shit, John. Are you crazy?'

'I couldn't very well leave it on the floor of my bedroom in Monaco,' said John. 'There was enough evidence stacked against me already.'

'Yes, but why didn't you chuck it in the sea. Or in Lake Geneva?'

'I told you. I thought Colette's Russian mafia boyfriend was involved in this. I'm not yet convinced he isn't.'

'Fair enough. But put that away, for Christ's sake, before you shoot someone.'

John put the Walther back in his Tumi.

'Is it loaded?'

'Of course it's fucking loaded.'

I glanced sideways at him.

'Did you sleep last night?'

'Not really. I kept thinking that Chief Inspector was about to turn up and put me in manacles.' He shook his head. 'Jesus, I need some air.'

'Why don't I lower the hood?'

'Are you kidding? I feel quite exposed enough as it is. Look, let's stop somewhere. For a coffee.'

'We've been driving for less than an hour.'

'I know, I know. But – let's just stop somewhere, okay? Please?'

'I've got an idea. We could have an early Sunday lunch. Perhaps with a glass of wine in you, you'll relax a bit. Maybe you could have a nap in the car afterward. We could go to the Colombe d'Or, perhaps. That's not far from here.'

'No. I couldn't go there. They know me. I used to go there all the time with Orla.'

'Of course. Somewhere else then. Somewhere they don't know you. There's a café up ahead. With parking.'

John nodded. 'I've got a better idea,' he said. 'Head a bit further north, to Vence. We can stop at the Château Saint-Martin. A couple of times I almost went there with Colette. They don't know me there but I hear they've got a pretty good spa and an excellent restaurant. Maybe I can have a massage. I really think that might help. I've got a bitch of a tension headache like you wouldn't believe.'

'All right. If that's what you want to do. But I don't know how you ever made it to Geneva. At this rate we're never going to get to Marseille.'

'I know. And I'm sorry. Look, I'll be a lot better when I've got rid of this headache, okay?'

'Okay, sure.'

The Château Saint-Martin was set amidst the ruins of an old fortress – an antiseptic sort of place in about thirty acres of grounds that looked like any overpriced luxury hotel in Southern California. The lawns were lush and green and so carefully cut they looked less mown than Brazilian-waxed. The Beverly Hills air was augmented by the staff's ill-fitting beige-coloured uniforms and there was a gift shop selling overpriced silk scarves and straw hats and lots of other stuff including some books you didn't want. It was the kind of place you went for your second honeymoon and read *Fifty Shades of Grey* to look for some ideas about how to make your stay more interesting; which was probably why the guests looked so very bored. Several women were doing some yoga in the sun and probably trying to work up an appetite for a light lunch. They were mostly Americans who liked the French but only if they spoke English good enough for them to wish someone a nice day.

John went and booked himself a deep-tissue massage while I sat in the garden restaurant in the shade of some old olive trees and chose a bottle of cold Meursault. Since John was paying I chose the Coche-Dury Meursault 2009, a snip at 500 euros; then I sat and read about another forest fire in *The Riviera Times*. There are always forest fires in the Alpes-Maritimes and Provence during the summer. This one was in the Forêt de l'Albaréa, near Sospel; 900 hectares of forest and several dozen houses had been destroyed, and the unidentifiable body of a man had been found. I wondered how badly you had to be burned for your body to be unidentifiable. Sometimes life in France seemed very much more precarious than in England. At last John returned from the spa and I waved over the maître d' and we ordered some gazpacho followed by two chicken salads.

'You were a while,' I observed.

'Got talking to the girl who's doing my massage,' he said. 'Nice-looking bird so I tipped her in advance.'

'Why?'

'To double my chance of a happy ending, of course.'

'Is that a possibility?'

'It is now. Besides, she's from Yorkshire.' He nodded. 'From Keighley. If there's one thing I know about it's women from fucking Keighley.'

'That's a surprise. A girl from Keighley, in a place like this.'

'Isn't it?'

'That's Brontë country, isn't it?'

'It is.'

But when the waiter arrived with our food, we were in for a bigger surprise. Because our waiter was none other than Philip French, who had been the fourth musketeer in John's *atelier* of Mike Munns, Peter Stakenborg and myself. And it was only now I remembered that French's home in Tourrettes-sur-Loup was only a few miles away from Vence and the Château Saint-Martin. If either John or I had ever accepted his invitation to visit him there, we would have known that and perhaps avoided the area altogether.

French regarded us both, but more especially John, with something close to loathing before laying the chicken salads very carefully on the table.

'*Bon appétit*,' he said quietly.

'Christ, Philip,' said John. 'What are you doing here?'

'As you can see, I'm your fucking waiter.'

'Yes, but why?'

'I should have thought that was obvious. I need the money, that's why. I have bills to pay. I can no longer do that with my writing because no one will publish my work. Rather more to the point, what are *you* doing here? You're the one who's wanted for murder by the police. Or was that just some cheap publicity stunt to help you sell more crappy books?'

'No. Orla's dead. I really didn't do it, Phil. I give you my word. Whatever you think of me, I'm not a murderer. We're on our way to Marseille. To look for someone who'll help to clear me I hope.'

'As if I care.'

'I'm sorry you think that. Look, Phil you won't – you won't call the police, will you? At least give me a chance to prove myself innocent.'

'That's a good one. You, innocent. An oxymoron if ever I heard one. Sorry. That's not a word we're allowed to use in one of your books, is it? Because most of your readers wouldn't understand it.'

'Please, Phil. I'm begging you. Don't give me away.'

'Did I say I would give you away? Did I?'

'No, you didn't. Phil, you've got every right to be angry with me. And I apologize if you think I treated you badly. All I can say is that I was under a great deal of pressure at the time. But look here, Don has found it within himself to forgive me. Can't you?'

French glanced at me and I shrugged back at him as if John was speaking something like the truth.

'Don was always the best of us,' said French. 'I'm made of less noble stuff than he is, I'm afraid.'

That made me smile. It's funny how people think they know you when in fact they don't know you at all. There is certainly nothing noble about me; but I'm no psychopath, just someone preternaturally disposed to killing, A hundred years ago, in the trenches, I'd have been up to my neck in death and – I wouldn't be surprised – quite comfortable with that.

'If I can clear myself I shall try very hard to make it up to you,' said John.

I almost laughed. John might have been trying his best to throw himself on Philip French's mercy but instead he only managed to sound pompous.

French shook his head and then glanced over his shoulder at the maître d'. 'Look, I can't talk now, but I'm near the end of my shift. Meet me in the underground parking lot at three o'clock and we'll talk then. All right?'

'All right.'

French walked quickly away without a backward glance.

'That's all I fucking need,' said John, and for a moment he buried his face in his hands. After a moment he looked up, tried to eat some lunch and then drained his glass empty. 'He's probably calling the police right now.'

'I don't think so.'

'No? He hates my guts. Why wouldn't he?'

I shrugged. 'Because he said he wouldn't. More or less. Philip generally means what he says. Besides, does he really want the trouble if he's working here? The management, the other guests – they might not appreciate it if a hundred gendarmes descend on this place. That might reflect on him, and if he does need the money he also needs the job.'

'Yes, good point.'

I ate my lunch, most of John's, lit a cigarette, ordered some coffees and pushed my face outside the shade of our umbrella and into the sun. I realized I was enjoying myself and decided I'd been a little unjust to the Château Saint-Martin. The Coche-Dury and truffle-poached chicken salad had been excellent and the gardens were nice, too. As usual I had more of a taste for expensive places and hotels than I would ever have let on. I decided that when I was in possession of a fortune of my own – which, I hoped, would be quite soon – I would come back to the Château Saint-Martin, perhaps with Twentyman's shapely young Russian friend Katya, and, in the hotel's best suite, fuck the arse off her morning, noon and night.

Meanwhile John had gone off and cancelled his massage. There didn't seem to be much point in having it now, since it seemed unlikely that he would ever relax again.

At three o'clock we both went to the hotel's underground car park where we had left the Bentley and found Philip French already waiting for us in the cool gloom. He was no longer wearing his waiter's uniform, but it wasn't just his own clothes that made him seem different; he was altogether more businesslike, even intimidating. He lit a roll-up and for a moment he just faced us in silence.

'So then,' said John, 'what did you want to talk about?'

French laughed. 'What do you think?'

'I really don't know why you're taking this tone with me, Phil,' said John.

'Don't you?'

'No, I don't.'

'Then I'll come straight to the point. The price of my silence is 250,000 quid.'

'Don't be ridiculous.'

'Fine. As soon as you've left here I'll call the police. I don't think they'll have too much of a problem finding a nice Bentley like the one you arrived in.' He walked over to the Bentley and sat on the blue bonnet. 'You see, I already checked that with the concierge. The Swiss number-plate should make it easy to spot. By tonight you'll be sharing a sweaty Monaco police cell with some Russian pimp and wishing you'd taken my offer.'

'So that's how it is,' said John.

'That's how it has to be,' said French. 'I can't afford it any other way. I'm skint, John. I owe money to all sorts of people down here. Which means I'm desperate. Maybe not quite as desperate as you are, perhaps, but that's how it is, *old sport*.'

'I don't have that kind of money right now,' said John.

French stroked the hood of Bentley and smiled. 'Don't give me that. This lovely car is worth at least a hundred K.'

'It's not mine. If I gave it to you the true owner would eventually report it stolen and then where would you be?'

'No worse off than I am right now and that's the truth. Caroline – my wife – she's left me. Taken the kids and fucked off back to England. All I have down here are debts and dead mosquitoes. I can't even afford to fill my swimming pool or switch on my air conditioning.'

'When I closed the *atelier* I gave you a generous redundancy payment,' said John. 'Maybe you've forgotten that.'

'That was taxable, since I am self-employed. Tax down here is something akin to demanding money with menaces. So the French government had more than half of it. But then you wouldn't know anything about tax, would you? Famously, you don't pay any tax at all. Besides, what you gave me, after writing all those bestsellers I wrote for you, it was fucking chickenfeed. You know it and I know it and Don knows it. I don't know why he's helping you after what you did to the four of us. Unless he has some other agenda. Your biography perhaps, when you're banged up in a Monaco jail. Yes, that might be it. No one has known you for as long as he has, which would make him best placed to write a book like that.'

'Please leave Don out of this,' said John. 'No one had a better friend than him.'

'Have it your way, Houston. But my price stands. Two hundred and fifty grand or I telephone the cops. And don't think I won't do it. I've been on the go since seven o'clock this morning so, believe me, it'll be the best job I've had all day.'

'You weren't listening. I simply don't have that kind of money. Look, use your loaf, Phil, I'm on the run. I've got a few thousand and that's it. The minute I use an ATM I'm toast.'

'He's right,' I said.

'Do you think I'm stupid? I looked at your fucking lunch bill. It was 650 euros. That's a week's wages for me. Including tips.'

'That was my fault,' I said. 'I ordered a bottle of Coche-Dury. I don't know what came over me. Touch of the sun I think.'

'In all the years I've known you, Don, you never once ordered a really expensive bottle of wine. Not once. Your thrift always impressed me because that's how I am myself. So if anyone ordered a 500-euro bottle of white Burgundy it wasn't you.'

'That doesn't alter the fact that I don't have two hundred and fifty grand,' said John.

'No?' French smiled. 'Then I tell you what, John. I'll take that famous watch of yours, on account. The Hublot Black Caviar. According to the *Daily Mail* it's worth a million dollars. So if I sell it I ought to get how much – maybe 150,000 euros? Who knows? These things are never worth as much second-hand as you think they are. Believe me I know. Lately I've had to sell a lot of my possessions on eBay: a nice guitar, a racing bicycle. I'll take that watch and whatever cash you can raise by nine o'clock tonight. But I'll be disappointed if it's not at least 20,000 euros.'

John said nothing.

'That's a good offer,' said French. 'Best deal you're going to get from me, anyway. I'd advise you to take it, Houston. Besides, you've probably got a whole drawer full of expensive watches at home. Me, I've got this fucking ten-euro Casio.' He held up his wrist to show us a strip of black plastic on his wrist. 'Matter of fact, why don't we swap?'

John took off his watch and handed it over to French, who put it on immediately. John looked at the Casio he'd received in return and then hurled it across the garage.

'Now that's just stupid,' said French. 'You know that watch probably keeps just as good time as your one. Which begs the question. Why spend a million bucks on a watch? It's not like you get any more time for your money, is it? And you'll forgive me for saying so, but it's a million dollars you could have spent giving decent bonuses to the people who made you rich. Mike, Peter, Don and me.'

'You bastard,' muttered John.

'On my new million-dollar watch I make it 3.15,' said French. 'I expect to see you both at my house tonight, with the cash. Shall we say nine o'clock?' He handed me a card with an address and a postcode. 'Here. Just in case you lose your way. The Villa Seurel. On the Route du Caire. A short way past the Hôtel Résidence des Chevaliers, and on your left. I'll be expecting you. By the way, don't count on me giving you any dinner. There's nothing in the fridge except ice.'

CHAPTER 8

After John had left Colette's apartment, I poured a glass of the Dom Pérignon he had left on ice in Colette's champagne bucket and sat down in the sitting room. At more than a hundred pounds a bottle it seemed a shame to waste it. Meanwhile she took a long shower and then went into the kitchen to make us coffee; it was late and she must have thought we needed to stay awake for the drive to Nice airport. But I think she mostly went into the kitchen because she hardly dared to meet my eye for fear that I would tell her some unpleasant detail that she didn't want to know about what had happened upstairs in the sky duplex. The sort of details you get in *Macbeth* about blood, and while the dogs didn't exactly count as Duncan's grooms I was sure she wouldn't have appreciated my shooting them: Colette loved dogs. I could easily understand her reluctance to deal with Orla's death, and so when she returned to the sitting room with a coffee pot and two cups I was happy to avoid the subject altogether. Indeed I was reading my Kindle when she came in and generally behaving as if the murder had never happened.

She was wearing a nice white blouse that was tight enough to show the swell of her breasts, a pair of neat black tailored pants, sensible ballet pumps, and a single gold bangle that resembled a snake. Her scent was Chanel 19 but I only knew that because there was a bottle of it on her dressing table and because it was exactly the same scent that Orla had worn; it would, I thought, have been typical of John to have given his mistress the same kind of perfume as his wife, just to avoid any cross-contamination. I admired him for that: John did adultery better than anyone I knew.

'What are you reading?' she asked.

'*The Information*, by Martin Amis.'

'What's it about?'

I thought it best not to mention that it was about two authors who hate each other.

'I think it's a revenge tragedy,' I said vaguely. 'But to be honest I really haven't figured what the fuck is going on.'

'I don't know how you can read at a time like this,' she said.

'I can read anywhere.'

I shrugged and watched her pour the coffee; and thinking it was now best to seem very ordinary indeed I told her something about my early life and my love of reading.

'My mother taught me to read,' I said. 'I mean really taught me, so that I could read to her. Like that bloke in *A Handful of Dust*. Her eyesight wasn't very good and there weren't any talking books back then. You might say that I was her talking book. Consequently I read a lot of books that perhaps I shouldn't have been reading at that sort of age. I mean I never read stuff like *Winnie the Pooh* or *The Lord of the Rings*. It was Edna O'Brien and Ian Fleming and Iris Murdoch right from the start. In spite of that I felt like a whole world had been opened to me. Not just a world of books but the world that those books described. As a child it was deeply liberating. As if someone had given me a ticket to a whole different universe. You might almost say I escaped having a childhood altogether. After that I found I could switch off and read at any time and in any place. I never had a problem about detaching myself from the reality of everyday life. It was usually people I had a problem with, not books, which is a common enough experience in Scotland. I was also drawing, playing the piano, or collecting things like stamps and shells and bottle-tops, and numbers of course – I was always collecting car numbers, which was a lot easier than collecting the numbers of trains, because the cars weren't moving – but in the end it always came back to reading. I'm the kind of person who if ever I were asked on *Desert Island Discs* would much prefer to be cast away with eight books instead of with eight records. Music I can live without, but reading, no. This is good coffee, thank you.'

'It's Algerian coffee,' she said. 'I get my mother to send it from home. What sort of books did you read?'

'I liked histories and biographies, or books about travel and nature. Still do. Oddly I was never much interested in fiction. The other boys were forever reading stories about the Second World War. Not me. I used to like books about wildlife.'

'You don't sound like someone who would have ended up in the army.'

'After school I meant to become a lawyer. I did a law degree, at Cambridge. But my father died, leaving my mother with not very much money; debts, mostly; and luckily for me the army was there to cover the costs of finishing university in return for three years of service as a soldier. At the time it seemed like a fair exchange, although most of my contemporaries thought I was crazy. But I was a rather better soldier than anyone would have imagined. Although not so much a leader of men as an intrepid warrior, so to speak. More your lone wolf. No, I can't say I was ever interested in leading a band of brothers.'

'I was never much of a reader,' she said. 'My father read the Koran a lot and certainly never encouraged me to read anything. I couldn't give a damn about the Koran now. It's not a book for women. The first man who ever gave me a book to read was John. I still have that book. It's *The Great Gatsby*.'

I nodded. I hardly liked to tell her that John gave a copy of *The Great Gatsby* to all of the women he had a thing with. I couldn't ever love someone who didn't like that book, he often said. He had a box full of the hardback Everyman edition in his study.

'Did you read it?'

'I tried,' she said. 'But I couldn't see what all the fuss was about.'

I smiled and looked at my watch. It was now 3.30 a.m.

'We'd best leave for the airport. Our cases are already in the car so there's nothing left to do except lock up and leave.'

'I can't find one of my earrings,' she said. 'John bought them for me. At Pomellato. They were expensive.'

'It'll turn up.'

I stood up and glanced out of the window. Monaco was gilded with light, like the golden collar on the neck of some embalmed princess. I wondered if this was the reason I felt so comfortable in that little principality: I am quite comfortable with the dead. They don't moan much about the cost of living.

I clapped my hands, businesslike, but rather too loudly for Colette's nerves, as she gave a start as if something had exploded behind her head.

'Now then. I've got you a ticket on Air France 6201 to Paris, which leaves Nice at 6.15 a.m. so we ought to get you there by 4.30 at the latest. That flight gets you into Orly at 7.40 a.m. I'll give you the ticket and some money when we get to the airport and you can send John that text saying you've gone to visit your sister in Marseille when you're sitting in the departure lounge. Yes, don't forget that, will you? This is important, Colette.'

'Why not now?'

'Do you want to risk having him come down here again? With me sitting here?'

'No, I suppose not.'

'Do it in the departure lounge. When you arrive at Orly take the train into the city – it's cheaper – and go to the Hôtel Georgette, where I've reserved a room for you. It's a family-run hotel in the Marais – Rue Grenier-Saint-Lazare, number 36 – and while it's not very expensive, it's clean and it's comfortable. I've stayed there several times myself and you'll find that I've paid for two weeks in advance.'

'Thank you, Don. That was very thoughtful of you.'

'Don't mention it. Then all you have to do is stick it out and wait for me to get in contact with further instructions. It might be a couple of weeks before I turn up in person. It could even be three. But we'll speak on the phone long before that. Until then I suggest you go and see some exhibitions. I'm sure I don't have to tell you about what there is to do in Paris. Only the dead have an excuse for finding nothing to do in Paris. A lot of tourists go to the cemetery of Père Lachaise, but as a writer I always find the one in Montparnasse rather more interesting and certainly less popular with the tourists. Samuel Beckett is buried there, as are Jean-Paul Sartre and Simone de Beauvoir, in the same plot, which is peculiar since they never actually shared a house when they were alive.' I smiled. 'Can you imagine?'

'And you're going to London?'

'That's right. My flight is a little later than yours. The BA 2621, which leaves Nice at 7.05 and gets into Gatwick at eight. I'll go back to the flat in Putney and wait for the news to break and then the cops to show up. Which they will. I'm certain of it. There's no point in us trying to see each other before that's happened. All of the people who knew John and Orla will be under a certain amount of scrutiny from the police and the press until things die down a bit.'

Colette nodded gravely; she didn't drink the coffee.

'Now make sure you've got your laptop with you, because I'm going to email you with details of what to say – when eventually you speak to John or to John's lawyer, depending on where he is. By then he should be a nervous wreck and ready to do anything you want. Once you've told him that you're prepared to say that he was with you for the whole evening, that should go a long way to putting him in the clear; but of course it will draw a whole shit storm down on your head when, eventually, you come back to Monaco to face the music. The police will be quite hard on you, I think. Why didn't you come forward before? Are you lying to protect him? Did you kill her? That kind of thing. You must be prepared to be bullied. But we've spoken about that.'

'Yes,' she said. 'I understand.'

'If they ask where the hell you've been you can say you were scared. You didn't know what to do. You thought you might be accused of complicity. You were frightened that they might send you to jail for something you had nothing to do with. You can tell the same thing to John. You can even remind him that you're French-Algerian, which means you come from a family and from a place where people never talk to the police – he'll believe that because he's a bit of a racist.'

'That's true. The fifteenth – where my family lives – is the *banlieue*. No one trusts the police in northern Marseille.'

'But you've thought about it now and decided to do the right thing. Because you can't bear to remain silent any more when a man's liberty is at stake, and so on and so on.'

She nodded again.

'Just remember why we're doing this, Colette. If you lie for him and say he was with you for the whole evening instead of – what was it? – ninety minutes? Then you'll have something over him. And if you have something over him the best way of making sure you never use that is for him to marry you. Leave it to me to put that thought in his head. After that, he'll be in the clear.'

We went down to the garage and got into her car, the new Audi A6 that Lev had bought her when he was still around. I sometimes wondered about Lev Kaganovich. Was he even alive? Now that really was a mystery story. She was just about to start the Audi's engine when I told her I'd forgotten my Kindle.

'Do you need it?' she asked.

'I can tell you're not a reader,' I said. 'It's got about a hundred books on it.' I was already getting out of the car. 'If I don't fetch it I'll have nothing to read at the airport and on the plane, and for me that would be a very particular kind of hell. I need a book the way some people need a cup of coffee.' I bent down and looked into the passenger cabin. 'Don't worry. I'll only be five minutes.'

I waited for a second, smiled and held out my hand. 'The key. You'll have to give me the key.'

'I thought I gave it to you.'

'You did. But then I gave it back to you.'

She looked in her Chanel purse and nodded. 'You're right. You did. I'm sorry. It's just that I'm so nervous that the police are going to turn up any moment.' She handed me the key. 'Please be quick.'

I nodded, returned to the lift, rode up to 29 and let myself back into Colette's apartment. But the first thing I did was not to find my Kindle but to fetch a bottle of Russian champagne from a bag I'd hidden under Colette's bed. I opened it, poured some of it down the sink, where it belonged, and then used the half-empty bottle to replace the bottle of Dom in Colette's ice-bucket. Then I added a few Chekhovian touches to the appearance of the apartment from the same bag: a recent Russian newspaper, some Russian cigarettes – smoked and unsmoked – a half-eaten fifty-gram jar of Beluga caviar (£353), an unopened bottle of Grey Goose vodka, and a packet of Contex condoms in Colette's bathroom; I even left a copy of *Piat` desiat ottenkov serogo* on her bedside table, which in case you didn't know is *Fifty Shades of Grey*, in Russian. That was a nice touch. It's surprising what you can get on Amazon.

When I was satisfied that the apartment showed every sign of a recent visit from Colette's absent Russian boyfriend – more than enough to severely unnerve John, who was convinced he was mafia – I fetched my Kindle from the windowsill where I'd left it and went back down to the garage.

Colette was biting her lip and looking anxious. I kissed her in an effort to reassure her. Was it my imagination or was there just a hint of semen I could taste on her lips?

'It's all right,' I said. 'We can go now.'

She winced. 'I'm sorry, Don. I left my iPad on the kitchen worktop.'

I shook my head. 'Not to worry. I'll go and fetch it now . . .'

'You're a very thoughtful man, do you know that?'

I took hold of the handle and opened the car door, but Colette clasped my arm and shook her head.

'On second thoughts, don't bother. I have my Apple Mac. I've got everything on there that I need. I really won't need the iPad.'

'If you're sure.'

'Yes. Besides, I just want to get away from here. Now.'

'Really. It's no trouble. And wait, suppose John finds the iPad. Won't he worry that you've gone away without it?' I shrugged. 'Won't *you* worry that he might go through your diary?'

'No,' she said. 'Besides he doesn't know the passcode.' She frowned, 'At least I think he doesn't.' She shook her head. 'I told him once – but no, he never remembers anything like that. He couldn't even tell you my mobile number.'

I shook my head. 'If you're sure.'

'I'm sure. Please, Don, let's just go, huh?'

'All right.'

Colette started the car and we drove slowly out of the Tour Odéon garage; but instead of turning up the hill and driving through Beausoleil – which would have been the quickest way to the airport – she drove down, toward the sea, and through the city.

'Why are we going this way?'

'Because the best time to see Monte Carlo is always in the summer, just before the dawn, at about four in the morning. In fact it's the only time it looks really beautiful and you have a sense of what it used to be like before money made it so – so nauseating. There aren't any sweaty tourists greedy for a celebrity at this hour and you can't smell the stink of gasoline from all those unbearably ridiculous Lamborghinis and Ferraris.'

I nodded and as we came into Casino Square I saw her point; what she'd said – it wasn't the first line of *Casino Royale* but still, it was all right. I put my hand on her knee and squeezed it gently.

'Yes, I agree. It's quite different. I don't think I've ever seen it like this.'

'You know something? I've never even been into the Casino.'

'Neither have I.'

'Let's do it now,' she said. 'Just for ten minutes. We'll leave the car out front, go in the *Salon Privé*, and have one spin of the roulette wheel.'

'Really, we ought to get to the airport. And besides, I'm hardly dressed for it.'

'Please, Don. I need to feel lucky again. And you are so English – you've left us loads of time to get to the airport. At this time of the morning it will take twenty minutes. And your clothes are fine. You're not wearing jeans. You have a jacket. You don't have to look like Daniel Craig any more to go in there, you know.'

I smiled at how much like a little girl Colette seemed; it was easy to see why John had fallen for her; I was falling for her, and I wanted to indulge her a little. To encourage her, to enable her to take her mind off things; she'd had a difficult evening and it seemed only fair that we should do something that was important to her.

'If you like,' I said. 'But just a few minutes, mind. We don't want to miss our planes.'

We parked out front – easy at that time of the morning – and went inside. The casino entrance hall looked more like a nineteenth-century opera house than a place to lose money; then again, when was the last time that opera made money? We presented our passports to the *caissier* – to prove we weren't Monégasques, forbidden by law to gamble in the casino – bought a couple of ten-euro tickets for the *Salon Privé* and passed into a large, high-ceilinged room that was still surprisingly busy with people sitting around blackjack tables and roulette wheels. Some of the gamblers and croupiers looked at Colette with open lust as if wondering how many chips it took to walk in with someone like her. They might have been surprised when I bought Colette a single 500-euro plaque and handed it to her.

'One spin of the wheel,' I said.

'I promise.'

She took a circuit around the room before stopping at one of the many roulette tables, where she put the plaque on black and waited while the croupier turned the wheel and rolled the ball; and when the ball hit black, she squealed so loudly you might have thought she'd beaten Le Chiffre and won millions instead of another single 500-euro plaque. She hugged me excitedly and then we cashed in and left before the temptation to roll again became too great for her to resist.

Outside the sweet early morning air was already warm on the face and the sky was the colour of manuka honey. It was going to be another hot day. A small truck was washing the street in front of the Hôtel de Paris. Consciences are cleaned with equal facility; take it from someone who knows.

'That was such fun,' said Colette, as we walked back to the car. 'I can't believe I won. Thank you. I feel so much better.'

'I'm glad,' I said, and before we got back in the car I kissed her again, only this time I let my hand make free with her breasts.

Less than thirty minutes later we were driving into the long-term underground parking lot at Terminal 2; with its signal-red walls, low ceilings, bright lighting and polished concrete floor, the Nice airport car park was a very pleasant alternative to its malodorous English counterparts. And at that early hour the car park was quiet, with no one else around.

I pointed out a space at the far end of an empty row. 'There,' I said. 'No need to drive any further.'

Colette turned smartly into the spot, switched off the engine and popped the trunk with a button on the driver's door.

'I'll get the luggage,' I said and jumped quickly out of the car. 'And I think because you're earlier than me, I'll walk you over to your check-in.'

'You don't have to.'

'Nonsense. Besides, I've got your ticket.'

I put Colette's bag on the ground, and then my own, and as she came around the back of the car I pointed at something lying on the floor of the Audi's big boot.

'Look,' I said, pointing at the back of the boot. 'There's something shiny lying on the floor. Is that – is that your missing earring?'

Of course, I knew it was her missing diamond earring; I knew because it was me who had placed it there in the boot.

'Oh, my God. You're right. It is my earring. How did it get there? Is this my lucky day, or what?'

'It's your lucky day, all right. You win five hundred euros and now you find your missing diamond earring. That means something else good is going to happen to you now because these things always happen in threes. Take my word for it.'

'I hope you're right.'

'Of course I'm right.'

Colette leaned into the boot to fetch her missing earring, and as she did I pulled out the silenced Walther P22 from under the back of my belt and shot her twice just behind the ear. She was probably dead before her face hit the carpet and all quite painlessly, I might add. It took only another second to sweep up her legs and tip the rest of her body into the trunk. I lowered the lid for a second, glanced around the car park and having ascertained I wasn't being watched, lifted the lid once more and shot Colette twice in the chest, just to make absolutely sure. The gun was so silent I might have been pulling the trigger on a gas barbecue. I chucked the gun after her, dumped her case in the boot beside her body and then closed the lid, permanently.

I went through her handbag, took some things I thought might come in useful later – including her laptop – turned off her mobile phone and then stuffed the bag under the passenger seat.

I locked up the car and checked in for my flight back to London.

It was a nice day to fly somewhere.

CHAPTER 9

Tourrettes-sur-Loup is an attractive higgledy-piggledy village that occupies a high space on the edge of the spectacular Loup valley and seems to grow out of the rocky plateau it's built on, like a huge and sprawling geranium; it put me in mind of that mystical albeit much colder place, Shangri-La, from James Hilton's *Lost Horizon*. I didn't know if the inscrutable locals enjoyed impossible longevity, as in Hilton's hugely successful novel, but they seemed no more interested in the outside world than if they had been Tibetans and, in a local restaurant close to the medieval town square where John and I ate an early dinner, the waiters seemed to regard our attempts to speak French as if they themselves continued to speak ancient Occitan, which was once the language in that part of France. Still, the food was good and there was a decent wine cellar from which we had chosen an excellent ten-year-old Bandol. We were sitting on a small terrace at a restaurant called La Cave de Tourrettes, with a view of the valley that would have given a Sherpa vertigo, and in the air was a strong smell of night-scented jasmine which quite overpowered the smoke from my cigarette. I'd just eaten a delicious terrine of crab and was now contemplating the arrival of a gut-busting cassoulet.

'That cunt,' muttered John.

'Who?'

'Phil. Who do you think? My friend and former fucking colleague.'

'Perhaps.' I shrugged. 'Good writer, though.'

'Yes,' John admitted. 'Good enough. Or at least he was.'

'I'm surprised he can't get published.'

'The whole business is changing. You've got to write exactly what they want or you're fucked.'

'Maybe. Still, I can easily see why he chose to live here. This is a nice little place – Tourrettes. It's a bit *Name of the Rose*, isn't it? Unlike the rest of this part of the world there's something completely unspoiled about it.'

'The same cannot be said of him.'

'No, perhaps not.'

'To be frank, I hardly recognized the bastard.' John shook his head. 'He's changed a lot since I last saw him. I had no idea he was quite so bitter. Thinner, too.'

'It's not just money that changes people for the worse,' I said. 'It's the lack of money, too. He's had a rough time of it, these last few months. That much is clear. I mean, I'd no idea that Caroline had cleared off with the kids. Or indeed that he was working as a waiter.'

'I think I told you that, John.'

He shrugged. 'Did you? I don't remember. Anyway, it's quite a comedown for any writer to endure.'

'There's nothing holy about being a writer, Don. And what's wrong with being a waiter? George Orwell worked as a waiter. Didn't do him any harm.'

'No, he was a *plongeur*. A dishwasher. And besides, the normal trajectory is that you wait on tables on your way to becoming a famous writer, not the other way around.'

'The world doesn't owe you a living just because you're a

writer. Besides, your wife cleared off. And it hasn't made you a cunt like him.'

'Kind of you to say so, John.'

'The way he was talking, you'd think his whole fucking life was my bloody responsibility. I mean, Jesus, he was supposed to be self-employed. When I wound up the *atelier* I was under no obligation to give him a penny. You know that better than anyone, Don. But I felt an obligation to him, for old times' sake. To soften the blow. Because he'd been with me for almost as long as you have. Twenty grand I gave him. Twenty fucking grand. And how does he repay me? With threats. Blackmail. The cops.' He frowned. 'Do you think it's true? That the French really took most of it in tax?'

'Depends how much he owed them already. But they're pretty good at getting tax out of people, the French. Much better than the Italians.'

I took a drag on my cigarette and blew the smoke toward an American woman who must have thought that every country in the world ought to have behaved like the United States and outlawed the habit; she tutted loudly and waved a napkin ostentatiously in front of her face as if I'd directed some neurotoxic gas in her direction. I toyed with trying to update Oscar Wilde's famous remark about a cigarette, to take account of this kind of thing: 'A cigarette is the perfect type of a perfect pleasure. It irritates Americans. What more could one want?' But it didn't really work; it's always a mistake to think you can improve on anything Oscar said.

'I read a rather good Elmore Leonard novel about a blackmailer once,' I said. '52 *Pickup*. Fifty-two is the amount of money in thousands of dollars that two blackmailers ask their victim to pay.'

'Then that guy got off lightly, didn't he? Me, I'm down a

million-dollar watch. Not to mention another twenty grand at nine o'clock.' John glanced at the tan mark where his Hublot Caviar watch had been, shook his head and cursed, again. 'I can't tell you how gutted I am about that watch. I bought it in Ciribelli. It wasn't just an impulse thing. It had sentimental value. It really meant something. To me, at any rate. It was a present to myself for selling one hundred million books. I was going to have it engraved to that effect, only I never quite got around to it.'

'I didn't know that. I'm sorry.'

'What really pisses me off is that he's probably going to sell it for way less than it's worth.'

I surveyed the red wine in my glass for a moment and then shook my head.

'Not without the box, he won't. These days, people who buy that sort of thing second-hand want everything that goes with it. The box, the certificate, the original receipt, the bloody carrier bag and wrapping paper for all I know. It's the same with books. Try selling a first-edition *Brighton Rock* without the dust-jacket and see how much you get. I know. I did.'

'Yes, that's a point. Without the box he'll be lucky if he gets a tenth of what the watch is really worth. But with the box it'd be worth at least twice that. Maybe more.' John laughed bitterly. 'That's a happy thought. Thanks, old sport. I'll be thinking of that tonight, when I hand over the twenty grand.'

'In *52 Pickup* the victim manages not to pay the blackmailers anything at all. That's why I mentioned it. He tricks them. In fact he goes a lot further than that.'

'Easier said than done.'

'I don't think so. It's just possible that if we were to offer to get Phil the Hublot box and all the Black Caviar paperwork for your watch he might be persuaded to give up on the twenty grand. That way he'd get much more money when eventually he sells it. And no questions asked, probably.'

'But I don't have the box or the paperwork. It's back at the apartment in Monaco. And there's no chance of getting it from there.'

'He doesn't know that. Look, John, if I went up to Phil's house on my own tonight I could sell him a story that the box is somewhere else. At the *atelier* in Paris, perhaps. That only I can get it; and that I'm ready to make a deal with him.'

'Go on.'

I glanced at John's Tumi bag, which was on the ground by his leg.

'Have you got the money in there?' I asked.

'Of course.'

'Give the bag to me.'

John handed over the bag and I took a quick look inside it just to check it was all there, like he said.

'I'll show him the twenty thousand, like we agreed. But then I'll suggest that if he lets me keep the money then I'll bring him the box and the paperwork. I get to keep the twenty thousand but he stands to make an extra hundred 150,000 when he sells the watch. Maybe more.'

'So he thinks you've double-crossed me for twenty grand?'

'Exactly. I'm figuring he's got nothing against me. In fact I'm sure I can persuade him that I'm his friend and that he owes me – *something*. Without you there to make things personal I'm sure I can get him to believe that the Bentley and the cash are what I've been after all along. I'll tell him I'd forgotten all about the watch. He'll want to believe that I really hate you as much as he does. And that I'm no better or worse than him when it comes to revenge.'

'But I already told him the Bentley wasn't mine.'

'Of course you did. Only I'll tell him I know different. Or that I know someone who'll buy the car with no questions asked, for fifty grand. I'll tell him I'm willing to settle for the cash and the car if he settles for your watch, in its box.'

'Yes, that might work. But why would he trust you to come back with the Hublot box?'

'Because I'm not you. He isn't a fucking criminal, John. He's actually quite law-abiding, only right now he's also desperate. I know him. Phil and I go way back. He used to work at J. Walter Thompson, remember? That's how he and I met. Besides, I didn't work in advertising for all those years without becoming just a little bit persuasive.' I shrugged. 'Anyway, what have you got to lose?'

'What happens when you don't come back to Tourrettes with the Hublot box?'

'It will be too late by then. Hopefully you'll have found Colette and your alibi. With any luck you'll be out on police bail. Facing trial, perhaps, but with every chance of being acquitted. Meanwhile, you can instruct your lawyers in Monaco to threaten Phil with jail unless he returns the watch.' I finished the wine in my glass. 'So, what do you say?'

'Give me a minute to think this over,' said John. 'I'm not saying yes. Not yet. Just – give me a minute, okay?'

The cassoulet arrived and I made short work of it while John – ignoring his own main course – concentrated on the Bandol. He was drinking more than was good for him but I could hardly blame him for that; given the strain he was under the surprise was that he wasn't drunk more often.

Then at 8.45 he ordered another bottle of Bandol and told me he would wait at the restaurant for me. 'I guess there's no harm in you trying to talk him around,' he said. 'It's not like I have anything to lose.'

'Good.' I picked up the Tumi bag and collected the car keys off the table. 'I'll be back as soon as I can.'

'You do that, old sport. If I'm not here I'll be at one of those bars on the Place de la Libération.'

CHAPTER 10

I walked back to the square in front of the church where we had left the Bentley and found some small boys next to it, taking pictures of themselves. One of them even crouched down near the exhaust and filmed the start-up on his mobile phone. Tourrettes wasn't like Monaco where expensive cars are ten-a-penny; it was altogether smaller and much less glamorous; to that extent it reminded me of Cornwall.

I smiled kindly, steered the car carefully away from the busy square and drove north onto the Route de Saint-Jean and then up the narrow, dry-stoned road that was Route du Caire, in the direction of Phil's villa. Once or twice I had to move quickly into the side as a van driven by some mad local came hurtling down the road the opposite way. There was no street-lighting, since this was rural France, but there were several houses along the way providing just enough illumination to help me navigate. Soon after the hacienda-style entrance of the Hôtel Résidence des Chevaliers on my right, the road narrowed even further until at the top of the hill, on the left, the Bentley's headlights picked out a rusting metallic sign that read '*Le VILLA SEUREL, Propriété privée*'; next to this was another sign from Immobilière Azuréenne which read '*À Vendre*'. I steered the car through an open gate and up a narrow twisting drive. Ill-kempt bushes brushed the dusty blue doors of the Bentley as the car crawled up a steep hill until the ground beneath the twenty-one-inch wheels flattened and widened and I was turning onto a gravel parking area in front of a two-storey cream house with pale green shutters. I turned off the engine, collected the Tumi bag off the passenger seat and stepped out of the car to find Philip French standing behind a zigzag wall with a glass of wine in one hand and a roll-up in the other.

'Where's John?'

'I thought it best if I came up here on my own,' I said. 'Things being what they are between the two of you it seemed best to avoid a scene.'

'That's all we've ever had – he and I. He'd think of a scene and I'd write it. Today, in the car park at the Saint-Martin was the first conversation we've ever had about something real.'

'He's not so bad. He didn't kill her, you know. He really is an innocent man.'

'I couldn't give a fuck if he killed her or not. Since I never met her I have no feelings about the woman one way or the other.'

'Phil. That's not worthy of you.'

'Come to do his dirty work, have you?'

'Not at all.'

'I hope you brought the money, for his sake.'

French turned on his heel and walked back onto the terrace, and as I followed him I noticed a strong smell of marijuana in the air.

The house occupied a good space at the top of a hill that provided uninterrupted views of the countryside to the south and probably the sea as well. The garden was not overlooked by anyone or anything as far as I could see, and about the only thing that gave a clue as to the parlous state of the owner's finances was the empty swimming pool and a second immobilière's sign that had been placed behind a garden shed, only this one read '*À Louer*'. A wrought-iron balcony ran the length of the front of the house, and underneath this was a refectory-style table on which sat a wine-box, a couple of glasses, some cigarette papers and next to a Rizla rolling machine a plastic bag containing tobacco and whatever else you needed to make a joint these days.

'Nice place you have here,' I said.

He smiled and I saw that his teeth were not in the best condition; they were the colour of the keys on an old piano. He was a thin man, even a little cadaverous, with skin as thin as the Rizla papers on his joints.

'How many square metres have you got?'

'It's 4,400 square metres of mostly olive grove. Originally we were going to make our own olive oil, but that was another pipe dream down a long borehole of pipe dreams.'

'But a great place for writing, I'd have thought.'

'It might be, if I had anything to write. But I'm all written out, Don. I fear my days of writing anything other than some newlywed's bloody lunch order are over.' Phil took a deep drag on the roll-up and I noticed he was still wearing John's Hublot watch. It stood up from his racket-shaft of a wrist like the lid on an Aga cooker.

'Yes, I know what you mean. Now that we no longer have John's outlines to work from I've found it hard to get going again myself.'

Phil smiled a cynical smile. 'Sure. Whatever you say, Don.'

'Look, Phil, I don't recall there being any bad blood between you and me. I always did my best for all the guys in the *atelier*. Perhaps you didn't know, but it was me who persuaded John to give you that redundo money. He needn't have given any of us any money at all, since we were all technically self-employed. But if you're going to behave like a cunt I'll fuck off now and save us both the emotional energy of an argument. Frankly I've got enough on my plate dealing with John without you as well.'

French nodded sullenly and took an asthmatic drag on the joint he was smoking as if he was hoping it might provide some actual nourishment. He looked as if he could have eaten a good meal.

'You're right,' he said. 'I'm sorry. And where are my manners? Would you like a drink?'

I nodded.

Phil fetched a glass of red from the wine box and handed it to me.

'Where is he, anyway?' he asked.

'Actually, he's drunk. I left him back at the Château Saint-Martin sleeping it off. The way he's been drinking, this might easily have become more unpleasant than it needs to be.'

'I'm sorry about this afternoon. I don't regret pinching his watch, but I do regret being so rude to you, Don.'

'Forget about it.'

I tasted the wine, which wasn't nearly as bad as it looked.

'You're selling the house?' I said, changing the subject.

'Have to. Unfortunately my missus left before I could murder her like John murdered his. Lucky bugger. But now she wants her half. Only the property market in this part of the world is fucked now that the socialists are in and screwing the last penny in taxes out of everyone. So, no one's interested. No one wanted to rent it. No one wants to buy it.' He looked at the huge watch on his wrist and smiled a fake sort of smile. 'Until I got this little gewgaw I was actually thinking of applying for the Society of Authors' hardship fund so that I could afford the fucking ticket home.'

'And now that you have that watch, what will you do?'

'Flog it, of course. See what I can get for it in Monaco if I can find out where he bought the thing. I've got a day off tomorrow so I figured to check that out on the internet.'

'Ciribelli,' I said. 'That's the name of the shop where he bought it. Actually there are three stores, but your best bet is probably the one in the Hôtel de Paris.'

'Oh. Thanks.' He frowned. 'Thanks a lot.'

'Don't mention it.'

'Listen, Don, under the circumstances I'm the last person to give anyone advice on their behaviour. But do you know what you're doing? Since I moved down here I've met a few French cops, and they play rougher than our own boys in blue. Aiding and abetting a man who's wanted for murder and all that; you're taking a bit of a risk, aren't you? If the police nick you, they'll throw the book at you. Not to mention the desk it was resting on. This is a high-profile case. It's been all over *The Riviera Times* and *Nice-Matin*.'

'I know. But I figure it's worth the risk. You see I'm not actually helping John. He only thinks I'm helping him. I've got plans of my own.'

'Oh? And what are they?'

'As a matter of fact that's what I want to talk to you about. Why I came up here on my own tonight.'

'You want to smoke a joint while we talk about it?'

'No thanks. I'll stick to cigarettes if you don't mind. For what I've got to say I need a clear head.'

'Sounds ominous.'

I sat down, opened my cigarette case and laid it open on the table like a little jewellery box before taking one and lighting it. I sat back and smoked it as if I had all the time in the world to get to the point.

'There's nothing I like more than smoking a cigarette on a terrace in the south of France,' I said. 'Unless it's fucking someone on a terrace in the south of France. But at my age it looks as if I'll have to settle for the cigarettes, I think.' I shrugged. 'Then again, maybe there's an alternative. Which is what I want to talk to you about.'

Philip French sat down opposite me and started to make another joint. 'So what is it?'

'First, the twenty grand you were demanding from John; to stop you going to the police and informing on him – and by extension me.' I reached into the Tumi bag and tossed the money onto the table between us. 'There it is. Paid in full.'

'Thanks.'

I shrugged. 'Of course, another twenty grand is nothing beside what you could get for that watch if you had the box and all the papers that came with it when John bought it. Without any of that you'll be lucky to raise a hundred grand, compared with maybe four times as much if you had everything you need to make the thing look kosher.' I took another drag on the cigarette. 'But I can get you all that. The box and the papers are in the safe at the *atelier* in Paris and I still have the key and the combination. The cops are probably keeping an eye on the place, so there's a risk factor involved. Which means it's going to cost you, Phil.'

'How much?'

'Twenty grand.'

'Oh, I see. I take the blame with John and you take the cash.'

'A bargain considering you might raise four hundred grand.'

He smiled.

'Did I say something funny?'

'Just that there was I feeling like a fucking criminal and now here you are dealing off the bottom. We make quite a pair.'

'That's why I'm here.'

'Wait. Why aren't you asking for half of what I can get for the watch?'

'Because I already have the Bentley.'

'What? He said it belongs to someone else.'

'It does. Only I have a buyer who'll give me fifty grand for it, no questions asked. You get the watch and the box and I get the car and twenty grand. That makes seventy grand for me.'

'Seventy versus four hundred. It still sounds to me as if you're coming up short, Don.'

'Perhaps. You can call it a sign of good faith, if you like.'

'In what?'

'First things first: do we have a deal about the money?'

'Sure. Keep it. If you can get the box and make the watch squeaky clean, so much the better. But don't take any unnecessary risks.'

'Okay.' I put the money back in the black bag. 'Thanks.'

'But I still think you're selling yourself short.'

'And like I said, that's a sign of good faith.'

Phil opened his hand as if expecting me to put something other than money in it. 'In what?' he repeated. 'Don't make me strip naked for it.'

'In you, Phil. In you. You see I've got a nice proposition for you that can make us both much wealthier than a few hundred grand a piece. Enough for you to pay off your wife and to keep this place, if that's what you want to do.'

'What kind of proposition? And don't say a novel, or a

script, or I'll laugh. It's only the people who've got almost nothing to say who are being paid the big money to say it in print: cooks and fucking footballers and national treasure actresses with backsides almost as big as their books. These days the Christmas bestsellers look like they were published by *Hello!* magazine.'

'Just hear me out. If you were describing my idea as a plot for a book, you would call it a simple reversal of fortune plot. You know? *The Prisoner of Zenda*. We put John Houston to work. For us.'

'And how would that work? He's a wanted man.'

'In a way, that's not true. John Houston no longer exists. John is using a false passport. That's how we're getting around without any trouble. At the moment he's someone called Charles Hanway.'

'I might have known he'd have done something like that. Yes, I remember him getting that passport for research when he wrote whichever fucking book it was. And he employed the Forsyth method to get it. So that's how he's managed to evade capture. He's nothing if not resourceful, is our John.'

'My plan is this: we get Charles back to England and we put him up at my place in Cornwall. It's so out of the way that everything but the rain avoids the fucking place. John keeps that beard going until he looks like all of the other hobbits who live down there. He'd be like the man in the iron mask. He stays there and continues to do what he does best, which is to write story outlines for us. And then we write the actual books. Simple as that. Just like before. Only this time it will be us who reap the benefits. We'll pay him what he used to pay us. Just enough to enable him to live, reasonably, in Cornwall. Which is to say not very much. Meanwhile you and I will become Philip Irvine – a pseudonym for our writing partnership. I would say Don French, but there's Dawn French, of course. And we wouldn't want to be confused with her. Not to mention another pseudonymous writing partnership called French: Nicci French.'

'Sean French and Nicci Gerrard. Yes, that's right.'

'So Philip Irvine it has to be. At least until we can come up with something better. We can write alternate chapters, like they do. It will take a few books and a couple of years to get ourselves properly established, but I reckon if we stick closely to the old Houston formula Hereward can make a deal with VVL. In less than ten years I see no reason why we shouldn't be as rich as John.'

'You're joking, aren't you?'

'No, I'm not. I'm perfectly serious. This can really work, Phil. I'm absolutely certain of it.'

'Suppose we get caught? Christ, Don, we'd go to prison. They'd give us five years for something like this. And the prisons down here are exactly what they say on the tin. There's none of that open-prison shit you get back home. You serve hard time in the south of France. There's no telly in a cell, just some jihadi with a hard-on and a welcoming smile.'

'There's a book in that, too, I shouldn't wonder. But I really don't see how we'd get caught. Like I say, Polruan – that's where I live in Cornwall – it's so quiet and out of the way that you could be living next door to Lord Lucan and have no idea.'

'Have you talked about this with John?'

'Not yet. I'm waiting for him to get really desperate before I broach the subject. Which he will when we travel to Marseille and fail to find the woman he's relying on to give him an alibi for where he was and what he was doing on the night Orla was murdered. That's where he'll have his meltdown and I point out the many advantages of living in Cornwall.'

'Suppose he says no?'

'Frankly, if it's a choice between a prison cell in Monaco and a life of freedom in Cornwall then Cornwall edges it.' I laughed. 'But only just. Seriously though. What would you choose? It's an offer he can't refuse.'

French nodded. 'That's quite a plot you've got there. Although a little far-fetched, perhaps.'

'It will work.'

He stood up. 'Come with me, Don. I want to show you something.'

I got up and followed him, pausing only to go back and fetch John's bag.

'It'll be all right there,' he said.

'With twenty grand in there, it doesn't leave my sight,' I said.

'Fair enough.'

I picked up the bag and followed French around the back of the house to a neat little cottage bungalow with a flat roof. He opened the door, switched on a light and showed me into an office with everything a writer would have needed: an Apple iMac the size of a window, a Herman Miller Aeron chair, a wraparound desk, a Dyson fan, a Flos Piani desklamp, an Eames lounger and ottoman, and all surrounded with floor-to-ceiling brushed aluminium shelves that were home to a library of beautiful books.

'This is what I call a writer's study,' I said. 'I'd love to have somewhere like this to work in. It's fantastic.'

'I don't know why,' he said, 'but I couldn't bear to sell any of this shit. Which is absurd when you think about it because I don't actually write anything. Not any more. I just come in here and read or stare at the walls. You see I meant what I said, Don. About writer's block.'

'Oh come on, Phil: writer's block. That's just an ignorant question for the literary festivals. Athlete's foot I believe in. But not writer's block. Do lawyers get lawyer's block? Do policemen get policeman's block? I don't think so. It's a bullshit excuse invented to cover up for one's own laziness. It doesn't exist.'

'Maybe not for you. But the thought of sitting down and writing something now fills me with dread. And it's more than just writer's block. I'm written out. Finished. I couldn't write another book if Erle Stanley Gardner was in here to dictate it.'

'Nonsense. You might just as well say that your heavenly muse has deserted you. There are no muses. All that stuff is for Virgil and Catullus and Dante, not you and me. You don't need a muse to write what we write any more than there could be a mental block that stops us from doing it. We're pros. That's what we do.'

French smiled wearily.

'This will explain it better, perhaps.'

He leaned over his desk, moved the mouse on its mat and chose a file on the iMac which had simultaneously come to life.

'It's an email I wrote to my wife Caroline and never sent. But it explains everything. Forgive the pet names and intimacies. But please read it.'

'You're depressed, Phil. That's all. And who wouldn't be? I know what I'm talking about because my wife left me, too. That sort of thing affects writers the same way it affects anyone. But it isn't writer's block.'

'Please read it.'

I shrugged and sat down in his chair. It was a nice desk. Everything felt just right.

Dear Mrs Cat,

Forgive my silence. It's not just you that I have failed to write to but rather that I have failed to write *anything at all*. Not one paragraph. Of course the urge dies hard but however much I try, nothing comes. Not even a trickle of words. It is as if there was no ink in my pen or ribbon in my typewriter. Faced with a blank page I feel as clumsy as if I was a savage who knew only grunts and sign language. I'm as blocked as if I was entombed inside a pyramid, sealed for ever. It is like being impotent except that there is no Viagra or Cialis that can fix this.

You'll remember that whenever my writing was blocked I would sit down and write a long letter to you – to kick start my writing. And so, here goes. It's probable that I shall never send this but if I do, then I apologize for any pain this might cause on top of so much pain I have caused you before. Please try to understand, I wish only happiness for you. Do you remember the first time we met? It was at Felicity's house, in Hampstead, and I told you then that I was going to dedicate my life to making you happy. I still feel that way.

Mrs Cat. How did it get to be like this between us? I don't know. And I have no words to explain it, not because there are no words but because what I feel is locked in a general sense of my own impotent wordless-ness. I don't think that it's that I have been trying to explain the inexplicable, just that I have learned that any explanation with words is now a task that is beyond me, Caroline. The craft or art of writing something has, like you, quite deserted me; and I am wise enough to know that if it can't be done – if I can no longer put something as important as you and me into any words – then perhaps I am no longer a writer at all.

I think a good writer always tries to overcome each and every obstacle, like a horse going over the fences. But there are many horses that refuse those fences that look to be impossible; those horses are often retired from racing for it is said they lack heart. Some are even destroyed. Unfortunately this has also happened to me. Since you left our home in Tourrettes I can no longer overcome the writer's everyday obstacles. I no longer have the heart for it. Every day I make an effort to write something – the same effort I always did – but without success. I do not seem to have the resources to do that simple thing I used to do with such facility. Of course, it's true that a man may change and become someone else, but if that has happened to me then I think the man who was the writer has now gone for ever, as perhaps you have done. I am not bitter. I do not blame you for anything. But I think that without you I am another man entirely – a man who cannot write a thing. And that is intolerable to me . . .

I stopped reading and shook my head.

'You've been smoking too much weed,' I said. 'You're depressed, Phil. That's why you can't work. It's evident in every word. You need to get away from here – from yourself, for a while. It's not Viagra you need, it's a fistful of Prozac. Come back to England with me and John. Forget being a writer for a bit. Do something else. And then, when you're ready, we'll give you a story outline and you can start work again. Just like before. Only this time you'll be working for yourself. Think about it, Phil. There will be lots of other women. Foreign book tours with willing publicity girls. Fancy cars. Expensive houses. You're not a bad-looking guy. I promise you this will seem like a bad dream in a few months' time. Just give yourself a chance.'

'Thanks, Don, but no. It's a kind offer and I wish you success with it, only I'm through with writing; even if I wasn't washed up as a writer I'm not sure I could take the pressure of writing two books a year. Not any more. But don't worry. I won't tell a soul. Your secret is safe with me.' He grinned. 'Besides, it's so far-fetched who would believe me? Seriously though. Mum's the word.'

I nodded. 'I know that, Phil.'

Of course, I didn't know it at all; I was thinking, 'Once a blackmailer, always a blackmailer,' and I could see no option now but to kill Phil as I had killed Colette. That's the trouble with murder. There's an exponential factor – the same one that Macbeth encounters. Blood will have blood. If I didn't kill Philip French then I would have killed both Orla and Colette for nothing. Because this had always been my goal, to have John working for me, just as I'd once worked for him. There was nothing spontaneous about this plan. I'd been working toward this ever since John had closed the *atelier*. The idea I'd just outlined to Phil had been quite genuine; even the offer I'd made him – that he and I should become writing partners – had been real. At the same time, ever since our unexpected meeting at the Château Saint-Martin I'd always known that killing Philip French was also a possibility; and now that I'd seen the email he'd written – but not sent – to his wife, Caroline, I recognized an opportunity to turn his death to my immediate advantage.

John would cease to be wanted by the Monty police if someone else was held responsible for Orla's murder. Not to mention Colette's.

I leaned forward on the desk chair and pointed at the Eames lounger.

'Sit down,' I told him. 'I want to say one more thing and then I'll leave you alone.'

He nodded and sat down on the Eames.

'When I've got the box and the papers, for the watch, I'll FedEx them here. All right? I wouldn't be surprised if the name of Ciribelli, the jewellers, is on them. So that should make things easier for you to get a decent sum for the Hublot.'

'Thanks a lot, Don.'

'And by the way, when you've got the money promise me that you'll fix yourself up. Buy some new clothes. Get a haircut. See a dentist. And quickly. All that dope you're smoking is affecting your gums.'

'It is?'

'Yes, I'm afraid so.'

'It's been a while since I could afford to see a dentist.'

'They're receding badly.'

Philip French touched his mouth.

'It's the first thing I noticed when I saw you again, Phil. You know it looks to me that you're suffering from the same thing Martin Amis had back in 1995, when he spent twenty grand on his teeth. You remember that? Talk about a mountain out of a molehill. The chattering classes thought it was vanity, but of course it wasn't; it was gum disease: Marty smokes roll-ups just like you. So, see a dentist, Phil. And soon.

You wouldn't want to get an abscess, would you? I'm not so sure you don't already have one on the way – your face is looking just a little puffy on one side.'

'What are you, my dentist?'

'No.' I smiled thinly. 'But you're forgetting that I once studied dentistry. So just occasionally I let my white tunic show.'

'I thought it was law you studied.'

'Don't you think I remember what degree I started?'

'I didn't know they did dentistry at Oxford.'

'They don't. I was at Cambridge. I couldn't afford to finish my studies so then I joined the army. That's why they put me on a toothpaste account when I went into advertising. Because I'd been a dental student.'

French nodded firmly as if he actually recalled my fictional early career as a dental student and said, 'Yes, I remember now.'

'It taught me one thing,' I said. 'Dentistry, I mean. Not the army. That didn't teach me anything. Dentistry taught me that there's so much physiological health that relates to the state of our oral hygiene. Did you know that a lot of heart disease is caused by dental caries? It's true. Simple flossing is a much more effective way of preventing a heart attack than cutting down on cholesterol. So, if I were you I'd get that swelling seen to as soon as possible, mate. If that's what it is. I can't be entirely sure from where I'm sitting.'

Philip French was exploring the state of his gums with his tongue.

'Look, forget I said anything. It's probably nothing at all. These things usually are.'

'Would you take a quick look before you go?'

I shrugged. 'Really, I'm not qualified, Phil. You should see a professional. If there is the beginning of an abscess you'll need it properly drained and you'll need an antibiotic. To stop an infection. Amoxicillin is generally prescribed and is very effective. But if it starts to become painful Nurofen is probably best.'

I knew all this because I'd already endured treatment for a dental abscess the previous summer. As John used to say, in preparing one of his story outlines, 'There's no research quite as effective as something you've experienced yourself.'

'Just humour me, Don, please. Just take a quick look and see what you think.'

'All right. But let me fetch a flashlight from my bag so I can see what's what.' I frowned. 'Have you got any mouthwash?'

'There's this,' he said and held up a bottle of scotch.

'That'll have to do.'

We both took a swig and I collected the Tumi bag off the floor.

'Just lean back on the recliner,' I said. 'Now then, open wide and let me take a look.'

He leaned back and opened his mouth.

'Wider.'

Behind my back I thumbed down the hammer on John's Walther .22 and slipped off the safety catch. I knew there was already one in the chamber because I'd seen him lock and load the gun when we were on the autoroute. Obviously I'd have preferred a 38 – or better still Hemingway's twelve-gauge – to shoot a man in the head; and I certainly wouldn't have trusted a .22 to trepan a male skull; but the soft palate at the back of his mouth was a different story: that was just muscle fibres sheathed in mucus membrane, after which the next stop was a really thin piece of bone the name of which I couldn't remember, and then the hypothalamus. A lot depends on the ammunition of course; but for what I had in mind the .22 would do just fine.

'Wider.'

I put the muzzle inside Philip's mouth – he probably thought it was a flashlight – and quickly squeezed the trigger, shooting him, Hitler style, like he'd actually meant to commit suicide. His body went into spasm for a moment as if the neurons that controlled his nerves had been fried with electricity; his eyes filled with blood and other stuff, and his legs twitched violently for several seconds – so violently that I was obliged to hold them down for fear that he might fall off the recliner and ruin the death scene I'd so carefully contrived. Then his head rolled slowly to one side. After another moment or two his breathing became laboured and messy as blood and cerebrospinal fluid started to drain through the open wound in the palate of his mouth, straight down his throat and into his lungs. A pink bubble formed on his lips and began to enlarge as if it was being inflated by some hidden pump. His chest was struggling to get a hold on the atmosphere. I stood back and waited for the bubble to burst and for him to drown.

As always when I kill someone I felt a tremendous sense of cosmic connection to the world, as vivid and sharply defined as if I had touched the forefinger of my maker. A *South Bank Show* moment. I don't normally believe in God, but it's at moments like these that I do experience a timeless force in the world that is Life itself. You only have to see a human life ebbing away in front of you to feel a tremendous relationship with all of nature, not just the omnipresent cicadas and the strong smell of violets in the air, but the shimmering leaves on the olive trees and the stars in the sky. It is as if life is enhanced and amplified to an almost deafening maximum by the witnessing of its departure. Human existence asserts itself most vigorously in the face of death. I expect that's why men and women used to attend public executions – as if, in an uncertain world, it was only by seeing someone put to death that they themselves could feel the truly fantastic sensation that is life itself. It is the most beautiful and shattering experience to find yourself so strongly underlined like a great passage of writing in a book that otherwise can sometimes feel just a little ordinary. That's a shocking admission, I know; but I feel true clarity most when I have a smoking gun in my hand. I've noticed how people in movies always do it with a long face and then beat themselves up about it afterward; that's not how it is at all. From everything I've read, most people get off on killing someone. Me, I was grinning like a loon. So much so I felt obliged to offer some sort of explanation to someone I'd known for more than a decade.

'Sorry, Phil. If you can still hear anything then I just want to say that I didn't want this at all. You do see that, don't you? Really. It was a genuine offer I made to you earlier this evening. I'd have much preferred having you as a writing partner, buddy. As it happens I think you were right about that and I was wrong. Now I come to think about it, you were written out. That last novel you wrote for John wasn't very good. I thought it was just a blip, but John recognized that something more fundamental had happened. So, it looks like I'm going to have to do this by myself, as I don't much like the idea of sharing anything with Mike Munns. I don't know about Peter Stakenborg. I'll have to think about him. He's harder to control. And I don't want to do this with anyone I can't control. That would defeat the whole object of the exercise.'

A sound like the drain in a sink – or perhaps a coffee machine – emanated from the depths of his throat and lasted for almost a minute before, like him, it died. I felt for a pulse, and not finding one I now considered the forensic picture I wanted to paint for the local police, much as I would have done if I'd been writing a novel. The difference was that this was real, although I have usually found that the best way to achieve realism within a text is to imagine oneself carrying out a crime, much like a method actor might have done; in other words, I have always tried to feel what it would be like to have done some dreadful thing in a novel, so much so that I sometimes have trouble separating those people I really killed from those I think I've only killed within the context of a story. So I finished my wine, and then began work.

Gunshot residue – GSR – is the burnt and unburnt particles of primer and propellant that are left on a gunman's hand after a shot has been fired: it's one of the first things scenes of crime officers look for in determining whether or not someone took their own life with a firearm. So I put the still-cocked automatic in Phil's right hand and fired the gun out of the open door and into the olive grove. Then I let his arm fall with the gun still in his hand; to my great satisfaction, with his finger hooked through the trigger guard the gun remained firmly in his grip.

Next, I searched carefully for both brass cartridges: two would have made the police suspicious. I didn't find two, but I found one and pocketed it carefully before seating myself in front of his iMac and typing a few extra lines onto the maudlin and self-pitying email he'd written to his wife Caroline. I added some stuff about John Houston that held him responsible for the things that had gone wrong in Philip's life; I drew back from a full murder confession, of course.

That would have been too much. Then I pressed send.

I wiped the Apple keyboard with some cyber-cleaning compound I found in his desk drawer and then, still carrying my wine glass – which was covered with fingerprints – I went back to the Bentley and dropped the glass into the boot, from where I now retrieved my backpack.

Back on the terrace I retrieved the butt of my cigarette from his ashtray and lit another to help me concentrate. I had all the time in the world, of course. Everything was quiet. The nearest neighbour must have been at least half a kilometre away. There was just the incessant noise of the cicadas and a dog barking in the distance to disturb the peace of the countryside.

Back in the house I placed Colette's car and door keys in the drawer of a fitted closet in a bedroom upstairs. In another drawer I left her laptop, but not before wiping it carefully, of course. I put her hairbrush beside the sink in the bathroom and one of her lipsticks in the bathroom cabinet. In the kitchen bin I placed the ticket for the parking lot at Terminal 2 of Nice Airport where I had left the Audi and her dead body.

I was on my way out to the garage to add the Tour Odéon in Monaco to the list of favourites on the satnav in Phil's car when I saw a copy of that day's *Riviera Times* on a pile of newspapers by the kitchen door, and I remembered the story about the unidentified body found in the ashes of the forest fire in the *forêt de l'Albaréa*, near Sospel.

Rereading the story I found that the police thought it unlikely the body would ever be identified, as it was so badly consumed by the enormous heat generated by the fire. This was very much to my advantage. So when I went into the garage to program the satnav I also added the coordinates of Sospel to make it seem as though Phil had visited both of these places. Then I circled the story in the paper and left it where I had found it, on a pile of old newspapers in the kitchen.

It was all circumstantial stuff but, in my experience of dealing with the police – and in particular, the RUC – the circumstances of collecting evidence are such that, short of a full confession on the part of a suspect, there's seldom any one thing that stands out to the exclusion of everything else. Most cops will tell you that circumstantial evidence will usually do very nicely thank you, and I'd left enough of it scattered around poor Philip's house to convince Henry Fonda and a whole room full of angry men. As soon as the police located Colette's body they would conclude that she and French had been co-conspirators; and if I got really lucky they might even conclude that they had killed John and dumped his body in the *forêt de l'Albaréa*, which was perhaps an hour's drive north of Monaco.

I went back into Philip's study to double-check that he was dead. There's an easy way to do this and it isn't a pulse. You just put your mobile phone under the victim's nostrils and then check to see if there's any condensation on the glass. There wasn't. He was as dead as the net book agreement.

I pocketed the twenty thousand euros but I left John's Tumi bag on the floor beside the desk; Tumi luggage and bags all have metal plates containing twenty-digit numbers permanently affixed to a pocket inside so that it's easy to trace them if they get lost. John's bag in Philip French's possession would be another piece of important evidence that he was dead. I'd been with him when he'd bought it in the Hôtel Métropole shopping centre in Monaco.

Another excellent piece of evidence was the million-dollar watch that French had extorted from John; with any luck someone at the Château Saint-Martin or in Tourrettes-sur-Loup might have seen him actually wearing it. Anyone disposing of John Houston's body would surely have taken an expensive watch like the Hublot Black Caviar.

But perhaps the best evidence of course was the murder weapon now in Philip's hand – the same make and calibre of pistol that had been used to murder Colette, not to mention the same ammunition: I'd been quite careful about that.

I walked around the villa trying to think of anything I'd forgotten; but the more I thought about it the more inclined I was to the conclusion that even Inspector Clouseau could have made a good case against Philip French with the picture I'd painted for the local police.

CHAPTER 11

I was about to get back in the car and leave Philip's villa when my mobile started ringing. To my horror the caller ID said it was Chief Inspector Amalric. I thought about not answering it but then he'd have only rung again; besides, as Michael Corleone once said, 'Keep your friends close, and your enemies closer.'

'Chief Inspector,' I said. 'I'm so sorry. I was going to call you, wasn't I? I completely forgot. I'm afraid it's been one of those days.'

'That's quite all right, monsieur. Geneva must be a lot more interesting on a Sunday than I remember it.'

'Not nearly as interesting as Monaco. As a matter of fact I'm going back to London, on Tuesday. It would be difficult to meet on Wednesday, but I could meet you any day after that, if you're still planning on going to London yourself.'

'Why don't I call you as soon as I get to Claridge's and we can arrange a dinner. Thursday perhaps.'

'I'm always delighted to have dinner at Claridge's. I take it that you haven't yet caught up with him, then. With John Houston.'

'I regret not. But there's someone else I'm seeing first thing tomorrow who might be able to help me catch up with

Mr Houston, as you say. Someone I haven't managed to speak to before.'

'Oh? Who's that?'

'Your old friend and fellow writer in Houston's *atelier*, Philip French. I have an appointment with him at ten o'clock.'

'You're going to Tourrettes-sur-Loup?'

'Yes. As a matter of fact I'm there right now. You see, I used to live in Tourrettes. My sister still lives here and I'm staying with her tonight. It's quite like old times.'

'Oh, I see.' I swallowed so hard I wondered if he heard it.

'Before I see him tomorrow, I wanted to ask you a little about him. What's he like?'

'I've known him for more than ten years. He's solid. Reliable.'

'Did you know that he's working as a waiter? At a hotel in Vence?'

'No, I didn't. I knew that since John wound up the *atelier* money has been tight for him. But I didn't know things were that bad.'

'Did you know that he owes the bank a lot of money?'

'No.'

'Did you know his wife has left him?'

'I didn't know that either. Look, it's been a while since we spoke.'

'Would you say that he was the type of fellow to bear a grudge?'

'Phil? No more than anyone else. Look, if you're asking me if he's the type to commit murder then the answer is absolutely not. Besides, if he did have a grudge against John why would he take it out on Orla?'

'Why indeed?'

'On the other hand.'

'Yes?'

'I was just thinking. No one has seen or heard of John in almost two weeks. To be quite frank with you, Chief Inspector, the last time we spoke I lied to you. I said I didn't think he would try to get in contact with me. The truth is, I did, kind of. And since he hasn't I've begun to fear the worst.'

'So have I,' said Amalric. 'So have I. Look, I'd better go. My sister is calling. She and I – we're supposed to meet some old school friends at a restaurant in town tonight.'

'Oh?' I was trying to conceal the panic in my voice. 'Which one? Just in case I ever go back there.'

'L'Auberge de Tourrettes. Do you know Tourrettes?'

'A little. It's very pretty. I've always rather envied Philip having a house there.'

'Yes, that's the restaurant I'd recommend, if you're ever back here.'

'As good as Claridge's?'

'In its own way, yes, perhaps.'

'When you see him, say hello to Philip from me.'

'I'll do that.'

'And enjoy your dinner.'

As soon as the Chief Inspector had rung off I called John to tell him to take a taxi back to the Château Saint-Martin, immediately. But he wasn't answering, so I sent him a text and asked him to acknowledge it straight away. He didn't.

At the same time I tried to do a Google search for L'Auberge de Tourrettes on my iPhone, but I had already exceeded my monthly data download limit and I had little choice but to go back into Philip's study and, ignoring his bloodshot staring eyes, to try and find the restaurant on his iMac. From the Google map it appeared that L'Auberge de Tourrettes, on Route de Grasse, was about 200 metres from La Cave de Tourrettes, on Rue de la Bourgade and on the opposite side of the town square where, earlier on, I'd parked the Bentley. As soon as I had located the restaurant where the Chief Inspector was dining I removed my Google searches from the iMac's browsing history, just in case some resourceful cop attending the murder scene decided to check that, too. Then I wiped the keyboard and tried to call John again.

The Chief Inspector hadn't ever met John, but he was a clever man and I was sure that if they did run into each other – in the Place de la Libération, perhaps – a thin beard wasn't going to fool him, even at night; when cops are looking for missing persons and fugitives they always construct photofits and facial composites of how that person might look with a beard, glasses, or a different hairstyle. Amalric would almost certainly have committed those pictures to memory, and if he hadn't he would certainly have loaded them onto his smartphone.

Once again John didn't answer his phone, so I called the restaurant and asked them if the Englishman was still there on the terrace. They told me he'd paid the bill and left about ten minutes before, and I guessed that almost certainly he was now sitting outside one of the many bars on the Place de la Libération, nursing a cognac, girl-watching and probably not even hearing his ringtone. It was more than likely that in just a few minutes John would see Amalric parking his car and – what was worse – that Amalric might see him.

Three murders are quite an investment and it was obvious that all of my efforts to turn John into my secret employee would be rendered futile if he was arrested. Realizing I now had little option but to go back into Tourrettes-sur-Loup and fetch him from under the Chief Inspector's nose, I cursed loudly, for there was just as great a risk that I myself might bump into him.

I jumped back into the Bentley and took off in a spray of gravel. Naturally I could have wished for a less noticeable car; but with the hood up it was dark inside the passenger cabin and there was every chance of not being recognized.

A few minutes later I entered the Place de la Libération and slowly made my way anti-clockwise around the square, steering carefully around the Sunday night tourists for fear of knocking one down, and pausing in front of one café and then another until I was back where I started, with no sign of John anywhere.

On my third trip around the square – and in front of the Café des Sports – I turned right and drove a short way along the Route de Vence, with still no sign of John. A hundred metres further on I steered the Bentley around a mini-roundabout and approached the square again, this time from the east.

'Where the fuck are you, John?' I muttered through clenched teeth as once more I entered the square. This time I followed the road into the car park that occupied the centre and circled again. All the time I was repeat-dialling his phone every ten seconds.

Then I saw him sitting on the edge of a water trough next to the Café des Sports like some feckless teenager, except that he had a brandy glass in one hand and a cigar in the other. He was talking to a bicyclist clad from head to toe in matching blue Lycra who was filling his water bottle from the public tap.

I tapped gently on the horn, lowered the passenger window and stopped the Bentley.

'Get in,' I said as urgently as I dared in front of the cyclist.

John drained his glass, laid it and a banknote on a table behind the trough, and opened the car door.

'Quickly,' I said.

John jumped in, hauled the car door shut and I pressed my foot gently on the accelerator.

'Where the fuck were you?' I said. 'Why didn't you answer your phone? I've been round this fucking square four times.'

'I was in the public toilet,' he said. 'Sorry. Is there a problem?'

I didn't reply. I'd meant to turn left again – around the square – so as to avoid the Auberge de Tourrettes further on, but the way into the main square was now blocked with traffic and the driver of the van behind me was too impatient to let me wait. So I drove on and, anxious to avoid going past the Auberge on the left, I turned right onto the Route de Saint-John, and along to the Route du Caire, which led up to Phil's villa. I had no intention of going back there, of course, and the Château Saint-Martin was in the opposite direction, but just then, beside a short rank of parked cars opposite the foot of the Route du Caire, I saw Chief Inspector Amalric get out of a blue Renault with a busty-looking blonde who looked much too young and pretty to be his sister; they paused and then, arm in arm, came toward the Bentley.

'Christ, there he is,' I muttered and pulling down the sun-visor, turned sharply up the Route du Caire.

In my rear-view mirror I saw him turn – to look at the Bentley? I told myself Amalric probably had other things on his mind at that moment, such as getting in the blonde's pants, but I couldn't be absolutely sure he hadn't seen my face.

'Would you mind telling me what the fuck is going on?' demanded John.

'That's one of those Monty cops back there,' I said.

John let out a curse and turned sharply in his seat to look back, but we were already round the corner.

'The detective who called me last night in Èze.'

'What the fuck is he doing here?'

'He's going to see Phil in the morning,' I said.

'I knew that bastard was going to sell me out,' snarled John. 'Fucker.'

'Relax,' I said. 'That's not going to happen.'

'How do you know?'

'Because I know Phil. Look, shut up and let me think for a moment, will you?'

I keyed the Château Saint-Martin's details into the Bentley's satnav and saw that there was no point in driving on much further, as the road we were on continued away from Vence for several miles; so a bit further up the hill, I turned the car around and drove back the way we came – but slowly, so as not to overtake Amalric and his girlfriend.

Finally, we were back on the road to Vence and the Château and I was able to put my foot down and do some thinking.

'Maybe we should check out of the hotel,' said John. 'Go somewhere else. Or even drive to Marseille tonight.' He looked at the empty space on his wrist where his watch had been, swore once again and then peered at the clock on the Bentley's dashboard. 'We can be at the Villa Massalia before midnight,' he said.

'No,' I said. 'We've both had too much to drink. Besides, that detective – Amalric – he isn't going to see Phil until ten o'clock tomorrow morning.'

'How do you know?'

'Because he called me again. While I was at Phil's house. Wanting to get the low-down on what kind of a bloke he is.

Whether he was the type to do you and Orla in. That kind of thing.'

'Jesus. And what did you tell him?'

'That he's not. No more than you are, John.' I shrugged. 'At least I think so. Frankly Phil seemed a bit suicidal. I think it was fortunate I went up there and spoke to him.'

'You'll forgive me if I don't set up a collection for him.'

I grunted.

'Did he go for the deal? The box and the papers for the watch?'

'The money's in the glovebox.'

'Really?' John opened the glovebox and found his twenty thousand euros. 'Bloody hell, old sport. How did you talk him out of it?'

'It's you he hates. Not me.'

'So what makes you think he won't grass me up when that cop goes to his house tomorrow?'

'Then he won't get the full bar mitzvah for the Hublot. He'll be out of pocket by a considerable margin.' I shook my head. 'Look, it's just a coincidence that cop coming here on the same day we did. Amalric hadn't managed to speak to Phil before, so he's doing it tomorrow.'

By now I'd decided not to tell John that Phil was dead; at least not for a while, until I had him somewhere less public; I'd had enough of panic for one Sunday evening. And I was dog-tired to boot – too tired to devise an edited version of what had happened. Nervous exhaustion, I imagine. It's amazing what one simple murder can take out of you. With a gun you'd think there'd be nothing to it. Just pull the trigger and stand back. But not a bit of it. Probably something to do with the adrenalin rush you get when you blow someone's brains out.

We arrived back at the Château and I dropped John at the front door.

'I don't know about you,' I said, 'but I need a drink.'

'I'll wait for you in the garden.'

'Order me a large Calvados, will you?'

One of the parking valets offered to park the Bentley for me – the way they do when they know there's five euros in it for them – but I needed a few minutes to myself. So I declined the offer and drove the Bentley down the ramp into the underground car park myself, and sat in the car's womb-like, dark interior for a few minutes with eyes closed. Had Amalric recognized me? If so then I would surely be his prime suspect when he found Philip French's body on Monday morning. Or had he just been admiring the Bentley, like those kids in the square earlier on? I would know which it was soon enough.

I got out of the car, and as I walked to the lift I heard footsteps somewhere behind me. It always makes me nervous when I hear footsteps in the dark. It's the one legacy of Northern Ireland I know I'll never be able to shake off: the nerves I get when I hear that sound. It always make me think about what happened to Robert Nairac, an intelligence unit British army captain who was snatched from outside a pub in South Armagh during an undercover op in 1977; he was tortured and killed by the Provos. Nairac is one of nine IRA victims whose graves have never been revealed, although it's rumoured he ended up being fed to pigs.

I got into the lift and breathed a small sigh of relief when the doors closed and the car delivered me into the hotel's air-conditioned lobby. At the reception desk, I asked for a six o'clock call in the morning. The girl on duty smiled at me in a way that made me think that I was a decent, law-abiding man; it's strange how no one can ever tell when you've just shot someone dead. It's one of the things that make life so interesting. I went to the spotless men's room and devoted a few lubricious thoughts to the receptionist and her panties while I washed my face and hands. I like the smell of gunpowder, in a nostalgic sort of way, but still, I saw no reason to make things easy for the cops in case they did come calling after all.

In the bar a couple of American newlyweds were sitting as close to each other as it was possible to sit without having sexual intercourse; a short distance away, a rather glum-looking couple and their pre-adolescent daughter were having a post-prandial drink with their bodyguard: it was the Cordura gun tote by his leg that gave his game away. He paid me no regard at all, which was a mistake given that I was the only one there – apart from him – who had held a weapon that particular Sunday evening. Even without the tote I would always have picked him out as a shooter; his eyes were always working the room, one way and then the other, like a ventriloquist's dummy. The tote bag looked like a bad idea: if I'd still had the P22 I could easily have shot his preppy, blazered boss in the time it took for him to unzip his handgun. It might have livened up the dinner for them; certainly the wife didn't look as if she'd have minded very much. She was probably dying to fuck the bodyguard anyway; the wives usually do.

Outside, the garden was full of the scent of flowers, orange blossom and violets and night jasmine, and made a mockery of the perfumed soap on my fingers. The sky looked like a painting by Van Gogh: yellow and blue with a rolling tsunami of cloud. Already I was feeling much better about what I had done. A large Calvados looked like the perfect way to end what had been an awkward sort of day. Shooting an old friend is always difficult.

John had one foot on a stool and his phone in his hand, out of habit I supposed, as no one but me was going to call him. Not for a long while. I sat down opposite him, fired up a cigarette and blew a couple of smoke rings around the moon and tried to imagine what Vincent would have done with an advertising brief for cigarettes: the world was a much less colourful place without cigarette advertising. I certainly missed the old Benson & Hedges Gold commercials when I went to the cinema. I decided that when my new career as a bestselling thriller writer was up and running I was going to quietly approach a few cigarette companies and offer them a discreet bit of product placement. The Ian Fleming estate were surely missing a trick not trying to get some money out of Liggett who owned Chesterfield, the preferred cigarette of James Bond. Who knows? With a few handsome covers on a new edition of paperbacks they might even have turned that brand around.

'I've been sitting here like that guy in Africa with gangrene,' said John. 'Harry what's his name, in a Hemingway story. Sitting under this yellow mimosa, just a little bit drunk and feeling a little sorry for myself and imagining all of the stories I'm probably not going to write because I'll be in a prison cell and won't have done enough research to write them.'

'*The Snows of Kilimanjaro*,' I said.

'That's right,' said John and toasted me with his brandy glass.

'Don't be so bloody dramatic. I told you before, Phil made a deal. And he won't talk. Or maybe you want me to write *that* down.'

'I wish I could believe that, old sport.'

'It's my ass, too. You can believe that, can't you?' I sniffed the Calvados, swirled it around the balloon glass a bit, and then downed it all in one mouthful. 'Besides, you're going to write those stories.'

'I am?'

'Sure you are. I know it in my bones.'

CHAPTER 12

We shared a room, again. This was a mistake as, on this occasion, John snored, loudly. I almost felt a twinge of sympathy for Orla, having to endure a sound like that. No wonder she'd taken sleeping pills. And in a way, but for John's snoring, she might still be alive. At six, not long after I'd finally got off to sleep, I was awoken by the early morning call I'd ordered the night before, and I got up feeling irritable and bad-tempered. Even the magnificent view of the rolling foothills of the Baou des Blancs from the little terrace where I ate breakfast could not improve my humour. And I certainly wasn't looking forward to a two-hour drive to Marseille – even in the Bentley. Only the prospect of staying at the Villa Massalia – which John had promised was excellent – filled me with any enthusiasm for the Monday ahead of us.

John was watching TV. Even before Orla's murder he had always watched a lot of television.

'I get more ideas watching daytime TV shows than any other way,' he was fond of saying. 'I always tell kids who want to become writers, you don't have to hang out with cops, or go to the joint and interview bad guys. And you certainly don't have to live in a garret in Paris, and have breakfast every morning at the Deux Magots. Sometimes, the best research you can do is at home, sitting on your ass, with a doughnut and a coffee in your hand. Shows like Jerry Springer, Montel Williams, and in the UK Jeremy Kyle, will introduce you to as much low-life, trailer-trash modern-day grotesques as you would ever want to meet in one lifetime.'

John – whose French was better than mine – had been watching an early morning repeat of *Ça Va Se Savoir!*, which was the French version of a tabloid television show, and it was one he loved; I heard him still laughing as he switched over to watch the seven o'clock news on France 3.

'What the fuck?' he exclaimed. 'Jesus fucking Christ, Don, get in here and look at this.'

I got up from the breakfast table and walked into the sitting room, where John was pointing at the screen and gibbering, and while I didn't yet know it, my day was about to get very much better.

'For fuck's sake,' he said, and folded his arms womanishly while keeping both eyes on the screen. 'She's dead.'

'Who's dead?'

'Colette Laurent.'

It seemed that Colette's body had been found at last in the boot of a car parked at Terminal 2 of Nice Airport. The Nice police had released very few details beyond Colette's name and the fact that she had lived in Monaco, but from what the TV reporter was saying, there was little doubt that Colette had been murdered and that the car had been at Terminal 2 for two weeks. But most of the report seemed to concentrate on the disruption the closure of the car park was causing to international flights to and from Nice airport.

'Jesus Christ,' muttered John. 'Poor kid. What a terrible thing to happen to a girl like that. I guess that Russian guy must have killed her after all. Maybe the same night he killed Orla.'

'It would seem so,' I admitted.

'That's the end of my fucking alibi, isn't it?'

I shrugged and said nothing. At times like this it was usually best to let his mouth make all the running.

'I guess there's no point in us going to Marseille now,' he said. 'From the sound of it, she was never there. She's been in the boot of her car for the last fortnight. Poor kid.' His nose wrinkled with disgust. 'And in this weather, too. That's not good. I mean, can you imagine what this kind of heat does to a body? To be in a space like that all this time? You never met her, Don, but take my word for it, she was so very beautiful.' He stopped and tried to swallow his emotions whole. 'Best lay I ever had.'

'I'm sorry, John,' I said. 'Really I am. But none of this alters the fact that we still have to leave here before nine o'clock.'

John stared at me blankly.

'That cop. Chief Inspector Amalric? From the Monty police? He's going to see Phil at ten. Remember? I mean Phil probably won't say anything. But why take the risk, right?'

John sighed a sigh as profound as the view outside, stepped onto the balcony, took hold of the railing with both hands and hung his head. For a moment I thought he was going to jump and I made as if to restrain him. Without him I had nothing. But instead of jumping, he sighed and said:

'I've made up my mind, Don. I'm going to give myself up. I've come to the end. I can't go on. Really I can't. I mean thanks for everything and I'll try to keep you out of it, old sport. But there's no point. Now that Colette has gone the only real option I have of proving I didn't kill Orla is to take my chances with a jury.'

'If it was just Orla's murder, I might agree with you.'

'What do you mean?'

'You know something? It might be good,' I said. 'The hot weather, I mean. Good for you, at any rate. That is, if you fucked Colette without a condom. Did you?'

'Of course I fucked her without a condom. I had a vasectomy, remember? What are you talking about?'

'I'm not exactly sure how that works. Did you ejaculate in her body?'

'Of course I did. Just not with sperm in the ejaculate. Why on earth do you want to know?'

'Maybe that Russian fucked her, too. In which case you'll be all right. Otherwise you'll just have to hope that the heat in the boot of that car has spoiled any of your DNA that might still be in her pussy.'

'Oh shit. Yes.'

'Because if there is any DNA in her pussy then there's every chance they'll charge you with her murder, as well. With two women dead – one your wife and the other your mistress – I'd say you've got even less chance with a jury now than you had before.'

John put his head in his hands and turned in a circle as if he had a terrible migraine.

'What a mess,' he said. 'What a fucking mess. If I knew where my bag was I might fetch my gun and shoot myself.'

'I gave your bag to Phil,' I said.

'What? Why?'

'But don't worry, I still have your new passport. I let him have the bag when he was still in two minds about taking the money. The gun was still in the bag I suppose. I forgot about it. After all, there are so many pockets in that bag. Anyway I forgot about the bag when he gave the cash back.'

John sat down abruptly on the floor of the balcony, took

hold of the railing again and then pressed his face against the bars.

'What are you doing?' I asked.

'Getting used to the view. This is what I'm going to be looking at for the next twenty years.'

I switched off the TV, fetched him a little bottle of The Macallan whisky from the minibar and tossed it to him. 'Here,' I said. 'Get that down your neck. Perhaps it will remind you of where your fucking backbone used to be.'

'Fuck you. Fuck you, Don. You're not the one facing life imprisonment.'

'Who says you are? I mean, really – who says you are?'

John unscrewed the little bottle cap, closed his eyes and emptied the contents into his mouth. I sat down on the floor in front of him and took hold of his jacket collar.

'Listen to me,' I said.

I slapped him hard, not once but twice, and when at last he opened his eyes they were filled with tears.

At last I had him where I wanted him.

'Listen to me, you stupid fuck. I didn't risk my neck to help you without first thinking through all of the possibilities. And I mean all of them. Now I promise you that there's a way out of this situation, but you're going to have to keep calm and pay close attention. If you listen to me and do exactly what I say there's absolutely no reason why you should ever see the inside of a prison cell. Do you understand? You won't have to go to prison. I promise you.'

He nodded, silently.

'Now then. Years ago you wrote a storyline for a book called *Hidden Genius*. Do you remember?'

He nodded again.

'You'd ripped off the plot from a book by Marguerite Your-cenar, called *The Abyss. L' Œuvre au Noir*, in French. The book – your book – was about a nuclear physicist, a genius called Jonathan Zeno, who decides to live under an alias somewhere quiet and out of the way after he decides that what he has discovered is too dangerous for anyone to know.'

'I remember,' said John. 'He gets a job teaching physics at a school near a nuclear power station in the West Country. But then he discovers something that makes him think there's been a leak of radioactivity and he has to choose between blowing his alias and saving all the kids in his school. Actually only part of it was ripped off from Yourcenar's book. It's also ripped off from Ibsen's *An Enemy of the People*.' He shrugged. 'Anyway, what about it?'

'There were some interesting observations about aliases and pseudonyms and *noms de guerre*, and it got me thinking about the whole business of having a pen name, a *nom de plume*. Samuel Clemens being Mark Twain, Amandine Dupin being George Sand, and more recently J. K. Rowling being Robert Galbraith.'

'It wasn't a bad book,' admitted John. 'Was it you who wrote that one, or Peter?'

'Me. And actually it was my best, I think. Not necessarily in terms of sales, but critically.'

'I suppose that's why we never did another,' said John. 'But what's your point, old sport?'

'Like a successful lie, a successful alias requires that you believe it yourself. That you never stop being that other person.'

John was nodding. 'It's what the shrinks call reflex conditioning. If you never step out of character you don't get
rumbled.'

'So then. You have a passport and a driving licence in
the name of Charles Hanway. Then why not live as Charles
Hanway? Provided you stick to the alias and keep your trap
shut you can live, quietly, at my house in Cornwall. And
here's the smart angle. You carry on writing storylines,
albeit anonymously, and I carry on writing the books. Just
like before. I'll get Hereward to make a deal with VVL. And
I'll pay you out of what I can make from them. That way you
won't ever have to meet anyone who remembers you. No one
but me. And this way we can both benefit. I stay in print, and
you stay out of prison. Simple as that.'

'Someone would be bound to find out.'

'Not in Cornwall. Nobody knows you in Cornwall. Frankly,
they hardly know what fucking day of the week it is down
there in the shire. You can go for days without seeing anyone
vaguely human. And when you do they tend to keep themselves to themselves. Frankly the place is so out of the way
that it's only the fucking mice who visit. It's like being back
in the 1950s. The very opposite of Monaco.'

'You really think it would work?'

'I know it would work, I've lived there. Believe me, I know
the place. Look, Manderley – that's the joke name on my
front door – is quite comfortable. There's a good broadband
connection, a widescreen telly, Sky TV, a decent wine cellar, a
good library, and a nice vegetable garden; the nearest neighbour is Bilbo Baggins, and he's more than a mile away.'

'Might work at that.'

'What's the alternative? Risk your future to a jury? Fuck
that. Rich bastard like you – they'd send you to the guil-

lotine, if they could. Especially in this economic climate. Who knows? After a while they might even declare you dead, which might take some of the heat off you.'

John nodded. 'You know, you're right. It might just work.'

'Of course, you'd have to lie low for a long time. Maybe for ever. No trips up to London. Penzance maybe. Or perhaps Truro. Certainly nothing east of Exeter. But what have you got to lose? It's me who's taking the bigger risk. The cops aren't after me. It's you they're after. Right now, I don't even have a bad credit rating. But if I get nicked hiding you then I'm facing at least five to ten, I reckon. To encourage the others.'

John fetched another whisky miniature from the minibar.

'I'm not completely convinced,' he admitted. 'But so long as the cops are looking for me I can't think where else to go. Bob Mechanic is bound to turn up in Geneva sooner or later, and if I know Bob the very last thing he'll want to do is to help a good friend. Not if it might imperil his reputation with the Swiss authorities. He'll deny he even knows me, if I know Bob.'

'A friend in need, eh?'

'That's Bob's idea of a nightmare. He's not in the least like you, old sport. I'm beginning to realize just what a good friend you are, Don.'

'All right then.' I glanced at my watch. 'My suggestion is this. Instead of driving west, to Marseille, we head north, back to England. We can stop overnight in Paris. We'll dump the Bentley there and take the Eurostar back to London first thing Tuesday. With any luck it might be months before your careless pal Bob Mechanic even notices his car is missing. Like that Porsche Turbo he left at the airport.'

John nodded.

'This is good of you, Don. I don't know what I would have done without you.'

'Forget it. That's what real friends are for, right?' I shrugged. 'It'll be just like old times. Me and you in a fast car on the A7 to Paris and the atelier, which we'll start up again, albeit on a rather more modest scale. In London. Only this time I'll be out front and you'll be in the backroom. Good for you, good for me.'

CHAPTER 13

The drive to Paris was uneventful with neither one of us saying very much. With me driving for most of the way we reached the outskirts of Paris just after five o'clock on Monday evening and I headed across the river, up the Champs-Élysées. Paris was the usual mess of traffic and attitude, tourists and metropolitan disdain.

'Where are we staying?' he asked. 'Not the George V. They know me there. Or the Crillon. Or the Bristol. The last time I was at the Bristol it was with poor Colette.'

'The Hôtel Lancaster,' I said. 'I stayed there a couple of times with Jenny on those rare occasions when you'd paid me a decent bestseller bonus. It's on Rue de Berri, near the Arc de Triomphe. There's an underground parking lot right next door and we can dump the car there. No one at the hotel will even know we arrived by car.'

'Good idea.'

We checked into separate rooms this time, and after I'd asked the concierge to book us a table at Joël Robuchon, across the Champs-Élysées – of course, in my mind we were celebrating – I lay down for a nap before dinner and went straight to sleep. I hadn't been asleep for very long when there was an urgent knock at my door. It was John, of course, and he was looking pale and agitated, again. He didn't say anything. He just pushed past me into the room, and switched on the television.

I guessed what he probably wanted me to see but I thought it was probably best to play dumb. So while he tried to find the right channel I yawned and said, 'John, if you don't mind, I'm not really in the mood to watch TV right now.'

He shook his head, silently.

'As a matter of fact I'm a bit tired after the drive.'

Finally, he found TF1 and stepped back from the screen as if he wanted me to see as much of it as possible.

This time the police line and the news reporters were in Tourrettes-sur-Loup. I recognized the rusting sign at the bottom of Philip French's drive – the Villa Seurel – but I pretended I didn't.

'What is this?' I asked.

'That's Phil's house.'

'Is it? Christ, what's happened?'

'Phil's dead,' said John. 'He's committed suicide.'

'That's impossible,' I said.

'No, it isn't,' insisted John. 'He shot himself. Not only that, but it seems there was some connection between him and Colette. In fact, the police seem to think Phil may have shot Colette. What about that for a fucking plot twist? Talk about truth being stranger than fiction.'

'You're joking.'

John pointed at the screen and, as the news report continued, it seemed that he was right.

'There. What did I tell you? Didn't you say that he seemed a bit suicidal when you saw him last night?'

'Depressed, certainly. I mean, he gave up on your twenty grand without much of a fight. Which was odd, yes. And of course Caroline had gone back to England with the kids leaving him to wait on tables. So, naturally he was a bit down in the dumps.'

'And he was in debt, right?'

'Yes. According to the cop – Chief Inspector Amalric – he was quite substantially in debt.'

'I want to ask you a question, Don.'

'Fire away.'

'Do you think it could have been him who killed Orla? That he and Colette were in cahoots? That it was Phil who shot her while I was downstairs fucking Colette?'

I shrugged. 'I suppose – given that he seems to have shot himself – it's just about possible. Tourrettes isn't so far from Monaco.'

'Fifty minutes away by car,' said John. 'And he did hate me. You saw how he behaved yesterday.'

'Yes, but if he hated you, then why did he kill Orla? That doesn't make sense. Orla never did any harm to anyone. Not that we know of, anyway. Who knows what her fucking Mick brothers did with her money? But why top her? Why not just top you?'

John wagged a forefinger, thoughtfully.

'Yes, but look here: when you kill someone then your revenge is all over with relatively quickly. Too quickly perhaps. A bullet in my head, and it's all over, right? There's no chance to really enjoy something as quick as that. But if you kill a man's wife, and make it look like he was the murderer, then that's revenge on a Shakespearean scale. It's something drawn out, dramatic, even operatic. You make him suffer like he's on the rack. Which is how I've been this past fortnight.'

I shook my head. 'That's a little far-fetched, even for you, John.'

'Is it? Is it? I don't know.'

'And what was in it for Colette? Why would she go along with something like that? She loved you, didn't she?'

'I think maybe she must have found out that I was planning to leave Monaco and move back to England. Perhaps it was Phil who told her. In the long run, I'd have made sure she was all right, of course, money-wise, but frankly I was looking forward to living a rather less colourful life, if I can put it like that.'

'All right. That's possible, I suppose. I didn't know Colette, so I can't say if revenge was in her character or not. But I did know Phil. Yes, he was angry with you for ending the *atelier*. And maybe he did hate you. But I can't see him hating you enough to do what you're suggesting. I think I liked Colette's Russian better for that.'

'If there ever was a Russian,' said John. 'I'm not so sure.'

'What's that you say?'

John was plotting now – plotting like he was planning a book. I think it was all he could do not to get out a notebook and start jotting down ideas.

'If I could come back to Phil's motive here, for just a moment. If we could focus on that, please.'

I smiled thinly; John might have been discussing a character in one of his books. He looked as if at any second he was going to have what he used to call a 'sumimasen moment' – after the word that Japanese waiters cry out to new customers – when he would punch a fist into the palm of his hand and shout a word of thanks to his muse for giving him the inspired plot twist that was going to stun and amaze his readers.

'Yes?'

'There's something I've never told you before, Don. Something that's relevant to all this, I think. A couple of years ago, I bumped into Phil's wife, Caroline, when she was shopping in Cannes. Except that she wasn't shopping. Not like any woman I've ever seen. Not for anything decent. She was looking for bargains in some cheapo place on the Rue d'Antibes. Zara, or somewhere equally ghastly, the sort of place where they dress women of a certain size and budget. So I—'

I groaned. 'Please tell me you didn't fuck her.'

John took a deep breath and looked very sheepish.

'Oh, for Pete's sake. You *did* fuck her, didn't you?'

'She was lonely, Don. Lonely and neglected by her clod of a husband. So I took her to Chanel on the Croisette, bought her a nice dress and a handbag, gave her lunch at the Carlton, treated her like someone very special and then took her to a room upstairs.'

'You cunt.'

'Yes, you're right. It was a despicable thing to do. And believe me I regretted it later. But you've no idea how much it all seemed to cheer her up. I mean, she was a very different woman afterward.'

'Yes. She was someone who had committed adultery.' I shrugged. 'But I don't suppose it matters now, does it?'

'No. Still, I thought I ought to mention it. Get it off my chest. It makes things easier to understand, doesn't it?'

'Yes. That's what I call a motive. You're right. The poor bastard had every reason to hate your guts. If he did know.'

'There's something else.'

'What?'

'No, it's just that – look, I'm not trying to vindicate what happened, but she was too fast for someone like Phil. Caroline French was someone who liked the good things in life. He couldn't ever have held on to a woman like her.'

I could see that he'd wanted to tell me something else in the way of a confession and then thought better of it, and in that very same instant I knew with one hundred per cent certainty that I'd been right about him and Jenny – that he'd fucked my wife, too. That he had done my office between my sheets. It was the way John had described Caroline as 'too fast' for Phil. Once, after Jenny had left me for her High Court judge, and John had tried to suggest that I was probably better off without her, he'd described her in those very same terms, as someone who was 'too fast' for someone like me. Of course this telling remark implied that by contrast with dullards like Phil or me, a man as sophisticated as John was more than equal to the task of dealing with fast women like Caroline or Jenny. And possibly he was, too. It's amazing how women behave in a posh shop when there's a rich man around with a limitless credit card. Either way this was, for me, a moment of both vindication and pain, and having been proved right in my suspicion that Houston had indeed fucked my wife it was all I could do not to punch him right there and then. I hated him now more than ever I had hated anyone who wasn't Irish and I was glad he felt he was on the rack. I was enjoying my own Richard Topcliffe moment and poor John was my Catholic recusant. But I was not and never have been the type to let a mere hors d'oeuvre of hatred come before the full banquet of my revenge: long ago I had decided that this was a painstakingly prepared dish that would be served with such anaesthetic cold my victim would not even know that he had eaten it.

'So, then,' I said. 'Maybe you're right after all. What is it Iago says about Othello? "I do suspect the lusty Moor Hath leap'd into my seat: the thought whereof Doth, like a poisonous mineral, gnaw my innards; And nothing can or shall content my soul Till I am even'd with him, wife for wife."'

'Precisely so,' said John. 'That's exactly what I'm on about, old sport. That silly bitch Caroline must have told him I'd shagged her, and when I put an end to the *atelier* he probably decided to pay me back in grief and pain. There's no other explanation for it.' He shook his head. 'I wouldn't be at all surprised if he was already waiting in Colette's apartment when I went down there, grabbed the key from my tracksuit pocket, nipped upstairs and shot Orla while I was still on the job. Nor would I be surprised if all that Russian stuff – the champagnski, the ciggies, the newspaper – was just set-dressing to make me think her Ivan had turned up and to put the wind up me so that I would go on the run. That was clever. Very clever.'

I nodded. 'And immediately afterward Phil drove Colette to the airport car park where he shot her? In cold blood? I suppose it's just about possible. But this only makes sense to me if they were both after money – to blackmail you in return for her admission to the police that she was your alibi.'

'Yes. That's right. She must have got cold feet about the whole idea. Threatened to go to the police with her story. Either that or she wanted more money. Or money up front which Phil simply didn't have.'

John grinned and started to jog on the spot, like a boxer, as if for the first time he could run toward some light at the end of the tunnel. His leather shoes squeaked like springs that needed oiling, but for a big man he was surprisingly light on his feet.

'This is good for me, old sport. This is a real break, you know. Now I can hand myself in to the police. It's obvious that if the two of them were acting together it leaves me in the clear. More or less. Don't you see? He was in possession of my watch. Not to mention my bag and my gun. Christ, Don, he must have used the Walther to kill himself. The police will have to conclude that he took them all from my apartment. I shall just tell the cops that I was shit-scared and took off to Switzerland to wait for the truth to come out; and that when I saw they were both dead I put two and two together and decided to give myself up.'

I nodded patiently and tried to remain calm. I hadn't reckoned on this. I went to the window and moving the net curtain I stared out at the hotel's small but elegant garden. Here and there were iron statues of peacocks, which I rather preferred to the real thing, they being so much quieter. The laurel bushes and tree ferns were such a brilliant, almost artificial shade of green that you half expected to see a man being stalked through the undergrowth by a tiger or a jaguar – which was pretty much how I felt, most of the time. As if at any moment my ambitious revenge might swallow me whole. I opened a window and lit a cigarette so that any other sharp intakes of breath might seem smoking-related rather than the corollary of my almost shredded nerves.

'Look, John, there's something I haven't told you. Because I didn't want to depress you any more.'

John stopped jogging and frowned. 'What's that?'

'I think you'd better sit down. Because you're not going to like this.'

John sat down on the edge of my bed. I turned off the TV and returned to the window.

'What the fuck is it? Tell me.'

'When I first met the Monty cops in London I maintained your innocence so vehemently that they felt obliged to share with me some forensic evidence they hadn't released to the newspapers. Apparently they found blood and gunpowder on the sleeve of your tracksuit.'

John shook his head. 'No problem. Phil could have put on my clothes while I was busy banging Colette. Yes, that's it. He must have been wearing my tracksuit when he shot Orla. To help implicate me.'

'If that was all there was then I'd agree you should hand yourself in to the cops and take your chances.'

'What else is there?'

I blew smoke out of the window; it was supposed to be a non-smoking room and I had enough trouble on my hands without setting off the alarm that was attached to the ceiling, blinking red like the tail light of an aircraft. I caught sight of my own reflection in a mirror on the inside of the closet door. Wreathed in a little halo of blue cloud I looked more in control of myself than I might have supposed. Like someone or some thing infernal. As usual the cigarette was having an effect, helping me to form ideas out of nothing more than smoke and mirrors.

'The fact is, John, it's not just your chances any more. It's mine, too.'

John shook his head. 'I don't follow you, old sport. I've said I'll leave your name out of it and I will. If it makes any difference you can keep that twenty grand when you fuck off back to London. There's no reason you should be involved in any of this. I'm more than capable of facing this on my own now.'

'But I am involved. Very much more involved than you know.'

'What are you talking about, old sport?'

'Last night, when I went to see Phil he was in an extremely difficult frame of mind. He'd been drinking a lot. Smoking a lot of dope, too. I didn't know he smoked weed, did you? Anyway, he told me that I could stuff your twenty grand because the Chief Inspector from the Monaco *Sûreté Publique* was coming to see him at ten o'clock on Monday morning and that he was going to tell him that you were staying in Vence, at the Château Saint-Martin. Yes, that's what he said. He told me he'd thought it all over and he couldn't bring himself to forgive you for destroying his life as a writer, not to mention destroying his life as a man. He told me then that he'd found out you'd fucked Caroline and said that no amount of money could compensate for the pain he'd felt – that a man he considered to be his friend could have betrayed him quite so egregiously.

'I tried to reason with him. I said that what was done was done. I'm afraid I even told him about my plan to hide you away in Cornwall and that we could reinstate the *atelier* with him as one of your writers. I said everything would be just like it was before and that in the fullness of time, if he was writing and making a decent living again, Caroline might even come back to him. But he wasn't interested in any of that. He told me the only writing he was capable of doing these days was jotting down a lunch order at the Château Saint-Martin. Tempers got a bit frayed and he started to shout at me.

'I only meant to threaten him with the gun – your gun, which I'd found in your bag when I was taking the money out to give it to him. I told him that he might manage to get you arrested but that he'd better think twice if I was going to allow him to grass me up. Or words to that effect. I said that if I did get nicked he could be sure that eventually I'd come back there and kill him. Anyway, he was pissed and stoned like I said – which is probably why he tried to take the gun off me. We wrestled a bit, in his study and that was when the gun went off. It seemed you'd left a bullet in the breech. I should have checked it before I pointed the thing at him but I didn't. There wasn't time.' I shrugged. 'It was me who shot Philip French, John. It was me who killed him.'

'Jesus.'

'After that I set about trying to make it look like a suicide. I put the gun in his hand, let off another shot for the forensics boys. I left your bag and your watch in the hope that it might persuade the police – as it seems to have managed to persuade you – that Phil had something to do with Orla's death. It was the same gun after all. There was an unsent draft of a rather self-pitying email he'd been composing to his wife on his computer which he'd insisted on reading to me as a way of explaining that he was finished as a writer; I don't think he'd ever intended sending it to Caroline; so I sent it, for appearance's sake, you understand. Then I left. That's why I was so fucking panicky when I came to fetch you in the village square last night. And why I started bricking it when I saw that copper and realized he was already in Tourrettes. Because I'd just shot Phil.'

John nodded. 'I see. Fuck me. You had quite an evening, didn't you? But where do you think the cops got the idea that Philip French had anything to do with Colette Laurent's death?'

'The circumstances, I suppose. You're the missing link, after all. You knew Phil and I dare say they'll have worked out that you knew Colette, too; and intimately. They must have found her laptop when they came across her body. It's just a suspicion I have, but I rather think Chief Inspector Amalric might be playing a clever game here. He could be hoping you'll hear on the news that the cops think Phil had something to do with Colette's death and that, as a result, you'll think it's now safe to hand yourself in. And look, for all I fucking know, they don't really believe that Phil killed himself either. I have no idea what kind of fist I made of making his death look like a suicide. My expertise in these matters only extends to writing thrillers. They're not stupid, these people. So it's not just you who's now facing jail, it's me, too.' I shook my head and added, 'They're not actually looking for me, of course. Not yet. And before you ask I have no more intention of handing myself in than you have. Or had.'

'Yes, I see.'

I flicked the cigarette into the guttering where it lay like an exploded incendiary device waiting to detonate and set the whole building on fire.

'I do agree with you about one thing, though, John. Phil and Colette certainly do look as if they killed your wife and framed you for it. For whatever reason. Money, revenge – we may never know for sure. But suspecting it is one thing; proving it is something else. With your gun and your bag and your watch all found at the scene of Phil's homicide a jury might just as easily be persuaded by a good lawyer that you killed all three of them: Orla, Colette and Phil. And make no mistake about it, I shall certainly deny that I had anything to do with Phil's death. In court. On oath. I'm telling you now, there's no way I'm going to put my hand up to that. Not while I've been assisting a wanted felon to escape from justice. You do see my problem, don't you? A jury might easily be persuaded that I shot Philip French on purpose. At your behest. To stop him from telling the cops about you. That's me in a conspiracy to commit murder, which probably carries a life sentence in France, just like in England. I'm not going to take that chance. Not for you. Not for anyone. Me, I'm going back to London on the Eurostar first thing tomorrow morning. You can do what the fuck you like, chum. Come with me. Stay here in Paris. It's entirely up to you. But I've had enough. I'm going straight to Manderley. It will nice to be in a place where nothing ever happens and no one ever does anything. And if you're sensible you'll come with me.'

John, who had remained seated on the edge of my bed all this time, got up and helped himself to a miniature of whisky from my minibar.

'I feel a little like Oscar Wilde,' he said, pouring the contents into a glass. 'You remember? At the Cadogan Hotel in 1895. Him being urged to flee for France by Robbie Ross before the coppers could turn up and arrest him for sodomy and gross indecency.'

'Thanks a lot, chum,' I said. 'I always saw myself playing Robbie Ross to your Oscar.' I smiled thinly. 'I should like it to be known now that in no circumstances are my ashes to be interred in your tomb, as his are, in Père Lachaise.'

John sipped at the whisky for a moment and then drained the glass.

'And of course fleeing to Cornwall is rather less glamorous than catching the boat train to Paris.' He shrugged. 'But it will have to be that way, I suppose. I regret I can now see no alternative to Cornwall.'

JOHN HOUSTON'S STORY

PART TWO

Last night I dreamt I was still at Manderley. It seemed to me that I stood by the rusting iron gate at the bottom of the short drive and could not leave, for there was a bloody great padlock and chain upon the gate. I called in my dream for someone – anyone – in the road outside to come and open it, and had no answer because no one was there. No one is ever there. *Because this is fucking Cornwall.*

It's two years since I came to live my secret life in Don Irvine's house in Polruan. It's a nice enough house, I suppose; Georgian probably, made of grey Cornish flint, with four bedrooms, several acres of garden and a nice view of Fowey harbour on the other side of a picturesque-looking estuary river. A view of Fowey is, in my opinion, rather better than a view of Polruan; but only just. Together, Fowey and Polruan are about the same size as Monaco, and in the summer the place is very popular with yachtsmen, although these are nothing like the kind of magnificent yachts we used to see in the harbour there. They're more your weekend sort of yacht – more of a polite letter from the bank than a statement. And when I say popular I don't mean popular like Monaco was popular. There's no money here and it's not remotely fashionable. Fashion is something that only exists east of Exeter. I think everyone in Cornwall must wear a shit-coloured fleece, even in summer. And hardly anybody who's anybody ever comes to Fowey and Polruan.

Frankly I think there are even fewer people living down here than when Daphne du Maurier was still alive. Back then she wasn't the only famous writer living in Fowey. Kenneth Grahame and Sir Arthur Quiller-Couch used to live down here, too. But today there's no one you've ever heard of writing in Fowey. Which is probably lucky for me. There's a small literary festival of course. These days no town with aspirations can afford to be without one of these. Not that the Du Maurier Festival is any good; it certainly doesn't surprise me that no writer of note can be bothered to travel five hours from London to sit in a rain-lashed tent in front of a small, unresponsive audience that looks like it has been hand-reared on fudge, clotted cream, cider and Winston fucking Graham. I sneaked into the back of the tent to hear some bitch no-hoper down from the Smoke bore us all to death with her so-called comedy novel about mother culture – whatever that is – but I left before I passed out with ennui.

I keep myself to myself, which is easy enough. Not long after I arrived in Polruan I read in the newspapers that a body was found in a forest north of Monaco; it had been burned beyond all recognition and it was generally assumed that this charred body was mine, dumped there by my murderers, Philip French and Colette Laurent, which means that the police aren't looking for John Houston any more. But this doesn't mean to say I can relax and go exactly where I want. Far from it. I keep away from London where people might recognize me, even with my Papa Hemingway-sized beard. If ever I was seen again then the whole case might be reopened and I might easily find myself under arrest; for me it would be a very short step from being a hapless victim to becoming an obvious suspect. I've been to Truro and Penzance a few times and Exeter once or twice, but one of my daughters is at university there now, so I tend to keep away, especially during term time. Of course, I'd like to see her, but I don't dare take the risk. Sometimes I feel a bit like Abel Magwitch in *Great Expectations*. And, truth be known, I probably look like him, too.

So I stay down here and knock out seventy-five-page story-lines just like before, only now I do most of my research online; there's not much you can't find out with a decent broadband connection and Google. I find I was more right than I ever knew that the internet connection and a TV are all you really need to see enough of the world to write a book. Hemingway describes sitting in the Café des Amateurs on the Rue Mouffetard to write, and truth be told that's how most punters still think it ought to be done; but the truth is that you can write a lot more if you just stay home and write. Travel might broaden the mind but it means you get less writing done. Besides, the world is all the same when you actually look at it. Denver looks like a smaller version of Chicago; Lyon looks like Cheltenham; Cagnes-sur-Mer looks like St Austell; and Athens looks like Sunderland. The so-called global village is just one huge shopping mall. I don't miss the world very much. It certainly doesn't miss me.

I write the storylines and Don writes the books – most of them anyway, and it's an arrangement that suits us nicely. Lately he has brought in Peter Stakenborg to write one of our new titles: *The Other Man from Nazareth*. Peter doesn't know anything about me, of course. As far as Peter's concerned it's Don who writes the storylines; and after all, it's Don Irvine's name that's on the books now. Don's become very successful doing it, too; not as successful as I was, but that's to be expected; besides, we've only been doing this for two years. Publishing has changed a lot in that time. There's less money sloshing around than there used to be. Publishers are feeling the pinch thanks to eBooks and the general ignorance of a public who seem to have a diminishing appetite for books – at least books for which you have to pay more than a couple of dollars. Even so, he's doing all right; he just signed a new contract with VVL that means he will deliver six books within three years for ten million dollars. And that's just in the US. I don't doubt that in three years' time when he comes to negotiate a new contract he could expect to make at least twice as much.

Don pays me thirty thousand pounds a year. That might not sound like much when you compare it with what he gets, but I don't pay any tax of course – I don't even have a National Insurance number – and down here thirty thousand a year is still a fortune. Besides, there's nothing to spend the money on anyway. The local shops are full of pasties and tourist tat – hideous ornaments and ghastly paintings of Cornwall. I get a Tesco online delivery once a week, paid for by Don, as is almost everything else: oil for the Aga and the heating, electricity, water, broadband charges, books and DVDs from Amazon, the car – even my Celestron telescope was paid for by Don. So that thirty grand is mine to do whatever I like with. But mostly the money just stays in the bank.

Yes, Don has been a good friend to me. But for him I'd be in prison, I've no doubt about that. True, I get a bit depressed, sometimes. It can be lonely here, especially in winter when the ferry across the estuary stops and if you want to get to the other side you have to drive all the way around the river, which takes exactly forty-one minutes. There's a woman called Mrs Trefry who comes in to clean and we chat a bit sometimes, and there used to be a gardener, too – Mr Twigg – only I discovered I liked doing the garden myself, so he stopped coming because there was nothing left for him to do; after a morning sitting in front of a computer there's nothing I like better than a bit of gardening. Kipling used his Nobel Prize money to add a rose garden and a pond to his house in East Sussex. I'm thinking of doing something similar so that I can see more of the bird life that is abundant in this part of the world. I've already built a small observatory in the old cider house, where with the aid of an eight-inch telescope I can look at the stars and the planets; the skies down here are remarkably clear. It makes me feel small but I don't mind that. I've discovered a kind of humility I never had before.

I also grow all my own vegetables and quite a bit of summer fruit; and I have a small boat to go fishing in. You have to sail out of the harbour to catch anything worth eating. Most of the decent-sized bass are gone now but there's still plenty of pollock and eel. To my surprise I've become quite an accomplished fisherman. Fishing makes you patient.

One thing I do miss about Monaco is the weather. As the people in The Bodinnick Arms are fond of saying, there's a reason Cornwall is so green; it rains a lot. When it's fine, it's very fine indeed, but when it's wet it's bloody awful. This is a place where rain really does set in for the day. The present summer has been especially bad. It seems that it has been raining for ever. So thank Christ for Sky TV, especially in the winter. I've a nice big widescreen set in my sitting room, with HD, and – like any writer – I like to watch the daytime scum shows and the footy, of course, when it's on. And I've managed to put together a complete collection of first editions by Daphne du Maurier and Q. But what I most like now are books on tape; I've become especially fond of listening to Dickens as read by people like Martin Jarvis and Sir David Jason.

Don comes down from London once a month, rain or shine, in his nice big Range Rover – which is the same model that I used to have myself – and stays the weekend. We go to the pub and talk about the storylines for the next novel, or I might hand over the edited manuscript of the last one; he still has a tendency to overwrite – to use three words where one will do, and to quote other writers like they're fucking saints – so I give him quite a lot of the blue pencil. He has a nicer flat in Putney now – a penthouse that overlooks the river – but he's just acquired a small apartment in Monaco where he's planning to live permanently when he starts to make the big money. Which he will, I've no doubt about that. I'm not bitter about this. Even before Orla died I'd already had enough of Monty. The place is about as shallow as a Martini glass. It's all supercars and fancy overpriced restaurants, private beaches, gala nights with royalty and ghastly film premieres. I've told him he isn't going to like it there but he won't listen. In Monaco there's just shopping and more shopping and always for something you don't really need; there are no art galleries or museums to speak of, no social life, and the women are just out for what they can get; Don says he likes women who know what they want and he'll be quite happy to let them have it. But everyone has to make their own mistakes, I guess. I should know, I made more than my fair share of them.

If he suspects that I once shagged his missus he's never mentioned it. Fortunately, he sees very little of Jenny – Lady Muck, he calls her – so I think there's no chance now that she's going to fess up to what she did with me. Which is just as well, as that would spoil everything. I had a small moment of panic last May bank holiday when I saw her and the judge in a tea shop in Fowey, but fortunately she didn't see me. I even managed to go back and get another squint at her. Frankly it was hard to believe that I'd ever fucked her at all. Her hair was so grey she looked like a High Court judge herself. Quite a contrast with the woman wearing a basque and suspenders and string panties who sucked my cock so enthusiastically in the Swan Hotel at the Hay-on-Wye Festival while Don was interviewing some crime writer from Baltimore. To my surprise it was the best blow-job I ever had.

In spite of that – the blow-job, I mean – Don is well out of his marriage. By contrast he looks like the bestselling author he now is. With a hair-transplant, dental veneers, a good tailor (I sent him along to Huntsman) and a permanent tan, he's hardly recognizable as the backroom boy who used to be my loyal writing devil. *GQ* magazine recently asked him to model some Philip Marlowe-style raincoats. His transformation has been quite startling.

And for once virtue has not been its own poor and always inadequate reward. Don was just made a Fellow of the Royal Society of Literature, which pleased him enormously; last year he won an Edgar Award for *Passing Strange*; and he's already shortlisted for this year's Golden Dagger from the Crime Writers' Association for *A Murder Not to Solve*. The material rewards have come his way, too. Quite apart from the Range Rover and the Aston Martin Vantage he drives in London, he seems to have a string of young and willing girl-friends. One of them, Serena, is half his age and looks like a model; but she actually works for *The Daily Telegraph* so I don't suppose I shall ever meet her in person, just in case she's the kind with a nose for a story.

If I need a woman there's a lady I go and see at her beautiful home near Padstow who looks after all my needs. She's very kind and thoughtful, and has a lovely personality. Her name is Myra. Do I envy Don? No, not at all. He's worked hard and deserves every success. Me, I'm just lucky to be at liberty. On the whole it's much better here in Cornwall than in some air-conditioned cell in Monaco. I'd have gone mad if I'd been cooped up all day, unable to see anyone or go anywhere. I've got much to thank Don Irvine for. He risks a great deal by hiding me down here. I'm better off here and no mistake. The dust and the damp here aggravate my allergies sometimes, and once I had a severe attack of asthma, but apart from that my health has been good. True, I've put on a lot of weight. I have a bicycle to try and stay fit, but the hills around here would defeat Sir Bradley Wiggins.

Don has kindly offered to equip one of the outhouses with a treadmill, but I told him that there's no one here to be in shape for. Certainly Myra doesn't mind what I look like. Besides, in this area of the world there's all the walking anyone would need, for miles around. He and I have really only disagreed about one thing since I came to live in Cornwall, and it was not about the plot of a book.

The fact is that early on in my time here at Manderley I tried to kill myself. Overcome with solitude I bought a length of good nylon rope from a ship's chandler in Fowey and, one midsummer morning, I tried to hang myself in the apple orchard. But as I was hanging there I learned two things: one was that strangling to death is a poor way to die; the other was that the boughs of apple trees are not sturdy enough to take a man's weight and, eventually, the one I'd chosen broke and I fell to the ground, spraining my ankle quite badly. It was Mr Twigg who found me and called an ambulance which took me to a hospital in Plymouth. It was Mr Twigg who called Don, who was very cross about what I'd done but came down straight away, and when I was feeling better we argued about it.

'I didn't save your fucking neck just so as you could put a rope around it and try to do yourself in,' he said. 'That was bloody selfish of you after all that effort I went to. What the hell were you thinking of?'

'I was thinking that life here in Cornwall seemed like a piece of shit. Will that do? I used to drive an Aston Martin and now I drive an old Fiesta. I had a mistress who belonged in the pages of a men's magazine. She and I used to drink Dom Pérignon at the Hôtel Negresco. Now I visit an ageing prostitute in Padstow and after seeing her I get fish and chips from Rick Stein's. In the morning I used to speak French to order a coffee and a croissant in the Café de Paris; but now, when I go to the village shop in the morning to fetch a newspaper and a loaf of bread, I could be speaking French for all the fucking conversation I get. They look at me like I'm a bloody alien. I know I said I wanted to live in England again but this isn't exactly what I had in mind. I feel like I'm living in Middle Earth. Besides, I rather think that it's my neck to wring, don't you?'

'Perhaps. But did you stop and think about what might happen to me if you killed yourself?'

'Oddly enough, I didn't.'

'Perhaps you should have done. You might have considered the job I'd have explaining to Plod just how it is that a man who everyone thought to be dead happens to be hanging in my bloody orchard like a Cox's Orange Pippin? No, I thought not. They'd have fucking nicked me for sure. I'd be in Vine Street Magistrates Court right now, facing extradition.'

'I can think of worse fates than a nice prison cell in Monaco.'

'Don't forget, two of those homicides occurred on the Côte d'Azur, so for helping you to escape justice the French police could probably claim priority for my extradition over the Monégasques. And I bet the Monty cops would be quite glad to yield authority to the French cops. It would save them the problem of having an embarrassing trial. I may not be nearly as famous as you, but the death of your wife still generates a lot of press. And while a cell in Monty might sound okay to you, the one at Les Baumettes isn't quite so appealing.'

'Les Baumettes?'

'It's a prison near Marseille. According to the *Daily Telegraph*, the EU justice minister has described it as a living hell and the most repugnant prison in Europe. The next time you feel like sending yourself to heaven, just remember that at the same time you'll be sending me to hell.'

'Point taken.'

'Look, old sport, it's bound to seem a little quiet down here at first. But things will get better.'

'You mean I'll get used to it being shit here.'

'Yes. If you like. Please, John. Promise me you won't try anything like that again.'

'Yeah, all right. Anyway, it's not something I want to try again. Hanging myself, I mean. It's not all it's cracked up to be.'

'Thanks.' Don nodded. 'It's difficult enough keeping you a secret as it is. But now the fucking hospital is wondering just how it is that you have no medical records.' He grinned. 'Next time pull the bung out of your boat while you're out at sea. Like Maxim de Winter. No body means no awkward fucking questions.'

'It didn't exactly work out for him, did it?'

'No. But he was an amateur. And besides, Rebecca left a note. I trust you won't be so careless.'

'Thanks, I'll bear that in mind.'

What is especially touching in retrospect is the way Don was so upset about my wish to die; indeed, he took it very personally, almost as if he had become my guardian, and I realized just what a true friend he is. Anyway, I'm over that now. I hardly ever think about suicide and I'm settling into life down here, like the rain.

Tonight I shall probably listen to *Little Dorrit* again on CD. There are passages in that book I can never hear without the temptation to weep.

DON IRVINE'S STORY

PART THREE

It's a tiny apartment I have in Monaco – about the size of a postage stamp – but that's okay. You don't own an apartment in Monaco to live large but to save millions in tax. There's just a bedroom, a sitting room (which serves as my office), a bathroom and a kitchen area. It's nicely decorated though; *Le Point* magazine are going to do a little spread on it, and me. It's a far cry from the sort of penthouse that John used to own in the Tour Odéon, but this apartment cost less than a tenth as much as that one did and does me for now. The pre-war, cream stucco building occupies the corner of the Rue des Violettes, and my apartment is on the second floor, above a chicken and pizza restaurant, which sounds awful but is actually quite handy given the size of my kitchen. From my bedroom window you can see across a picturesque series of steps that lead up onto Rue des Roses, and straight into the sitting room of the apartment opposite. It's not very private but at this price I can't really complain. Not when I consider how much money I'll be saving when, eventually, I move out of London and live here permanently. The apartment opposite is owned by a woman who I think must be a prostitute; she spends ages getting ready to go out and all sorts of men seem to visit her at various times of the day and night. People-watching:

it's one of the things that make Monaco so fascinating. At night the delivery motorcycles for the chicken and pizza restaurant can get a bit noisy as they rev up like angry mosquitoes; and the electrical wholesaler next door to the chicken and pizza place seems to open pretty early in the morning when several white vans collect outside to load up with various bits and pieces; but that's just the penalty you pay for living in an interesting part of town. Other than that, everything is working out just fine.

Whenever I'm in Monaco I'm always up early to catch the best of the day; so, most mornings at around six o'clock, I put on a pair of Bose noise-cancelling headphones and start writing on my iMac. I work through until midday, when I go to *Le Neptune Plage*, which is a private beach on Larvotto. In the summer *Le Neptune* is always busy and it's usually advisable to reserve a sunbed, which costs about twenty euros a day. That's where I eat my lunch. I have the set menu, which is about forty euros. They know me there and I like that. The water is nice but right now it's best not to swim at all because of the many jellyfish. I stay at *Le Neptune* until about four, when I go and do another five hours at my desk before going out again to have dinner somewhere. Usually I go to the Hôtel Columbus, which is a pleasant half-hour walk – if you don't mind all the tourists. You get used to them – even the large coaches that deliver them in their hundreds just outside Casino Square. Anyway I'm not really here often enough to mind them very much. My books are already published in forty-seven languages, so I'm frequently touring a new title abroad. It's a rare month when I don't have to go to another country to promote something; this year I have a book being published somewhere, in translation, *every week*.

It's all a marked contrast to my life in Putney, where I have a penthouse flat in Putney Wharf Tower that overlooks the river, and which is where I conduct my business when I'm in London. It's there that I have meetings with Neville – the web-master I've employed to look after my Facebook, Twitter and website – and Tiffany – the PR person who I have on a monthly retainer to handle all my print and broadcast media publicity. The first thing I do every morning is send Neville a little publishing or philosophical *aperçu* that he can put up on my Facebook page. These are especially popular in France. Don't ask me why but they love me in France. Right now I have two books on *Le Nouvel Observateur*'s list of top twenty bestsellers.

Naturally, when I'm in London I see a lot of my new agent, Hereward – I sacked Craig Conrad – and the small but dedicated team at VVL who are now publishing my books. Of course, I have contractual approval of all jacket designs and I write all my own blurbs for the VVL catalogues. On the back of a television sale that CAA – my film and television agents in Los Angeles – have made, Hereward predicts great things for us in the spring of next year. HBO bought my latest book, *Devils Offended*, while it was still in manuscript. So I've taken on Peter Stakenborg to pen one of my future titles, as the pressure to tour the books often means that I now have less and less time to write them; and I'm looking for an additional writer, which ought to be easy enough; the state of British publishing means there are plenty of good writers around who nobody wants to publish any more. What with writing, dealing with an almost endless series of editing queries, book tours, and general publicity, I find I have little or no time to myself.

And, of course, once a month I have to drive all the way

down to Cornwall to see John, to collect a new story outline or an edited manuscript for submission to the publisher, and to try to keep him sweet, of course. Which isn't easy. John always was an awkward customer, even when we were working in advertising. Fortunately, if ever I have need of such a thing, I have a fail-safe guarantee to ensure his continuing cooperation: a plastic bag containing some forensic treasures incriminating him which would certainly be of interest to the Monty police.

He still asks questions about what happened in Monaco and France. How was it that Phil and Colette ever met, since John only ever saw the former in Paris and never in Monaco? Why was Colette killed at all? Why didn't they try to get in contact with him to extract some sort of ransom in return for an alibi? And how was it that Phil – who had studied theology before becoming a copywriter and had even once considered entering the priesthood – could become the kind of person who was capable of murdering two people in cold blood?

'Listen,' I said. 'Half of the SS were judges and lawyers.'

'That you can understand. But a priest is something else.'

'Priests can kill, too,' I insisted. 'I wouldn't let the fact that Phil studied theology persuade you otherwise. History is full of priests who were also killers. The Templars. The Holy Inquisition. Josef Stalin.'

'Stalin was a priest?'

'He certainly trained to be one. At least according to Simon Sebag Montefiore's biography, *Young Stalin*. You should read it. Besides, if our latest novel is to be believed, anyone is capable of murder. Any man, at least. Isn't that what we were saying? That it's quite normal for men to kill. That it's a rare moment in history when men aren't killing each other. That this is why we have wars. That war is not, as Clausewitz says, the continuation of politics by other means but rather a normal expression of male psychology. This was the premise of your storyline; and a jolly good one, too, if I may say so. We're going to make millions off that book when it gets on the telly.'

'I'm just saying that you wouldn't have tipped Phil to become a murderer,' said John. 'But you, on the other hand . . . You must have fired your SLR in anger when you were in Ireland.'

'For sure. I'm not sure I ever hit anything, mind.'

'Orla thought different. She always said you had a dark past. That she'd had you checked out by someone who used to be an IRA intelligence officer, and that you'd been with some secret black ops outfit in the late Seventies.'

'Did she? I never knew.'

We were in the sitting room, in front of the wood stove which was blazing away; it might have been summer in Europe but in Cornwall it was something else; I always felt you need a fifth season to properly describe the climate in Cornwall. I'd brought some new books and some good wine and a box of the cigars that John liked and was now enjoying.

'Were you?'

'Oh yes.' I grinned. 'Can't you tell? I'm a natural born killer. That's why I became a writer. Kill your darlings. Isn't that what they say? Well, I do. And I have. And I enjoy it.'

'But you do know guns.'

'Everyone who's been in the British army knows guns. It comes with the job, John. It's called basic training. And you were the one with the gun collection, not me. Orla might still be alive if you hadn't given her a bloody gun for Christmas. She was shot with her own gun, wasn't she?'

'That's another thing. How the fuck did Phil know where it was?'

'You must have told him.'

'I don't remember it.'

'John, when we had the *atelier* in Paris you used to say all sorts of things you probably don't remember now. I do remember you telling us all you'd bought her a gun for Christmas. You even told us what kind of gun it was. You made a joke about it. Frankly, I was a little surprised that Mike Munns never mentioned it in that hatchet job he did on you in the *Daily Mail*. He managed to mention everything else about you that was incriminating.'

'Which one? The piece that followed on from Orla's death? Or mine?' He shook his head. 'I don't remember making a joke about my buying her a gun.'

I nodded. 'You said you'd bought her two things for Christmas. A new Ferrari and a gun. And if she didn't like the Ferrari you would fucking shoot her. Words to that effect.'

'I really said that?'

I nodded.

'Jesus. I can just see that one playing in court.'

'Exactly.' I shook my head. 'Anyway, you said you bought it for her because she got nervous when you went away on book tour. Therefore, it wouldn't be such a stretch of the imagination to suppose that she kept it in the bedside drawer.'

'No, I suppose not. But look here, Phil loved dogs. He used to have a dachshund and a beagle. At least before Caroline took them back to London. I can't imagine him shooting the boys any more than I can imagine him shooting Orla herself.'

'Someone shot them.'

'That they did. And perhaps we'll just have to await the book to find out what really happened. And then the inevitable film of the book for television.'

'What book?'

'I thought you knew.'

'Knew what?'

'That Mike Munns is writing a book about the murders. Mike Munns. You didn't know?'

'A book? What kind of book?'

'A true crime story. That's the sort of thing he does these days.'

'True crime?'

'Yes. His book is about me and Orla and Phil and Colette. About you, too, for all I know.'

'Me? I can't see why he'd want to write about me.'

John shrugged. 'It's called *The Man Who Shot the Bitch in Monte Carlo*. Good title, don't you think? If a little unfair to poor Orla. I mean, she could be a bitch. But then what woman isn't like that sometimes?'

'Who's this book for?'

'For John Blake Publishing. They do a lot of that kind of thing. I don't think we're talking about *In Cold Blood* here. Mike's no Truman Capote, that's for sure. Or *The Executioner's Song*. No, I imagine it'll probably be his usual sleazy exposé of life among the super-rich, with plenty of gore and gratuitous sex thrown in. That's what sells these days. Like that book he wrote last year about the gay Saudi Arabian prince who murdered his man servant. What was that called?' John snapped his fingers. '*The Prince and the Toyboy*. Which was pretty good, even though I say so myself. He's a useful turn of phrase, has our Mike. And gratuitous sex and violence was always his strong suit. Anyway, I saw it on *Publisher's Lunch*. You know? Today's publishing news and gossip that's on the web. Who knows? He might actually find something out. Something the police missed, perhaps. I wouldn't be surprised. Mike is quite tenacious when there's a fast buck to be made.'

'Yes, he might. And he is.'

'Now that's one publishing party I'd like to go to. Just to see the look on his face as I ask him to sign my already redundant copy.'

'He hasn't been in touch with me about a book,' I said. 'And I'm sure Peter would have mentioned it if he'd asked him to help.' I shook my head. 'Matter of fact, I haven't seen him in ages. Last I heard he and Starri were living in Brighton.'

'Perhaps he figures neither of you trust him enough to help him.'

'I don't. And nor does Peter.' I lit a cigarette. 'But what the fuck does he know about what happened? He doesn't know anything.'

'Nor do you,' said John. 'At least that's what everyone believes.'

'I haven't spoken to him since we had lunch in Wandsworth, on the Tuesday Orla's death was on the TV. Not after that stitch-up piece he did on you. And it's not like her family would have helped. Not with a title like that. They're not the kind of people you'd want to betray. So. It has to be a cuttings job. Returning to his own vomit. Speculation. Without speaking to you, or me, he has nothing. The only other people who knew anything are dead. Orla. Colette. Phil.'

'Maybe the copper is going to offer some new ideas. Chief Inspector Amalric. Do you ever see him around? In Monaco?'

I shook my head.

'He doesn't know anything either. He couldn't know anything. Could he?'

'Don't ask me, old sport. I'm dead.'